Praise for the Novels of Susan Donovan

NOT THAT KIND OF GIRL

"Refreshing and open, *Not That Kind of Girl* is a story straight from the heart."
—*Romance Junkies*

"*Not That Kind of Girl* has it all—mystery, romance, and laughter."
—*Single Titles*

"Will keep you reading late into the night and rooting for happy endings all around."
—*Fresh Fiction*

THE NIGHT SHE GOT LUCKY

"This second in Donovan's stories of dog-walking friends is a wonderful combination of love and laughter, with serious moments as well as some intrigue. The animal characters are a delightful addition to the story."
—*Romantic Times BOOKreviews*

"*The Night She Got Lucky* is a sexy, sweet, and simply delicious contemporary romance." —*Joyfully Reviewed*

"A cute, funny, and sexy tale from beginning to end."
—*Romance Reviews Today*

AIN'T TOO PROUD TO BEG

"Donovan whips up a fine frappe of romantic comedy and suspense."
—*Publishers Weekly*

W9-BRH-268

"A fun and sexy 'feel good' story and a 'must' title to add to your current romance reading list." —*Bookloons*

"A story of rioting emotions, wacky weight challenges, and lots of love. This is one story you will be sad to see end. Kudos to Donovan for creating such a believable and realistic story."
—*Fallen Angel Reviews*

"*He Loves Lucy* has everything: humor, sweetness, warmth, romance, passion, and sexual tension; an uplifting message; a heroine every woman . . . can empathize with; and a hero to die for."
—*Romance Reviews Today*

"An extraordinary read with intriguing characters and a wonderful plot . . . fantastic." —*Romance Junkies*

"Lucy is a humorous delight . . . fans will enjoy this fine look at one year of hard work to find love."
—*Midwest Book Review*

"A great romance . . . a top-rate novel . . . with its unforgettable characters, wonderful plot, and excellent message, *He Loves Lucy* will go on my keeper shelf to be read and re-read a thousand times . . . Donovan has proven that she will have serious star power in the years to come." —*Romance Reader at Heart*

TAKE A CHANCE ON ME

"Comic sharpness . . . the humorous interactions among Thomas, Emma, and Emma's quirky family give the book a golden warmth as earthy as its rural Maryland

setting. But there are also enough explicit erotic interludes to please readers who like their romances spicy."
—*Publishers Weekly*

"Donovan blends humor and compassion in this opposites-attract story. Sexy and masculine, Thomas fills the bill for the man of your dreams. Emma and Thomas deserve a chance at true love. Delightfully entertaining, *Take a Chance on Me* is a guaranteed good time." —*Old Book Barn Gazette*

"Full of humor, sensuality, and emotion with excellent protagonists and supporting characters . . . a wonderful tale. Don't be afraid to take a chance on this one. You'll love it." —*Affaire de Coeur*

"Impossible to put down . . . Susan Donovan is an absolute riot. You're reading a paragraph that is so sexually charged you can literally feel the air snapping with electricity and the next second one of the characters has a thought that is so absurd . . . that you are laughing out loud. Susan Donovan has a very unique, off-the-wall style that should keep her around for many books to come. Do NOT pass this one up." —*Romance Junkies Review*

"Susan Donovan has created a vastly entertaining romance in her latest book *Take a Chance on Me*. The book has an ideal cast of characters . . . a very amusing, pleasurable read . . . all the right ingredients are there, and Ms. Donovan has charmingly dished up an absolutely fast, fun, and sexy read!" —*Road to Romance*

"Contemporary romances don't get much better than *Take a Chance on Me* . . . such wonderful characters! You want sexual tension? This book drips with it. How about a love scene that is everything that a love scene should be? There's humor, a touch of angst, and delightful dialogue . . . *Take a Chance on Me* is going to end up very, very high on my list of best romances for 2003."
—*All About Romance*

KNOCK ME OFF MY FEET

"Spicy debut . . . [A] surprise ending and lots of playfully erotic love scenes will keep readers entertained."
—*Publishers Weekly*

"Donovan's blend of romance and mystery is thrilling."
—*Booklist*

"*Knock Me Off My Feet* will knock you off your feet . . . Ms. Donovan crafts an excellent mixture to intrigue you and delight you. You'll sigh as you experience the growing love between Autumn and Quinn and giggle over their dialogue. And you'll be surprised as the story unfolds. I highly recommend this wonderfully entertaining story."
—*Old Book Barn Gazette*

"From the beginning I was hooked by the author's fast-paced writing and funny situations . . . I highly recommend this debut book by Susan Donovan. You'll just have to ignore the ironing and vacuuming and order pizza for the family until you've finished being knocked off *your* feet by this saucy, sexy romp."
—*A Romance Review*

Also by
Susan Donovan

Cheri on Top

Not That Kind of Girl

The Night She Got Lucky

Ain't Too Proud To Beg

The Girl Most Likely To . . .

The Kept Woman

He Loves Lucy

Public Displays of Affection

Take a Chance on Me

Knock Me Off My Feet

I Want Candy

SUSAN DONOVAN

St. Martin's Paperbacks

This is a work of fiction. All of the characters, organizations, and events portrayed in this novel are either products of the author's imagination or are used fictitiously.

I WANT CANDY

Copyright © 2012 by Susan Donovan.

For information address St. Martin's Press, 175 Fifth Avenue, New York, NY 10010.

ISBN: 978-0-312-53622-0

Printed in the United States of America

St. Martin's Paperbacks edition / March 2012

St. Martin's Paperbacks are published by St. Martin's Press, 175 Fifth Avenue, New York, NY 10010.

10 9 8 7 6 5 4 3 2 1

This book is dedicated to Celeste Bradley—creative coconspirator, fellow dreamer, travel companion, and friend.

. . . Remember, no matter where you go, there you are.
—Buckaroo Banzai

Chapter 1

It was time to hit the road—again.

Candace Carmichael wrestled with the gearshift until it slipped into reverse and the car began to lurch into the darkness. Sure, navigating this crooked driveway would have been a hell of a lot easier with headlights, but that wasn't an option, since she was trying to escape Gladys Harbaugh's house without being detected.

And, okay. Fine. So this wasn't the most mature way to deal with a roommate conflict. But there was just no way Candy could handle another scene with eighty-year-old Gladys. The old gal had been kind to let her stay rent-free for the first two weeks she'd been back in her North Carolina hometown, but when Gladys started to "borrow" Candy's lingerie, it was definitely time to move on.

Almost there.

She squinted into the dark, delicately adjusting the car's course as it scraped against a row of bushes. Not that a few extra scratches would be noticeable on this beast, a 1997 discarded police cruiser she'd bought at auction with her last three hundred bucks. Candy sighed. Sometimes, she couldn't even *believe* how fast—and how spectacularly—her perfect world had imploded.

Was it really just a year ago that she'd cruised down her private drive in her shiny new Infiniti, admiring the way the blue waters of the Gulf of Mexico set off the pristine white stucco of her five-bedroom home? All that seemed like some other woman's life.

Just a few more feet.

The Chevy's rear end finally cleared the driveway. Candy forced the gearshift into drive and pressed down on the gas, praying she could make it to the state highway before the damn thing backfired . . .

Bam!

"Oh, shee-it." Candy floored it. The car's worn tires screamed against the asphalt as the engine released a series of cannon-fire belches, each one more obnoxious than the last. A quick peek over her shoulder showed Gladys's bedroom light was on.

There was nothing to do now but put the pedal to the metal and head to Highway 25, which would get her out of Bigler. Her heart pounded in her chest. Her hands shook. And suddenly, it occurred to her that she was having difficulty seeing. *Well, duh!* She'd forgotten about the headlights! With a groan of frustration, she turned them on. That's when red and blue flashing lights appeared in her rearview mirror.

"You've got to be kidding me!" Candy's gaze darted from the alarming swirl of color in her mirror to the contours of the winding country road. Exactly *where* was she supposed to pull off? It was guardrail and woods as far as the eye could see. The quick blast of the siren made her jump in her seat.

"Okay! Okay!" she yelled out. "I'm fixin' to pull over, you idiot! Give me a minute!"

Suddenly, in her peripheral vision, she noticed an open patch by the side of the road. It happened to be on the *other* side of the road, but she decided it was still her best bet, and whipped the car around to a skidding stop. Unfortunately, all the whipping and skidding hadn't sat well with the engine, which began to spew smoke into the air along with another volley of backfires.

"Uh-oh," she whispered. It seemed the officer wasn't happy with all the commotion, either, and the large black SUV did a U-turn, the siren now *whoop-whooping,* and slammed to a stop in front of her, blocking any attempt she might make to get back on the road. Then a spotlight flashed on, so blindingly bright she had to shield her eyes.

Briefly, Candy thanked God for small favors. At least the person pulling her over wouldn't be her life-long friend Turner Halliday. He was the actual sheriff in Cataloochee County, and the sheriff didn't work nights. He had deputies to take those less desirable shifts. So at least Candy would be spared the additional humiliation of being pulled over in the middle of nowhere, at four in the morning, by her childhood buddy.

The siren went silent. Candy heard the door of the SUV slam shut and she blinked against the intense light. She could barely make out the figure of a man advancing toward her, but she heard him cough and saw him wave his hand in front of his face, chasing away the smoke. She cut the engine, thinking . . . wondering . . .

Since this wasn't going to be Turner strolling up to her window, she might be able to buy herself some mercy. She decided to get out the big guns. Shameless? Oh, absolutely. But what choice did she have? Candy began undoing two additional buttons of her blouse and arranged her weapons to their best advantage. Then she fluffed her hair and licked her lips. She hated to do this, but she didn't have the money to pay for a simple parking ticket, let alone a moving violation. She took a deep breath and prepared herself for the dumb-blonde-recently-from-out-of-town defense.

That's when the officer reached the driver's side window, leaned in, and grinned at her.

"License and registration, ma'am," Turner said, his bright eyes and white smile gleaming in the spotlight. "And you can put your ta-tas away. They're not gonna do you much good in this particular situation, and besides—I'm more of an ass man, myself."

Candy groaned and fell back against the driver's seat. "Ah, come on, Turner. Have mercy on me."

He shook his head and chuckled. "Candy Carmichael, this car you're driving is a public safety hazard of the first degree—and that's *with* the lights on! Lord have mercy, girl! What are you doing driving around in the dark in this piece of shit with no headlights? You could've killed someone, or gotten *yourself* killed!"

She sighed as she reached up to button her shirt. "Yeah. I know. Sorry. I was trying to escape Gladys and forgot to turn on my lights once I hit the main road."

Turner laughed again and leaned an elbow on the open window. "She finally scared you off, huh?"

Candy rolled her eyes. "I had to get out of there. She's a nice old lady, but she has absolutely no respect for my personal space. Thirteen days was all I could take."

Turner made a soft humming sound in his throat and looked away. He began to nod. "Coming out to the lake house tonight?"

"Of course," Candy said, smiling, hoping that this detour into small talk meant Turner had decided to take pity on her. How could he not? The idea of the four of them hanging out at the lake house was downright sentimental. It was what they'd done from grade school to graduation, just Candy and her best friend, Cheri Newberry, along with J.J. Decourcy, and Turner. Clearly, if Turner had a tender bone in his body, he'd have to let Candy slide for this little infraction. She was practically family! "I hear Cheri's making some kind of new chicken thing," Candy added.

"You bringing a cake?"

"Uh . . ." Candy bristled at the question. She hadn't picked up a measuring cup in a dozen years, but if it would get her out of a ticket, she was willing. "You want me to?"

"Hell, yeah."

Candy exhaled with relief. "So . . . what kind of cake would you like?"

Wait.

What was Turner *doing*?

She peered over the open window and her mouth fell open with disbelief. The whole time they'd been chatting about baked goods, Turner had been scribbling on an official-looking pad of paper.

"You know I've always been partial to your chocolate cake," he said, signing his name on the bottom of the form. "That shit is so good it makes my head spin." He carefully pulled the top layer of paper from the pad, smiled, and handed it to her.

She narrowed her eyes at him. "Really. You ask me for a cake and then give me a ticket?"

His smile softened. "I was teasing about the chocolate cake and it's just a warning, Candy, but it's not for the headlights. You've got a serious exhaust problem, and I'm ordering you to have your North Carolina emissions inspection completed within seven days. Plus, you're not wearing a seat belt." He shook his head, slowly scanning her. "You're a hot mess, girl."

"Yeah," she said meekly, accepting the piece of paper. *Truer words had never been spoken*, she thought as she looked away.

Candy refused to cry. There was no way she'd let her old friend see her fall apart. That had never been her style. She was a survivor. A fighter. Hell, she was a woman who'd started eight profitable businesses in the last decade! She would simply laugh this whole thing off. That's right. That's what she'd do.

Candy looked up again—and stared in astonishment. While she'd been busy with the self-coaching routine, Turner's entire demeanor had changed. The corner of his full mouth had curled up mischievously. His hazel eyes smoldered under the brim of his dark blue sheriff's department baseball cap. His latte-brown masculine face had softened and he'd tilted his head slightly.

Okay. She'd known this guy since elementary school. Sure, she'd noticed that Turner Halliday had taken the route from cute boy to handsome teenager to helluva hunky man, but something about the sight of him right at that moment was a shock to her system. Exactly what was going on here? Was it the light? Was it the fact that Turner was an authority figure actually being decent to her, offering her the first break she'd had in what seemed like *forever*? Was it the way he was trying his best not to smile? Trying not to look down her shirt?

Maybe it was just the alluring shape of his mouth, that little dip in his top lip, the strong, full line of his bottom lip, those little dimples that bracketed both.

Who knew? But the fact remained that Turner Halliday was leaning into her car window all big and brown and sexy and powerful—and wearing that cute little badge—and Candy actually heard herself suck in air at the impact of it all.

Just then, he moved in a little closer. His gaze dropped to her mouth.

And before she could give any decent amount of thought to what she was about to do, she tossed the traffic warning to the car seat, pushed herself up, grabbed him by his fine-looking face, and planted a big, juicy kiss on her lifelong friend's lips.

Hello.

This was interesting.

The kiss kept going. That hadn't been her intention. This was supposed to be a simple, friendly, spontaneous expression of gratitude, a genuine burst of affection for a fellow human being who had been kind enough to cut her some slack.

Right?

Which was perfectly understandable given the context. Candy was practically penniless. She'd lost millions in the Florida real estate crash and was about to declare bankruptcy. She'd foreclosed on that luxury home in Tampa. The Infiniti had been repossessed. She'd stupidly borrowed money from a less-than-savory character who wanted it back, like, *yesterday*. She had no job. She'd mishandled her mother's retirement nest egg, a pesky detail Jacinta remained blissfully unaware of. And Candy had recently crawled back to her hometown in the western hills of North Carolina, where she'd been taken in by her best friend's receptionist, an octogenarian floozy who couldn't seem to stay out of her guest's underwear drawer.

Was it any wonder she felt compelled to kiss an old buddy who'd just shown her a modicum of kindness?

Fine.

Then why were her arms now around Turner's neck and her eyes closed in bliss? Why was she hanging out of the car window with her boobs arched out and pressed up against his hard, muscled chest? Why was one of Turner's hands buried up under her hair while the other was on its way down her spine, headed directly to her—

"Holy hell, girl."

"Hmm?"

Candy felt herself being pushed away from the heat, pressure, and exquisite juiciness of Turner's mouth. She opened her eyes and the spotlight nearly blinded her, making her wonder where, exactly, she was, and why, exactly, she was there.

Turner stared at her, his eyes wide with surprise. He

removed one hand from her hair and the other from the small of her back and slowly backed away from the car.

Candy slid down into the driver's seat. "Oh, God. Sorry," she mumbled.

"No," he said sharply. "*I'm* sorry. My bad."

She glanced up in time to see Turner yank off his ball cap, sweep his hand across his close-cropped hair, then smash the cap back on his head. Next he rubbed his chin and mouth, shook his head, and tapped his feet in the dirt. This strange routine was topped off by an adjustment of his gun holster.

"Drive safely," he said as he turned away.

Candy peered out the driver's side window and watched him practically jog to his SUV, her eyes shamelessly riveted to the grade-A specimen of man-booty tucked in those uniform trousers. "Uh, thank you!" she called out, feeling ridiculous. What exactly was she thanking him for, anyway? Not arresting her?

Or was she thanking Turner Halliday for giving her the finest, hottest, most bad-ass openmouthed kiss she'd ever had in her freakin' *life*?

Chapter 2

"Well, hurry up, now! No sense in dawdling! I knew you'd end up here sooner or later!"

With a sigh, Candy headed up the sidewalk of Vivienne Newberry's home on Wilamette Avenue, her best friend, Cheri Newberry, at her side.

"Just eat whatever she puts in front of you," Cheri whispered, still giving her survival tips for living with her great-aunt. "And if she gets cranky, offer to make her a risky slush and go heavy on the vodka. Don't try to reason with her. Offer to clear the supper table but be aware that she'll never actually let you, but she'll bitch about you behind your back if you don't at least make an attempt. Go to bed as early as possible. And—like I really have to tell you this—privacy is going to be damn near impossible in this house, so don't say anything on the phone that you don't want to become common knowledge."

"Come on, now!" Viv called again, waving her fleshy arms from the porch step. "I just made ya'll a scalloped potato and ham casserole and I've already called down the street for Tater Wayne to unload Candy's things from the car!"

Cheri and Candy exchanged a quick glance. No words were necessary. It was only about six weeks ago that Cheri was subjected to a nearly identical welcome-home ritual, complete with calorie-dense casseroles and an immediate attempt to set Cheri up with Viv's handyman, Tommy "Tater" Wayne, a perfectly nice guy who happened to sport about seven teeth and an eyeball that went schizoid in the company of attractive women.

"It's gonna be all right," Cheri whispered, throwing an arm around her shoulder. "It's just temporary."

Candy swallowed hard and nodded. "It's not like I got many options."

"I told you you're welcome to stay with us out at the lake house!" Cheri bumped her hip against Candy's and laughed. "How many times have I offered?"

Candy laughed, too, but obviously her best friend was just being sweet. There was no way in hell she'd be bunking out at Cheri and J.J.'s lakeside love nest. They'd only been engaged a couple weeks!

"I adore you for offerin', but don't you dare bring that up again. You and I both know that wouldn't work." Candy waved back at Viv and smiled, slowing her step so she'd get just a few extra seconds with Cheri. "At least your granddaddy Garland will be here as a buffer, right? You know how well we get along."

Her friend nodded. "I think he's more excited about you moving in than Viv is, honestly. God knows he can use the distraction."

The two women paused briefly in front of Viv's ever-present lawn jockey, a formerly dark fellow who'd recently been painted the same mauve pink as the house. Apparently, it was Viv's nod to the changing times.

"Good Lord," Candy whispered. "Has Turner seen this?"

"Not sure," Cheri said, laughing softly. "But I bet he'd have a few choice words."

"No doubt." Candy shot a quick glance at Cheri and felt herself frown. She hadn't told her friend what had happened with Turner earlier that morning. She thought it was best to keep the details to herself. Besides, what exactly would she say? *Oh, by the way, I tried to dry-hump Halliday from the open car window! Doesn't that just beat all?*

"You okay?" Cheri squeezed her shoulder.

"Oh, sure. I'm great."

"You'll find a job soon. Or you'll come up with one of your fabulous start-up ideas and you'll make enough money to get set up in a cute apartment in town. It won't be long. You'll see."

"Of course," Candy said.

"Maybe you could even start that bakery you used to dream about. Bigler would be perfect for something like that—God knows we could use it!"

Candy faked a smile while thinking about how best to respond to that bit of insanity. First off, she'd have to be careful not to sound too down on Bigler, since Cheri was here to stay, but the idea of starting a brick-and-mortar business in this town made her downright queasy. And secondly—a bakery? What the hell? Candy cleared her throat. "Well, you know I don't plan to be here long-term," she said sweetly.

"Oh, I know." Cheri sighed. "I was just being selfish."

"And you realize the last time I mentioned the bakery thing I was still wearing a B cup."

Cheri giggled. "I know, but I figured now that you were back you'd think about it again. I mean, it's almost like you threw away that dream the second you left for college."

"Almost," Candy said, nodding.

"I'm just saying that I know things are going to turn around for you. They always do."

Cheri was being outrageously optimistic, of course. It was true that Candy had always managed to come up with a business idea that got her on her feet again, but this time it was different—she was beaten down as far as she'd ever been beaten in her life. Her entrepreneurial juices didn't flow well while being hounded by bill collectors. Go figure.

Even finding a menial job was proving to be impossible in the current economy. The entire country was in a major recession, but Bigler had gotten the life choked out of it. With her business degree and résumé, Candy had positioned herself right out of a small-town job market. She'd already been told she was overqualified for every job she'd applied for in Bigler—assistant manager at the Piggly Wiggly, a bank teller position, waitressing, even a shift on the production line at the tannery. In desperation, she'd responded to an ad for a nanny position. But, like everyone else, they told her they feared she'd only quit the moment she found something better.

Better? Right now, anything was better than what

she had, which was sixteen dollars, about three days' worth of mascara, and a car about to die a hideous—and noisy—death.

That wasn't counting Sophie, of course. It was far too early to even *think* about selling Sophie. The bracelet was her last defense against utter ruin, her ace in the hole, and her good-luck talisman. When the Florida housing market came crashing down, Candy refused to part with the twenty-two thousand dollars' worth of platinum, sapphires, and pavé-cut diamonds. Even Cheri didn't know she still had the bracelet.

That's because when it came time to sell everything for pennies on the dollar, Candy just couldn't bring herself to do it. She'd purchased that bracelet for herself right after making her first million-dollar real estate deal—just strolled right on into Hayman Jewelers, tapped her finger on the glass case, and whipped out a roll of cash. And now, six years later, Sophie was the only remaining link to a lifestyle Candy was determined to have again. One day soon, when the time was right and the big idea was big enough, Sophie would finance Candy's ticket back.

As casually as possible, she touched the inside of her left thigh to make sure Sophie was in her customary place, strapped securely inside the small travel belt just below the leg opening of her panties. All was well.

"Have you called Jacinta yet? Does she know you're in town?"

Candy stopped in her tracks and Cheri's arm fell from her shoulder. "I told you. I don't want to talk to her and she doesn't want to talk to me. It's the only thing we've ever seen eye to eye on."

"But she's your mother."

"I hope you haven't eaten lunch!" Viv called out, clapping her hands in excitement and looking none too sorry to have butted in on their conversation. "Look at you, Candy! I swear you look more like Marilyn *Mon*roe every time I lay eyes on you! Ya'll come on up here." Viv ushered them onto the wide, wooden porch.

"Be strong," Cheri whispered in her ear.

"Now, let me just say up front that all we've got at the moment is a twin bed, seeing as how Cheri took the big mattress and box spring with her to the lake house when she left without any warning."

Candy had to hand it to Vivienne Newberry—she was a passive-aggressive *goddess*. It didn't matter to Viv that her grandniece was insanely happy with J.J. Decourcy and had been a spectacular success replacing Garland as publisher of the *Bigler Bugle*. Viv still couldn't resist a poke at Cheri for moving out to the family lake house after just a few days of living under her roof.

As they headed through the front door, Candy grasped at Cheri's hand and gulped. She wondered how long *she'd* last at Land of the Lawn Jockey. She hoped to hell she was strong enough for this, because until she found employment, Viv Newberry was surely her last shot at free room and board in this town.

"'Sup, Sheriff?"

Turner extended a leg out of the SUV and smiled at his best friend, hanging out in his usual workday spot, holding up the back wall of the Bigler Municipal Complex.

"Haven't you got anything better to do? Loitering is against the law in these parts."

J.J. Decourcy laughed as he extended his arms wide. "What in the world would be better than this? I'm the managing editor of the freakin' *Bigler Bugle,* baby, and I'm out hobnobbing with the powers that be, looking for another award-winning scoop!"

Turner shut the door of his cruiser and headed up the back steps, the weariness settling in his shoulders and back. "You're sure as hell chipper today."

J.J. fell in step with him. "Yeah? And you look like you been run over."

Turner shrugged. "Pulled a double shift. Pauline called in sick for the overnight again."

"Ah, man, that's rough. Sorry to hear it."

As they strolled down the hall, Turner and J.J. waved at the usual daytime crowd that inhabited the public safety wing of the municipal building—the 911 call center employees (all two of them), the fire chief, the animal control officer, and the sheriff's administrative support personnel, including Turner's secretary, Bitsy, who handed him a hefty stack of paperwork as he passed by her desk.

"Thanks, Bits." Turner gestured for J.J. to have a seat in his office. "So what's up at the *Bugle*? How's the new publisher working out?" Turner glanced up in time to see a wave of ecstasy wash over his friend's face. He'd become immune to it over the last few weeks. Mostly, anyway. It wasn't like he wasn't thrilled for J.J. and Cheri—they'd been in love since middle school, and it had been one hell of a long and convoluted path to happiness for them. He knew that better than anyone.

But once in a while—okay, like right at that moment—Turner didn't much care for the lovesick look that had taken up residence on his buddy's face. It made him slightly irritable, in fact.

"Cheri is incredible. Simply incredible." J.J. sighed with contentment as he settled into the simple chrome and vinyl chair across from Turner's desk. "Damn, Halliday. I'm a happy, happy man."

"Uh-huh."

J.J. laughed. "Sorry. I don't mean to be obnoxious about it. But you did ask."

"Yep. I asked." Turner turned his attention back to the stack of paperwork Bitsy had just handed him. The ongoing North Carolina Rural Drug Task Force investigation of Bobby Ray Spivey was starting to heat up. An undercover DEA agent had infiltrated yet another methamphetamine manufacturing and distribution ring headquartered in Cataloochee County, this time in Preston Valley, and the next month or so would mean lots of man-hours for Turner's department. Or, more accurately, for *Turner*. Budget cuts had left him no choice but to hold off on the two new hires for the fiscal year, and with Pauline ready to go on maternity leave, he knew he'd better start getting used to a life of extra hours and not enough sleep.

But to Turner, this wasn't just another case. It was probably his last shot at linking Spivey to Junie's death, and he'd have to do it before the meth investigation came to a close.

"So. Anything good going on?"

Turner looked up at J.J. and smiled. This was their daily dance, and by now, they were damn good at it. He

and J.J. Decourcy had been best friends since kinder-
garten. After high school, Jay had gone away to UNC
to study history and political science, then he'd run off
to travel the world and eventually work for a news service in New York City. Since he was a country boy at
heart, that hadn't lasted long, and J.J. came back to
work for Garland Newberry at the *Bugle,* where he'd
been ever since.

Turner, on the other hand, had done two years with
the Marine Corps, then went to Western Carolina on
the G.I Bill, majoring in criminal investigation sci-
ences. He'd married Junie right after graduation and
joined the department as a deputy. Within three years,
he was the boss. And not long after, Junie was dead. In
a flash, his beautiful wife—the only woman he'd ever
loved with all his heart and soul—was gone from the
world.

Turner let his gaze wander to the small silver frame
he kept on his desk. Junie looked back at him with those
dark, almond-shaped eyes and her trademark smile. He
never got used to it, really, the idea that a spirit so full of
joy could exist one instant and vanish the next. But he
knew she was gone. He was called to the scene of the accident. He saw his sweet, funny, passionate wife slumped
over the wheel, lifeless. Dead.

Turner kept living. J.J. liked to point out that it was
more like *existing*—just a cycle of breathing, eating,
sleeping, and working—but somehow, he'd managed to
keep going.

He checked out his friend now, sitting where he sat
nearly every weekday morning, primed for the mental

tug-of-war in which Turner would play coy and J.J. would try to get him to reveal more than he intended. After years of this, they considered themselves at a tie. They both knew the daily standoffs were more about friendship than work, anyway.

"Pretty quiet," Turner answered him. He shoved the task force reports into a file—that was one topic that would never come up with his best buddy during one of these chats. Although J.J. had been privy to Turner's suspicions that Spivey was involved in Junie's death, his friend would hear about the meth ring only about an hour before everyone else did—when the task force called a press conference to announce an arrest. Anything else would compromise the investigation and put an undercover agent's life at risk. "But something kind of interesting went down early this morning," Turner added, nodding slowly.

"Oh, yeah?"

"Oh, yeah. I pulled some chick over for not having her headlights on, and she tried to flash me to get out of the ticket."

J.J. roared with laughter. "Damn, man. You have the best job in the world! You let her go with a warning, no doubt."

Turner felt himself grin at the memory of that spectacular sight—lots of creamy, milky, ivory-white cleavage, messed-up blond curls past her shoulders, and a pair of the pinkest, wettest lips he'd ever seen.

Candy Carmichael drove him fuckin' *crazy*. Always had, always would, and for good reason. That girl was a sweet treat that had continually been dangled just out of his reach. Intentionally or not, she'd flat-out tortured him in high school. The memory of her had left a permanent, voluptuously shaped indentation on his libido. And now, suddenly, all these years later and for no apparent reason, she decided to kiss him.

It had damn near short-circuited his brain.

"Yeah," he said to J.J., sounding as nonchalant as possible. "I gave her a warning. And then she gave me a little somethin' to show her appreciation."

J.J. sat up straight in the office chair, alarm on his face. Quickly, he looked over his shoulder, making sure Turner's office door was shut. "Uh, is this going to be a *Penthouse Forum* kind of story? Because if it is, I need to prepare myself psychologically for this watershed moment."

Turner laughed aloud. Along with reminding him that he was still alive, J.J. had made it his mission to try to convince Turner to start dating again. He'd never even been tempted. It was as if that part of him had died with Junie.

That was, until about six hours ago, near mile marker 47 on the shoulder of westbound State Highway 25. "Sorry to disappoint, but all the woman did was lean out the car and give me a kiss."

J.J. blinked. He waited. He shrugged. "And? Then what? Did you charge her with assaulting an officer? Can I run this on the front page?"

"No, and no."

"So what happened?"

"I kissed her right back."

His friend collapsed against the chair and his jaw fell open. "Wanna tell me who the woman was?"

"I'll give you a hint." Turner felt a sly smile spread across his lips.

"Yeah?"

"She agreed to make me a chocolate cake in exchange for her freedom."

"Candy Pants?" J.J.'s voice lowered to a whisper. "You kissed Candy?"

Turner nodded.

J.J. suddenly looked panicked. "You know you two are supposed to come to the lake for dinner tonight, right? Cheri's making some kind of marinated chicken thing. You can't cancel on me, man."

"Yeah, I remember."

"But isn't that going to be a little awkward? How are you going to handle this? What's your plan?"

Turner shrugged. "Same as my plan's always been with that girl, Jay. I'm going to keep on walking."

"But she kissed you." J.J. shook his head in confusion. "You're going to walk away after she kissed you? Just pretend nothing happened?"

"She was only thanking me. She's been through a lot this last year or so—she was just being friendly."

"So it was a dry peck."

Turner bit the inside of his cheek before he answered. A peck? No. Dry? *Hell,* no. That kiss had been all about slick tongue, wet lips, and possibilities. And he couldn't lie to himself. It may have started out as a "thank-you" kiss, but it was well on its way to becoming a "fuck-me" kiss when he'd put a stop to it.

"It was on the moist side," Turner said.

"Moist." J.J.'s voice was flat.

"Yeah, man. Moist and friendly."

"Okay, so let me get this straight." J.J. adjusted his position in the chair and cleared his throat. "Candy Carmichael—who's been yanking your chain since before you even knew you *had* a chain or what it was for—just laid something moist and friendly on you and you're going to walk away from it? Why? You're single. *She's* single. You're both adults. I don't get it."

Turner took a deep breath. "You're missing the bigger picture."

"Which is?"

"How many times do I have to tell you? I'm not ready for a woman in my life. Period. And besides, this is Candy Carmichael we're talking about. *Candy,* man. I grew up with her. She's been a friend of mine forever. That would just jack everything up something awful, especially if she decides to stay in town for a while."

"Rrriiight," J.J. drawled. "First off—at the risk of sounding like a broken record—you need to start dating. It's been over four years. You *know* Junie would have wanted you to have love in your life."

"But—"

J.J. cut him off. "And secondly, since I'm fixin' to marry one of my oldest friends in the very near future— a woman I've been nuts about my entire life—if you think I'm going to sit here and agree that a good friend can't become a great love, you're out of your damn mind."

Turner opened his lips to say something, but couldn't manage it.

J.J. grinned. "Who's missing the bigger picture now?"

* * *

The instant the shiny black SUV pulled into the drive-way, Candy yelled *"Bye, Viv!"* while grabbing her purse and trying to shut the big oak door behind her. Oddly, it wouldn't budge.

That was because Vivienne had wedged her chubby leg in the door.

"Yoo-hoo!" Viv called out to Turner, nearly knocking Candy down to get to the top of the porch steps. "How sweet of you to swing by and give her a ride! These girls just don't have much luck with their cars, now do they?"

Candy squeezed her eyes shut in mortification. It was bad enough that her damn car had stopped work-ing that afternoon, but the idea that Cheri had recruited Turner to drive her to the lake was just wrong, wrong, *wrong.* How weird was this going to be?

"Oh, don't you look handsome tonight," Viv said, beaming at Turner. "Sounds like ya'll are going to have a lovely time. Cheri's making some kind of fancy chicken dish I never heard of, so I can't really vouch for it, but it's supposed to stay muggy after sunset so ya'll might want to take a nice swim."

Turner seemed to follow Viv's rambling just fine and nodded politely as he strolled down the front sidewalk. He was out of uniform now, wearing a faded pair of jeans, a white and neatly pressed cotton oxford shirt with the sleeves rolled up, a pair of sneakers, and his ever-present sheriff's department ball cap pulled down tight. He had one hand in his jeans pocket. He had a little smile on those lips. He had one of the smoothest man-swaggers Candy had ever had the privilege to witness.

Why hadn't she noticed this before?

It was almost as if Turner Halliday had stepped from the shadows and started walking around under some kind of personal sexy spotlight. When had this happened? She'd been back in town for nearly two weeks and she'd certainly seen Turner enough—out at the lake house, in town, and she'd even run into him in the *Bugle* newsroom a few days ago when she'd gone to visit Cheri. He'd always been perfectly sweet. Polite. Helpful. Witty. Charming. In other words, he'd been the same Turner Halliday she'd always known.

So why the sudden change in him? Or was it simply a change in the way she *saw* him?

Just then, Turner's eyes flashed at her, his smile spread, and it all became clear.

It was the kiss. The second I decided to kiss Turner Halliday, everything changed.

Because up until that morning, she'd never kissed him. Not once. She'd liked him, of course—he made her laugh, he listened when she complained about boyfriends, he'd helped her out of more than a few jams over the years—but she'd never even thought about him that way, not the whole time they were kids and certainly not since she left Bigler a dozen years before. Candy had never figured Turner for dating material, let alone kissing material.

How wrong could a girl get?

"Good evening, ladies," Turner said, coming to a stop at the bottom of the stairs. "A swim sure sounds nice, Miss Newberry, but I can't stay out late tonight. I have to get some sleep before I go back in to cover the last half of the night shift."

"Oh, that's right! Pauline's about to pop, isn't she?"

Turner chuckled. "Yes, ma'am."

Viv shook her head. "How a woman is supposed to uphold the law and raise three little ones I'll never know."

Turner gave Viv a quick kiss on her cheek, then turned to look at Candy. "Ready?"

Candy froze. She felt her breath go shallow. Her hands started to sweat. She clenched her thighs together, squeezing the life out of Sophie. *Ready?* Ready for what? Ready to admit that Turner Halliday suddenly turned her on like all hell?

"Yes," she said, clomping down the steps in her sling-back sandals so fast she nearly lost her footing. "Let's go." She reached back for Turner's hand and pulled him to the sidewalk.

"Y'all have a good time tonight! I won't wait up!"

Viv's words echoed, then rattled around in her head with sentiments like *Oh, hell,* and *Oh, damn,* because Turner's hand had just latched onto hers and it was big and warm and she didn't want the touch to end.

This was not possible. Candy had absolutely no desire to complicate her life. She wasn't even sure it could *get* any more complicated! A man was the last thing she wanted. Sex might be nice every once in a while, but a *relationship* was out of the question. Especially with someone like Turner—a decent guy, a guy with ties to this town, a guy who'd been widowed at the age of twenty-six. He deserved more than a fling. He deserved a lot more than Candy could ever give him.

They got to the SUV. Turner opened the passenger

door for her and she climbed up, acutely aware of the view she must be providing him. She shouldn't have worn a skirt.

And she suddenly wondered . . . how many times over the years had she switched her ass in front of Turner? How many years had she pranced around him in a bikini without a second of self-consciousness? Had he ever noticed her? Had he ever thought of her as anything but his buddy?

Turner came around and hopped in the driver's side, immediately starting the car. He gave her a sideways glance. "Seems every time I see you, you're running away from someone."

She laughed, a little uncomfortable with that observation, since it wasn't the first time she'd heard it. "I can't stay with Viv. I've been there a matter of hours and she's already driving me nuts. She tried to pimp me out to Tater Wayne in exchange for him working on my car. And just before you showed up, she made me a skillet of scrambled eggs, telling me I'd need something on my stomach in case Cheri's recipe didn't turn out."

Turner swung the SUV onto Wilamette Avenue, waving good-bye to Viv. "Well, I've got a spare room at my place, if need be. Just give me enough notice to clear out some of the junk. I swear I won't try to pimp you or make you eggs."

Candy turned her head away to look out the window, feeling her eyes bulge out at the thought. Yesterday, that offer might have seemed perfectly innocent, and even doable. Today, it caused her to break out in a sweat.

"Thanks, but I'll figure something out." It embarrassed her that her voice sounded smaller than she'd intended, maybe smaller and sadder than she'd ever heard it. That was probably because she was thinking the unthinkable—that she might actually attempt to stay with her mother for a little while. After all, she'd survived in the same house with her for eighteen years. What would a few more weeks hurt?

Turner cleared his throat. "Hey, listen, we've known each other a long time, Candy. We all go through rough patches now and again and I know I couldn't have made it through mine without my friends. All I'm saying is if you need anything, I'm here."

Slowly, Candy swiveled around. She found Turner looking at her, those impossibly beautiful lips turned up slightly, those gentle hazel eyes shining under the brim of his hat. And she knew that whatever she might be struggling with was nothing compared to the heartbreak Turner had experienced in his life.

Candy could always make money again. Junie was never coming back.

She returned his smile and nodded in silent understanding, holding out her hand to him should he accept it. He did, and Candy took his big hand in both of hers and squeezed tight. She couldn't stop the wave of emotion suddenly crashing through her chest and belly.

"I am so sorry about Junie," Candy said, her lip trembling.

He shrugged and said nothing, but he kept his hand in hers as he kept an eye on the road.

In silence, Candy contemplated Turner's offer to help her with anything she needed. He couldn't live up to that promise, of course, since what she needed most was to magically turn back the hands of time to early that morning, so she could remember to flip on the damn headlights.

It would have made everything so much simpler.

Chapter 3

Red, yellow, and orange flames flickered from the fire pit and sent sparks into the night air. Turner stretched out in the lawn chair and let the pleasure of the moment sink deep into his bones. He'd enjoyed a fine meal with his oldest friends. Tom Petty tunes wafted from the iPod dock on the porch. And suddenly, he found himself caressed by waves of female laughter so sweet it made his skin tingle. That was a sound he didn't get to hear much these days. It was a sound he sorely missed.

There were countless things about Junie that Turner longed for, but the loss of her laugh had been particularly painful. Sometimes it seemed a hole had been punched through the world with the absence of that sound. The ring of Junie Pickett's laughter was what first drew his attention from across the college dining hall, a joyous sound that was clear and rhythmic. It sure didn't hurt that when he tracked down its source he found a sweet, open face the color of mocha, a head of shiny black curls, and a curvy, petite body. And later, he would discover all the things about Junie that lived under the surface—her capacity for love, her ability to forgive, and her fierce dedication to teaching.

It had always amazed Turner how much Junie loved her rowdy middle-schoolers—the most awkward and unlovable stage any human being could go through, in his opinion. Those kids were drowning in hormones, their bodies and brains growing too fast for them to keep up. But in the three years she was given to teach, Turner knew Junie made a difference in the lives of those young people, especially those living in the worst kind of poverty. She'd finagled food donations from the local grocery stores and sent her kids home with boxes of canned goods. She managed to conjure up clothing and shoes. And she often drove out to the homes of her students to "sit a spell" with the parents, just to tell them she was there if they needed anything.

Junie's love of children meant she looked forward to having her own someday. Of course, they'd both been beyond thrilled to find out she was pregnant, and that's why Junie headed to Chicago the very day after school let out for the summer. She wanted to share the news with her family in person.

Turner leaned his head back and gazed at the starry night sky above him, taking in a breath of lake air and wood smoke. For over four years now, Turner had carried the sickening truth on his shoulders. The weight pushed down on him every morning when he woke up, every day while he worked, and every night when he tried to sleep. He was supposed to have gone with Junie to Chicago, but canceled at the last minute because of work. He would have been behind the wheel that day.

He could've handled whatever caused Junie to lose control and plummet into the ravine. He should have been there.

For more than four years now he'd known that if he'd chosen family over his job—just that once—Junie would still be alive, and his world would still be intact.

He would still *have* a family. He would still have a world.

A raucous wave of female laughter dragged Turner back to the moment. He looked up to see J.J. shaking his head and chuckling, obviously enjoying the tale the two women were recounting from their glory days in Tampa. Turner hadn't been paying much attention to the thread of the story, but he thought it had something to do with a real estate open house gone horribly wrong. Candy and Cheri had left Bigler after high school and never looked back. They went to college, started careers, and eventually made it big in the Florida real estate bubble. They lost it all in the crash, and both had come crawling back home, Cheri first, and a few weeks later, Candy.

From what Turner could tell, Cheri was well on her way to rebuilding her life—she'd taken over the reins of the *Bugle* when her grandfather retired, then got engaged to J.J. For Candy, however, the transition hadn't been so smooth. In fact, it seemed she was barely keeping it together.

But she could laugh at herself, and her lightheartedness was contagious. Turner found himself smiling as they wrapped up their story.

"And everything was made worse by how flippin'

hot it was that day," Cheri said. "Do you remember? Without the air-conditioning, it had to have been over a hundred and ten in that house."

"Oh, damn, at least!" Candy said. "I swear I was so hot I could've grilled a panini between my thighs, right there in the master suite."

The women busted out into guffaws, and J.J. chimed in. Turner laughed, too, but in the back of his mind all he could think was that he was damn jealous of that sandwich. It certainly wasn't the first time he'd fantasized about the friendly confines between those long and luscious thighs, and it probably wouldn't be the last.

As subtly as he could, Turner spent a moment simply appreciating everything about Candy Carmichael. She glowed in the firelight, her skin golden, her blue eyes flashing as she laughed, all that thick blond hair curled tighter by the humidity, those gorgeous legs crossed at the knee. She was at least five foot ten. He'd heard her described as "statuesque" over the years, but he'd always thought that word suited a woman with sharper edges, the kind of woman who fell just short of being flat-out feminine. Okay, so she was tall, but Turner always thought Candy was too soft, too curvy, too *pretty* for a word like that.

He'd always seen her as juicy. Ripe. A succulent blond sex bomb.

Turner shook his head at his own idiocy, damn glad Reggie wasn't there to witness his drooling over Candy Carmichael, all these years down the line. After the fiasco of his junior year in high school, his big brother hadn't hesitated to set Turner straight. He'd taken Turner outside to the backyard, pointed for him to sit on the fence rail, and said simply, *"Let it go, little bro. That girl's daddy would skin your black ass just as soon as he'd give you the time of day. Ain't no tail worth that kind of grief."*

Neither of them had to point out the irony of Reggie's advice. Their own parents hadn't taken an easy road—his mother was black and their daddy white—but the boys learned early that in backwoods North Carolina, the rules got a whole lot stickier the other way around.

Things were different now, of course. The country had a biracial president. Turner and Candy were adults, not kids. And that bastard Jonesy Carmichael had died many years before, taking his bigoted ways with him to the grave.

But, Turner wondered, were things different *enough*? This was still the western boonies of North Carolina, after all, and as the county's first black sheriff, he knew he had no room for error. His only option was to play everything perfectly straight, all day, every day. Even if he were ready for a woman in his life, Candy Carmichael wouldn't be the smartest choice he could make. She would only bring complications. Trouble.

Suddenly, she turned his way and her smile softened. She must have felt his gaze on her body, because he didn't miss the flash of embarrassment in her pretty blue eyes. J.J. had been right—this was going to be awkward. Unless Turner addressed the situation head-on and talked to Candy about that kiss.

"You sure I can't get you another beer, Turner?"

"Naw, man, thanks. One was my limit tonight." Turner nodded subtly to Candy before he moved his focus to

J.J. "In fact, I probably should be heading out. I gotta get a little rest before I go back to work."

Turner pushed himself up from the lawn chair, hugged Cheri, and thanked her for a lovely evening. He slapped J.J. on the back and told him he'd see him tomorrow. Turner felt Candy's eyes on him.

"Would you like me to drop you back in town?" he asked her.

"Oh! Sure. That would be great." Candy grabbed her bag and hugged J.J. and Cheri good night. They walked together to Turner's SUV and he opened the door for her, averting his eyes from the backs of her bare thighs and the luscious curve of her ass as she climbed up.

God *damn*, she had it going on.

Candy remained silent during the ten-minute ride through the dark woods. Turner knew that it would be up to him to start the necessary conversation.

"Please don't feel uncomfortable about what happened this morning. I understand completely, Candy."

Very slowly, she turned her head and shot him an undecipherable look. "You do?"

"Sure," he said. "You were relieved that I didn't cite you. You didn't mean anything by that kiss, and I didn't make more of it than it was."

"Okay," she said, not entirely convinced.

"I mean, right?" A flash of alarm went through Turner's body. It had been a long time since he'd tried to decipher a woman's way of communicating, and perhaps he'd lost his ability. Was she toying with him? Was she trying to tell him something without actually saying it? What was going on here? He tried again.

"What I'm saying is you made it clear to me a long time ago that you weren't interested in me that way—you know, as someone you'd want to date—so I figured the kiss was just a . . . well, you know. A fluke."

Candy made a clicking sound with her tongue that sounded to him like annoyance. She was annoyed with *him*? He almost burst out laughing.

"What the hell are you talking about, Halliday?" She turned abruptly in her seat to face him. "You and I never discussed the possibility of dating. It never even came up. You always seemed perfectly happy being my friend, so I figured that's what we'd always be."

He tried not to choke as he peered at her in the dim light. The thing was, Candy looked perfectly sane and she sounded completely rational, like she believed the words she'd just spoken. How a person could be that delusional and look so normal he had no idea. "So that's how you remember it, huh?"

Candy swung her arm up over the back of the driver's seat and leaned closer to him. Her blue eyes were huge in the glow of the dashboard. "What exactly are you getting at?"

Turner chuckled, turning the vehicle down Main Street into Bigler. He knew Viv's house was no more than two minutes away. There would be no way they could sort out this mess by then, but he couldn't stop himself from setting her straight.

"I'm talking about that night I called your house and your father answered."

Slowly, a puzzled frown pulled at Candy's brow. She shook her head very slowly, sending her pale curls brushing across her shoulders. A stray lock slipped down over the top of her breast. "You called my house all the time, Turner."

"I did, but it was usually to tell you where we were all headed or what time we'd swing by to pick you up. The night I'm talking about was different."

Turner didn't see any sign of recollection in her expression. She tipped her head to the side and lowered her chin. Still nothing. Was it possible she really didn't remember that conversation and the fallout from it?

His mouth fell open in disbelief. "It was May of junior year. You actually don't—"

"No." She shook her head definitively. "I don't know what night or what phone call you're referring to. It's obviously a big deal to you, and I'm sorry if I'm forgetting something major, so just tell me what you're talking about."

Turner turned onto Wilamette, stunned. And angry, truth be told. "We'll talk about it some other time." He pulled the truck into Viv's driveway, and he could've sworn that damned bleached-out stable boy was giving him a "what the fuck did you expect?" kind of look. "I really gotta get some sleep."

Candy removed her arm from the seat back and pulled away. As she moved, the sweet scent of perfume and female flesh flooded Turner's nostrils. It occurred to him that maybe the best way to handle this was to not handle it at all. Maybe he should just stay away from Candy. Period. Not even try to maintain their friendship. Just forget about the kiss. Forget about the past. Forget about *her.* Maybe he should just decline any future invitations out to the lake and wait for her to get tired of her little hometown reunion experiment and hit the road, which probably wouldn't take long.

Maybe her friendship wasn't even worth the effort—especially if one of the most painful moments of Turner's life had meant so little to her that it had slipped her mind.

He hopped out of the SUV and jogged around to the passenger side, knowing he couldn't get Candy out of his vehicle fast enough. "Good night," he said, holding the door open for her, avoiding eye contact. "Take care."

Candy was frowning as she swung her long legs to the side, bent one knee, and dropped a sandaled foot to the asphalt. She shook her head at him and walked away. "Good night, Turner," she whispered.

As he drove away, he saw Candy glance over her shoulder. She was still shaking her head.

Chapter 4

Cherokee Pines Assisted Living was a single-story, red-brick complex with razor-sharp landscaping, a grand semicircular drive, and a white-pillared portico framing the main entrance. A network of white-pebbled walkways led from the main building to the gardens, tennis courts, and swimming pool. The property was surrounded by towering old evergreens that had likely inspired its name.

Candy blinked in surprise. She had no idea Jacinta's retirement home was this posh. Then it hit her—her mother might have to move out when she realized her nest egg had been fried to a crisp.

She parked the beat-up Chevy at the far corner of the parking lot, making sure it was hidden behind a line of senior citizen vans. She didn't want anyone making note of the condition of her car. Or of its contents. That morning, as soon as Tater Wayne had it running again, Candy began loading all her crap back into the trunk and the backseat. She'd had no choice. When she'd walked in the house after that incredibly strange drive home with Turner, Viv was lying in wait. The conversation that followed had been the last straw.

"You're probably starving." Viv started in on Candy the instant she stepped into the house. "There's a plate in the oven for you. You shouldn't go to bed hungry."

"Thanks, but I'm fine, Viv. The dinner was excellent. Good night." Candy started up the stairs.

"He's always had a thing for you, you know," she said, folding her arms over her chest. "Ever since you'uns were little."

"What?" Candy froze on the second step. She looked down at Viv.

"Now, your daddy had some narrow-minded ideas, that was for sure, and I remember him complaining to me once about how you were being too friendly with a colored boy, which was just plain silliness considering how your daddy and Turner's daddy had been friends back in the day, before he went and married Rosemary. Oh, it was a scandal at the time, let me tell you. A shock, really. Nobody knew what to think."

Candy turned around on the staircase so she could see Viv square on. "What is all this about, Viv?"

"Why, it's about you and Turner." She smiled brightly. "You know I've always loved that boy like one of my own. And he's grown up to be a fine, fine man, of course."

Candy waited until it was obvious Viv wasn't going to embellish that thought. "I'm going to bed."

Viv shrugged. "All I'm sayin' is you should think long and hard before you get yourself mixed up in that kind of arrangement. Just ask Rosemary. She'll be the first to tell you. It was no picnic for them in this town, being married to someone outside their own race."

"Married?" Candy nearly choked out the word. "Are you talking about me and Turner Halliday being *married*? Are you out of your mind, Viv? I've been back in Bigler five minutes! I haven't seen Turner in more than five years! This is complete lunacy!"

Viv gave a quick wave of her hand, swatting away Candy's reaction. "Now calm down. I noticed the way you two looked at each other this evening, and anybody can see what's coming down the pike if you're not careful. Turner's always wanted it, honey. I figured I should give you my two cents' worth."

Candy had to laugh. "Oh, Lord," she said, sighing. "Look, Vivienne, as much as I appreciate you letting me stay here temporarily, I do not want your two cents. I don't need advice about my love life. I'm a thirty-year-old woman and I've had my share of men in my life and I can make my own decisions. But, for your own peace of mind, I can assure you there's nothing going on between Turner and me. We're friends. That's all."

"Well, then." Viv sucked in her bottom lip in offense. "I meant no harm."

"Good night," she said yet again, continuing up the stairs.

"So you'll be free to keep Tater Wayne company while you're in town, then? He said he'd fix your car."

And that was how Candy came to be walking across the parking lot of the Cherokee Pines Assisted Living complex, the noonday sun beating down on her head, everything she owned cooking in the back of a 1997 Chevy Caprice.

She just needed a freakin' break. She needed a job. A place to crash where she could be left alone. Enough money in her pocket that she could think straight and figure out where she was headed and what she was going to do next. One thing was certain, she wouldn't be staying in Bigler one more day than was absolutely necessary. In fact, if it weren't for Cheri being here, she never would have considered returning to this town in the first place.

Candy smoothed out her skirt and raised her chin as she approached the entrance. She could do this. She could deal with Jacinta. All it would require was a bit of friendly chitchat. A dash of forgiveness. Some pathetic begging thrown in for good measure.

As the automatic glass doors opened, a delicate *bing* announced her arrival. A pimply-faced guy no more than twenty looked up from the raised front desk. Candy didn't miss the flash of surprise in his eyes when he saw her.

"Uh, may I help you?"

Candy smiled pleasantly and approached the reception area. "Hello. Yes. My name is Candace Carmichael and I am here to visit my mother, Jacinta Carmichael. She's a resident here."

The boy peeled his stare from her cleavage and looked up at her face, his pale blue eyes narrowed with mistrust. Candy knew he reminded her of someone, but she couldn't quite put her finger on it. He quickly tapped at the computer keyboard and said, "She isn't expecting any visitors today. You're not on the list."

"Yes. Well, she didn't know I was coming." Candy leaned in and whispered, hoping she could get this weasel boy on her side. She gave him a big smile. "It's kind of a surprise. She doesn't even know I'm in town."

"Hmmph."

"And what is your name? Are you the manager here?"

He straightened. "I'm Gerrall Spivey. And I'm the night-shift front desk manager. I don't usually work days."

"Gerald, you said?"

"No." His mouth formed a thin line of irritation. "Gerr-*all*. No *d*."

"Oh!" *I'm failing miserably.* "What an unusual but wonderful name!"

"Right," he said, picking up the phone and dialing a few numbers. He turned away, his shoulder to Candy. "Mrs. Carmichael, you have a visitor at the front desk. You weren't scheduled for anyone, so if you'd like I'll ask her to—" Gerrall stopped. He turned and frowned at Candy again, then let his eyes roam from her forehead to her shoes, with another brief derailment occurring at her boobs. "Yeah," he said into the phone. "That would be her. Okay, Mrs. Carmichael."

Gerrall—no *d*—hung up and pointed to an uncomfortable-looking settee in front of the bay window. "Have a seat. She'll be out in a minute. But it's almost lunchtime, so I can't promise she'll be much interested in visiting."

Candy didn't understand that bit about lunch, but nodded anyway. "Great. Thank you."

She was so nervous that her tummy felt like it was home to several dozen butterflies and small birds, all crashing around in the tight quarters. She sat down on the sofa and pressed her knees together, comforted by the feel of Sophie stuck to the inside of her left thigh. She began looking around the place. Dusty rose carpet.

Muted striped wallpaper. Real crystal chandeliers. Fresh flowers. Oil paintings of sun-dappled landscapes that had to be straight from the starving artists' sale in the Howard Johnson's ballroom.

She tried to smile at the sour and pimply Gerrall, who continued to glare at her over the raised reception desk, when it dawned on her—*Kid Rock*. Gerrall looked like a young Kid Rock after a shave, shampoo, and cut. But not a good cut.

His glare darkened.

Wasn't it the same everywhere? she thought. A dorky dude who's accustomed to lurking near the bottom of the food chain gets a hold of a little power and gets drunk with it. *Not on the list.* Of course she wasn't on any damn list! That would mean she had advance permission to show up here, that her mother was actually looking forward to her visit.

Maybe she should have just stayed with Viv. She could probably find a way to live with the pimping and the poking around in her love life. Or, maybe she could move back with Gladys! Hell! Now that she thought about it, the old lady could *have* her underwear. In the scheme of things, would it really matter all that much?

"Is there a problem?"

A rotund, middle-aged man stuffed into a suit and tie came around the corner and hovered near the reception desk. His question was for Gerrall but his eyes were on Candy. She stood up.

"She *says* she's Jacinta's daughter," Gerrall whispered.

"I see."

The man blinked with annoyance and took a few steps toward Candy. She could smell his aftershave from twenty feet. His thinning and too-long black hair was slicked back away from his ruddy face.

"Wainright Miller, here. Executive director of Cherokee Pines."

"Oh, hey, Mr. Miller." Candace held out her hand and smiled. "A pleasure to meet you. I'm—"

"Candace!"

Jacinta swept into the foyer with a sense of purpose, the sleeves of her Hawaiian-print caftan drifting behind her like flags in the wind. The first thing Candy noticed about her mother was that she didn't look a day older than the last time she'd seen her, which was well over five years ago. Her hair was still a blond bouffant, her blush still applied with a spatula. The next thing Candy noticed was the scowl in her eyes.

Mr. Miller stepped aside as Jacinta approached.

"How nice to see you, dear," she said, coming to an eye-to-eye halt before her only child, her hands on her hips. "I'm assuming you're here to return my nest egg plus the ten percent interest you promised."

Before Candy could open her mouth to produce an answer, a series of digital beeps rang out from an intercom system and a gaggle of senior citizens appeared out of nowhere, rushing toward the open double doors across the lobby.

Jacinta's head spun around and she sighed with irritation. "I guess you better just go ahead and sign her up as my guest for lunch today," she told Mr. Miller, grabbing Candy's hand. "Come on. We'll have to hurry or that hussy Lorraine Estes will try to steal my seat."

*   *   *

Turner pushed away from the dining room table, already regretting that he'd stopped by his mother's for lunch. The combination of too much home cooking, a shortage of sleep, and Candy Carmichael on the brain would make it nearly impossible to stay focused on work that afternoon.

Reggie grinned at him from across the table. "Anything new in your world?"

Turner shrugged. "Same shit. Starting another drug task force operation out in Preston Valley. I swear to God, it seems like the only new businesses opening up around here are meth labs."

Reggie laughed and gathered up his dishes. "Good to know the entrepreneurial spirit is alive and well in Cataloochee County."

"Right. How about the dealership? Business picking up?"

"No," Reggie said, frowning. "Let's just hope it doesn't get any worse. We only moved fourteen cars and three pickups last week. Worst week this fiscal year."

Turner glanced quickly toward the kitchen, making sure his mother was occupied. "So, listen. Check this out—the task force is looking into what's going on out at the Spivey place."

Reggie's eyes got big and he leaned forward across the table. "Bobby Ray Spivey?"

He nodded.

"Oh." Reggie pursed his lips. "And?"

Turner looked at his brother like he was crazy. "You know full well what the *and* is, Reg. This might give me the break I've been looking for with Junie."

"Ah, man." His brother groaned softly and peeked over his shoulder at their mother, still busy at the sink, her back to them. Obviously, Reggie didn't want Mama getting all riled up by the topic of conversation any more than Turner did. "You've already been all over that," Reggie whispered, crossing his big arms over his chest. "You spent *years* looking, Turner, and you never found a thing linking that slimeball to what happened to Junie. Come on, now. I know it would be a relief to have something—*somebody*—to blame for her death, but—"

"I don't want relief," Turner snapped. "I want answers. I want the truth."

After a few silent seconds, Reggie muttered something indiscernible under his breath and stared at the tablecloth.

"What?"

When his brother looked up again he shook his head back and forth. "Junie drove out to that place to give that idiot a piece of her mind about how he treated his kid, who was in her class, right?"

"Right."

"Then she left. She lost control of the car and ran off the road, T. Just because that Spivey loser was the last person to see her don't mean he did anything to her. The man was found at home watching TV, right? His kid cried when he heard about Junie—she was his favorite teacher—and all this time you and J.J. never found a shred of evidence that the Spiveys had anything to do with the accident. I think maybe . . ." Reggie's voice trailed off. "Ah, hell. Forget it."

Turner laughed bitterly. "That's it? I don't get the punch line? Why stop now?" The heat of anger began to rise up his neck. Reggie was the only person in the world he trusted with work-related shit. Reggie had been an MP in the army for eight years before he came home to run their dad's Ford dealership, so he knew his share about law enforcement. And Reggie and J.J. were the only two people who knew of his suspicions about Spivey. So it pissed him off that this was the kind of reaction he got. The truth was that having a multiagency task force poking around Bobby Ray Spivey's life might unearth something that Turner had missed, especially now that an undercover DEA agent had wheedled his way inside that group of lowlifes who hung out in Preston Valley.

"I just think it's time, is all," Reggie said, his voice deflated. He uncrossed his arms and laid his hands flat on the table. "You gotta let her go, little brother. Please. It's time you move on with your life."

"What the fuck do you think I'm trying to do? Finding out once and for all if Spivey had anything to do with—"

Their mother chose that instant to return to the dining room, a smile on her face and two servings of strawberry-rhubarb pie balanced in her hands. "This is such a treat having both my boys here on a plain old Monday!" She set the plates in front of the men.

"Thanks, Mama," Turner said, shooting Reggie a sharp look.

"Looks delicious," Reggie said, his eyes throwing daggers right back.

"I heard Candy Carmichael is still in town," Mama said, raising her teacup to her mouth, a move that didn't quite hide the remnants of her smile. She wagged an eyebrow at Turner. "Have ya'll been getting together with Cheri and J.J. often? Do ya'll get along like you used to?"

Reggie coughed delicately and held a napkin up to his lips. Turner rolled his eyes at his brother.

"Once in a while," he mumbled, digging into the pie. As always, the tart-and-sweet filling meshed perfectly with the rich, flaky pastry crust. "Mama, you still make the best pies in all of Cataloochee County."

She shrugged like the compliment didn't mean anything to her. "As long as you boys enjoy it, then I'm doing all right, I suppose."

"So what's Candy up to these days?" Reggie's question sounded innocent enough, but the way his eyes danced with laughter made Turner want to stand up and smack him upside his shiny head.

"Not much. She's only passing through, probably be leaving any day now."

"Now, that's odd, because I heard she's been putting in applications for jobs all over town." Mama looked truly puzzled. "Word is she even applied for a spot on the line out at the tannery, and that's no work for a young lady with a college degree."

"Jesus," Reggie said. "She sounds desperate."

Turner focused on his pie.

"Where's she living?" Mama asked.

Turner continued to focus on his pie.

"Turner?"

He looked up at his mother. "Uh, with Vivienne Newberry."

"Oh, my." Mama made a hissing sound with her tongue against her lips.

Reggie chuckled.

"Does Candy still make those mouthwatering cakes?" she asked. "Remember those cakewalk fund-raisers the cheerleaders used to put on for the football team? Candy's cakes were always grand prize, right? Remember that? Oh, my, they were as delicious as they were beautiful."

"Mmm, mmm," Reggie said. "Delicious *and* beautiful."

Turner was damn near ready to stick a fork in his brother's bare skull. "I don't know if she still bakes, Mama," he said, though in his heart he sure hoped to hell she did. She owed him a chocolate cake.

"Well, the next time you see her, tell her to stop by the Quick E Mart. If she's really that desperate for work I'll put in a good word for her with your uncle Earl."

"That's sure nice of you, Mama," Turner said, finishing up with his dessert, "but I doubt I'll be running into her any time soon."

"Oh? And why is that?"

"Work. Things are pretty busy. Don't have a lot of time for socializing." Turner stood up and took his dirty dishes out to the sink, then swung through the dining room, grabbed his ball cap from the back of the chair, and kissed his mother good-bye. "Thank you so much for a wonderful lunch, as usual, but I gotta run. I'll call soon."

By the time Turner made it out the front door, he knew his brother was behind him. Two hundred seventy pounds of six foot five couldn't exactly sneak up on a person.

"Hold up."

Turner ignored him, and climbed in the SUV and turned the ignition.

Reggie banged on the door until Turner rolled down the window.

"What?"

His brother gave him a crooked smile and leaned in. "You don't still got a thing for Candy Pants, do you?"

By that point, Turner had had enough of his brother. "Don't call her that, okay? I need to go, man."

"Hey, I don't mean anything by it. You and J.J. used to call her that all the time back in school. I remember—"

That made Turner perk up. He cut the ignition and gave his full attention to Reggie. "Tell me what you remember."

"All right." His brother nodded and pursed his lips in thought. "I remember how much you secretly liked her. Hey, I didn't blame you, man. It was obvious that she was going to be a brickhouse when she grew up."

"Anything else?"

Reggie frowned. "You talking about that night I heard you on the phone with her dad?"

"Yeah."

"Well, let's see. I was back home for Thanksgiving break right after my Achilles tendon surgery, so that was my senior year at State, right? So you had to be, what, about seventeen?"

Turner nodded.

"And I saw your face fall when her daddy answered. And then Candy came on the phone and gave you some kind of bullshit answer while that racist son-of-a-bitch father of hers breathed down her neck."

"Uh-huh."

"And you got really upset. You were shocked more than anything. You just couldn't believe that someone you'd known all your life could freak out like that the second you wanted to date her. But since I'd been down that road once or twice myself by that time, I took you out into the backyard and—"

When Turner busted out laughing, Reggie stopped talking. "Did I say something funny?"

"Nope," he said, letting his laughter die down to a bitter chuckle. "Thank you, Reg." Turner patted his brother on the shoulder. "See, I was starting to think maybe I'd made the whole thing up in my head or exaggerated it all out of proportion, because when I asked Candy about it last night, she didn't even remember the conversation. She said I'd never asked her out."

Reggie's mouth fell open. "You're shittin' me."

"I am not." Turner sank back into the headrest.

"So you asked her out again last night? Did she say yes this time?"

Turner's head popped up. "*Hell,* no."

"She said no again?"

Turner sighed and started up the SUV once more. "I didn't ask her out, all right?"

"Well, why not? Jonesy Carmichael was wrapped up in his pointy-headed white sheet and laid in the ground a long time ago. This is God giving you a second chance, little brother. You need to jump on that."

"I am not ready to date," he said, backing out of the drive even though Reggie was still leaning in the window. "And if I were, you think I'd be fool enough to start with Candy Carmichael?"

Reggie began to jog along by the side of the vehicle, pivoting when Turner put the gearshift into drive. "Whoa! Damn, T! Why are you still touchy about that chick?"

Still touchy? Hardly. Until she came back to town a few weeks ago, she'd barely crossed his mind. The last time he'd seen her had been more than five years before, at J.J.'s ill-fated wedding to Cheri's flaky sister, when Turner and Junie had exchanged pleasantries with Candy. More importantly, Turner hadn't had a decent conversation with Candy since before she went away to college and he joined the corps, which had been seven years before *that*.

So as he drove back to the municipal complex, Turner thought about his brother's fool question, and decided Reggie could be a real ass sometimes. Ridiculous! Of course Turner wasn't *still touchy* about Candy Carmichael.

He was touchy all over again.

In fact, as he picked up his messages from Bitsy, he decided "touchy" might not even cover it.

Turner closed the door to his office. He sat down in his desk chair. He nodded to himself. He wasn't touchy. No. It was far worse than that.

His fuse was lit and he was damn near ready to detonate.

Chapter 5

"All right then," Jacinta said, smoothing her caftan around her in the easy chair. "First off, no men in the apartment. Also, no late-night phone calls. No alcohol. No smoking. You'll have to sleep here." Jacinta pointed at the cream and white floral tufted-back sofa. "And two weeks is the absolute maximum you can stay. It's in the tenant association contract—only immediate family can spend the night and only for a total of fourteen days per year."

Candy nodded, dropping her overnight case on the plush carpet of Jacinta's sitting room. From what she'd gleaned in the last hour—at the lunch table and from her mother's ongoing commentary—this place had more official and unofficial rules than a federal prison.

"And I'll expect you to busy yourself on Monday and Friday evenings. That's when I play bridge. And you'll need to find somewhere to go every Tuesday and Saturday evening from between seven and ten, so that I can have my privacy."

Candy stared, then blinked.

"I entertain, you know."

No doubt.

Candy had seen evidence of that at lunch, when it became clear she'd landed in some kind of wrinkle in the space-time continuum where the plot lines for the movies *Cocoon* and *Mean Girls* had merged, where the cattiness far surpassed anything she'd experienced as a Tri Delta pledge at Florida State, and where the laws of supply and demand had gone haywire when it came to the most precious commodity of all at Cherokee Pines— *men.*

She'd counted seven male residents in the dining room during lunch, each surrounded by a dedicated harem of females. The coveted seat Jacinta had feared would be snatched up was at the left elbow of Hugo Stevens, cock of the walk. He was a retired plumbing contractor who still had all his own hair, sported a pencil-thin mustache, and was partial to ascots. Candy had watched, impressed, as Jacinta managed to bat her eyes at Hugo while simultaneously beating off the competition with vaguely threatening hand gestures and snide remarks.

So, sure. Candy would find something—anything— to do while Jacinta "entertained" Hugo on Saturday nights. Maybe she'd take up bowling.

"Anything else I should know?" she asked her mother.

"I'm sure there's something I'm forgetting, but we'll cover it as we go along."

There was a knock at the open door to Jacinta's apartment, and Gerrall poked his head in. He was carrying a box that Candy had intended to fetch from the lobby.

"You didn't have to do that," she told him, reaching out to take the cardboard container from his hands.

Gerrall laughed. "Oh, yeah I did. Mr. Miller was freaking because it was sitting on the floor near the entrance. He said it looked unteamly or something."

"Unseemly?"

"That was it."

"But I was coming right back for it," Candy said.

Gerrall actually smiled at her. "Miller can be a little stiff sometimes. Just try to ignore him."

"God knows we all do," Jacinta said.

Candy laughed as she put the box down by her suitcase. She'd already decided to leave the rest of her stuff in the car, since she was getting sick of packing and unpacking. Besides, she already doubted she'd last a whole fourteen days at the Senior Citizen Sing-Sing. It wasn't intentional, but she let go with a loud sigh as she plopped down on the sofa.

"Here. I snuck this out of the kitchen for you."

Gerrall reached down over her shoulder and gave Candy an up-close view of a piece of greasy chocolate cake wrapped in a napkin. Gerrall must have been carrying it around in his pants pocket, since it looked flattened.

"Oh!" she said, accepting the gift, trying not to make a face. "How nice of you!"

She'd attempted to eat a piece of this cake at lunch, and it had tasted like Styrofoam frosted with peanut-butter-flavored wallpaper paste, and she'd decided that no one—no matter how catty they were—deserved desserts that bad. In fact, the entire lunch had been lousy.

Candy put the brakes on her racing thoughts, very

nearly laughing at herself. Eighteen months ago, she was dining at Florida's finest restaurants, drinking exotic cocktails at the best Miami Beach clubs, partying at private estates from Ocala to Key West. And now she was back in Bigler, an itinerant unemployable person, lucky to have food and shelter of any kind. And she was bitching about the cake at her mother's retirement home?

She needed to get a grip.

"Thank you, Gerrall. I'll just stick this in the fridge."

"Oh, that reminds me," Jacinta said. "Any leftover food goes in a Tupperware container. No exceptions. It's part of the bylaws."

"Got it."

Candy took a moment to check out Jacinta's tiny but chic kitchenette, noting the quality tile, countertops, and cabinetry. Then she poked her head into the bathroom, where she found the same attention to detail. Her mother's bedroom was large, featured two walk-in closets and a built-in window seat. She estimated that the apartment had to be close to a thousand square feet.

Yep. This place was expensive. Candy swallowed hard at the prospect of telling Jacinta that she'd squandered the sixty thousand her mother had given her to invest in real estate.

"I'll catch you later then," Gerrall said, waving good-bye to Candy as Jacinta shoved him out the door.

"Little pecker-head," her mother mumbled under her breath.

"He seems nice enough," Candy said, revising her original opinion of the guy as she came back to the sitting room.

"He doesn't come from good people, Candace. Keep an eye on him. Do not trust him. And that goes double for Miller." Jacinta pointed to the sofa again. "We might as well get down to business. Have a seat. I want to know how it is that my big-shot daughter has shown up on my doorstep without a dime to her name."

"Uh, well . . ."

"Your daddy always said you'd shoot yourself in the foot." Jacinta settled into her chair once more, spreading her caftan in an arc around her. "Thank God he's not alive to see this. That man was insufferable when he turned out to be right."

"Why the *hell* didn't you say anything?" Cheri's voice was sharper and louder than usual. It was so loud, in fact, that Candy feared Jacinta could hear her best friend's phone voice all the way through the closed bedroom door.

"I'm sorry if you're mad 'cause I left Viv's," Candy whispered. "I appreciate you getting her to let me stay for a while, but I just couldn't stand it."

Cheri made a hissing sound of impatience. "Oh, Lord, Candy. I don't blame you one bit for leaving—she told me you two had a run-in when you got home last night. I'm talking about *Turner*! Why didn't you tell me about what happened with Turner when he pulled you over yesterday?"

"Oh." Candy sat up on the couch, slipped into her flip-flops, and tiptoed across her mother's sitting room to the door. "Hold on a sec." As silently as possible, she unlocked the dead bolt and crept into the hallway. It was nine-fifteen and the place was silent as a tomb. "Yeah, about that," she said, leaning against the wall and sliding down until her butt hit the carpet. "It's kind of a weird story, actually."

"Where are you?"

"At Jacinta's place," she whispered. "Believe it or not."

"Not," Cheri said. "But I'll get to that in a minute—why are you whispering?"

"Because she said 'no late-night phone calls' and I'm sitting out in the hallway."

Cheri paused. "It's nine-fifteen."

"Around here, that's the middle of the freakin' night."

"Right. So what did she say about the nest egg?"

Candy gulped, not looking forward to sharing the details of that unpleasant conversation, even with Cheri. She wasn't entirely sure which part was more painful—the part where her mother told her she never expected to get the money back in the first place or the part where she accused Candy of being incapable of staying put long enough to be successful at anything.

"It took you three colleges to get one degree," she pointed out. "You've started and ended a dozen businesses over the years. And Lord knows how many boyfriends you've run through that were never quite good enough to marry."

"I sold many of them, actually," Candy said by way of clarification.

Jacinta looked horrified.

"My businesses, Mother. In the last eleven years, I've sold eight businesses for a profit, and I always rolled it over into the next venture. It's called 'enterprise.'"

Her mother had pursed her lips. "Yet here you are, your enterprising ass on my couch and your possessions in a cardboard box. Obviously, something ain't right."

Candy looked up and down the hall again to ensure there were no eavesdroppers before she answered Cheri. "Jacinta wasn't thrilled, but she wasn't surprised. She took the opportunity to lecture me about my lack of stick-to-itiveness."

"I'm sorry you had to go through that."

Candy shrugged. "It's the price I gotta pay if I want to crash here. But I can only stay two weeks—it's in the resident bylaws."

"I saw a HELP WANTED sign in the window at Lenny's Diner today."

"Seriously?"

"Keep your voice down or I'll report you to Mr. Miller!"

Candy nearly jumped at the sharp command coming from her right. She glanced up to see Lorraine Estes stick her pink sponge-rollered head from her open door. Candy had no idea her mother's archenemy in man-chasing also happened to be her next-door neighbor.

The plot was thickening.

"You shouldn't be here in the first place," Lorraine added. "This here is a high-end place, not a flophouse. And what you did with your mother's nest egg is a sin! Shame on you!"

Candy rolled her eyes, pushed herself up from the carpeted hallway, and headed out toward the front lobby. "Hold on again, Cheri," she said, noting that Gerrall was watching some action-hero movie on his laptop at the front desk. She waved at him and pointed to her cell phone. "I'm going to take this call outside."

"I'll buzz you back in," he said with a smile.

"Now tell me about Turner."

Candy sighed, settling onto a bench near one of the white-pebbled walking paths, stalling, wondering how she would be able to avoid mentioning that she shoved her twins in Turner's face. In retrospect, it had been a stunningly bad decision. "Uh, what exactly have you heard?" she asked.

"J.J. told me the whole story, including the part where you flashed your boobs at the sheriff," Cheri said matter-of-factly. "That was just before you reached up and grabbed his cheeks and kissed him. Now, would you mind telling me what I'm missing here? Because I had no idea you've been harboring lust for Turner Halliday all these years."

Candy laughed. "That's because I haven't! I mean, I didn't *know* I was. Do you know what I mean?"

"No, I do not."

That hadn't come out right.

"You're telling me you're hot for Halliday?" Cheri's voice squealed a little.

"No. Yes. I know I shouldn't be. Would it be a problem if I were?"

Cheri laughed. "The only problem is that I was the last to know!"

"Sorry." She propped her forehead in her palm and sighed again. She felt like an insane person—a homeless insane person. "I swear I would've given you a heads-up if I'd been aware of it myself, but it just kind of hit me. I looked up and there he was and it was like I was on autopilot."

"Just like that?" Cheri asked. "You pulled out one set of headlights because you forgot to turn on the other?"

"I didn't even know it was Turner at first."

"So it was a *random* flashing event."

Candy groaned. "Fine. I deserve this. I should have told you as soon as it happened, but I guess I was just embarrassed. Forgive me."

"Forgiven," Cheri said. "So."

"So," Candy replied.

"J.J. says that Turner really enjoyed the kiss. In fact, J.J. thinks Turner likes you."

Candy sat ramrod straight on the bench. "What, are we suddenly in seventh grade again?"

Cheri laughed loud and long. Truly, it was a beautiful sound and Candy couldn't help but join in. How could she not be thrilled that her friend was so outrageously happy? It had only taken Cheri a month to figure out she'd always loved J.J. and was destined to be the newest Newberry to serve as publisher of the *Bugle*. If Candy envied Cheri anything, it was how simple and straightforward the transition to happiness had been for her.

Their laughter eventually died down. That's when Candy was suddenly hit with an appreciation for just how ridiculous her situation was. Last year at this time, her biggest dilemma was deciding whether to straighten her curls with a Brazilian blowout. And tonight she was freeloading in a retirement home, nine dollars and eleven cents in her pocket, talking on a cell phone that Cheri had paid for.

The instant Candy felt the tear hit her cheek, she wiped it away.

"How did we get here, Cheri?" she asked, her voice suddenly heavy with sadness. She knew her friend understood what she was asking, no matter how abrupt the subject change had been. And she knew Cheri didn't mind answering her, no matter that they'd had this discussion a hundred times.

"We were on a roll, girl," Cheri said with a sigh. "It was a thrill to buy and sell and watch our net worth skyrocket. We were smart and we acted decisively. It was like a game for us. It got to the point where it was easy to make money."

"Too easy," Candy said. She stood up and began to wander through the pines, her fingertips brushing against the cool, flexible needles. "It didn't even seem real sometimes."

"I know what you mean."

"Like play money."

"Yeah."

"But we were good at it, weren't we?"

"Damn good," Cheri said.

"Then the rules changed, just like that."

The two women were quiet for a moment, and the only sound was the crunch of Candy's flip-flops on the pebbles and the chirping of nighttime bugs. She closed her eyes against the remembered pain of those awful months, where they could do nothing but watch as banks tanked, property values evaporated, and the market died on the vine. Candy heard the words burst from her lips before she even knew she planned to speak.

"I'm so sorry for my part in what happened," she

said. "I was always the one pushing for more, telling you about some new property we could flip or cookin' up some deal. I know I can go off on a tangent sometimes, and I think my grand schemes—"

"That's nuts and you know it." Cheri cut her off. "We were a team. I made the numbers work and you had a knack for seeing the potential in properties. Whatever we did, we did together."

"But the commercial deal—"

"Even that."

Candy raked a hand through her hair and tilted her head back. The pines rose straight above her, piercing into the wispy night clouds and the stars beyond. She took a deep breath and wondered to herself once more— what would have happened if she hadn't talked Cheri into moving from residential to commercial? If she hadn't pushed to leverage their entire net worth on a single strip mall property? If she'd been satisfied with what they'd already acquired?

Sure, they would have suffered when the real estate bubble burst, like everyone else who owned property in southwestern Florida, but it wouldn't have been total annihilation. Maybe they'd still have *something* left.

"I just . . . no." Candy heard her voice break. "I think sometimes it's my fault, that I got you into this mess."

"Hey, Candy?"

"Yeah?"

"Everybody should be in the kind of mess I'm in."

Candy sniffled. "I guess it turned out pretty good for you, didn't it?"

"Uh, *yeah*."

Candy began to laugh outright, and Cheri joined her, then said, "And it will work out for you, too. Just wait and see."

She nodded in silence.

"Now is not the time to give up, babycakes."

"I know."

"You're Candy Freakin' Carmichael."

She snorted with laughter. "Hell, yes, I am—currently residing at the Cherokee Pines Assisted Living facility, thank you very much."

"Oh, Lord, girl . . ." Cheri said with a sigh. "Are you going to be okay tonight?"

"Of course. The couch is comfy. Tater got my car working again. I'll go to Lenny's tomorrow and see about that job."

"I'm here. Always. I love you to death."

Candy felt herself smile. That was one thing that had never wavered, regardless of the wheres and the whys and the hows of her life—she could always count on Cheri.

"I love you right back. Oh! And just one last thing."

"Yeah?"

"Do not tell Turner where I am, okay? Don't let J.J. tell him where I am, either. Let him assume I'm still at Viv's. I need some space. I need to figure this out."

"What if he asks?" Cheri sounded torn. "You want me to lie to him?"

"Ah, hell, I guess not. If he asks, tell him, but if he doesn't ask, don't bring it up."

"If you say so," Cheri said.

Candy ended the call and shoved her phone in her pocket, strolling toward the front door. She pulled on the handle but it was locked tight. Gerrall looked up from his laptop, grinned, and buzzed her in.

"You have a good night now," he said. "It's sure nice to have a new face around here—especially one as pretty as yours."

"Thank you," she said with as much politeness as she could muster, considering that Gerrall hadn't been looking anywhere near her face when he'd said that. *Do not trust him . . .*

Candy reached Jacinta's apartment door and tried the knob. It, too, was locked tight.

"Shee-it," she hissed. She gently tapped her knuckles on the varnished wood. No response. She knocked a little louder. "Jacinta?" she whispered, looking up and down the hallway. "Jacinta? *Mother?* Open up!"

"You know what they say—you can take the girl out of the trailer park . . ."

Candy slowly turned toward the voice. Once again, she encountered the neighbor lady's pinched little face framed in the halo of pink sponge rollers, and just had to laugh.

"Lorraine, honey," she said, "I'd freakin' *kill* for a trailer right about now."

Jacinta flung open the door and glared spitefully at her neighbor. "Carmichaels do not live in trailer parks, you nosy old floozy!"

"I *never!*"

"That's not what I heard!"

As Candy staggered through the door and back to the couch, she told herself that tomorrow was another day. As soon as she was horizontal, she pulled the blanket over her head.

* * *

Gerrall grabbed the duffel bag from the trunk and made his way across the junk-strewn grass to the barn. The light was spilling out from the cracks in the old sliding doors and he sniffed the air for the telltale tang of meth production. It was nearly two A.M. and they were still cooking in there, which meant they were behind on product, which meant his daddy would be mean as hell. With the new organization pushing them so hard, his daddy was worse than he could ever remember. Gerrall figured the best he could hope for that night would be to drop the shit on the worktable and get out before his daddy decided to beat him black and blue. Maybe he'd sleep in the old tree house instead of the trailer tonight, just to be on the safe side.

He pushed the door open a crack. Immediately, four sawed-off shotguns were aimed at his face. "It's me," he said, hearing the exhaustion in his own voice. He wondered how long it would be before one of these assholes started sampling the goods and got so jumpy they just shot his head off for the fun of it.

"Well, looky who it is!" His daddy grinned at Gerrall and ground out his cigarette in the dirt floor of the workroom.

The new cook screamed at him. "Fuck, Spivey! Stop your fucking smoking out here! How many times I gotta tell you this whole place and every one of us in it could blow up because of your fucking cigarettes!"

His daddy chuckled, then pulled out a handgun and pressed it into the cook's temple. "Talk to me like that again and I'll put a hole in your brain."

Gerrall sighed. The cook looked like he was going to crap his pants. It was almost a done deal that this guy—who didn't even have a name yet as far as he knew—would be gone in the morning and Gerrall would be looking for another college chemistry major dropout to run the shop. It wasn't as easy as it sounded, since everybody and their uncle was trying to get in on the meth business out here. Anyone with a working knowledge of chemistry was a hot commodity.

Gerrall smiled to himself. If he were really, really lucky, he'd come home one night to find the barn blown to all hell and his daddy's body parts scattered all over the property like pieces of confetti on Main Street at the Fourth of July parade. His daddy deserved it. He was a worthless human being and too damn stupid to live. Nobody would miss him. That was for sure.

Gerrall looked around the room. "Hey, everybody." He swung the duffel bag up to the work surface, unzipped it, and began unloading boxes of cold and flu medicine.

"Any trouble tonight?"

Gerrall shook his head at his daddy's question. "Everything's good. But the new guy from across the Tennessee line seems kinda slow in the head if you ask me."

"Nobody asked you." Bobby Ray walked over to Gerrall and slapped him on his ear by way of greeting, then began to riffle through the boxes with his filthy fingers. "This is it? This is all you got?"

"Yeah. That's everything they had tonight. Seven drop-offs."

"What the fuck?" His daddy slammed his palms down on the wooden worktable. "This isn't anywhere near enough!"

"I'm always looking for more smurfs, just like the Fat Man told me, but you know it's getting harder and harder for them to make buys," Gerrall said.

Bobby Ray threw a box of cold medicine against the barn wall. His face went purple with rage. "What I *want* you to do is bring back more shit than this! I don't care if you have to go out yourself and get it! Do you fuckin' understand? These people we're workin' for now don't fuck around!"

The dozen or so men in the barn remained silent. It was like this a lot lately. Most of the losers who worked for his daddy figured if they didn't speak and didn't move then Bobby Ray Spivey would be less likely to notice them, so less likely to shoot them.

Gerrall turned toward their new delivery driver, a big, rough-looking Hispanic dude who called himself "Dan." He'd been working for his daddy for two weeks now and had hardly said a word. Gerrall didn't even know if he spoke English, but he always made the deliveries to the Florida state line and always came back on time with every dime accounted for. His daddy seemed to think he was some kind of good omen for their business, since they'd got their new big-time backing right after he came on board. Though the Fat Man took credit for that.

The Fat Man took credit for everything.

The driver ignored Gerrall.

"We'll do better tomorrow night," Gerrall said, heading for the door. He kept on walking, right past the trailer and into the woods. He used the light of his cell phone to locate the foot and handholds on the old syca-more tree, then began to climb in the dark. When he pulled aside the plastic covering to the tree house door, a flashlight nearly blinded him.

"What the fuck?"

"Sorry! Sorry!" The little girl he'd seen hanging around the property dropped the flashlight and shot up out of the sleeping bag, her eyes as wide as Frisbees. She gathered up her backpack and some matted-looking stuffed animal and scurried right past him out the tree-house door. Gerrall shook his head and watched as she skillfully scampered down the tree and hit the ground running.

"If I catch you up here again, I'll kick your ass! Understand?"

"Okay! Okay!"

"Fuck." After Gerrall checked to make sure nothing was missing, he took off his shoes and crawled into the already warm sleeping bag.

He hated the idea that some lab loser's kid had found his hideaway. He also felt sort of bad that the kid was now out in the woods alone. But hey . . . not his problem.

Chapter 6

Turner glanced around the small sheriff's department conference room and prepared himself to referee the latest disagreement. He was used to it. Though the newspaper headlines stressed only cooperation, the truth was that power struggles were a daily affair in joint task force investigations. It had been that way for last year's big cocaine bust in Waynesville and the Spivey case was turning out to be no different. Turner figured anytime there were multiple law enforcement agencies working together, strutting and territorial pissing would be part of the bargain.

The group that had gathered that morning represented seven separate government agencies. The current argument was about who would ultimately foot the bill for cleaning up the meth "superlab" once the suspects were hauled off in handcuffs and enough evidence had been collected to tie them in with a Mexican drug cartel. They'd discovered that the makeshift methamphetamine lab in Bobby Ray Spivey's old tobacco barn had recently received an infusion of organized-crime

capital, which meant bigger and more sophisticated
equipment for the chemical "cooking" process, dra-
matically increased output, and a whole lot more traffic
coming and going through the rural Preston Valley
region. It was now apparent that when it was all over,
there would be a veritable toxic waste site to deal with.

Of course, Turner and the head of the Cataloochee
County Health Department had already made it clear the
local government couldn't pay for it. Seven years ago,
the county busted four meth labs. Last year, the number
was forty-seven, and twelve of them met the criteria of
"superlabs."

"Can't get blood out of a budget-mashed turnip," his
comrade in the health department had explained.

How about the U.S. Marshal's office? "We see our-
selves in more of a supervisory role here. Besides, we've
already exhausted our annual cleanup budget for the
entire state and it's barely the end of May."

The North Carolina National Guard? "We've always
left that to the DEA. We're really here to do the aerial
and ground surveillance."

The FBI? "Hell, no."

Well, what about the U.S. Drug Enforcement Agency?

One of Kelly O'Connor's perfect dark eyebrows rose
high on her forehead. She folded her manicured hands
on the table in front of her. Turner smiled to himself,
already knowing that whatever she was about to say
wouldn't match the prissy way she held herself.

"I will remind you that it's my guy in there risking
his 'nads every day with those hillbilly knuckleheads,
and if he doesn't get his ass blown up before we're
ready to go in, it'll be a fuckin' miracle." She tapped

her ink pen on the tabletop. "Somebody else can pay for the damn cleanup."

"I don't think we have any choice at this point but to call in the state Environmental Protection Agency," Turner offered. "We know from the aerial video that they're pouring all kinds of toxic stuff in the creek behind the barn, right?"

His health department coworker nodded. "Acetone, toluene, xylene, and corrosives like hydrochloric and sulfuric acids—and that's only the stuff we've been able to identify so far. It's going to be your basic cocktail of death if it leaches into the groundwater around here."

"Spivey's property is starting to look like the Wal-Mart parking lot on a Saturday afternoon," added the FBI agent in charge.

"They're cooking tens of thousands of doses a day at this point," O'Connor said.

"That's a great idea," said Trent Marshner, the special agent in charge for the North Carolina Bureau of Investigation. "Have the state EPA pay for the cleanup."

"So where do we stand with the Spivey kid? Any chance he'll turn?"

Turner knew that question from the assistant district attorney was directed to him. He'd known Gerrall Spivey since he was in Junie's seventh grade class. Back then, he'd been a dirty, underfed wild child three years older than his classmates, uncomfortable making eye contact with adults. Junie had taken a liking to him, of course, since she always gravitated toward the most desperate cases. The kid had even been over to the house for dinner a few times and he'd shoveled in food with the manners of a stray dog. Turner had driven him home on those occasions, and that's how he made his first acquaintance with Bobby Ray.

A twenty-foot-high flagpole sat at the end of a long, steeply declining gravel lane, proudly displayed the stars and bars of the Confederacy, which provided yet another clue that Gerrall's father might not be the most evolved of men.

"Y'all shouldn't be feeding my boy," was how he greeted Turner and Gerrall. Turner tried to keep his disgust hidden—the Spivey place was nothing but a twenty-acre junkyard. Out of the corner of his eye he thought he saw a dead cat lying in the grass.

"We don't mind, Mr. Spivey."

Gerrall kept his head down as he moved silently from the shiny county-issued SUV to the broken front door of the family trailer.

"I can take care of my own. I don't need no help from your kind, even if you *are* the sheriff."

Turner was fairly certain the "your kind" label did not refer to college-educated professionals who showered on a daily basis. "I hope you do make an effort to provide for your son, Mr. Spivey. My wife has noticed that Gerrall comes to class in the same clothes most every day, and that they haven't been washed. She said he's often hungry in the morning. A lot of people are struggling, and there's no shame in that. If you'd like, I can have social services stop by and—"

"You and your uppity badge can get off my land. I know my rights as a private citizen."

From then on, Turner dropped Gerrall at the end of the lane. He never again spoke to Bobby Ray until a few days after Junie died, when a fellow teacher mentioned to Turner that Junie had planned to stop by the Spivey place on her way out of town.

The news crushed him. He'd told Junie to never go out there. He'd warned her. But she'd gone in secret. *I would have gone with her! Why didn't she tell me?*

"She didn't want you worrying," the teacher added. "She knew you were busy at work."

Before he could answer the DA, Turner steadied himself by taking a deep breath. "I don't think Gerrall is going to help us. He's doing great, considering his home environment—even got his GED last fall and obviously he's working the night desk at Cherokee Pines—but he's still living with his father. I spoke to him a few days ago when he stopped by my uncle's convenience store."

"What did he say?" the FBI agent asked.

Turner laughed a little. "Not much of a talker—not to me, anyway. But I don't get the feeling he'd trust anyone to keep him safe from Bobby Ray. He certainly doesn't trust *me*—not after what happened with child protective services."

Everyone in the task force knew of Turner's past involvement with the Spiveys. Just before Junie died, he'd filed a report with the state's child welfare agency, asking them to open an investigation into possible abuse and neglect. Six months after Junie's death, the agency deemed the results "inconclusive." Gerrall had turned sixteen by then, and had dropped out of school.

"Dante says the kid is pretty beaten down—does whatever his daddy tells him to, and lately that's been collecting from the smurfers," Kelly said.

Kelly was referring to DEA field agent Dante Cabrera, a guy in his early thirties more used to the New York streets than the North Carolina hills. But he'd finagled his way into the group as a regional driver. For the last couple weeks, his job had been to take shipments from the lab to the Florida state line and hand them off to the cartel for distribution. The detailed information Cabrera had provided now formed the backbone of their case, though Turner and everyone else knew the longer they kept him inside the greater his chances were of being exposed.

Turner was troubled by that news. It was the first time he'd heard that Gerrall was actively involved in the meth operation. He turned to the state bureau of investigation agent at the table. "You guys still tailing Gerrall?"

"Yeah," he said. "He's making four to five pickups a night after he gets off his shift at the nursing home."

"But he's not accepting deliveries at Cherokee Pines?"

"Not that we've seen."

Turner barely had time to register his relief when there was a knock on the conference room door. Bitsy stuck her head in. "Sheriff, I'm sorry to disturb you, but you wanted me to remind you when it was time to think about lunch."

"Right. Thanks, Bits." Turner looked around the conference table, almost afraid to ask. "What'll it be today? Lenny's? The sub place? Pizza?"

Candy smoothed down her hair and pointed her chin high. She grabbed the HELP WANTED sign taped to the front window of the diner and ripped it off the glass on her way in the door.

"Hi, Lenny," she said, leaning on the counter, waiting for him to look up from the cutout window between the dining room and the kitchen. When he did, he smiled. Then started laughing.

"Candy Carmichael? Am I seeing things?"

"Nope." She held up the sign and smacked it down on the countertop. "Your newest employee is here."

One of Lenny's eyes narrowed as he frowned. She decided he hadn't changed much in the last dozen years—still half bald and all round. His laugh hadn't changed, either, and it rang through the mostly empty restaurant, which also looked exactly the way it had when she'd been in high school. If the place had been sparkling clean, it might have been considered retro. In its present condition, it looked just plain worn out.

"You don't want any job I got," Lenny said, shaking his head and throwing a dish towel over his shoulder. "Last I heard you went down to Florida and got your degree and became a business tycoon or some damn thing."

"Hmm," she said, fiddling with the tape still stuck on the sign. "I did, yes, but that was then and this is now. I've decided to reinvent myself."

"I see." His eyes sparkled with amusement. "And you want to reinvent yourself as a dishwasher?"

Candy couldn't hide it. She was disappointed, since she'd hoped the opening was for a waitress. There she was again—shooting for the moon. "Sure," she managed, trying to keep her smile in place. "Sounds perfect."

"Aw, girl, I'm just messin' with you. Hold up a minute." Lenny came out the swinging door and made his way around the lunch counter. Before she could mount a defense, Candy found herself pressed up against his apron-covered belly, swallowed in his beefy arms. When he was done, he planted her in front of him and looked her in the eye. "I was pulling your leg. It's a cashier job, seven A.M. to four P.M., with counter duties at lunch and a half hour paid break."

Candy felt herself bust out into a grin. "I'm in."

Lenny shook his head again. "I heard you were back in town. So where are you living now?"

"What do you mean?" Candy didn't like the way that sounded.

Lenny scratched his chin and thought about it. "Well, first I heard you was stayin' out at Gladys Harbison's place, but that she kept stealing your underpants so you left. Then you landed at Vivienne Newberry's but only lasted long enough to convince Tater to fix your car. And then you went out to Cherokee Pines and—"

"Yes! Yes! Whatever!" Candy hadn't meant to shout. At least she'd managed not to scream in frustration. This was just the way it was in Bigler, so what was the point in overreacting? It wasn't like she had any more secrets to keep anyway—the whole world knew she was a broke failure who'd squandered her mother's nest egg. What was there to keep private? "I'm staying with my mother, but only temporarily. I'm hoping that having a job will lead to better things, you know, like my own place."

Lenny didn't bother to hide his surprise. "You're staying in town? I assumed you were only passing through. I didn't think you were serious about the job, honey."

"But I am!" Candy felt her eyes widen. "Lenny, I am serious about the job. I need this job."

He scratched his chin again. "Well, I'd have to have a three-month commitment from you, honey. This here ain't a revolving-door kind of establishment."

"I understand." Three *months*? She was thinking more along the lines of three *weeks*! "I promise I'll give you three months. I'll take the job."

"You don't even know how much it pays."

"I'm assuming minimum wage."

Lenny chuckled. "You assume right."

"When can I start?"

Lenny put his hands on his hips and stared at her. "You still bake? 'Cause I remember judging the county fair bakeoff the year you submitted that chocolate praline turtle cake. Honest to gosh, I thought I'd died and gone to heaven when I took a bite of that thing."

Oh, Lord. Is that all anyone remembered about her? Candy plastered a smile on her face. "I don't really bake anymore, Lenny. Just not into it the way I used to be."

"A shame," he said, shaking his head. The phone next to the cash register began to ring. "Lenny's," he said into the receiver, moving around to the other side of the counter. "Uh-huh. Sure, doll. Fire away." He shoved the phone under his chin and looked up at Candy, suddenly gesturing wildly for her to join him. He pulled a pencil from behind an ear and started scribbling on a pad of paper while he pointed at a stack of freshly washed aprons.

"You want me to put one of these on?" Candy whispered.

He nodded. "You want cheese on that?" More scribbling. "And what kind of dressing on the chef's salad? Uh-huh. No problem. See you then, doll."

Lenny hung up. "Consider yourself punched in!" he said, heading into the kitchen. "We'll get to your paperwork after the rush."

Candy looked around her—there was an elderly couple sipping coffee at a table by the window, and a man, alone, stooped over at the end of the counter, reading the *Bugle*.

What rush?

"Here, let me help you with all this." The receptionist smiled at Candy and relieved her of two of the four shopping bags full of food. "I'm Bitsy Stockslager, by the way."

"Oh, hello! I'm Candy Carmichael."

"The sheriff has mentioned you. How nice to meet you."

Candy smiled weakly, realizing she'd begun to perspire, and it wasn't just the stifling heat and the trip from the municipal complex parking lot with eleven lunches in her arms. She was nervous—horrified, really—that she was about to walk into Turner's office in the capacity of a diner delivery boy.

She looked down at herself, suddenly unable to remember what she'd chosen that day from the extensive haute couture wardrobe stored in her overnight bag next to Jacinta's couch—jeans, silver hoop earrings, a light coat of mascara, flip-flops, and a simple white cotton peasant blouse that might have been a smidgen seethrough and might have the tiniest stain near the hem. She should have kept the apron on!

Why did it even matter? Turner had seen her a million times, wearing everything and anything and sometimes close to nothing. It wasn't like she was trying to impress him.

Was it?

Bitsy held the door to the conference room open for her and she stepped inside. Immediately she was greeted with the expectant faces of what were obviously a bunch of law enforcement types, mostly guys in suits and one strikingly beautiful woman with dark hair, creamy skin, and piercing brown eyes. She was very feminine, but looked like she could whup Candy's ass without rising from her chair. Shockingly enough, the woman was the one who smiled warmly and spoke first. "Oh, thank goodness you're here!" she said.

Candy froze. If she hadn't felt Bitsy poke her gently, she probably wouldn't have known to move into the conference room.

Why was she melting down like this? She was dropping off bags of grilled cheese and coleslaw, for God's sake. In her other life she'd negotiated real estate contracts, set up limited liability corporations, and intimidated lazy contractors, all in the course of a single day's work.

Just then, she felt Turner's eyes on her. She glanced his way. He was seated in a conference chair, his big body leaning back, his lips parted and his arms hanging at his sides like he'd just been knocked backward by a stiff punch. The look in his eyes was a mix of surprise and pleasure.

She glanced away and tried to catch her breath, her whole body tingling from being in the same room with him. And the strangest flood of feelings went through her—guilt, desire, regret, longing, sadness—followed by the most maddening thing of all, the awareness that she had no idea where any of it was coming from.

"Okay, then. Bon appétit!" Candy unceremoniously dumped the bags on the large rectangular table and began to back out of the room.

"Here. Wait." One of the suits stood up and started rooting around in his front pocket. "This includes a tip, because I'd really like to tip you."

"Me, too," said another guy. "Please. Take this."

Candy glanced at the pretty woman who mouthed the word "sorry" and rolled her eyes. It made her chuckle.

"No, thank you," she said, stepping backward. "Enjoy your lunch."

Once she was out in the hallway she managed to catch her breath, which was good because she needed the oxygen if she was going to run out to her car as she planned. She'd just made it outside when she heard Turner's voice.

"Candy! Wait up!"

She didn't.

"Hey! Hold on a second!"

She saw her trembling hand fumble for the car door. She felt Turner come up behind her. She watched Turner's fingers slip around the circumference of her wrist, his wedding ring glinting in the sunshine, his flesh hot against hers. And when he spun her around, she couldn't seem to resist.

The lust burned in Turner's beautiful green-brown eyes, pure and fierce. But it didn't quite hide the underlying sorrow. And Candy told herself that, yes, he was gorgeous and sexy and sweet, and, yes, she was incredibly lonely, but this could not happen. It *should* not happen.

She didn't plan to stay in this town a moment longer than necessary. And Turner was still in love with his dead wife!

So. No. Just . . . *no.*

It all seemed so clear and convincing inside her head, but she wasn't able to say the word with her lips. Instead, she blinked, fidgeted in the rush of conflicted feelings, and stared at him. Then she began to surrender to the pull of Turner's lust, drown in the depth of his eyes, fawn over all the wonders of his handsome face—that powerful chin, those sensual lips, the strong cut of his cheekbones.

"What's going on here, Candy?"

She regained her focus. "Okay. Well, I just got hired at Lenny's Diner and he asked me to deliver your lunch."

He laughed. "That's not what I'm talking about and you know it."

"I gotta go."

"No more running." Turner's grip tightened on her wrist and she felt her arm being bent and pressed into the small of her back. She wasn't sure if she was being arrested or seduced, but the sweet shiver she felt between her legs made her think maybe it was seduction.

Then he nudged her butt against the car and pressed the front of his body into hers, chest to chest, belly to belly, pelvis to pelvis.

Now she was *sure* it was seduction.

"You make me fuckin' crazy," he whispered, his

face pressing close to hers, his gaze searching hers before dropping to her mouth, her throat, her chest.

She nodded.

"You've always done this to me, Candy."

She frowned. "What do you—"

That's when Turner closed in and kissed the living sweet hell out of her mouth, pushing harder against her, and his lips and thighs and everything in between began seeking, pressing, wanting, taking . . .

Candy brought her free hand around his waist and spread her fingers wide, moving up along his sides to his back, fusing the flat of her palm against his muscles. Turner felt so solid in her grip, so real and warm. Her knees began to give.

He grabbed a handful of her hair and tipped her head back so that his mouth could have full control of hers, so that his need was the dominant force. It was all fire and slippery wet hunger and it seemed to go on forever.

When the kiss got rougher, she heard herself moan.

Turner released her wrist, but only so he could slap both his hands on her ass. He lifted her up against the car. She spread her thighs and threw her legs around his hips.

"Lord have mercy, girl," he groaned, dragging his lips across her cheek, down the line of her jaw, across her throat. He pushed her harder, trapping her body between the old car and his tight body.

"Oh, my God," she whimpered. "Oh, my God, Turner. You feel so good."

"You feel fuckin' incredible." His hands slid up her sides, across her ribs and up to her breasts. He cupped them gently, then rougher, his thumbs grazing over nipples that were far too erect for public.

And then it was over.

Candy was suddenly, shockingly, sliding down the side of the car to her feet. Turner began backing away. He rubbed his face, took big gulps of air, blinked his eyes. "Oh, damn," he mumbled.

Candy suddenly felt foolish. She pulled at her top. Smoothed her hair. "Uh, was it something I said?"

Turner closed his eyes and laughed. It was a low and sexy laugh, and Candy wanted nothing more than to feel him on her again, but clearly, the moment had inexplicably passed.

"Yes? No?" she asked.

He opened his eyes and smiled sheepishly. "Sorry to tell you, but that whole encounter was captured on video. There's a security camera trained on this lot at all times. I completely forgot."

Candy looked up at the building, noting the small black unit mounted at the corner just under the roof. "Fabulous," she said, sounding especially sarcastic. "I've always wanted to star in an adult video—especially one set in Bigler. Preferably in the police station parking lot. It's been a lifelong dream, really."

"We need to talk."

Candy pulled the car door open, shaking her head. "I'm not sure talking is going to come naturally to us at this point, Turner." She got inside. "I think maybe we should just keep our distance. You're lonely. I'm lonely. But screwing around with a man I truly like and respect just doesn't seem like a smart move at this point in my life."

Turner raised an eyebrow.

"Oh, you know what I mean!" Candy turned the ignition and waited for engine to catch in its embarrassingly loud fashion.

"Have dinner with me."

"I can't. I'm busy. Good-bye." She backed out of the parking lot, the engine backfiring as if to add insult to injury, and she looked back only once. Turner stood with his palms out and his eyes wide.

When she returned to the diner, Lenny was waiting for her. "Just got a call from Bitsy over at the sheriff's department. Seems you ran out of there without letting them pay for their food. Sheriff Halliday gets a free slice of pie every once in a while, sure, but a hundred-dollar takeout order ain't free."

"Oh!" Candy felt like a complete idiot. "I'm really sorry, Lenny."

He laughed. "Hey, everybody has a first day." Lenny patted her on the back. "Bitsy said she'll drop it off on her way home."

Candy didn't have much time to dwell on her mistake. The rest of the afternoon at Lenny's went by in a blur, and she got her first taste of lunch-hour rush. In the process, she learned all there was to know about the cash register, the daytime cleaning checklist, the menu, and the two lunch-shift waitresses. Afterward, she filled out her paperwork, picked out a couple medium-sized Lenny's T-shirts that would serve as her uniform—to be paired with jeans or a skirt that was no more than one inch above the knee, as per Lenny's instructions.

"This here ain't a Hooters," he'd pointed out.

At five, she clocked out and headed home to Cherokee Pines.

An unfamiliar face was at the front desk. Candy introduced herself and the woman pursed her lips and
said, "Yes, I've heard all about you."

Feeling thoroughly unwelcome, Candy continued
down the hall to Jacinta's apartment and found the door
unlocked, which was a relief. All Candy wanted to do
was collapse on the couch and try to sort out everything that had happened that day.

She was confused. Aroused. Unable to shake the
fantasy she'd been carrying around in her mind's eye all
afternoon—Turner, naked and glistening with sweat,
sprawled out in all his milk-chocolate, muscled glory, in
relief against a set of bright white sheets. That image
had shaken her so badly that she'd barely been able to
sort Lenny's clean silverware.

Jacinta greeted her immediately, looking particularly fetching in a chartreuse and magenta sundress.

"You look very nice," Candy said. "Are you going
out?"

"No, you are." Jacinta looked at her watch. "You'll
need to be gone right after dinner."

"What? *Why?*"

She smiled. "It's Tuesday, dear."

Chapter 7

"I heard your car coming a mile away," Cheri said, giving Candy a warm hug. "You want a beer?"

"Oh, God, yes. Thank you." Candy collapsed into the porch rocker and sighed with the relief of being somewhere she was wanted. She'd forgotten how good it felt. While Cheri was inside the house, Candy enjoyed the lovely sunset over Newberry Lake. This cottage had been in the Newberry family for four generations, and it had been a second home for Candy when she was a kid. All four of them—J.J., Turner, Cheri, and Candy—had spent every summer of their lives swimming, boating, and fishing out here.

The partying had come later, in high school, and by then Cheri and J.J. were an item. Candy started bringing her boyfriends into the mix. Turner brought his girlfriends. And she'd never once thought it should have been different.

Why, then, did Candy suddenly remember that arrangement with a twinge of shame? Was there something more to this? And why was she suddenly *sure* it had something to do with that phone call Turner mentioned the other night, the one she couldn't remember.

"Here you go." Cheri handed Candy a cold bottle of Miller and took a seat next to her. "I'm so glad you got the job at Lenny's. What are your hours going to be?"

"Uh . . ." It took a second for Candy to drag herself back to the present moment. "The day shift Monday through Friday and an occasional Saturday half shift. I think it'll be fine. I'll just have to save every penny to put toward an apartment."

"Too bad Tanyalee is still in rehab," Cheri said, a wistful smile on her face. "She'd hook you up with a place no problem."

"Maybe when she gets home," Candy offered, knowing full well that was unlikely. Tanyalee had run her boyfriend's real estate leasing office, but now that the boyfriend was in the federal slammer, it was doubtful Tanyalee would have much pull in that area when she returned.

Cheri sighed. "There's sure gonna be a lot of shit to sort out when my little sister gets home."

Candy patted her friend's hand, deciding she'd let the understatement go by without comment. Tanyalee had checked herself into a six-week inpatient program in Arizona to deal with her self-proclaimed kleptomania, love addiction, and codependency. The girl had gone berserk with jealousy when Cheri returned to become temporary publisher of the family newspaper, especially when it appeared that Cheri and J.J. were picking up where they left off after high school.

In fact, a whole mess of secrets began to unravel with Cheri's return. A forty-year-old murder mystery reemerged. Tanyalee admitted that she'd once trapped J.J. into marrying her simply to get revenge on Cheri. And Cheri's granddaddy—after a few too many trips to the keg—blurted out to his retirement-party guests that he and J.J. had lured Cheri to the publisher's chair knowing she'd lost her fortune and wanting to give her a hand without bruising her pride.

As if all that weren't enough, the drama was topped off by a hostage situation, where Tanyalee, Cheri, and Candy nearly got themselves killed.

No wonder Tanyalee checked herself into rehab a few days afterward. Candy would have gone along if she'd had the cash. So, yes, Cheri was right—there was going to be a lot of shit to sort out when Tanyalee got home.

She decided to change the subject to something much happier. "Have you decided what you're going to do about your engagement party?"

Thankfully, the question brought a smile to her best friend's face. "Yes!" Cheri said, perking up. "J.J. and I thought we'd have a get-together out here, you know, something casual. Live music and swimming. Tater Wayne can barbecue. And would you do me the honor of making cupcakes?"

Candy felt her rocking chair come to a halt.

"No?" Cheri's eyes widened. "I realize you haven't done much baking lately, but I figured—"

"Of course I will," Candy said, managing a smile as she resumed her rocking. She wouldn't be touchy about this, she decided. If her best friend wanted cupcakes for her engagement party, she'd have cupcakes. "Just let me know as soon as you've picked a date. Speaking of which, have you chosen a date for the actual wedding yet?"

Cheri shrugged. "Probably late fall. We're not in any rush. J.J. said he always wanted to get married by an Elvis impersonator in Vegas, and I told him that sounded great and to send me a photo of him and the lucky lady, whoever she might be."

Candy howled with laughter. "Where is J.J. tonight, anyway?"

"Working late at the paper."

Candy rested her head against the rocker and took a sip of cold beer. She kicked off her flip-flops. It wasn't long before they both took note of her bare feet, then looked at Cheri's bare feet, and started to laugh.

"We've become barefoot mountain women," Cheri said.

"Oh, Lord, I just realized I haven't worn a pair of outrageously expensive shoes for over a year," Candy said, sounding pitiful. "I doubt I would even remember how to walk in them."

"Tell me about it. Sometimes I fantasize about just fondling a pair of Christian Louboutins."

"Oooh, or a good Coach bag."

"Forget Coach—how about a Birkin?"

Candy moaned. "Now you're just being a purse tease."

The women laughed again, until the laughter ended in identical sighs. They sat in quiet for a few moments, listening as the sounds of an evening by the lake enveloped them.

"Thanks for letting me hang here while Jacinta and Hugo get their freak on."

Cheri chuckled. "You know you're welcome here

anytime—all the time. I told you to come *stay* with us, remember?"

Of course she remembered—and she'd refused the offer every time. Candy shook her head in silence, and instead of responding, she decided to watch the orange, red, and pink ripples of sunset dance on the water. "Moving right along—I need to talk to you about Turner."

Cheri sat straight up in her rocker, planting her feet flat on the wooden porch as if she were bracing herself. "Okay," she whispered.

Candy lolled her head to the side and gazed at her friend. "He still wears his wedding ring."

"I know. He hasn't gone on a single date since Junie died."

"He doesn't seem to want to talk about her, though. At least not with me."

Cheri hissed. "He doesn't even open up to J.J. much about her and they're still practically joined at the hip. Turner is an extremely private person, you know. J.J.'s tried to get him to open up, but Turner hasn't done his grieving in front of anyone, apparently not even his brother and mother."

Candy nodded, mulling that over. "Cheri?"

"Hmm?"

"You would remember if Turner ever asked me out in high school, wouldn't you?"

Her friend scrunched up her brow. "Of course I'd remember! *Did* he? You never mentioned that he did, though J.J. claims he always wanted to date you."

Candy placed her beer on the porch and dropped her face into her hands.

"What?" Cheri touched her arm. "Did something else happen with Turner? What's going on?"

Candy raised her eyes again and shook her head. "I wish I could tell you what's going on, but I don't know how to describe it. I'm having these feelings for Turner that I just don't get. We kissed again today."

"Seriously?"

Candy sat up straight and took a moment to gather her thoughts. "No. You're right. I don't think calling it 'kissing' is accurate. We *attacked* each other today. He initiated it this time, and we went from zero to out of control in seconds. I swear I could have ripped the man's clothes off and done him right there in the parking lot, video or not."

Cheri's eyes got big. "Um, what parking lot? What video?"

"The municipal complex. After I delivered his lunch."

Cheri sucked in air. "Whoa," she whispered. "That's crazy."

"You have no idea," Candy said, shaking her head in bewilderment. "I've never felt this out of control with a man. It's like it doesn't matter what's right or smart because my body knows what it wants and doesn't give a damn about anything else."

Cheri gasped again.

"But honestly, I can't be messin' with Turner like that. Casual sex would ruin our friendship, and even if he was ready for it, I couldn't start anything real with him because I don't plan to be here long."

A sad look crossed Cheri's face and she scrunched up her mouth.

"You know I'd never be able to carve out a life for myself in Bigler the way you have." Candy hated that she had to say all this aloud, but it had to be put out in the open eventually. "It's obvious that Jacinta and I will never connect, and she's my only family here. The job market is nonexistent. And you know I love you, but you're going to get married soon, and you'll have your own family to focus on. I'll come visit. I promise."

Cheri nodded, trying not to cry.

"We'll always be a part of each other's lives."

"I know."

Candy reached over and hugged her friend.

"But then again . . ." Cheri tipped her head.

Candy waited.

"Maybe you shouldn't write Turner off so fast. Maybe there's something there. Maybe there's always been something there with you two, and your body is just trying to get you to pay attention to what's in your heart. Maybe this is your opportunity to figure it out."

Candy bit her lip and stared at the lake again. Admittedly, she'd never thought of it quite that way. Cheri could be right. But still, if she and Turner ended up having an insanely hot fling—and it was obvious that would be the kind they'd have—where would it lead? Even if she found some kind of professional work nearby, was she ready for a committed, long-term relationship? Had she *ever* been?

"I don't have such a great track record with men," Candy said. "You know that better than anyone."

Cheri shrugged. "I didn't, either, but I'm pretty sure the past is only good for one thing and that's getting a person where they are at the present."

Candy smiled. "You sound like a wizened old newspaper publisher."

Cheri started to laugh, but it was cut short when they both heard tires crunching on the gravel lane.

"Huh," Cheri said, craning her neck. "That doesn't look like J.J.'s truck."

That's because it wasn't. Within ten seconds both women realized that Turner had just arrived.

Chapter 8

"Oh, shee-it," Candy whispered.

Cheri stood up and waved as Turner hopped down from the vehicle. He'd taken two steps toward the cottage when he saw Candy in the rocker, then swiveled his head to find her car parked in the shadows.

"Oh," Turner said, sheepishly shoving his hands in his uniform trousers. "Hey, listen, let J.J. know I swung by. I assumed he'd be around . . ." Turner took another quick glance at Candy. "Ya'll enjoy your evening. Sorry to disturb."

"Wait." Candy jumped up from the rocking chair and ran down the front steps in her bare feet. Before she knew it, she was standing directly in front of Turner, their eyes locked in the twilight. She grabbed his hand. "You got a minute to talk?"

"Sure." He revealed just a hint of a smile.

"I'll be inside if ya'll need anything," Cheri said, a bit too cheerfully.

Candy led him to the dock, painfully aware of the warm bulk of his hand in hers. The dock would be as good a place as any, she guessed, since she had no idea what she was doing or what she was going to say to him. Hadn't she just declined Turner's offer for dinner a few hours ago? Hadn't she just dismissed his suggestion that they talk? Yes, she had. But when she saw his beautiful face just now, that mix of sorrow and desire in his expression, she knew dealing with him was her only option.

No matter what else came of this, she cared for Turner. He was one of her oldest friends.

Candy squeezed his hand. She looked up at him as he walked by her side, and smiled.

Female. Luscious female. She was female in every respect—her scent, her soft touch, her laughter, her intangible energy. The essence of Candy reached out and caressed his body, poured into his being, flooded his senses.

Turner allowed himself to inhale long and deep, letting all that she was settle deep inside him.

God, how he loved women. Damn, he'd gone too long without feeling the pleasure of simply being in a woman's company.

Truth be told, he hadn't *allowed* himself to experience this. There were women everywhere in Turner's world, every day, and some of them had been less than subtle about what they wanted from him. But it had been as if he were deaf to their call, no matter how sexy they were, how smart or funny or appealing. Nothing— *no one*—had tempted him since Junie's death.

No one but Candy, the woman here at his side. Her

thigh pressed against his as their feet dangled over the edge of the dock, occasionally knocking together. They both pretended it was accidental. They both knew it wasn't.

They'd been sitting in near silence for about ten minutes. It was as if they were getting used to being in each other's presence at a lower frequency. They were doing pretty good—so far, there'd been no wild kisses, or gropes, or thighs flung around his hips.

"Turner?"

"Yeah."

"We're both adults, right?"

"I sure as hell hope so, 'cause what I'm thinking is for mature audiences only."

She giggled just a little, but he watched her struggle with her feelings. When she bowed her head, that stunning curtain of blond curls obscured the side of her face. As much as he loved her hair, he needed to see her expression. So Turner used his fingers to push the thick waves aside and tuck them behind her ear.

She looked up, wariness in her eyes. "You are a very good man," she whispered, and though the words were pleasant enough, a large lump had already formed in his gut. He already heard the "but" coming . . .

"I've always known you're considerate and honest and *loyal*," she added, just before she took a lightning-quick glance at his wedding ring, still visible in the near dark.

Ah. So that's what it was.

"And I only recently figured out that you're the sexiest man I've ever known."

Okay. I hadn't seen that coming. "Thanks," he said, slightly embarrassed. "And you're incredibly—"

"Wait—I'm not finished with you."

Turner laughed, and he figured that since she saw him as such a stud, she wouldn't mind if he slipped his arm around her waist and pulled her a little closer.

Apparently, he was wrong.

Candy peeled his hand from her body, then gave it a friendly pat as a consolation prize. Somehow, it didn't seem like the move of a woman overcome with his sex appeal.

"Turner, it's fairly obvious that you're still grieving for your wife. I don't want to interfere with that. And the truth is, I'm not sticking around Bigler any longer than I absolutely have to, so as much as I'd enjoy rolling around in bed with you, I don't think that kind of fling would be good for either of us."

Turner leaned back, propped himself on his hands, and gave her statement some thought. There was nothing unkind about what she said. In fact, it was downright noble. She was protecting his heart. She was interested in doing the right thing—both for him and for herself. He admired that.

There was just one problem—he wasn't feeling anywhere near as decent. In fact, since that white-hot make-out session in the parking lot, he'd been walking around mostly indecent, with the majority of his blood supply backed up in his boxer shorts. He hadn't been able to shake the feel of her soft body against his, the way she melted into him, fit around him, surrendered under him. He couldn't shake the taste of her sweet mouth or the rich scent of her arousal.

For the rest of the day, Turner had felt like a sex-addled zombie, stumbling through the joint task force meeting while every cell in his body continued to vibrate from his encounter with Candy. By three o'clock, he realized he might be ready to move on, to let Junie go. By five o'clock, he realized the time had come for him to live again—he was sure of it.

In fact, right at that moment, he'd have to say his vote was for rolling around in bed—and fuck the consequences.

"What are you thinking?"

Turner tried not to laugh. He really did. But it was just too funny—the reason he'd driven out here was to tell J.J. he'd made up his mind to ask Candy to date him. Officially. And here she was, turning him down before he could even spit out the words! So when he laughed, it had come out sounding pretty bitter.

"I was just being honest with you," she said, obviously hurt. Candy brought her legs up under her and began to push to a stand. "I should go."

He touched her arm, stopping her. "It wouldn't be just a fling and you know it."

She stared at him with wide eyes, but didn't move.

"I haven't been with anyone since Junie passed, and if you and I did end up in bed together, it wouldn't be just some kind of hookup. It would be special. *You* are special. You have always been special." Turner paused a moment, weaving his fingers with hers and staring down at the sight, dark and light laced together. "*This* is special, Candy."

She nodded softly, but Turner swore she looked like she was about to cry. That would be a first.

"Thank you," she whispered.

"So could we just—"

She placed the fingers of her free hand over his lips to shush him, shaking her head gently. "Let's just leave it at that, okay? Maybe if things had been different, if the timing had been better . . . I don't know."

He pulled her fingers from his lips. "You owe me an explanation, Candy. Why now, all of a sudden?"

She cocked her head in confusion.

"Why did you suddenly notice me? After all these years?"

Her eyes flashed with something close to embarrassment. "I've always noticed you. I've always liked you. A lot."

"But you said yourself that you just now saw me in a different light."

Candy grinned. "No. What I said was that I just realized you're the sexiest man I've ever known."

"Yeah. I just wanted to hear you say it again."

She laughed. "I'm not sure why, Turner, okay? But there you were, pulling me over with your flashing lights and your bright smile and it was like I was seeing you for the first time. That probably doesn't make much sense."

"Oh, yes it does," he said, "I was suddenly out of context. I wasn't your childhood running buddy, hanging out with you and J.J. and Cheri, like always. Plus, you were practically naked from the waist up, and that might have given you a slightly different perspective."

"That's an exaggeration."

Turner laughed. Very carefully, he leaned in closer to her, now gripping both her hands in his. "The point is I think you saw *me,* just a man, for probably the first time."

Candy frowned slightly and turned away, moving her eyes to stare at the water. "Tell me the rest of that story," she said, a hesitance in her voice.

"Which story?"

Candy glanced at him again, the corners of her mouth turned down and her chin trembling. "When you drove me to Viv's you mentioned something about the night you called and my dad answered the phone."

Turner pulled back, surprised. He studied her for a moment, but saw nothing but sincerity in her eyes. "All right."

"It's just that I think I'm starting to remember some of it," she said, her voice barely above a whisper. "I need you to fill in the blanks, if you don't mind."

Turner treed his hands from hers, turned his body square with the edge of the dock, and gazed out over the lake. "All right," he said. "It had taken me months to summon the courage to ask you out on a date, but I finally decided that the moment was right. You had just broken up with Petey Swanson, remember?"

A vague smile touched her lips.

"But your daddy picked up the phone. I was very polite. I said, 'Good evening, sir. This is Turner Halliday. May I please speak to Candy?'" He turned toward her again, and saw the pain in her expression, but he continued. "Your father asked me why I wanted to talk with you, and, since I knew I'd have to go through your father one way or another, I told him I wanted to date you."

"Oh, no," Candy murmured. She shook her head and closed her eyes.

"He called me 'boy.' " Turner heard the stiffness in his own voice. "Your father asked me who I thought I was and said I'd never get anywhere with you because you'd been 'raised right.' Then he told me to stay within my own race."

Candy gasped. She slapped a hand over her mouth and widened her eyes.

Turner chuckled bitterly. "Yeah, I know. But when he finally put you on the phone, I went ahead just as planned. I asked you to go out with me that Friday night. Do you remember what happened?"

She shook her head quickly, her hand still covering her mouth.

"You pretended you didn't hear me. You started laughing even though I hadn't said anything funny, and that's when I knew for sure your daddy had to be standing over your shoulder. You told me you had to go because your family had company and that you'd see me at school. Then you hung up on me."

Candy's hand fell away from her mouth but she continued to shake her head from side to side, like she didn't want to believe it. Then she bit down so hard on her bottom lip that Turner half expected to see blood.

"Now do you remember?"

"I . . . I didn't hear what my daddy said to you before I got to the phone. I didn't know he—" Candy struggled for air. Her entire body began to shake, like she was freezing. "I just knew what he'd do if I . . . no wonder he . . . that whole night was so awful and . . . Oh, God, Turner. I am so sorry!"

He nodded. Somehow, after all this time, her apology didn't bring any relief. It hardly seemed to matter, in fact. Candy's reaction had been so intense that he was more worried about her. "Are you all right?"

"I'm fine. I'm glad we got that out in the open. I better go."

"What?"

She grabbed her sandals and popped to a stand. "Please forgive me," she said stiffly, looking down at him. "I had no idea I'd hurt you like that. It makes me sick to know you've been carrying that memory around all these years."

Turner retrieved his shoes and socks and stood up with her. "Hey, that's life."

"Yeah, and life can suck, especially any part of it that involves Jonesy Carmichael. The happiest day of my freakin' life was the day I drove out of this town and . . ." Candy stopped herself, her jaw tightening with the effort. "My daddy wasn't a good person. Let's just leave it at that."

She began to walk away, heading down the dock, her long and curvy body outlined in what little twilight remained. Turner stared at her retreating form. "So that's it?" he asked. "You're just going to run away from me, too? Just like you run away from everyone?"

Candy turned around. He knew right away that she was crying. "The last thing I ever want to do is hurt you again, and that's what would happen if I gave in to this, Turner. I am not staying in Bigler. I can't. *I won't.* And you have this whole *life* here, Turner, this important, real, wonderful—"

He'd only taken a few steps when she straight-armed him. "Don't. Please. Just let me go."

Turner stopped. It was plain to him that whatever

pain he'd been harboring all these years from his brief contact with Jonesy Carmichael was probably nothing compared to what Candy carried, and yet she'd always seemed so carefree, so joyous and fun-loving. He'd never guessed.

"Please don't go, baby," he said.

She laughed, wiping away her tears. "I'm not anybody's baby and, like it or not, I'm not going anywhere for three months. I promised Lenny I'd stay on at the diner that long. So you'll see me around." She forced a smile. "Take care of yourself and keep your eyes open for happiness, because I know you'll find it. You're the kind of person who deserves it."

Candy turned and began to jog toward her car. For a moment, Turner remained frozen where he stood, her last comment echoing in his head. And then it hit him— she was absolutely right. He did deserve to be happy. And the only thing that had brought him any happiness in the last four years of his miserable life had been Candy's touch. Her kiss. The feel of her body pressed against his. The sound of her laugh.

He ran, catching up to her immediately. He spun her around by the shoulders. She stared up at him, her face shining wet with tears and her lips quivering.

"I don't care about any of it, Candy. I want you, and I'm not letting you walk away."

She shook her head in refusal even as she grabbed him by the back of the head and crushed her mouth to his.

Turner dropped his shoes to the ground. His immediate thought was that if this were a good-bye kiss, then nothing in the world made any sense. Candy's lips were hungry and determined. Her tongue slid over his, hot and wet and greedy. Her hands were everywhere—his ass, his back, his thighs. So he gave it all right back to her, and then some.

Turner's brain exploded with yearning as his body burned with desire. He wanted more. He wanted it harder. Hotter. He was suddenly aware of how simple everything was, how the whole vast, complex universe suddenly fit into that small spot of grass on the edge of Newberry Lake where he stood in his bare feet, where everything Turner had ever wanted and needed and everything that had ever mattered to him just narrowed down to the sensation of her body against his. The kiss they shared was seamless, flowing, full of need and sadness and joy. It was full of love.

And then it was over.

Candy slapped her palms against his chest and pushed him away, hard. "No more," she sobbed, looking around to locate her car in the darkness. "I can't do this. I would rather die than hurt you, Turner. This can't happen. Do not—"

He took a step toward her.

"Do *not* come after me. Promise me you won't."

He couldn't do it. He wouldn't. Turner shook his head.

"This is not what I want, don't you get it?" Candy swung her arms out to her sides as the tears streamed down her cheeks. "This is not the life I want! *You* are not what I *want!*"

With that, she turned and ran to her car. He was so stunned by her words that this time, he didn't follow.

Candy pulled into the Cherokee Pines parking lot and checked the time on her cell phone—eight fifty-five.

She had a little over an hour to kill before she could return to Jacinta's apartment, not counting the extra fifteen minutes she'd need to add as insurance. She didn't want to walk in on anything Hugo-related. She was strong, but she wasn't *that* strong.

Though the night air was hot and heavy with moisture, air-conditioning wasn't an option in her car. Even if it worked, which it never had, she didn't have the gas to keep the engine running. She'd be cruising into work tomorrow on fumes as it was. So Candy found a blanket from the assortment of personal belongings in the backseat and spread it out on the hood of the old Chevrolet. She climbed up and stretched out, folding her arms behind her head against the glass windshield. She took a deep, deep breath, and felt her belly quiver.

She'd been crying the whole drive back from the lake house, and felt strangely alive from the experience, like her nerves were overly sensitive and her blood was overly oxygenated. Maybe she just wasn't used to it. Maybe that's what crying did to people. All she knew was she hadn't cried that hard in her whole life, and it had swept through her like an electrical storm.

In fact, while driving past the tannery, trying to see through her tears, it occurred to her that this might be why she swore she'd never come back to Bigler—because she'd end up face-to-face with all the crap she'd left behind.

That's why she'd made that deal with herself twelve years before and had never looked back. She'd told herself that the day she and Cheri left Bigler, North Carolina, was the day her life began, that none of what happened in Bigler had been real. When she arrived at

Florida State, Candy had had her first intoxicating taste of creating an identity for herself from scratch. No one there knew her as Jonesy and Jacinta Carmichael's girl from a nothing town in the middle of nowhere—the pretty cheerleader who baked cakes. She discovered she could be anyone and anything she chose, and that's what she did.

She got to do it again when she transferred to Miami and again at Central Florida. She was hooked. And she was aware that she'd looked for the same kind of thrill after college when she began building businesses only to sell them. The beauty of it was she got to start with a blank slate every time. Each new venture was a fresh start. No history. No past decisions she'd have to make room for in the present.

The pattern continued in her and Cheri's real estate endeavors. Candy had seen each new property as a new beginning. Each house could be renovated, redecorated, and resold, and the profits would pay for the next go-around.

It was the rhythm of Candy's life. And she'd *loved* it.

So of course staying in Bigler wasn't an option for her. Of course this place would never bring her satisfaction.

Her eyes darted to the single-story brick structure lit up like the governor's mansion. She chuckled to herself. It was actually a perfect place for her mother. She seemed truly happy here. As happy as Candy had ever seen her, in fact.

Candy stretched out her long legs and laced her fingers over her stomach. It was true that Jacinta had never been a horrible person or a bad mom. She wasn't Mother

Teresa, but she'd always been there for Candy, working at the family insurance office only during school hours. Her mother did all the usual stuff—helped her with homework and drove her to cheerleading practice and taught her the fundamentals of baking. The problem with Jacinta was that even when she was with Candy, she was only half present. The other half was all about Jonesy. Her mother was either mulling over how she'd succeeded or failed at managing Jonesy's temper at the office that day, or planning ahead about how she'd manage it when he got home that evening, or actively engaged in managing it. The result was that Candy always felt like an afterthought to her own mother.

Her father had been mostly a mystery to her, and the older she got the more she realized he was doing her a favor by not being home much. Owning an insurance agency gave him cause to work long hours, as her mother always reminded her, and part of being a self-made man was being an active member of the community. So there were Lions Club meetings, Rotary Club, the Salvation Army board of directors, the chamber of commerce, and his many years on the Cataloochee County Board of Commissioners. It always struck Candy as odd that out in the world, people considered her father an important man.

At home, to Candy, he was just an angry man. All the time. At the cable news broadcast. At the editorial page of the *Bigler Bugle*. At the two Bs Candy got on her report card. At high taxes. At stupid customers. At the blacks. At the Mexicans. At her mother for making his Jack and Coke too strong or too weak. Jonesy Carmichael was mad at life.

Candy suddenly shivered, though there was no breeze and it was so warm that a thin sheen of perspiration covered her face.

No, she told herself. She wouldn't go there. Not now. Not ever. It was a long time ago. It was over. And in the scheme of things—compared to what some girls had been through—it wasn't all that bad. All her daddy ever did was give her a few slaps to her face. Sometimes he took the strap to her backside. Or the hawthorn branch to the back of her legs. There were a few hurtful words, yes, but never much blood.

She knew the act of harming her wasn't his favorite, anyway. What he enjoyed most was the buildup, describing to her in vivid detail exactly what would happen if she crossed him. That was Jonesy Carmichael's forte.

So when Candy learned that her father had died of a heart attack behind his desk in the middle of a rant against someone or something—no one seemed to remember the topic at hand—her reaction had been one of numbness. Jacinta called with the news. She told Candy he was being cremated and that it wasn't necessary for her to come home for the memorial service if she was too busy.

She was too busy.

Looking up at the newly dark sky, Candy thought again about the evening so long ago, when Turner called to ask her out. Now she understood why the phone call had slipped her mind. It was just a small piece of what became a long and horrible night—the worst of her life. Turner's brave and sweet request had been the spark that set off a chain reaction of explosive rage. No wonder Candy had forgotten all about it. Compared to everything that followed, Turner's call was nothing.

Of course, there was another reason she'd forgotten all about it. The night had never happened, right? It was part of a life she'd convinced herself hadn't been real. It was a lot easier that way.

And yet . . .

Candy placed her hands behind her head and adjusted her position on the hood of the car. She couldn't help but wonder—what if?

What if Jonesy hadn't answered the phone that night? What if she'd had a chance to talk to Turner without her father standing over her? Would she have agreed to go out on a date with him? What were her real feelings for him all those years ago? What would she have said if the words she spoke were *her* words, not those of Jonesy Carmichael?

That was a no-brainer, Candy knew. She would have said *yes*.

Just then, out of the corner of her eye, she saw a shooting star jet across the horizon. The flash was so bright and clear that she sat up in surprise, her mouth open in wonder. It was several moments before Candy could stop grinning. She hoped Turner had seen it.

Oh, no. Candy let her face drop into her palm. What had she done? Only an hour before she'd told Turner she didn't want him. *Didn't want him!* When had she become a flat-out *liar*?

Because here she was, wishing he'd seen what she'd seen, wishing he'd experienced the same beautiful, magical moment she had. That meant she'd made a wish on a shooting star, and her wish was for him.

What a giant mess she'd made of this.

Candy took a few minutes to fix her face as best she could, using a corner of the blanket and some lip gloss, then headed into Cherokee Pines. Gerrall buzzed her in, all smiles, and came around the edge of the front desk with a big bunch of daisies in his hand. He held them out to her.

"Pretty flowers for a pretty lady," he said.

"Oh!" Candy didn't reach for them right away. She didn't want to take them because she didn't want to give him the wrong idea. But she was going to have to deal with him for two weeks, and so far he was the only human being in the joint who seemed happy to see her. Maybe he was just being friendly. So she took them with a simple "thank you."

Gerrall had noticed her hesitation, however, and something dark passed through his expression. It made the hairs stand up on the back of her neck.

"You surprised me is all." Unfortunately, Candy knew she sounded as stiff as she felt.

"Well, you don't have to take them if you don't like them," he snapped. His thin shoulders sagged as he returned to his desk chair.

"No. No, I like them. It's just I wasn't expecting flowers. Thank you very much, Gerrall."

He shrugged.

"Well, good night," Candy said, heading down the

hallway, knowing that she was so exhausted that it wouldn't even matter if her mother was still "entertaining" the hell out of Hugo in there. She'd just put in a pair of earplugs and call it a night.

Chapter 9

Life began to settle into a pleasant enough routine for Candy, considering she was stuck in Bigler.

Every morning, she joined Jacinta and her friends for an early breakfast of oatmeal, eggs, and orange juice. Some of the women proved to be quite sweet, and invited Candy to join in their bridge games on Monday and Thursday evenings. Jacinta didn't seem thrilled with the idea but didn't object, either, which struck Candy as some kind of breakthrough. The men, including the always dapper Hugo, asked Candy if she'd like to join them in a game of bocce ball out on the lawn.

Each Tuesday and Saturday evening Candy made herself scarce, as agreed. Since she couldn't afford a movie or even a box of popcorn, she rediscovered the joy of the second-floor public reading room of the musty old Cataloochee County Public Library on Main Street, where she spent hours thumbing through magazines, poring over cookbooks, and eventually registering for a library card—using Cheri's lake house address as her own. She roamed around town, too, checking out the art galleries and craft shops that catered to tourists headed into Smokey Mountain National Park. She idled away a few hours stretched out on the hood of her car, thinking, remembering, and keeping an eye out for another shooting star.

And each morning on her way out the front door, at six forty-five on the dot, she exchanged pleasantries with God's gift to retirement home management—Mr. Wainright Miller—who managed to remain unpleasant every damn time. One morning, he informed Candy that her rights as a temporary guest were limited. "Any planned leisure or recreational activity is designed for the benefit of our senior residents *only,*" he said.

"So no bocce or bridge for me?"

"That's correct," he said, his upper lip twitching.

"Even if I'm invited?" Candy asked, keeping her smile in place.

"They'll forget they invited you. I suggest you do the same."

"Have an awesome day, Mr. Miller," she said, deciding that if that chubby tight-ass ever had the audacity to set foot in Lenny's Diner, Candy would personally see to it that his coffee tasted funny.

And every evening when she returned, Gerrall was waiting for her—with a gift. First it was a DVD of some TV crime show she'd never heard of, about some middle-aged teacher who learned he has cancer and decides to sell drugs for a quick profit. Next, it was two Almond Joy candy bars and a can of Fresca, which Candy figured was just about as mixed a message as you could give a girl. Then it was a solid silver key chain featuring a big letter *C,* and she decided she had to put a stop to it.

"Gerrall, please don't buy me gifts. You are very sweet, but I don't want you spending your money on me, okay? You're a young man starting his career and you should be saving whatever you can."

He produced an odd smirk and said, "Oh, yeah? Well, maybe one day you'll come home and that key chain will be holding the key to your brand-new Lexus, which will be sitting out front, and you can get rid of that piece of shit you call a car. You're too pretty to be drivin' a car like that anyhow." Gerrall's smirk expanded into an all-out grin. "Whad'ya think of that?"

Candy laughed a little uncomfortably. There had been something vaguely threatening about the way he'd spoken. But the guy just kept grinning. She placed the key chain on the desktop and said her good-nights.

The days at the diner went by quickly, and Candy found herself truly enjoying her work. She ran the register and takeout counter at breakfast, helped with kitchen prep during late morning, then worked as both counter server and cashier at lunch. It didn't take long before she'd figured out how the regulars took their coffee, how they wanted their burgers cooked, and what kind of salad dressing they preferred. She made six more lunch delivery runs to the Bigler municipal complex, but only two of those were to Turner's office, and she called ahead to arrange for Bitsy to collect the money and meet her in the lobby. Candy claimed it was necessary because she couldn't be away from the counter for more than a few minutes. The real reason was so she wouldn't run into Turner.

She didn't necessarily like the arrangement. She missed Turner, truth be told. She missed his soft, hazel eyes and his remarkable mouth, and the way his hips moved when he walked, all loose and relaxed and sensual. *Damn.* She'd never seen a man move like he did! Then there was the way he chuckled low and husky from down in his chest. And of course she missed the way he got all flummoxed and started fidgeting after she kissed him—or he kissed her.

So *hell, yes,* it was best she didn't run into Turner Halliday. She had enough to worry about. Her first paycheck didn't come until the end of her first two weeks, which meant she was borrowing against her wages just to put gas in that huge wreck of a car. By the end of the first week, she already owed Lenny thirty-two dollars. But what really ticked her off was that she'd been forced to start rationing her mascara, applying only a single coat each morning. When business was slow, Candy sometimes found herself daydreaming about all the options that would be available to her in the health and beauty aisle of the Piggly Wiggly on payday. Which would she choose? Maybelline? Cover Girl? Revlon?

So it wouldn't be Dior or Lancôme—who cared? Anything was preferable to living without mascara of some sort. The idea was alarming. The last time Candy had been in public without mascara had been in the eighth grade.

On Thursday afternoon of her second week, Candy clocked out after her shift, tossed her apron in the dirty linen hamper near the back door, and went in search of Lenny. She found him bent over in the walk-in pantry, mumbling to himself as he pushed around commercial-sized condiment containers on shelves.

"Looking for something?"

He shook his head slowly and sighed. "I forgot to reorder pimentos. I can*not* believe I forgot the pimentos." He straightened and stared at Candy with a perplexed look on his face. He threw up his hands. "I've been makin' grilled pimento and cheese sandwiches for thirty damn years and this has never happened before. I must be losin' my mind. Pretty soon I'm going to forget to order the damn white bread!"

She quickly scanned the pantry shelves and smiled. "Third row from the top, to your right."

Lenny whipped his head around and grabbed the giant-sized plastic jar, his grin spreading from ear to ear. "You're all right, girl."

Candy took advantage of her opportunity. "I have a favor to ask," she said.

"Honey, whatever it is, the answer is yes. You need more gas money?"

She shook her head. "No, but thank you. I'd like to use your kitchen and baking supplies to make a cake for my mother's bridge club tonight. I'll reimburse you when I get my first check. Would you mind?"

Lenny paused, the jar of pimentos cradled in his arms. He considered it for a moment and said, "I don't see no reason why not, and no need to pay me back. You go have yourself some fun."

So for the next three hours, Candy did just that. It was like remembering the steps of a lost dance or seeing an old friend after a long time away. The remembered steps rose out of nowhere. The love was right below the surface.

First, she pulled potential ingredients and set everything out on the countertop. After a few minutes of study, she decided she had everything she needed for one of her all-time favorites—a praline turtle cake—the very cake Lenny had mentioned the day she came looking for a job. The thought of that made her smile. She went in search of parchment paper, and when she found some, Candy knew it was *on*.

She set the oven to 350 degrees, then buttered the bottom of three round cake pans, cutting the parchment to fit about an inch up the side of each pan. She heated up a saucepan on Lenny's large gas stove and tossed in more butter, brown sugar, and sweetened condensed milk. Once that was the perfect temperature—hot but not boiling—she poured three equal portions of the mixture into each cake pan and sprinkled with a handful of chopped pecans, setting it aside to cool.

Next, Candy used Lenny's stand mixer to create the cake batter, mixing flour, cocoa, and granulated sugar with baking powder, baking soda, and a pinch of salt. To that she added eggs, sour cream, oil, vanilla, vinegar, and hot water, mixing everything together on low speed. When the batter was smooth and silky, she divided it evenly into the three cake pans, using a spatula to get every dribble.

Once she had the pans baking in the center rack of the large oven, she began to wash the bowls and utensils. It was then, her hands wrist-deep in the hot suds, that she realized how happy she suddenly felt, how her soul felt lighter somehow.

By the time she began making the fudge layer and the chocolate frosting, Candy was humming and dancing around the kitchen, her nostrils alive with the richness of her imagination. She laughed to herself. She smiled. She spun around a few times with delight. She couldn't wait to see the look on the ladies' faces when they took a bite out of this triple-layered nirvana. After all, they were accustomed to cardboard and wallpaper paste.

The oven timer hadn't rung out yet, but she could tell by the scent in the air that the cakes were baked to perfection. She removed the pans from the oven and placed them on a wire rack, sticking a toothpick in the center of each to be sure. She had to admit feeling the teeniest bit smug when she discovered she'd been right.

"Uh-huh," she whispered to herself. "Guess the girl's still got it." Then she broke into her version of the happy dance.

After the pans cooled for ten minutes, Candy ran a knife around the edges and carefully turned each layer out onto a cooling rack. She removed the parchment with caution, doing her best not to skin off any cake in the process. Once that step was complete, Candy found herself compelled to stand there for a moment, hand over heart, taking in the praline-infused flawlessness of each fluffy chocolate circle.

About a half hour later, she was in the middle of drizzling melted chocolate over the thick layer of pecan frosting, when Lenny burst through the kitchen swinging door.

"That looks . . ." He gasped, staggering backward.

"You okay, Lenny?"

"Is that . . . help me, Lord! Is that a praline turtle cake?"

Candy smiled. "I'll bring you back a piece if there's any left."

"The hell with that, honey!" Lenny smacked his thigh and laughed. "You should be baking these for *me*. If that cake tastes anywhere near as good as the one you made back in school, I could charge damn near three dollars a slice for it, maybe even three-fifty."

"You think?" Candy said, smiling to herself as she dropped the frosting knife in the soapy water. A slice of this cake would sell for at least twice that in Tampa, she knew.

"Hell, yeah." Lenny patted her on the shoulder. "And, by the way, I'm giving you a raise."

She spun around, slack-jawed. "Seriously?"

"Yup. You're a natural at customer service and I haven't seen one error on the cash register tapes yet. Plus you found those pimentos for me. You keep this up and I just might make you assistant manager."

Candy felt herself bust out into a huge smile, and suddenly, it occurred to her how long it had been since she'd heard encouraging news—about anything. True, being assistant manager at a worn-out hillbilly diner wasn't exactly her dream career, but it was at least a step in the right direction. She had to fight to keep from blubbering.

Lenny looked alarmed. "Hey, now," he said, sucking in his gut and standing straighter. "Don't go doin' none of that. I can't handle crying females."

Candy shook her head. "I won't. I promise. I'm fine." She turned away quickly, rinsed her hands in the big sink, and pulled herself together. When she turned around again, she couldn't help it—she gave Lenny a tight, fast hug. "Thank you so much. I have to get going, but tonight, why don't you make a list of some of the desserts you'd like to offer and we'll talk about ingredient costs tomorrow."

"Really? You'll make cakes for me?"

"I'll think about it, Lenny." Candy grabbed her purse and tossed her apron in the hamper. "I'm still a little out of practice. I'm slow. But I could start with one or two cakes at a time and see how it goes, okay?"

"Shee-it, that's one or two cakes more than I got on the menu right now. Besides, it's high time I jazzed things up around here."

Lenny gallantly carried the cake to the car, taking great care to balance the cutting board as he walked. He gently placed it on the floor of the passenger seat. "Baking has never been my fore-*tay*." He lowered his voice to emphasize the gravity of his statement. "As you probably noticed, I save my skill for the grill."

The feel of all that silky blond hair brushing against his chest was too much to take. Turner felt his spine arch and his hips lift off the bed and he knew he wouldn't be able to last much longer—and this was before her lips had gotten anywhere *near* his cock! What the hell was he going to do once he felt her mouth on him, all silky and wet and sweet and wrapped around the swollen head of his dick?

Right. Like he was going to last three seconds once that occurred.

He clenched his eyes shut with the immense pleasure of anticipation. Candy's lips and tongue began to snake down his solar plexus, leaving juicy little kisses all over his skin, moving lower, so close to his navel now, and— oh, *oh,*—she just stuck the tip of her delicate tongue

into his belly button and he was afraid he was going to
blow right there.

Fuck! How was a man supposed to survive this?
How was a man who hadn't made love to a woman in
over four fuckin' years supposed to maintain his dig-
nity in this situation? How much longer could he possibly hold on?

He let his eyes open. He was so close. "Stop, baby.
Please," he heard himself whisper. "I'm about to explode."

But she simply smiled up at him. *Oh, damn.* He
shouldn't have opened his eyes. The visual was too
much to deal with. Candy's big blue gaze sparkled and
teased as her silky, full breasts hovered over his body.
Her hard pink nipples just grazed his skin. Her thighs
spread wide as she straddled his calves. Oh! Her little
pink tongue just darted out of her lips! Any second now
and he would feel the exquisite torture of that sweet
tongue, flicking and licking at him . . . and then her lips
would open . . . and she would welcome him inside her
hot little mouth . . . so vulnerable . . . so wet . . . so *fucking incredible*—

"Sheriff?"

Turner rocketed up from a deep place, yanked from
an abyss of rapture and shoved into—what the hell *was*
this? He blinked at his too-bright office, his hard desk,
his worried-looking secretary.

Reality. This was reality.

He became aware that a sheet of paper was stuck to
his damp cheek, and he ripped it off impatiently.

"I think you were asleep."

"No. Not at all," he lied, pressing the heels of his hands into his burning eyes. What had he just been dreaming? Oh, right—Candy Carmichael was about to give him the blow job of his life. Not to be confused with the other dreams he'd been having lately—like the one where Candy lay beneath him with her legs open, begging to be penetrated, or the one where she was crawling up the bed on all fours wearing nothing but a see-through macramé thong and a smile.

Turner dropped his hands and stared at Bitsy, who had by now assumed her customary position, arms crossed over her chest and lips tight. He knew damn well what was coming.

"You're working too many hours," she said. "You're going to make yourself sick. You need some kind of life, Sheriff. It's not normal for a healthy young man to do nothing but work. I think you were even having a nightmare this time. It sounded like an arson or a bomb threat or some other terrible scenario unfolding in your exhausted mind."

Silently, Turner thanked God that his hulking, gunmetal-gray desk blocked Bitsy's view of anything below his waist. Talk about a nightmare. "That's ridiculous," he said. "Why in the world would you say that?"

Bitsy clicked her tongue. "Because you kept saying, 'Stop, please stop,' and then you were moaning, warning people that something was going to 'explode!'"

"You must have misunderstood."

Bitsy rolled her eyes.

"Really. I was only resting for a minute."

"Uh-huh. Anyway, Kelly O'Connor is here and wants

to see you. And Sheriff . . ." Bitsy tapped her finger against her own cheek. "There's still just a smidgen of drool just above your—"

"Thanks." Turner grabbed a tissue and made no attempt to hide his annoyance. "Bitsy, would you mind—"

"Coffee's already on," she said. "Should I send Special Agent O'Connor in?"

"Sure. Why the hell not?" Turner closed his eyes for a split second and took a deep breath. He needed to switch gears, and fast. At least with Kelly O'Connor about to stroll into his office he knew his hard-on wasn't long for this world.

"You look like shit on a stick, Sheriff," O'Connor said, shutting the door behind her and taking a seat across from Turner.

"How kind of you, Agent O'Connor."

She chuckled. "What can I say? Charm shoots out of my ass pretty much twenty-four-seven whenever I'm out this way."

"And don't think we haven't noticed."

"You all right?"

Turner sat up straighter. Was there more drool on his cheek? Another piece of paper stuck to his skin? He quickly rubbed his hand over his face. "Of course I'm all right. Why do you ask?"

O'Connor scanned him as thoroughly as possible, even craning her neck to see over the desk. She raised an eyebrow. "You're kind of glazed over."

"Glazed?"

"You know, out of it. If I didn't know better, I'd suspect you were strung out on a woman."

His breath caught. He tried to laugh. Instead, all he managed to do was sound like he was choking.

"None of my business, obviously." O'Connor leaned an elbow on the desktop and wagged a dark eyebrow at him. "All I know is that whoever she is, I hate the lucky blond bimbo. Should have been me, but, hey, turns out I'm not your type. Turns out you prefer busty, blue-eyed, coffee shop babes, so what's a skinny chick with a black belt in jujitsu to do?"

Turner was used to Kelly O'Connor by now. He'd worked with her on a dozen cases over the last five years, and had put up with her good-natured ribbing for much of that. But last year she began hitting on him so hard that even a distracted widower would have to sit up and take notice. Turner never regretted the way he handled the situation. He'd been quick, honest, and so blunt that there could never be the tiniest bit of confusion about how he felt. It was the only way to deal with O'Connor. And she'd taken it well—never bothered him since. He figured that same approach would be effective now, as well.

"I'm not interested in discussing this. What can I do for you today?"

O'Connor grinned at him. "I'm here to talk about the busty, blue-eyed coffee shop babe."

Turner felt himself frown in confusion. It almost seemed like O'Connor wasn't joking. "Excuse me?"

"Turns out you aren't the only one strung out on that girl. You've got competition—Gerrall Spivey's got himself some big plans for Miss Candace Carmichael."

Turner nearly shot out of his desk chair. Every muscle fiber in his body began to twitch. It was all he could do not to lose his cool with O'Connor. "Want to tell me what the hell you're talking about?"

"Sure." She stood up and began moseying around his office, surveying his bulletin board, peering at the family pictures on the walls, fingering a few wanted posters. Whatever she was up to, she was enjoying it way too much. "Dante's field notes report that Gerrall's in *love*," she said. "Apparently, all he does is talk about this girl, Candy, and how he's seducing her with gifts and plans to marry her. I thought you should know, in case you didn't already."

Turner felt his jaw unhinge as he continued to stare at O'Connor. Not a damn thing about what she'd just said had found footing in his brain. It didn't make a lick of sense.

She quickly turned toward him, catching his open-mouthed stare. "You *didn't* know! Hot damn!"

"What the fu—" Turner stopped himself. He regrouped. "Okay. Let's start over. What did you just say about Gerrall Spivey and *Candy*?"

O'Connor chuckled. "Want me to talk slower?"

Turner was suddenly in no mood for O'Connor's bullshit. His displeasure must have been broadcast on his face because she held up her hands in a defensive gesture and began to give him the information without further delay.

"Right. So Cabrera's field notes indicate Gerrall Spivey has recently become obsessed with a woman staying with her mother at Cherokee Pines. That woman is Candace Carmichael. We checked her out, of course, and discovered she's the very same Candace Carmichael who delivered our lunch last week to your conference room, an incident I recall in great detail due to the fact that every man in the room lost at least a hundred IQ points the second she walked in."

"When the fuck did Candy move into Cherokee Pines?" His question was directed to no one but himself, and Turner had already begun reaching for the phone. *"Candy was supposed to be staying with Viv Newberry!"* He'd already started dialing J.J.'s desk at the newspaper. All he could think was how ridiculous it was that he hadn't known about this. After all, he knew about everything else in this damn county—who was three months behind on their mortgage, who'd just gotten a partial plate, who drank too much at the VFW's Monte Carlo night fund-raiser, and who was stepping out on their husband, with whom, and with what frequency. Why the hell hadn't someone had the presence of mind to tell him that Candy was staying with her mother, who happened to live where Gerrall Spivey worked?

But then again, why would they? No one had a clue it would matter to him this much. No one person knew how everything was connected—that the task force was investigating Bobby Ray Spivey and tailing his kid, that Turner would give a rat's ass that Jacinta had moved to Cherokee Pines and that Candy was staying with her, or that he was still strung out on Candy, just like O'Connor had said.

Not even J.J. knew how bad he had it for Candy.

Turner slammed the phone down before the call could go through, his brain honed in on the word O'Connor had just used—"obsessed." "I need to see a copy of Cabrera's field notes."

She shrugged. "Figured as much." O'Connor reached into the briefcase she'd brought along and handed Turner a manila folder.

"Has he threatened her in any way?" Turner asked, already flipping through Dante's transcribed notes, feeling the tension coil in his belly and chest as he read the undercover agent's report. His heart pounded like he'd just sprinted up the side of a mountain. "Is she in any danger?"

"Not that I can see, but you'd know better than I would. I mean, is she the type who'd jump at the chance to take a romantic drive up to Preston Valley to see Gerrall's etchings?" O'Connor laughed, clearly amusing herself. "And, hey, if she is, you might want to reassess your interest in her."

Turner didn't bother to look up from the report. Sweat had broken out on his forehead. His stomach had clenched. The idea of Gerrall Spivey being in the same *state* as Candy made his skin crawl, but reading of how he talked about her constantly, gave her gifts, and claimed she returned his affections made him want to throw up.

He had to get Candy out of there.

O'Connor sat back down in the chair across from Turner's desk. "Anyway, as you're probably reading right about now, Dante thinks it's all in the kid's head—a fantasy. And thank God there's nothing illegal about fantasizing, because if there were, I'd be serving several consecutive life sentences—if you know what I mean."

Turner kept reading. Dante's notes on Gerrall were more detailed than ever before, and they revealed the kid's expanded role in the operation. Apparently, Gerrall was now managing the dozens of "smurfers" his father paid to travel all over the southeast buying small quantities of cold medicine from mom-and-pop pharmacies. It was a way to bypass laws meant to curb meth production by stopping one person from buying large quantities of its essential elements—ephedrine and pseudoephedrine—found in common cold medicine. According to Cabrera's notes, Gerrall returned from work every night about one-thirty A.M. with up to a hundred boxes of over-the-counter cold and allergy remedies. He met the smurfers at various points between Cherokee Pines and Preston Valley, including the Tip Top Truck Stop, Cabrera said.

The field notes mentioned that Gerrall spoke often about what kind of car he planned to buy for Candy, and carried a photo of her on his cell phone. Whenever he showed it to someone, he referred to her as his fiancée.

Turner felt his throat close up with rage and grief. If the Spiveys ever *touched* Candy, he'd shoot them where they stood and he'd deal with the ramifications later. "I need to keep this report," he told O'Connor. He heard the agony in his own voice.

"Hey, have at it, but it's in the task force database, like all our field notes."

Turner looked up. "Thank you," he said. "The state bureau is still tailing Gerrall, right?"

"Right." O'Connor narrowed her eyes at him and was about to make some other biting comment when her pager went off. She snatched it from the waistband of her fitted trousers and frowned. "Gotta run," she said, grabbing her briefcase and heading for the door. "Now you can make that call in private," she said, smiling. "But have mercy on whoever dropped the ball on this one, okay, Sheriff? Ta-ta for now!"

Chapter 10

J.J. glanced up from his desk and did a double take, obviously not expecting to see Turner barging through the center of the *Bigler Bugle* newsroom, heading straight for him.

Turner's best friend grinned, pushed back his chair, and stood to greet him. "What an unexpected . . ."

"Ain't a social call, DeCourcy."

". . . pleasure." J.J.'s smile faded along with his enthusiasm. He raised an eyebrow. "What's up?"

"Cheri in?" It was a rhetorical question. Turner cocked his head toward the publisher's office at the other end of the newsroom, where he knew Cheri would be holed up.

"Sure is." J.J. moved around his desk and started walking in that direction, with Turner right behind him. He tapped on the closed door while looking over his shoulder quizzically. "Everything okay, man?"

"Nope."

"Come on in!" Cheri called out, her voice light and chipper from behind the door. Turner had to suppress a groan of frustration, because right at that moment, he was predisposed to fuckin' *hate* "chipper." In fact, he figured anything remotely "chipper" could just kiss his ass.

"Turner!" Cheri said, her eyes opening wide. "We've missed you lately! How've you been? Can you come out for dinner this week?"

Before he could stop her, she'd popped up from her desk and embraced him, then she gave him a friendly peck on the cheek. Cheri Newberry was so sweet. She smelled so nice. He'd always adored her. He still did.

But she wasn't Candy.

He wanted Candy.

And for the ninety-fifth time that hour, Turner tried unsuccessfully to keep the sexual dreamscape from invading his brain—Candy's little pink tongue and luscious lips, her long pale curls brushing down his brown skin, those thighs spread open over him.

Lord have mercy! Turner wiped his brow and sighed at his own pointless, pathetic stupidity. He had to pull himself together.

Cheri peered up at him. "You all right?"

"I wish everyone would stop asking me that damn question," he snapped, immediately regretting it. Cheri hadn't done anything—or had she? That was why he was here in the first place, right?

"Care to tell us what's on your mind?" J.J. motioned for Turner to have a seat in one of the chairs but Turner shook his head.

"Thanks, man, but this will only take a minute."

"All right," J.J. said.

His two friends then waited for him to elaborate.

When he didn't, they crossed their arms over their chests simultaneously, which annoyed Turner something awful. A month of living together and they'd become a matching set of bookends? Did they now walk and talk alike? he wondered. Were they going to start completing each other's sentences? Good God above, these two were irritating the living hell out of him lately.

"Turner?" Cheri lowered her chin and frowned. "You're starting to worry me. Has something happened? Are Rosemary and Reggie okay?"

"Yes. Everything's fine." He cleared his throat. "Except for one tiny little thing."

J.J. shrugged. "What?"

"It's Candy! Would y'all be kind enough to tell me *why* you didn't think to mention that Candy had moved in with Miss Jacinta out at Cherokee Pines? Would y'all tell me exactly *how* that little nugget of news slipped your damn minds?"

Once again, Cheri and J.J. reacted in stereo. Both sets of lips parted in surprise as they turned to stare at each other.

Perhaps that question hadn't come out as nonchalantly as Turner intended.

"Well . . ." they said together.

He was getting a headache.

"Hold up now," Cheri offered, propping her hands on her hips. "If you must know, we didn't mention it to you because she asked us not to tell you."

His eyelid twitched. "Say what?"

"In fact," J.J. said, "Candy made us promise that unless you came right out and asked, she preferred you didn't know where she was staying. She figured—"

"She wanted some space to figure things out," Cheri said, completing his sentence. "She thought it would be safer this way, you know, less of a temptation for both of you."

Turner stood stock-still, hands at his sides, the heat rising in his face. "You gotta be kidding me." He shook his head and laughed. He'd never heard anything so ridiculous in his life! God only knew what could have happened to her while she was trying to avoid him—no, Gerrall Spivey was no criminal mastermind, but he was mixed up in his daddy's twisted business and keeping company with a bunch of Mexican thugs that would as soon shoot you as shake your hand, and now he was obsessed with her!

"She doesn't want to hurt you," Cheri added. "She and Viv had a disagreement and she figured she'd just stay off your radar a bit. You know—put a little distance between the two of you so things could cool down."

"You don't say?" Turner nodded, wondering if he'd experienced any cooling sensation since the last time he laid eyes on her, touched her, smelled her, kissed her . . . and the answer would have to be *hell,* no. He'd only managed to make himself crazy thinking about her. Dreaming about her. Wanting her. "That's what she said, huh?"

"Yes." Cheri looked at him suspiciously.

Shee-it. Turner knew full well that Viv Newberry could drive a person to drink with her constant chatter and gossip, but at least she wasn't keeping company with members of a drug cartel. Why couldn't Candy have just stayed put?

J.J. jumped in. "Why are you so jacked up about this, Halliday? It's just a retirement home. She's hanging out with a bunch of senior citizens and you're acting like you're worried she's wandered into a den of iniquity or some—"

As J.J. talked, Turner stared at his best friend. It took a few seconds, but he saw J.J.'s eyes widen in understanding, then narrow in concern as the reality of the situation dawned on him.

"Spivey," J.J. whispered. It wasn't a question.

"Exactly."

"You mind telling me what y'all are talking about? Who's Spivey?" Cheri rested her butt on the edge of her desk and folded her hands in her lap. She looked like she was making herself comfortable, settling in for a long story, which Turner knew was unnecessary, since he planned on making it real brief and real sketchy on the details.

"You might say I've got some history with the Spiveys." Turner nodded at J.J. and took a moment to send him a silent warning—*let me handle this*. J.J. didn't know about the task force investigation, of course, but he sure knew all about how Turner had tried to link Bobby Ray Spivey to Junie's death. J.J. had helped him interview half of Preston Valley, in fact. But Cheri and Candy didn't need to know about that.

Turner refocused on Cheri. "Gerrall Spivey is the twenty-one-year-old guy who works the front desk at Cherokee Pines in the evenings. Back when Junie was teaching, he was one of her students."

Cheri's brow crinkled. "Okay."

"He lives out in Preston Valley with his daddy, Bobby Ray, a man who probably hasn't done a decent day's work since the first Bush was in the White House. The kid went to school most days hungry and dirty and beat down. Junie . . . she used to get all up in people's business when it came to those kids, you know. She fought for them, made sure they had everything they needed, and tried to help Gerrall as much as she could. His daddy resented the intrusion something terrible." Turner had to stop. He felt his throat begin to close up, and his eyes flew to J.J. for an instant, aware that he'd just said more about Junie in the last four seconds than he had in the last four *years*. J.J. smiled at him and nodded slowly, and Turner decided to continue.

"I had some words with Bobby Ray, and just before Junie died, I ended up having to sic Child Protective Services on him. They've never liked me much since, and the feeling's mutual."

"All right," Cheri said, still puzzled. "So you don't like the idea of Candy being around this Gerrall guy?"

"I suppose you could say that." Turner had already sensed that J.J. was getting fidgety, waiting for an opportunity to add his two cents, which Turner couldn't allow. "Jay. Walk me outside, would you, man?"

"Uh, sure."

"That's it?" Cheri's hands flew up by her sides. "You come storming in here mad as a hen because we didn't tell you where Candy was staying—and that's it?"

"That's it," Turner said, already heading for the publisher's office door.

"Don't even try to bullshit me, Halliday," Cheri said from behind his back, the chipperness back in her voice. "It's not exactly a secret that you're interested in Candy—and we think that's great—but don't you think it's kind of silly for you to be jealous of some Preston Valley yahoo?"

Turner stopped. He froze. He turned around to face Cheri and could tell by her grin that she was enjoying the hell out of having a bird's-eye view of all of humanity from way up in the publisher's office. Turner shrugged and said, "You know what? You're absolutely right." Turner gave her a quick kiss on the cheek. "Thanks, Cheri."

J.J. was all over him as they raced down the wide front stairwell of the *Bugle* building. "What the hell was that?" he asked. "You're seriously worried about that Gerrall Spivey kid being around Candy? Because of your suspicions about Junie?"

"Maybe," Turner said, suddenly feeling a little defensive.

"But we've never found anything that connects the Spiveys with Junie's death, man. We talked to damn near everyone in Preston Valley! We've gone over every detail a thousand times. I know it would be a relief for you to have somebody to blame for—"

"Not this shit again," Turner said, laughing bitterly. "That's just what Reggie said to me recently, that I need to blame somebody for Junie's dying to make sense of it, but that's not it at all. I want the truth, Jay. That's all I've ever wanted. And part of the truth is that Candy is living where Gerrall Spivey works, and—believe me when I tell you—that kid is not to be trusted and I don't like it one damn bit."

By this time, the two men had pushed their way out

of the newspaper building's front doors and were on the sidewalk. Turner was headed to his department-issued SUV parked at the curb when J.J. put a hand on his arm.

"Are you falling in love with her?"

Turner spun around. "That's crazy."

J.J. scrunched up his mouth and shook his head. "You know what's crazy, man? To lie to yourself about how you feel. Now that's some crazy shit. Not to mention lying to your best friend in the whole world, which is just plain dumb. So just don't do it—don't be crazy and don't be dumb."

Turner looked up and down the sidewalk to make sure no one could overhear this conversation before he spoke. "It doesn't even matter, Jay," he said, hearing the surrender in his own voice. "Candy's already told me I don't have a chance in hell with her because she's leaving town as soon as possible. The girl can't stay put in one place to save her soul. So that's it. It doesn't matter what I feel or what I wish was possible. There's nothing to be done about it."

The police radio on his belt suddenly squawked to life. Turner was needed at the scene of an accident on Highway 25. "Gotta run."

"You're wrong, man."

Turner looked up at J.J. and laughed. "No, I'm pretty sure I gotta run out to this motor vehicle accident, since it's my *job*."

"You're wrong about Candy."

"Really?" He sighed and looked up at the sky for patience. "How do you figure?"

J.J.'s smile was sly. "There is definitely something you can do."

"And what would that be?"

He rested his hand on Turner's shoulder. "Don't let her go, man. Simple as that. You make it worth her while to stay."

"I've always liked to lick the frosting," Hugo said, wiggling his eyebrows as he raised another forkful of cake to his mustachioed lips.

"This is exquisite! So light but so flavorful," said Mildred Holzmann. "Would you make us another one for Friday's bridge club? Do you know how to make pineapple upside-down cake? My mother used to make that during the Depression—such a lovely combination of sweet and tart. Do you think you could, Candace?"

"Now why would she go and waste her talent on something like that?" Jacinta scraped the last few crumbs from her dessert plate, then used her fingertip to remove a fleck of frosting stuck on Hugo's chin. "Pineapple upside-down cake is a throw-together kind of cake, Mildred. Anyone can make it. But this cake is a real bakery confection. Something like this takes time and skill."

"I'd be happy to," Candy whispered to Mildred, who looked near tears after mentioning her departed mother.

"And after that, you'll make a German chocolate cake," Hugo decided. "I'm cuckoo for anything coconut."

Jacinta giggled like a sixth-grader. "You are the funniest man," she said, pressing the sweetheart neckline of her muumuu against his upper arm.

Candy decided the time was right to step out into the lobby and give Gerrall the cake she'd promised him. He'd made such a fuss over her this evening when she'd arrived with the dessert, insisting that he help her find a spot for it in the dining room, telling her how delicious it looked, how amazing she was, and how long it had been since he'd seen something so beautiful. By that point, Candy knew if she didn't promise the guy a slice it would have been an obvious swipe.

She walked toward him as he sat at the front desk, watching some TV show on his laptop as usual, his thin shoulders hunched over and his mouth open like he was in a trance. "Here you go, Gerrall!" she said. He spun around at the sound of her voice and jumped to his feet.

"I knew my girl wouldn't forget me," he said, a huge smile breaking out on his pimply face. "My girl is the kind who keeps her word, isn't she?"

Candy offered the plate to him and he snatched it, plopping back in his chair. Did he just call her "his girl"? What the hell?

Gerrall began digging in. He leaned back and let his head drop back as he savored the bite. "Oh, my God," he mumbled, chewing. "This is the best thing I've ever tasted in my life. You're amazing, Candy!"

Since that was the second time he'd called her "amazing," he'd now racked up two "amazings" and two "my girls" in the course of a single day. Candy took a step back, feeling a little sick to her stomach.

"You enjoy now," she said, suddenly worried that she'd somehow led Gerrall on. But how? She'd been kind but distant. She'd returned his gifts. Maybe he was just the kind of guy with so little game that he couldn't tell the difference between sociable and sexual. He wouldn't be the first man she'd encountered with that problem.

Candy gestured toward the dining room as she continued to step away. "I should probably be getting back to the bridge club. Please remember to put the fork and plate in the kitchen—I don't want Mr. Miller on my case for anything else. Have a good evening."

"Speaking of which . . ." Gerrall set the half-eaten cake on the desk and winked at her. "Tonight will be our little secret, so don't worry about it."

"Excuse me?"

"You know. Tonight—the bridge club. I know you were back there playing cards even after Miller told you not to, but I assure you that your secret is safe with me. I'll never tell."

Candy cocked her head to the side and gave Gerrall a look she hoped could not be misinterpreted.

His face fell. His smile collapsed. "Are you mad at me?" he asked, his voice deflated. "Did I say something wrong? I'm only trying to help you, let you know that there's nothing I wouldn't do for you, Candy. Nothing."

She stood frozen for an instant, feeling so awkward that all she wanted to do was run. It suddenly occurred to her that this Gerrall Spivey kid was more than just odd—he was off. There was something wrong with him. Yet again, she felt a hint of a threat in the way he spoke to her. She didn't like it.

"You know your two weeks will be up soon," he

said. "Miller mentioned it today. I'm worried about you, Candy. Where are you going to go? Do you have a plan?"

"Of course I do," she fibbed.

"Do you need some help moving?"

"No, thank you. I better get back." She produced a smile and told him good night as she moved toward the dining room.

Gerrall was right, of course. She had exactly three days until Miller was going to kick her ass out of there, and she faced a dilemma. She wouldn't get her paycheck until the following Monday, and she had no way of knowing what she'd be bringing home after taxes. She'd been glancing at the *Bugle*'s classified section nearly every day, and saw that it might be possible for her to rent a room or a studio apartment in town for about $350 a month. But every place required a security deposit and first month's rent, which she knew she couldn't swing with a single paycheck. Once again, she was going to have to brainstorm her way out of a tight spot.

The bridge club welcomed her back with smiles and cheers. Even her mother grinned at her with what Candy swore was a hint of pride. She was pretty sure she'd never seen that in Jacinta's expression before.

Candy knew she'd find a way out of this latest jam. She always did. And as she stood in the formal dining room turned card lounge, she squeezed her thighs together for an instant, comforted by Sophie's sapphire and diamond awesomeness, the promise of all that was still possible in her life.

*   *   *

"Candace?"

She jerked awake, for an instant unsure where she was and who was speaking. That was the one problem with being a rolling stone—sometimes it took a minute for her to remember where she'd last rolled off to.

"I'm up. I'm up." Candy threw off the blanket and started to rise from the couch, ready to start the day, but felt her mother's hand on her shoulder, urging her to stay prone.

"Oh, it's not morning yet. You only just lay down half an hour ago. I didn't realize you were already asleep."

Candy rubbed her face with her hands and tried to focus. Jacinta's tone of voice sounded alien, almost tender. "Is something wrong?"

"I think maybe there is."

Candy watched her mother flip on the floor lamp near the set of plush swivel chairs and make herself comfortable in one. Jacinta's bouffant was restrained in a hairnet. Her face was coated in a clear sheen of night-time skin product Candy had to admit was doing the trick. Her mother was in her mid-sixties but looked at least a decade younger. Maybe it was simply the lack of Florida sun damage she'd grown accustomed to seeing on older women's faces. Candy smiled to herself at the thought—she'd finally stumbled upon something good to be said about spending your life in the North Cack-a-lacky hills! An abundance of shade!

"I was thinking," Jacinta said.

Candy pulled the covers up around her and sat cross-legged on the sofa, letting her eyes adjust to the light. "Yeah?"

"It has been good to see you."

Candy made a quick check for video cameras mounted around the room—because this had to be a joke. "Okay," she said.

"I've enjoyed your visit. I've enjoyed seeing you again and the two weeks have gone by quite fast."

Ah. So that was it. "You're kicking me out."

"No!" Jacinta shook her head so violently the hairnet slipped. She put it back in place. "In fact, I was thinking that it would be nice if you could stay a little longer. I've liked having the company, and it's reminded me that you and I were never as close as I would have liked. I bet that comes as a shock to hear."

Candy blinked a few times. "Uh, which part—the part about how we weren't close or the part about how you would have liked it to have been different?"

"That second part," Jacinta said. "I think I owe you an apology, Candace. And an explanation."

This conversation was so unexpected and so far beyond the norm that Candy didn't know what to say. Her mother had never spoken to her like this—directly and honestly, adult to adult—and it felt dreamlike. "What's the apology for, exactly?"

Jacinta shrugged. "Oh, you know, I always felt as if you didn't like me much, and I can't say that I blame you. I wasn't the most *involved* mother in town, I realize, and I was always glad you had Cheri's mama and then after she was gone you had Viv Newberry. I knew that you were getting that warm and fuzzy stuff from *someone*."

Candy frowned. What a damn strange way to apologize.

"Anyway, I just wanted you to know that I did the

best I could, considering what I had to offer you at the time." Jacinta turned her face away, and for a split second, Candy swore her mother was going to cry. Never, ever, no matter how bad things got with her father, had Candy seen Jacinta Carmichael shed a tear.

"Mother? Are you all right?"

"Of course I am!" She waved her hand through the air, then flicked off the light and rose from the chair. "Sleep tight. See you in the morning. Tomorrow's Saturday, in case you've forgotten, so I will be needing my privacy in the evening, of course."

"Right," Candy said, watching her mother leave the room. "Hey! Wait! You said you wanted to explain something!"

Jacinta looked over her shoulder and shrugged. "That's enough for one night. We'll talk some other time." And she was gone. Candy heard the sound of her door shut and her TV come on.

She sat there in the dark for what had to have been fifteen minutes, not moving, breathing slowly, letting her mind wander and her heart crack open. She couldn't wait to tell Cheri about this monumental occasion. Her mother actually spoke to her about something real! Her mother acknowledged that she'd let her daughter down! It was a miracle! So what if it was awkward? Her mother had actually made an attempt to *connect* with her! She felt like laughing out loud!

Candy's thoughts immediately went to Turner. She thought of the weight of everything he carried in the deepest part of his heart. His loss. His grief. His loneliness. She wondered how he'd survived it. She wondered if his life here in Bigler made him happy. She felt herself tremble at the memory of his lips against hers, his hands all over her body, the heat and solid strength of all he was.

Candy smiled sadly in the dark. She missed that man something awful.

Chapter 11

"Counter order up!"

"You have a nice day now," Candy said, handing Mr. Creswell his sixty-one cents in change and shutting the register drawer. "Come back and see us tomorrow, all right?"

"Wouldn't miss it for the world," the old man said, reaching for her hand and putting the change right back in her palm. "That's for you, sweetheart."

"Oh, gosh. Thank you!" Candy tossed the coins in the front pocket of her apron and smiled at him. As far as tips went in this place, sixty-one cents on a four-ninety-nine senior citizen lunch platter (plus tax) wasn't all that bad, especially since Mr. Creswell was a counter regular, and most of the customers who ate at the counter figured they didn't need to tip because it took only three steps to deliver food instead of the fifteen required for a booth or table. Besides, it all added up, Candy knew, and she was proud to say that with tips alone she'd been able to pay back Lenny every dime he'd given her for gas, fill the tank on her own once, *plus* sock away over thirteen dollars! And today was payday!

Life was definitely getting better.

Candy spun around to retrieve the plates Lenny had just set out.

"How's it goin' out there today?" he asked Candy, not looking up from his work as he spoke.

"Pretty smooth," she said. "Are you managing to keep up back here?"

Lenny laughed and shook his head as he assembled three BLT sandwich platters so quickly his fingers were a blur. "Good Lord, girl, I could do this with a hand tied behind my back, both eyes swole shut, and a dog humping my leg."

Candy laughed, turned around to serve her customers, and nearly dropped everything on the floor.

Turner was seated at the counter. He was smiling at her—one of those bright, white, big, sexy smiles.

It took her a couple seconds to recover from the shock, then she managed to nod in his direction, deliver the food orders, and ring up a departing customer at the register. That gave her enough time to develop a plan of action—and her plan was to be cool as a cucumber—and run down a mental inventory of what she might look like to him at that particular moment. Stained apron. Small silver hoop earrings. Hair pulled back in a ponytail. A single coat of mascara and not a trace of eyeliner or lip gloss.

Your basic hillbilly diner employee.

She completed the register transaction and reminded herself that it didn't matter. So what if she didn't look particularly alluring? She wasn't interested in luring

Turner in any form or fashion. He was her friend. He was a paying customer. And the man had obviously come here for lunch and nothing else, because when she glanced at him he was studying the single-page laminated menu, not her.

"Hey, Turner. Nice to see you." Candy stood on the other side of the counter from him, poised to take his order. "Anything look good to you today?"

Oh, God. Oh, shee-it. That might have been her standard greeting to normal customers, but the instant those words escaped her lips she knew it would have an entirely different meaning with Turner, a man who couldn't seem to keep his hands off her in public places. She swallowed hard. She waited for how he'd respond.

Ever so slowly, he looked up from the menu and pinned her down with those gorgeous hazel eyes. A barely visible smile tugged at the corner of his mouth. And then he whispered, "You, Candy. You look good enough to eat."

She heard herself make a squeak of helplessness, which was embarrassing. She wanted to bolt out the kitchen door and into the alley, where she could hide behind the Dumpster.

But all she could do was stare at that mouth of his. Those lips were a work of art—masculine lines, soft curves, and supple berry-brown flesh. The fact that all this could be found on one man's mouth just wasn't fair. It was too much. She'd never known a man with a mouth that beautiful, a mouth that taunted you to lick it and nibble on it and pry it open with your wet—

"Counter order up!"

Candy jumped. She turned around to retrieve the

food and found Lenny frowning at her. "You got a line at the register, girlie."

"What?" Candy peered over her shoulder. How long had she been frozen where she stood like that, pen in hand, staring at Turner's mouth? What the hell was wrong with her?

"You look like you just saw a ghost."

"Of course not."

"You must be running from the law, then."

"Huh? No!" It was then that Candy noticed Lenny laughing. "Oh, just mind your own business!"

It took her about three minutes to return, and she found Turner waiting patiently. That little smile was probably still on his lips but she would never know because she refused to look. Instead, she focused her attention on the restrooms at the opposite end of the diner, which she decided were fascinating.

"What'll it be? Can I interest you in one of our specials?"

Turner bit his tongue. The special he was interested in wasn't on the menu. The tension between them was so thick and the attraction so heavy that they should be laughing their asses off at how ridiculous it all was. But Candy stared off into the distance, looking at anything but him, and she seemed so skittish that he had to take pity on her.

So he wouldn't answer the way he wanted to. He wouldn't confess that the only thing that interested him was making his X-rated dreams a reality, that he was especially interested in seeing Candy nekkid on all fours, wiggling that perfect round ass as she begged him to ravish her.

"I'll have the meat loaf," he said, stifling a chuckle. Honestly, he felt like a junior high kid. He couldn't remember the last time he'd felt so lighthearted and goofy.

"Anything to drink?" Her big blue eyes continued to focus on anywhere that didn't include him.

Lord have mercy. Yes, he wanted a drink. He wanted to put his mouth on her sex and lick and suck and slurp at her until she came all over his face, draining her sticky juices and getting her sweet pussy nice and ready for his dick.

"Mr. Pibb, no ice, please."

"You got it."

When she turned away and reached up to clip his order on the little metal wheel, he thought he'd choke. Her jeans looked like they'd been painted on her ass. Those two incredible globes of flesh were split right down the center by double-stitched goodness. He felt actual physical pain just looking at her, because he knew how that ass felt cradled in his palms, each half firm but soft, a luscious handful of perfection, and he ached for another shot at it.

Turner had to adjust himself on the diner stool.

"Here you go—Mr. Pibb, no ice," she said, delivering his drink. Before she could take her hand away, Turner touched her wrist. She gasped. Her eyes widened.

"Thank you," he said, just before he raised the pop to his lips and gazed over the rim of the glass and right into her baby blues.

Candy licked her lips.

Who were they kidding? It was obvious that given the right set of circumstances—such as no one else around and a room with a door—they'd eat each other alive.

She pulled her arm from his touch and walked away. For the next few minutes, Turner observed Candy do her job. Her smile was genuine. She joked with the customers and had a special tenderness for the older folks. She even let the old men flirt a little without biting their heads off. Candy worked fast at clearing dishes and wiping off the counter and refilling waters and coffees. She really looked like she enjoyed what she was doing. For a moment, Turner couldn't picture her in the kind of life she apparently had led down in Tampa. That kind of wheeling and dealing seemed too cold for a woman like her, a woman whose smile affected everyone around her, a woman so soft and sweet and real.

"Bon appétit," she said, placing the meat loaf special in front of him.

"Hey, Candy?"

She crossed her arms over her chest and raised one eyebrow. She was trying so hard not to let him know she still craved him as much as he craved her. What if J.J. were right? What if the answer to this mess was finding a way to make her want to stay? How would he do it? What could he possibly offer a woman like Candy Carmichael that she couldn't get anywhere else?

That's when he remembered there was a reason he came to Lenny's and it wasn't necessarily to win Candy's heart. It damn sure wasn't for the meat loaf. It was to get a feel for whether she was safe around Gerrall Spivey.

"So you doing okay out at Cherokee Pines?"

She raised her chin. "Fine, thanks."

"No problems with anyone out there?"

"Of course not. Everyone's very nice—well, not *every*one, but I'm enjoying my visit with Jacinta, surprisingly enough."

"So nobody's bothering you?"

She frowned at him. "Wainright Miller is a real horse's ass. Why? You gonna arrest him for me?"

Turner chuckled. "That particular shortcoming doesn't violate either county code or state law, which is a good thing, because I'd be hauling in about ninety-nine percent of the population of Cataloochee County if it did."

Candy tried to fight it, but she smiled, and at that very instant, Turner swore to heaven above that she'd be doing a lot more of it and he'd be there to see it. Maybe someday he'd even be the reason for it.

"Nobody else givin' you a hard time?"

Candy shook her head. "Lorraine Estes is a trip. Not the most pleasant chick I've ever met."

Turner nodded. "That grumpy old hen could start an argument in an empty house."

Candy laughed. "Meat loaf's getting cold." She leaned a hand on the counter and shifted her weight to one hip, which accentuated her already killer curves. Turner had to drag his eyes away.

"Right." He dug his fork into the too-firm hunk of mystery meat.

Candy sighed. "And then there's bizarro Gerrall Spivey."

Turner put the fork down. "Oh, right." Turner managed

to sound casual. "He works out there, doesn't he? So he's buggin' you, too?"

Candy shrugged. "Gerrall's harmless, I suppose, but sometimes he creeps me out just the littlest bit, you know, going overboard with the compliments and stuff. He doesn't mean anything by it. I think he's just kind of clueless, and because I'm nice to him he's under the mistaken impression that I'm hot for him. It's a little awkward."

Turner nodded as if he were barely interested in what she was saying. The truth was, he was so pissed off that the top of his head felt like it was going to blow off. If that little motherfucker even came close to touching Candy, he'd bust him up something awful.

"You might want to try to avoid him as much as you can," Turner said with a sigh, hoping his words sounded like friendly advice and not an official warning.

"Seriously? Why?"

Turner shrugged. "Oh, nothing really. That it must be kind of uncomfortable for you is all."

"Counter order up!"

"I should get back to work." Candy straightened and smiled at Turner warmly, the skittish discomfort gone from her expression. "Anything else I can get you? Everything okay?"

"It's incredibly good."

Her gaze wandered to his plate and she laughed. "You haven't even tasted it yet, Turner."

"I mean it's incredibly good to see you, Candy. I've missed you."

His words seemed to catch her off guard. She got all

flustered again, and began wiping her hands on her apron. "I—"

"You're not doing me any favors by keeping your distance." Turner surprised himself. It wasn't his style to come on this hard, but for some reason it seemed like the natural way to handle this situation, to handle her. "And I damn well know it's not what you want, either."

Candy paused for an instant. Her lips parted in shock. And Turner watched a dozen different emotions pass over her expression before she seemed to snap out of it. "I really have to get back to work," she said, slapping his check down on the counter in front of him.

When Candy turned away, her blond ponytail flipped across the back of her neck, and right there in the middle of meat loaf central, Turner caught a whiff of the delicate, feminine essence of everything Candy.

Two more praline chocolate turtle cakes. An angel food cake. A devil's food cake with fudge icing. A carrot cake with cream cheese icing. And the pineapple upside-down cake Mildred Holzmann had requested, already perched on a foil covered piece of heavy-duty cardboard and readied for delivery.

The cakes were lined up on the prep counter in Lenny's kitchen like girls in cotillion dresses, all fluffy and lacy and exactly as she'd envisioned them in her head. Candy felt immense satisfaction at the sight.

"You're a damn genius," Lenny said. "Seriously. If these taste as good as that mouse-sized crumb you brought me this morning, you can slap me upside my head and call me silly."

Candy laughed. "I told you, the bridge club ate nearly every bit of it! I had to run for my life just to bring you in that little sliver!"

"No matter," Lenny said, reaching out to pinch a piece of devil's food. "I can eat as much as I want now, right?"

Candy smacked his arm. "Don't pig out on your profit, Lenny!"

"All right, now. No need to get violent."

Candy grabbed the pineapple cake and her keys and headed for the employee exit. "I gotta run if I'm going to look at that apartment and get to Cherokee Pines in time for dinner. See you Monday!"

"Yes you will!"

She'd barely taken three steps through the parking lot when she decided to turn right around. Candy peeked through the glass window of the back entrance, only to see Lenny sticking his finger in the cream cheese icing, just as she'd suspected.

"Stop it!" Candy yelled, pounding on the glass with her free hand.

Just a couple minutes later, Candy arrived at the old Victorian house on Chester Street. She felt ridiculous driving, and would have been happy walking if she didn't have Mildred's cake to worry about. As she headed up the steps to the house, Candy calculated how much money she would save without a gas tank to fill every week, and the thought made her giddy.

She knocked on the door. A harried-looking woman a few years older than Candy answered, three wide-eyed kids clustered behind her legs. The scent of spaghetti sauce wafted out onto the porch.

"I'm sorry," Candy said. "I hope I'm not disturbing

you, but I'm Candy Carmichael. I called about seeing the—"

"Oh, sure!" The woman welcomed her inside. "Follow me upstairs. It's on the third floor."

About fifteen minutes later the two women were on the front porch, and Candy was so frustrated she was near tears. The place was completely perfect! It was exactly what she needed! The apartment was furnished—nothing fancy but not threadbare, either—and available month to month. It featured a small bedroom, a sitting room, a compact galley kitchen, and full bath, plus it was privately tucked away from the rest of the house. All this for only $400 a month!

But the woman insisted on first and last month's rent up front, and Candy couldn't swing it.

She tried one last time to make a deal with her. She reached into the pocket of her jeans and pulled out the roll of bills that had been burning a hole in her pocket since about ten that morning, when she walked to the First National Bank of Cataloochee County on her break and cashed her paycheck.

Candy held out the cash to the woman. "This is six hundred and ten dollars. I've got another thirteen stashed at my mother's. And it's all yours, right this very minute, if you'll only let me pay the rest two weeks from now, when I get paid again."

The landlady crossed her arms over her chest and shook her head. "I wish I could," she said. "Please don't take this the wrong way, but I've been burned giving people breaks like that before. I hope you understand."

Candy shoved the money back in her jeans pocket. "Can you hold the apartment for me, then?"

"No. I'm sorry. I just can't. But if it's still here in two weeks, it's yours." The woman snapped at her oldest child to close the screen door, then returned her attention to Candy. "Listen," she said. "You seem like a nice girl and I'd like to rent the place to you but I learned a long time ago that if a tenant has trouble scraping together the rent at the start they're gonna struggle every month after, and I just don't have the energy to mess with that."

The woman wished her luck and went into her house.

By the time Candy reached Cherokee Pines, any payday elation she'd felt had disappeared. The sense of accomplishment from baking was gone. All the whirling thoughts of Turner had been pushed aside. All she could think about now was what she'd do in two days, when her time was up at Cherokee Pines. Where would she go?

Candy parked her junker of a car in its usual spot, hidden behind the senior vans at the edge of the lot, and trudged inside, balancing the cake in one hand as she entered the double glass doors.

She was greeted by Mr. Miller.

"Just what do you think you're doing?"

At first, Candy wasn't even certain she was the target of his attack. "Pardon me?"

He flicked his fingernail on the foil-covered cardboard she was holding. "This. This . . . *cake.* Just who do you think you are, bringing unauthorized food items into the dining hall?"

"Uh . . ." Candy's first instinct was to laugh. This guy could not be serious. *Unauthorized? Food items?* Who talked like that? "It's a dessert, Mr. Miller."

His lip curled. Sweat began to bead on his bulbous

forehead. "I have never liked you, Miss Carmichael," he hissed. "You are a condescending girl, which I find particularly odd seeing as how you are a guest here only because I allow you to be."

It was right then that Candy realized she'd be sleeping in her car that night if she couldn't find a way to deal with Mr. Mean-n-Chubby standing in front of her. And the truth was, she was dog tired. She was heartbroken about the apartment. She was still all worked up from seeing Turner at lunch. And dammmit, she did not want to sleep in her car again! She'd slept in her car for three nights before finally agreeing to stay with Gladys Harbison—something she'd never admitted to anyone! She'd parked in a deserted warehouse parking lot and taken showers at the Tip Top Truck Stop for a dollar-fifty a pop. Compared to that, Jacinta's couch was pure luxury, and that's where she planned to stay that night. After Hugo had been thoroughly entertained, anyway, since it was Saturday.

Oh, shoot—it was *Saturday*! Candy rolled her eyes at the realization that it would be many hours before she could relax.

"You think this is some kind of joke, don't you?" Mr. Miller asked.

Just then, Candy noticed the usual predinner-bell crowd beginning to gather outside the dining room doors. But on that particular evening, she and Mr. Miller were more interesting than the menu posting, and several residents began to move closer in order to hear what was being said.

Candy answered his question politely. "Not at all, Mr. Miller. I meant no disrespect."

The crowd continued to inch closer. Out of the corner of her eye, Candy saw Mildred Holzmann pushing through, her stare focused like a laser on the large rectangular-shaped cake topped with rows of brown-sugar-drizzled pineapple slices.

Mr. Miller wasn't finished. "As executive director of Cherokee Pines, it is my duty to see that our residents receive the highest-quality meals and snacks . . ."

Uh-oh. Mildred looked really excited. And now Hugo and Jacinta were advancing from the other direction.

". . . and our qualified staff sees to it that meals are designed . . ."

Miller was too busy lecturing Candy to notice that about three dozen old people were now giving him the stink eye. It was all Candy could do not to laugh out loud.

". . . with the specific nutritional needs of the elderly in mind. And that's why you cannot go around tempting our residents with just any old high-fat, high-calorie, sugar-coated—"

"Step away from the pineapple upside-down cake and no one will get hurt," Mildred said from her position, which was all up in Mr. Miller's face.

Though he gasped in surprise and tried to retreat, Hugo and Jacinta blocked his escape. Mr. Miller scanned the hallway to discover he was outnumbered.

Mildred shook a knobby finger at him. "This young lady was nice enough to bake that for me and you're not going to take it away. Do you understand? I haven't had a decent dessert since I moved into this place!"

"Besides," Hugo added, his nose in the air. "We're

old as dirt and we're gonna die anyway, so let us at least die with a smile on our faces."

"The food here stinks!" someone yelled.

"The tapioca pudding tastes like glue!" Candy was almost certain that complaint came from Lorraine Estes.

Just then, the intercom system rang out with the series of electronic beeps that signaled dinner was served, and the crowd began to shuffle toward the open dining room doors. "I'll take this," Mildred said, relieving Candy of the cake. "We'll save a seat for you at our table, dear."

Mr. Miller's lip was still twitching when Gerrall Spivey arrived for his Saturday shift just moments later.

"What's happening?" he asked, setting his laptop on the front desk and staring at Mr. Miller and Candy as if they were the oddest sight he'd ever seen.

Miller pointed at him. "In my office—now!"

Chapter 12

After the library reading room closed, Candy passed a good thirty minutes in the health and beauty aisle of the Piggly Wiggly, trying to decide between the mascara brand that promised length and definition and the one that would plump and curl. What if she wanted all those things? What if, as a modern American female consumer, she wanted mascara that plumped, curled, lengthened, *and* defined the living hell out of her lashes?

"Shit outta luck, I guess," she mumbled to herself, tossing her lackluster selection into her little handheld shopping basket. She wandered around the rest of the store, snagging some off-brand deodorant, shampoo, conditioner, and moisturizer. Then she compared prices on disposable shavers, thinking back to the old days when you didn't need a quadruple-blade, pivoting-head, no-slip-grip wonder of engineering to scrape the stubble off your kneecaps.

In a last-minute surge of wildness, Candy grabbed a bag of caramel corn from the snack aisle and headed for the checkout. *Damn*—she shook her head as she handed over the cash—more than twenty-seven dollars for a grocery bag of no-name toiletries and high-fructose corn syrup. That seemed like an awful lot of money to waste on stuff that didn't amount to anything, that wouldn't get her any closer to renting her own place or getting out of this town.

As she walked to the car, Candy tried to recall the orgy of the senses that was once her lifestyle, the best of anything and everything, and all of it taken for granted. Chanel perfume had been dabbed on her wrists. Perfectly prepared cuisine was paired with just the right wine. Only the richest fabrics and butter-soft leathers brushed against her body. Cleanly designed fine furnishings filled her home. Then there were the decadent *services* she'd convinced herself she couldn't function without. Exfoliating scrubs and silky body wraps that left her skin like velvet. Aromatherapy massages that loosened her muscles and relaxed her mind. The pedicures, the manicures, and the dancing fingertips of spa professionals upon her brow and cheekbones. God, she'd wasted so much of her life shopping for—and living in—luxury.

Now she shopped and lived in Bigler.

Candy tossed the Piggly Wiggly bag in the passenger seat of the Chevy and decided to take a walk around town. She still had an hour to kill before she could even think of going back to Jacinta's, and it was a warm, still summer night, the kind she'd loved when she was a kid. Candy laughed with delight as every one of Main Street's historic streetlights flickered on at once, as if putting on a show just for her, turning the old downtown into a storybook scene. She gazed up just in time to see the very last flash of orange before the sun settled behind the dark mountains.

All right, so her hometown had its own kind of subtle charm—Candy admitted it. If a person actually wanted to live in a small Appalachian mountain village with no obvious purpose for existing, she supposed they could do worse than Bigler.

She strolled along, though most everything in town was closed. Lenny's Diner was dark and Lenny was no doubt home watching TV while chowing down on a piece of his profit. The sewing shop, the hardware store, and the half-dozen mountain craft stores were shuttered, along with the chamber of commerce office, the electronics repair shop, and the . . .

Candy stopped, sticking her hands into the back pockets of her jeans and standing in silence. She'd driven past this storefront every day since she'd returned to town, but she could honestly say that tonight was the first time she'd really noticed her father's old office. The painted lettering was still visible on the glass display window—JONES CARMICHAEL INSURANCE, AUTO, HOME, AND LIFE—though it was beginning to peel away from the effect of weather and time. Obviously, the place had sat empty since his death, and Candy wondered why that was. She also wondered who owned the three-story brick building. She'd have to ask Jacinta.

Candy continued down Main Street and was pleasantly surprised to see that the corner ice cream parlor was open. She quickened her step, drawn by the shop's bright white light pouring onto the curb and the remembered taste of the butter brickle of her childhood.

She passed by the wide marble steps of Trinity

Lutheran and its gated courtyard garden, then reached the corner, stepped into the ice cream parlor's open door, and Turner nearly knocked her over.

"Candy!"

She grabbed onto him to keep from falling on her behind, and screeched when an ice-cold blob landed on her bare chest and began to slide down into her cleavage. "Ohmigod!" she yelped, bending and pulling at the neckline of her stretchy cotton T-shirt, trying to prevent the painfully cold confection from slipping down her belly.

"I am so sorry!" he said. And then, unbelievably, Turner just reached down into the opening of her shirt to retrieve the ice cream, which had come to a stop in the vee between her underwires. In doing so, his fingers brushed over the swell of her breasts. What the *hell*? All Candy could do was stand there on the sidewalk with her eyes bugging out, breathless from the shock of cold ice cream and the touch of Turner's fingers on her flesh. She watched as he doubled over in laughter and tossed the melting scoop in the trash can, along with his now useless sugar cone.

"Glad you think it's funny," she said, still holding the neckline of her shirt away from her skin. "Can you get me a napkin or something?"

"Of course. Sure. Sorry." Turner continued to laugh as he jogged into the shop and came out with a handful of napkins and a couple packages of moistened towelettes, which he displayed proudly.

"I sincerely apologize," he said, looking sheepish. He tried to stop laughing but wasn't particularly successful.

Candy shook her head. "Whatever," she said, fighting her own laughter as she reached out to snag the napkins from his grasp. But Turner pulled away.

She frowned at him.

"What are you doing here, anyway?" he asked.

Candy snorted, thinking that a sheriff should be able to figure that one out. "I wanted some ice cream."

"Ah, just as I suspected," he said, and then . . . oh, damn . . . right there under the historic streetlight, Turner let his gaze drop to the now stretched neckline of her shirt, and his mouth began to turn up at the corners in that sultry, sexy, oh-so-slow way that it did, the way that made Candy lose her ability to think straight.

"Did you have a particular flavor in mind this evening, Miss Carmichael?" he asked, his eyes not straying from her ice-cream-coated breasts.

Candy felt her heart pound and her breath go shallow. Why didn't she have the presence of mind to smack him? Why didn't she bring the two-inch heel of her gladiator sandal down on his instep? Why didn't she simply spin around and march down the sidewalk to her car in protest against the completely over-the-top way that Turner enjoyed hitting on her.

Because she'd lost her damn mind—that was the only possible answer—and all she managed to do was stand there and let him eat her up with his eyes. In fact, she had the urge to take off her shirt completely, followed by her bra, then her jeans and panties, all so this beautiful man could continue his visual feeding unencumbered.

"Mocha latte," she whispered, her voice all breathy and sexual.

Well, that did it. Suddenly, he was up against her, his face inches from hers, close enough that she could feel the heat pulsing off his body. She felt a fistful of napkins at the small of her back as she was directed down the sidewalk toward the Lutheran church. By the time Turner unlatched the wrought-iron gate of the courtyard and gently nudged her forward, Candy's vision was swimming. His hand returned to her lower back, and he must have ditched the napkins somewhere because she felt the flat of his palm and the wide spread of his fingers against her body. And suddenly, his hand slid up under her T-shirt, pressing hot and firm against her bare skin as it traveled up, up . . . then quickly back down, down . . . into the waistband of her jeans and panties and right smack onto the naked flesh of her ass.

In a single motion, he scooped her close, spun her around, and pressed her tight up against the front of his body, all the while pulling her farther into the shadows of a large beech tree.

Turner's lips were so close they were nearly touching hers. "Sorry for getting you all sticky," he whispered, gripping her ass tighter and making sure she could feel what she was up against. Candy counted three notice-able bulges poking against her body, and figured one had to be his gun, one was probably the wad of napkins, and the other was nothin' but Turner. The fun part was going to be figuring out which was which.

Candy leaned her head back and looked up into his face. She melted at the sight of his heavy-lidded hazel eyes, dark lashes, and that overtly sexual mouth, pulled into a wicked smile. Right at that moment, she wanted nothing more than to feel that mouth on her. Somewhere. Anywhere.

"You made the mess," she said. "You should clean it up."

Turner's eyes flashed in the shadows. "You sure about that, girl?"

Am I? Of course she wasn't sure. In fact, she was sure she *shouldn't* want that. So why was she allowing this to happen? Honestly, sometimes she wished she were a stronger human being. "Just hurry up before I change—"

His lips touched down on her breastbone, and the sensation was so achingly wonderful that Candy leaned her head back to offer her throat and chest to him. She felt her hair swing down her back.

"Oh, Gaaaawwwwwd," she groaned. Turner began tenderly licking and kissing and removing every trace of ice cream on Candy's chest, his lips and tongue making soft smacking noises as he worked. The moans of pleasure escaping from his mouth vibrated against her wet skin.

"I haven't been able to think straight since you came back to town," he mumbled in between kisses, slurps, and licks. "I can't work. I can't sleep. I can't relax. I gotta have you, Candy. You make me fuckin' crazy."

She gasped. She hadn't been this turned on since, well, since the last time Turner had his hands and lips on her. "Wait," she managed to say. "Maybe you should . . . please . . . oh, Lord, don't stop! Thatfeelssodamn*good*!"

Candy brought her hands to his head, and as he continued to feast on the delicate flesh at the top of her breasts, she let her hands roam over the contours of his perfectly shaped head and close-shorn hair. She memorized the feel of him—the smallish ears, the strong ridge of muscle at the nape of his neck, the lovely round curve of his skull. There was something quite tender about the feel of Turner's head in her hands as his mouth made love to her skin, and Candy suddenly felt a warm tug in her belly and a pulling in her heart. She felt tears forming in her eyes. Her lips began to quiver.

Of course she couldn't be doing this. She had real *feelings* for Turner. He was her friend and she cared for him. He was a man who'd lost a wife who'd cherished him, who'd likely held his head in her hands just like this, and that's what he wanted and deserved again—love. Committed and tender love that was right here in Bigler for him to come home to every night.

She wasn't the girl for that job and they both knew it.

But he'd just nibbled at her breast with his teeth. It hurt a little—and it turned her on *a lot*. His mouth was now dragging across the fabric of her T-shirt, searching for a nipple, finding it, and latching on. It felt as if a tiny fiber-optic cable connected her hard nipple to her clitoris, and as soon as Turner sucked, she jumped.

"You like that, don't you?" he asked, not moving his mouth from her nipple. "What else do you like?"

"Oh, God," she breathed.

"I bet you like this." Turner took his free hand—the one that wasn't cupping her ass and pushing her close to him—and began to unzip her jeans. In no time at all his fingers had insinuated themselves inside and were playing with her through her underwear, pinching at her pussy lips, teasing them, burrowing up into the fabric between them. "You're already so wet, Candy. So wet, baby."

Well, duh! It wasn't every day she got fingered in the Lutheran church meditation garden by the sexiest man on earth.

"Turner?" she whispered, trying to push herself away. Just then his fingers slipped inside the crotch of her panties, and her knees collapsed. He managed to hold her up, but a finger had found its way up inside her in the melee. Then two fingers. And now they both moved slowly in and out of her, two big fingers, slowly, so slowly, out and in again . . .

"Fuck," Turner whispered, dragging his mouth from her nipple to her ear. He bit down on her earlobe. "Are you always this wet, baby?"

"Oh, God, no. I mean, I don't know. I don't remember it ever being an issue."

He chuckled, then pushed his fingers up in her harder and back out, steady, deep, his knuckles now bumping against her clit. Candy's leg muscles started to shake.

"Are you going to come all over me?" Turner asked, dragging his lips from her ear to her mouth. He kissed her then, his tongue pushing apart her lips the way his fingers pushed open her pussy. In the back of Candy's mind, she knew something wasn't right about this. Maybe it was the church setting. Or the fact that Turner was in uniform. Or maybe it was just that she was about to have a screaming, soul-shattering orgasm within a hundred feet of her hometown ice cream parlor, which struck her as irresponsible.

"Please! Stop!" She pressed her palms to his chest. "We shouldn't do this."

Turner stopped. "All right," he said. He pulled his lips away. He straightened. He removed his fingers from her swollen pussy, and the sudden pullout made a sucking sound Candy found a little embarrassing. It only made him smile.

Then he zipped her up. He slid his other hand up and off her ass. And he gazed down at her with those intensely beautiful eyes while he licked his wet fingers. "This is better than any flavor they got next door," he said, smacking his lips.

Candy panted.

"Sorry. I got carried away."

She whimpered.

"You do this to me."

"You do it to me, too."

"I think we should just do each other and get it over with."

Turner shoved a hand up into her hair, and pulled her mouth to his once more. He kissed Candy until she couldn't stand up, until whatever clear and rational conclusion she'd reached only seconds before had vanished, flattened by the rush of desire in her, lost to the demands Turner made on her lips and tongue and her spirit. How could it be wrong to kiss Turner Halliday like this when it felt so right?

"Come home with me," he said, pulling his lips from hers, gazing into her face.

"I—" Candy blinked. "What? I can't."

Turner's police radio crackled to life, shooting a loud volley of static into the quiet garden, followed by the clipped voice of a dispatcher. As Turner used his cell phone to call in, Candy stepped away. She fixed her shirt the best she could, straightened her jeans, and ran her fingers through her hair. When she wiped her lips she discovered that Turner's licking and kissing might have felt incredibly good, but it was a lousy substitute for soap and water—the sweet stickiness from the ice cream had only been smeared around.

She probably looked a mess.

"You are the most beautiful creature I have ever seen," Turner said, once again standing so close to her that she could feel his energy and heat. "Candy, I gotta go."

"Me, too."

He placed his hands on her upper arms and held her steady in front of him. She looked up, unapologetic as she let him study her hair, her eyes, her mouth . . .

"I'll see you tomorrow," he said. Then he lowered his mouth and gave her a warm but restrained kiss. "Where are you parked? Let me drive you to your car."

Candy shook her head and took his hand. "I'm just down at the Piggly Wiggly. I'll be fine."

"I'll make certain of it," Turner said, his voice suddenly all business.

They walked out of the church garden, hand in hand. Candy kissed his cheek and began to turn down the sidewalk when Turner tugged her back.

"I thought you wanted ice cream," he said, his eyes wrinkling up in a smile. "It's still open."

Candy laughed. "I think I've had enough for one night."

The humor left Turner's expression, to be replaced by something hungry and serious. He shook his head and opened the door of the big SUV. "That's a damn

lie, Candy Carmichael. Neither of us got enough tonight and you know it."

She walked, and though she didn't look behind her,
she was well aware that Turner was driving along at
about two miles per hour. The thought that he was worried about her made her smile, and suddenly, she realized she couldn't remember the last time someone had
cared enough to worry about her.

Or was it that she never *let* anyone?

She reached her car, started the engine, and pulled
toward the Piggly Wiggly exit. Only then did Turner
wave good-bye and speed off down Main Street, lights
flashing.

The whole way back to Cherokee Pines, Candy told
herself she could handle whatever it was that had just
happened to her. Because something most definitely had.
She'd let Turner in. Once again, she'd reveled in the feel
of his lips and hands on her body. But this time, there'd
been more to it than just the physical. She'd allowed a
rush of affection and compassion to course through
her—all directed at and because of Turner—and the
newness of it felt reckless. The intensity of it was ter-
rifying. And she knew damn well that there was no
happy ending here but it didn't even matter—it was as
if she were powerless to prevent any of it from happening.

As Candy reached the entrance foyer to Cherokee
Pines, she realized she'd never before felt this out of
control of her own life—professionally, financially, or
emotionally. Even when she'd lived under Jonesy Carmichael's roof and according to his rules, she'd not felt
this powerless. That's because she'd had a solid plan

back then, and she was sure that nothing and nobody was going to keep her from it.

A dozen years had passed. Where had that brave, bold, confident girl gone? she wondered.

"Good evening, Candy."

She'd been so lost in her thoughts that she'd almost walked right past Gerrall without a word. "Oh!" she said, startled, not just because he had spoken but because of the way his voice sounded. And the expression on his face.

Oh, boy, he was pissed at her.

Gerrall let his eyes roam up and down her body and back again, his lips pulled tight. "Where have you been?"

There were a lot of things she didn't like about that question, and the biggest was the way Gerrall had asked it—with a sense of ownership, as if he had every right to know where she'd been. Which, obviously, he didn't. Candy tried to make light of the situation, and held up her grocery bag. "Been to the Piggly Wiggly," she said. "Pretty dang exciting down there, let me tell ya."

He wasn't buying it. He glared at her. "What happened to your shirt? You look like you were attacked or something."

"What?" She looked down and almost cursed at herself for forgetting all about how she must appear. "Oh. It's nothing," she said. "I spilled ice cream down my front and tried to clean it up and my shirt got all stretched out."

"Hmm," Gerrall said, leaning forward in the desk chair. "Well, I'm afraid if there's food in there I'm not going to be able to let you bring it in."

"Food?" Candy started to laugh, then realized Gerrall must have been drinking some of Mr. Miller's "unauthorized food item" Kool-Aid. "Right," she said with a sigh. "No food. Just shampoo and stuff."

"Mind if I have a look?"

Hell, *yes,* she minded! Candy was just about to tell him he could kiss her ass when she realized now would not be the best time for that kind of thing, since she needed to ask Gerrall for a really big favor.

"Of course. I know you're just doing your job," she said, nearly choking on her own words. She held out the plastic bag by the handles and opened it so he could peer inside. She saw him frown, reach in, and snatch the small bag of caramel corn. "What's this?"

"Oh, shee-it," she mumbled. She'd forgotten all about her spontaneous purchase. "Whoops," Candy said, deflated, exhausted, and thoroughly sick of living in senior-citizen lockdown. "Just throw it away."

Gerrall peered into the shopping bag again, then began to riffle through her items. That was all she could take. Candy yanked the bag back. "So, Gerrall, listen. I have a really huge favor to ask."

He smiled smugly, tossing the caramel corn onto his desk, which Candy took as a sign that he'd be enjoying the confiscated treat once she was gone. "What can I do for you?"

"I need a few more days to figure out where I'm moving. I thought I had a nice place lined up, but, well, it fell through this afternoon."

Gerrall raised his eyebrows. "I'm not sure I understand what you're asking for."

This was so demoralizing that Candy wanted to

scream. "Look, Gerrall, I know I'm supposed to move out on Monday but I don't have a place yet. I need a couple more days. Do you think you could let me in at night without saying anything to anybody? I'll leave super-early in the morning, before Miller gets here. I'll skip breakfast. Please? I need your help. I don't have anywhere to go."

Gerrall just *loved* this shit. She could tell by the way he puffed out his chest and grinned. "You could come stay with me for a while," he said.

"Uh, gee. No. But thanks."

"I can't make any promises," he said, suddenly quite serious.

"Oh, thank you, Gerrall!" For a split second she had an urge to hug him, but it passed quickly, thank God. "I can't tell you how much this means to me!"

He looked around the foyer, as if checking for spies. "You can't come in until after ten every night, and you'd have to be gone by six-thirty in the morning. You know you already almost got me fired because I let you bring in that cake, right? So you *know* I'm putting my ass on the line to do this for you."

"I won't let that happen. Thank you!" She pressed her palms together in thanks and started to walk away.

"But it's gonna cost you," he added.

Candy stopped. She slowly turned around to see Gerrall staring at her ass. She wasn't sure how much of this she could take. "What do you want?"

"A date."

"No."

Gerrall sighed heavily. "All right then. A cake. I

want you to bring me a cake every night you need to stay here."

"But I'm not allowed to bring any more cakes!"

"Oh, they'll be just for me," he said. "Miller will never know."

Candy rolled her eyes. She felt as if she were starring in a horribly scripted reality show where she was being forced to bake for everyone in town. It would be called *Hillbilly Cake Slut*.

"Fine. Whatever," Candy said. "I'm tired and have to get some sleep. Thanks for your help, Gerrall,"

"I want a lemon cake first. From scratch. No artificial colorings or flavorings or anything. That stuff's bad for my skin."

"Right," she said, staggering down the hallway to Jacinta's door. It was locked. Of course it was locked. If it were open, that would make things far too simple, and today's theme had been bedlam, not simplicity.

Candy tapped on the door. No answer. She knocked a little harder. Still no answer. It was well after ten! Those two couldn't still be going at it, could they?

"Such a tramp," said a sharp female voice.

Candy closed her eyes for an instant to gather her strength, and when she was ready, she turned to face the harpy in pink sponge rollers from next door. "Fuck off, Lorraine," she said, the weariness obvious in her voice.

Jacinta's door flew open as Lorraine's slammed shut, and Candy stepped back in surprise when Hugo tiptoed through. "Fell asleep," he whispered, with an apologetic shrug. Candy then noticed he was holding his shoes in his hands, along with his shirt and pants. Which meant . . .

Hugo scampered down the hall in his print boxer shorts, wife-beater undershirt, and black socks held up with garters. Candy was duly impressed. For an old, bowlegged dude, he sure could book it.

Chapter 13

Turner stood in the center aisle of the empty Tip Top truck stop restaurant, feet wide apart, staring down at the twisted body on the worn linoleum floor. The deceased lay in a puddle of dark red blood. Male. Caucasian. Age anywhere from eighteen to twenty-five years, but that was just a guess, since they'd found forty-five boxes of cold medicine in his backpack and what was obviously a fake ID. And though they were still waiting for the medical examiner to arrive, Turner was fairly certain he could call this one—the cause of death was the bullet hole smack in the middle of the poor kid's forehead.

Fortunately, they had more witnesses than they knew what to do with. The state police had set up two interrogation stations out in the parking lot, where fourteen truckers, two waitresses, and a busboy were in the process of giving their statements. So far, everybody seemed to agree on the basics: the victim arrived after midnight and ordered a bottomless cup of coffee. He didn't say much to anyone, not even the waitress, and sat in a booth that afforded him a good view of the entrance.

And then at twelve-seventeen A.M., the restaurant door opened, and a man wearing a ski mask took one step inside, raised and pointed a rifle outfitted with a fancy scope, and shot the kid as he tried to run.

The shooter jumped in a car waiting at the curb and was gone before anyone could think to get a look at the vehicle, let alone a plate number. But one trucker claimed he'd seen the suspect get into a full-sized pickup, probably a Ford or Chevy, which Turner knew would narrow things down to about half the population of the state of North Carolina.

He heard the restaurant door open and Turner nodded in Kelly O'Connor's direction. Right behind her was Trent Marshner from the State Bureau of Investigation. Both of them looked particularly grim.

"This kid was one of Spivey's regular errand boys," O'Connor said.

"We see him here at least a couple times a week hooking up with the Spivey kid," Marshner said.

O'Connor nodded. "This is a standard calling-card execution—just your basic howdy from one cartel to another, letting them know they're in town."

"What?" Turner felt sick hearing that information. "You're telling me there are now *two* Mexican cartels fighting over Cataloochee County's meth output? Are you shittin' me?"

"Spivey's output, more specifically," O'Connor said. "He's gotten big enough that he's worth fighting over."

Turner shook his head. "We've got to shut those bastards down. *Now.* Before innocent people get hurt."

Turner waved his hand around the truck stop dining room. "Any one of those witnesses could've been gunned down tonight. This is insanity. What exactly are we waiting for with the Spiveys? Why can't we go in right now and just bust the place up?"

Marshner and O'Connor shot each other a look before they gave him an answer.

"Listen, Sheriff," Marshner said. "We are well aware that your main concern here is protecting the citizens of your county."

"You're damn right."

"Turner, we are very close to snagging a much bigger fish than just Spivey. You know that." O'Connor touched his arm. "That's been our goal from the start, and Dante is getting excellent stuff, more every day. We're close to having enough evidence to indict some of the regional big guys, arrests that will make a real dent in the meth trade in this part of the country. Just a little longer."

"This shit is getting too rough," Turner said, shaking his head. "We need to shut them down. Now."

"You're tired." O'Connor shrugged.

Turner glared at her. "And you're gonna get people killed."

The minute he exited the restaurant, he spotted J.J. over by the diesel pumps. He waved for Turner to come over. This was the last thing he wanted to deal with, as usual.

"Hey, Jay."

"TV crew from Asheville been here yet?" J.J. asked.

"Nope."

"Good. Don't talk to them." J.J. grinned. "So what have we got?"

Turner looked around the crowded parking lot and knew this would be the hottest topic in town in the morning. "Looks like a drug-related killing. A young kid, probably mid-twenties, no ID, was shot inside the restaurant. The unknown suspects drove off. We don't yet have a specific description of the vehicle."

J.J. stopped scribbling in his notebook and frowned at Turner. "That's it? You got nothing else?"

"Not at the moment, Jay. You can just say the investigation is ongoing."

J.J. sighed and shoved his notebook in his back pocket. "I swear to God, Halliday—you are the only man I know who can make a bloody murder sound downright boring."

Agent Dante Cabrera stood silently against the back wall of the barn that served as Bobby Ray's meth lab. Spivey's men were putting together the latest shipment, which Dante would spend the rest of the night driving to the drop-off point at the Florida state line.

Dante considered himself the very definition of cool under pressure, but after the recent hit at the diner, he couldn't help feeling jittery. Full-scale gang warfare was a real possibility, and since he was responsible for the latest transport and exchange, he was directly in the crosshairs.

The rest of Spivey's men seemed just as tense. No one had said a word since Dante got there, and the tension in the room was palpable as they did a final count of the product.

Just then, the Spivey kid sauntered in with a cake in

his hand, a dopey grin on his face, and not a care in the world.

"You baking now, Gerrall?" one of the guys said. "I hope you didn't get any icing on your panties."

The rest of the guys laughed, and Dante could tell they were relieved to get a break from the day's tension.

Gerrall clearly didn't appreciate being the butt of their joke. His cheeks turned red and his nostrils flared. "For your information, my *girlfriend* made this for me. You didn't believe she was real, but if she wasn't, how would I have gotten this?"

"Please," one of the guys said. "There's no way an actual woman made that for you. You probably got that from the supermarket."

"Yeah," another guy said. "Nice try, kid. But it's obvious that the only pussy you've ever seen is the one between your legs."

The room erupted in laughter, and Gerrall's cheeks grew even redder. But before he could respond, his old man came charging in, heading straight for him.

Gerrall must have known what was coming, because he swiftly set the cake on a wooden counter just seconds before his father backhanded him, sending him sprawling across the floor. There was a sharp crack as the kid's head hit the ground, and then a groan as Bobby Ray delivered a sharp kick to the ribs.

"That's what happens when you get one of my smurfs killed, you dumb little shit," Bobby Ray said. "Haven't I told you that as one of my outside guys, it's up to you to keep an ear to the ground so you can prevent shit like this from happening? You hear me, boy?"

Dante cringed inwardly as Bobby Ray gave his son another kick, and Gerrall groaned in pain. The agent wished he could intervene, but he couldn't risk blowing his cover.

"Apparently your smurf had a whole lotta cough syrup on him when he was shot," Bobby Ray continued. "You know what that means? Huh? Answer me before I—"

"No," Gerrall gritted out. "I don't know."

"It means the cops are going to come sniffing around, and they're going to find out that your dead smurf had an appointment to meet *you*. But he never made it, 'cause he went and got himself shot first. And it ain't going to take a genius to figure out that as my son, you're connected to me. If that happens, if I go down because of you, then I'm going to show you a whole new world of pain. You got that, shithead?" He gave Gerrall a final kick, then ordered his men to go outside and start packing up the vehicle for the night's run.

Dante stayed inside with the kid, who gradually caught his breath and hoisted himself to his feet. Gerrall's eye was already beginning to darken and swell, and a pool of blood formed at the corner of his mouth, which he wiped away with his sleeve.

Dante maintained his position against the wall, arms crossed in stoic silence. It was an essential part of the persona he'd constructed for this latest undercover job, where he cultivated an image that was hulking, silent, and menacing. It allowed him to remain part of the scenery and freed up the men around him to talk openly. It also prevented him from drawing unnecessary attention or slipping up, which could lead to a slow and painful death.

"Asshole," Gerrall muttered as he bent over and coughed, then winced from the exertion.

"I wish I could get out of here till this all blows over," he continued, as much to himself as to Dante. "Too bad I got nowhere to go. I would stay with my girl, but she doesn't have a place either. But that's gonna change. I'm gonna get us a real nice house where we can build a life together. Our very own love nest. And we're gonna be happy, too. Want to see her?"

Gerrall took out his phone and pulled up a picture of the woman Dante knew to be Candy Carmichael. It was taken from the side, which was more than a little creepy because the woman clearly didn't know she was being photographed.

"She's real pretty, huh?" Gerrall said. "She's the reason I've gotta get away from *him*. So I can start a family of my own. And when we have our own kid, I'll never treat him how my dad treated me. That kid's going to have the best of everything. I'd rather die than turn into my dad."

Dante's heart went out to poor Gerrall. There was no denying that he was misguided. But he'd never stood a chance, growing up with Bobby Ray and suffering years of abuse like he had. Dante wished he could help somehow, maybe help set him up with some professional help. But it wasn't the time or place to concern himself with the kid's mental well-being. He had a job to do. He had to keep his eye on the big picture or a lot of innocent people would wind up dead.

Monday morning right after breakfast, Candy made a big show of carrying her boxes and overnight case to

the car and saying her good-byes to the residents of
Cherokee Pines. Mr. Miller watched the spectacle from
the open door of his office, a smug smile on his fleshy
face. Mildred Holzmann cried. Hugo told Candy he'd
miss her and really seemed to mean it. Jacinta acted
like she was devastated that Candy was leaving, which
would seem odd considering her less than thrilled reaction to her arrival. So when Candy kissed her cheek in
a fake good-bye, she whispered, "Tone it down, Mother.
See you tonight."

The highlight of Candy's day was when Turner came
in to Lenny's for lunch. He ordered the chili and a side
salad and she felt his eyes on her while she worked. His
attention caused her to put a little extra zing in the way
she moved. She felt alive, desired, sexy—even in a jeans
skirt and a diner T-shirt. She couldn't seem to stop smiling. The only downside to Turner's visit was that she
wasn't able to touch him.

"How was everything?" she asked when he came to
the register to pay his bill.

"Beautiful," was all he said.

Among the dollar bills he placed in her hand was
a folded piece of paper, but by the time she noticed it,
Turner was already on his way out the door. The note
remained unread as she watched him leave, time stood
still, and her legs went wobbly. Truly, watching Turner
Halliday walk was like seeing waves crash upon the
sand or witnessing the sun rise over the mountains—a
natural wonder so raw and powerful that it made a person damn glad to be alive.

Then he was gone. With a sigh, Candy unfolded the
note, and read three words in his cursive handwriting:

"I want you." With a shaking hand, she tucked it away in her apron along with her tips.

On her afternoon break, Candy went to look at three more apartments, all of them pigsties. As it turned out, there weren't many clean, quaint, and furnished apartments in Bigler going for four hundred dollars or less a month. She returned to work feeling dejected. Her mood improved while she baked six cakes—two devil's food, one spice, one carrot, one yellow, and the lemon cake for that little Spivey weasel. She hung out at the library for a couple hours, then sat on a bench in the Trinity Lutheran garden, remembering the feel of Turner's kiss. When she returned to Cherokee Pines at ten P.M., she followed Gerrall's instructions and went to the kitchen delivery entrance in the back, where she found the door wedged open with a rolled-up brochure. She locked the door once she was in, tossed the brochure in the trash, and left Gerrall his lemon cake on the counter. She managed to sneak down the hallway without attracting his attention.

On her second day of living a secret life, Candy took a quick shower and escaped out the back door before the Cherokee Pines kitchen staff arrived. She worked all day, went to look at two more apartments—both gross—and baked five cakes. Once again, the highlight of her day was Turner's visit for lunch.

"I'm mad at you," he said as soon as he sat down at the counter.

She felt her heart drop. *"Why?"*

"Because it seems everyone in town has tasted one of your cakes in the last week except me."

The relief poured through her, so glad that he was

teasing. "Now that's something that can be easily fixed, Sheriff."

Candy rested her elbow on the counter and propped her chin in her hand as Turner devoured that cake. With each forkful, he closed his eyes in pleasure and made a humming sound deep in his throat. "Damn," he said when he was finished.

"Still mad at me?"

"No way."

"Did you enjoy it?"

Turner shook his head and smiled. "I got no words for how much I enjoyed it."

Candy smiled so big she worried her face would break.

"So," Turner said, pushing the dessert plate to the side and leaning in on his forearms. He flashed those eyes up at her and produced one of his trademark smiles, and Candy forgot how to breathe. "You got any other talents I should know about?"

"Counter order up!"

She was back at Cherokee Pines at ten, where she found the back door propped open again. She left Gerrall's cake on the counter and was scurrying toward the hallway when she let out a yelp—someone was there, in the dark, waiting for her!

Gerrall flipped on the kitchen lights. Candy gasped. His face was all bruised. One of his eyes was blackened and swollen shut.

Candy waited for her heart to stop thudding. "What the hell are you doing stalking me like that? You scared the living *shit* out of me!"

"Just having some fun. Did you bring my applesauce cake?"

"Uggh!" Candy slapped the swinging door open and tiptoed down the hallway counting the doors until she reached Jacinta's, sixth on the right. As a precaution, she ducked below peephole level when she passed by Lorraine's door—that woman would jump at the chance to report Candy's illegal status to Miller. Jacinta was waiting and opened the door in silence, much to Candy's relief.

"Whew!" she said to her mother once she was inside. "Living on the down low's harder than it looks."

Jacinta smiled. "That's what Hugo always says."

"And I'm starting to really wonder about that Gerrall Spivey guy—he's creeping me out big-time."

"I think you made a mistake trusting him with your secrets," Jacinta said, shaking her head. "Like I said—he's not from good people."

Wednesday started the same way. Turner came for lunch and ordered a chef's salad. Candy put some extra croutons on for him. He had a piece of her white chocolate almond cake for dessert and when he was done he laughed and wiped his mouth with a napkin.

"Good?"

"Candy, you should open your own bakery. Seriously."

"Right."

"Hey, Bigler's only bakery closed up years ago and the town needs one. Why not?" The suggestion was so earnest and his smile so sweet that it almost sounded less than completely ridiculous.

Candy pressed her thighs together as if to check on

Sophie. *No,* she reassured the bracelet and herself, *not in this lifetime.*

"Can I get you anything else?" she asked him.

That's when Turner reached across the counter and took Candy's hand in both of his. She was so surprised that she froze, sure that everyone was staring. Public displays of affection in this town were significant statements, no matter who was on display. But public displays with the town sheriff during the Lenny's lunch rush had to be considered an outright spectacle.

Turner didn't appear the least bit concerned. "You know, I won't be working these crazy hours for the rest of my life," he offered. "I want to spend time with you. I want to take you out—you know, for real, once things slow down at work. I just wanted you to know that it's not always going to be this tough."

Candy brought her other hand up to wrap around his. "I'd like that."

"Dating a cop can be a challenge sometimes."

"Hmm. I noticed," she said. "Ice cream interruptus and all that."

Turner lowered his head and laughed. When he looked up, she leaned across the counter and planted a quick kiss right on his lips.

Once Turner had left, she enjoyed the sensation of floating for a few minutes, right until Cee-Dee Creswell shuffled over to the register to pay for his senior lunch special.

"How was everything for you today, Mr. Creswell?" Since that was her standard question and the old guy was one of her counter regulars, Candy didn't even raise her eyes to him until she noticed he didn't answer. "You okay?" She looked up and held out his change.

Mr. Creswell glared out the windows of the diner, as if intentionally ignoring Candy. Maybe he was becoming hard of hearing. That had to be it, Candy decided. She'd known this man her whole life. He went to the same church as her family. He'd been a client of her father's. And Mr. Creswell held a special spot in her childhood, since the hardest whupping she ever got was after she, Turner, Cheri, and J.J. got caught doing belly flops in the mud pit out behind his smokehouse.

"Are you all right, Mr. Cresswell?"

The old man slowly turned his face in her direction. For an instant, Candy didn't even recognize him. He looked ugly. His mouth was pulled down at the corners and a mean squint had replaced his usually kind eyes. A red welt of anger had discolored his skin. "You should be downright ashamed of yourself," he hissed, ripping the change from her hand. "Your daddy would disown you if he was still livin'."

And suddenly, the lightness she'd held in her heart was replaced by confusion and anger. What the hell had that been about? She couldn't seem to close her mouth while watching Mr. Creswell walk out of the diner.

Lenny's large hand landed on her shoulder. "I heard what he said. You okay?"

"What's wrong with people?" she whispered. "Really! What is it with people around here? It isn't 1850 anymore! For heaven's sake—our country's president is a man of biracial heritage! All I did was give the sheriff a peck! What is their *problem*?"

"Maybe you should take a break."

Candy nodded at Lenny's suggestion, ran into the kitchen and out the back door, where she took big swallows of fresh air. Her tears came fast and hard, and it didn't take long for her to understand that they weren't about Mr. Creswell. They were about her father. They were for the way her father had spoken to Turner all those years ago. About everything that happened that night—the night she swore hadn't happened, hadn't been real.

What a bastard Jonesy Carmichael had been. What a sorry excuse for a man.

Eventually, Candy cried it all out. She threw cold water on her face and went back to the counter, and made it through the rest of the rush without incident. In fact, a couple of her regulars told her to not pay any mind to old Creswell.

"Meaner than a skillet of rattlesnakes," said one customer.

"So *ignernt* he couldn't piss his own name in the snow," said another.

Later that afternoon, while she sorted silverware, Candy told herself she had to be the stupidest girl on the planet to get all excited about the way Turner made her feel—she was leaving Bigler in two and a half months. While she folded aprons, she decided she wouldn't worry about what was down the road, but would focus on enjoying the ride instead. The only thing that mattered was that she was completely, perfectly honest with Turner.

While Candy baked seven cakes, she talked herself into going back to the Victorian house on Chester Street to try negotiating with the landlady one last time. She wanted that apartment. She wasn't going to take no for an answer. This was one of those things in life she would just have to make happen.

It was close to five P.M. when Candy knocked on the door. The same woman answered and the same kids gathered behind her legs.

"Oh!" she said, looking surprised.

"I know you weren't expecting me, but I'm back," Candy said. "I am begging you to reconsider my offer. I can get you letters of recommendation if you'd like— from my boss and the publisher of the *Bugle,* who happens to be my best friend. I can provide copies of my last paycheck. And my tax returns for the last few years. It might be hard to believe, but at one point my net worth was—"

The woman put her hand on Candy's arm. "I rented it yesterday. I'm sorry."

Candy wasn't sure she'd heard correctly. The apartment was rented? But she was supposed to have that place. It was perfect. It was *her* place.

"I'm very sorry to have bothered you," Candy said, turning away and heading down the steps.

"Good luck!" the woman called after her.

After last call in the library reading room, Candy again headed for the church garden. When it began to rain, she raced back to her car in Lenny's parking lot and used the time to brainstorm by the glow of the overhead security light, jotting down some business ideas in the notebook she kept in the glove compartment. That little exercise segued into a list of pros and cons for getting involved with Turner. The cons she'd already gone over a million times in her head and began and ended with the fact that she was L-E-A-V-I-N-G. How much simpler could it get?

The pro column ended up being pretty long. Turner was a good man. He was available. He was sexy. He was sweet and kind and compassionate. He was doing something to make the world better. He believed in something more than his bank account balance or how much he could bench press. He loved his job and worked hard at it. He made Candy feel special, beautiful, desired. He made her laugh. His kisses caused her to levitate. She could watch that man walk till the end of time and never grow tired of the view.

She had to stop writing when her hand began to cramp.

Chapter 14

Candy headed home, and since it was raining hard when she arrived at Cherokee Pines, she decided to take the risk and park adjacent to the rear entrance. Her usual spot behind the senior citizen vans would require a long run to the building, which would certainly ruin Gerrall's cake. She'd just have to remember to leave a few minutes early the next morning to make a clean getaway.

It hardly mattered. Candy was sopping wet by the time she reached the door. The cake looked more like pudding. She yanked hard on the door handle, finding solace in the fact that she'd be inside in seconds. But it didn't budge.

"What the—?"

She tried again. Nothing. She tried harder. It was *locked*! Uh-oh.

Candy knocked. No one came. Where the hell was Gerrall? She knocked harder but stopped before she reached a full-out pound, knowing that if she banged hard enough for Gerrall to hear from the lobby then everyone else in the place would hear, too. That left her no choice but to make a run for the front entrance.

Shoving her car key in her pocket and balancing the cake in both hands, she ran through the rain, glad that she wore gym shoes, grateful for the brief dry pavement she found beneath a stand of evergreens near the building. But as she rounded the corner and hit the front lawn, a brilliant flash of lightning crackled so close she could feel the hairs on her arms stand up, and the loud *boom!* that followed made her lose her footing on the wet grass. She fell forward, the cake shooting out of her hands and skidding to a stop on the wet pavement, where it split into pieces and collapsed in a pile. Another crack of lightning, another loud *boom!,* and Candy struggled to her feet, her only goal now to get inside before she got toasted like a campfire marshmallow. But as she staggered headlong toward the entrance doors, she saw that Gerrall wasn't at the front desk—*Miller* was!

"Shee-it!" Candy ducked low and ran quickly past the double glass doors, hoping Miller wouldn't look up and see her. Now what? She plastered her back against the red brick exterior of the building and caught her breath, then checked her arms and legs for charred flesh. She stared out through a curtain of rain, thinking . . . thinking . . .

Candy suddenly looked to her left. The window! She could climb in Jacinta's window! It should be easy enough to find. Hers was the sixth apartment on this side of the building.

She crouched down low and counted her way along—a bedroom and a living room window for each unit—until she reached the sixth apartment. Unfortunately, the window was just a bit too high to reach from the ground, so she jumped up and quickly tapped her fingers on the glass. The light remained off. She jumped again. Still dark. Clearly, she needed to make a more regular tapping sound to get Jacinta's attention, so she whirled around and looked for a stick or twig in the mulch, but since the property had been landscaped to within an inch of its life, she found nothing sticklike anywhere. So Candy decided to break off a limb from one of the shrubs, an idea that sounded simple enough but involved several minutes of bending and ripping and pulling. Right when she began wishing she'd joined the Girl Scouts instead of the cheerleading squad, the branch snapped off. "Yes!" she whispered.

Candy began rhythmically tapping the branch on the window, hoping her mother would get the message that she was locked out and couldn't come in the standard way. But nothing. Oh, no! Maybe she'd fallen asleep!

"Jacinta!" Candy hoped her loud hiss could be heard over the rain and through a closed window. "Open up! I'm outside! Jacinta!"

Candy had no choice but to climb. Dammit—she sure picked a bad day to wear a skirt to work, but there was nothing she could do about it now. So Candy pulled up her denim skirt to mid-thigh, reached up to grip the brick window ledge, and lodged her gym shoe into a groove of mortar. She pulled with all her might and rose above the ground, only to hang there in midair, too weak to pull herself all the way up. She tried again. Still couldn't manage it. She banged the branch on the window again, harder this time, and still got no response. This was ridiculous. She was ready to cry from frustration.

"Get it together, Carmichael," she said aloud. "You can do this. This is *nothing*. You can climb in one little freakin' window. Now stop your blubbering and do it. Just *do* it!"

Candy gritted her teeth in determination as she reached up, jammed her toe against the brick, pulled. And pulled harder. And soon her chin cleared the window ledge, and even though her arms were shaking she let go with one hand and clutched at the vinyl window frame while walking her toes up the wall. She did it! She was there! And as soon as she pushed against the window frame it moved. Unlocked! Thank God! Finally— something had gone her way tonight.

Candy balanced all her weight on her left big toe and raised her right leg. If she could only get her knee on the ledge, then she could push her body up and over. She could get the top half of her body inside and then—

Suddenly, the whole world flooded with a flash of light, and Candy winced, expecting to hear another crashing *boom!* explode all around her. Instead, she heard Miller's voice.

"There she is! Arrest her!"

Candy ratcheted her neck to look behind her, and what she saw was a spectacle that made no sense. A half-dozen police vehicles were pulled onto the lawn, lights flashing in the rain, spotlights aimed directly up her skirt.

"Oh, my God!" Candy tried to push herself off the ledge but something was stuck. She couldn't move!

"Get me down!" she screamed. She flailed around with one hand and discovered that her skirt had bunched all the way up to the middle of her back, which meant her entire ass was exposed! "Oh, my God!" she yelled out again, trying desperately to pull her skirt down.

Suddenly the lights went on in her mother's apartment, and Candy felt something smack her on top of the head. Once. Again. And again and again.

"Thief! Trailer park trash! She's probably armed!"

Lorraine Estes?

She'd climbed in the wrong window. And Lorraine was beating her on the head with a rolled-up newspaper.

"Candy. Let me help you."

Turner? "Oh, God, get me down from here! Please! I'm hung up on something and I can't move. Help me!"

"It's gonna be all right," he assured her, his voice slow and steady. "I'm gonna reach up under you now and see if I can help you get unstuck."

The soothing sound of that mellow voice in the middle of all this crazy shit was almost too wonderful to be real. Then she felt his hand reach up under the front of her body and rub against some extremely sensitive places before he squeezed it between her belly and the brick.

"I think . . . wait . . . your belt loop is twisted around the window latch. Here. Hold on." Turner's forearm and hand began to twist and turn, doing some pretty amazing things to places on her body that had nothing to do with belt loops.

Candy shut her eyes and wanted to die right there. She swiveled her head around again in the hopes that the audience had dispersed, only to find that over a dozen residents had wandered out, clustered under their umbrellas, hoping to get a look at the crazy woman stuck ass up in a freakin' window. Among those whose mouths were hanging open were most of the law enforcement types she'd delivered lunch to a couple weeks back. The pretty woman with dark hair looked horrified. A guy who'd tried to tip her was smiling like he'd won the lottery.

That's it—she was going to cry now.

"Candace?" Her mother popped her head out the window just to her right. "Oh, dear Lord! What are you doing, child?"

"Here, Sheriff." Miller scurried under his umbrella and held out a utility step stool to Turner, not bothering to hide his glee.

"Thanks." Turner climbed up and got face-to-face with Candy. He stroked her hair and whispered in her ear. "Candy baby, you're a hot, wet mess. What in the world were you thinking?"

"Just get me down, Turner." Her gaze latched onto his and she saw his eyes crinkle up in amusement. "You can poke fun at me later, but please, *please* get me down *now*."

"You got it. Now, you're going to try to unsnag the belt loop when I lift you, okay?" He grabbed her by her hips and lifted enough for Candy to reach underneath and rip the small denim loop off a hook-shaped piece of metal.

"Got it!" she said.

Turner immediately pulled her skirt down to cover the lower half of her body.

"Thank you," she said, feeling the tears start to stream down her face.

"Stay there just a second and I'll help you down." Turner climbed off the utility stool and stood on the ground with his arms out. Candy lowered herself down the wall and he caught her. She was so ashamed and worn out that her legs didn't hold her.

"Come on," Turner said, propping her up and walking her toward his SUV parked in the grass.

"I am filing charges!" Miller screamed. "Don't think you're getting away with this, Miss Carmichael!"

Candy felt herself start to collapse. A sob escaped her shaking lips. She was soaked to the skin and the rain dripped from her hair into her eyes. At least it would mask the tears.

Turner opened the door and helped her inside the passenger seat. He put his hand on her cheek and looked at her with concern. "Just stay put. I'll take care of Miller and then we'll get you dried off, okay?"

She nodded, wiping the water out of her eyes, feeling herself start to shake all over. Candy sat in the silent SUV and with the windows sealed. She could hear her own heartbeat. She could hear rain pound and her teeth chatter. But she couldn't hear a word Turner was saying to Miller. Candy could only watch him touch Miller's arm to calm him down, nod patiently as the nasty man yelled and complained, and reassure Miller that he had the situation under control. At that moment, she was immensely grateful for Turner's people skills.

Suddenly, she panicked. *Sophie!* Candy groped around under her skirt to find that the bracelet was still in place—oh, thank you, God!—but felt sick with the knowledge that everyone must have seen the belt around her thigh. She'd have to come up with a viable explanation. Maybe she could say she didn't trust banks, which would be accurate enough, and chose to carry her pay under her clothes.

She watched all the law enforcement people start to get in their cars and drive off, the pretty woman stopping to speak with Turner before she flashed a look of pity in Candy's direction and left. What were all those cops doing here, anyway? Candy was just a woman overstaying her welcome at a senior citizen home! You'd have thought that kind of all-out response would be saved for a dangerous terrorist or something!

One by one the residents went back inside, some waving to Candy before they disappeared. It took a good fifteen minutes, but Turner eventually finished his negotiations with Miller and jogged back to the car. He got in the driver's seat and backed up.

"Take me to my car," Candy said.

Turner put the gearshift in drive and frowned at her. "Where is it?"

"Just out back." She pointed toward the rear of the building, and as they drove she noticed the remains of Gerrall's orange crème cake oozing all over the pavement. She busted out laughing.

"Something funny?" Turner looked sideways at her.

She pointed to the wet blob. "I was thinking of that stupid old song Viv used to put on her record player when we were kids. Remember? 'Someone left the cake out in the rain and I don't think I can take it'—"

" 'Cause it took so long to bake it . . .' "

Suddenly, they both exploded in laughter. Turner seemed to be enjoying himself as much as she was, at least until her guffaws turned into sobs and she bent over from the weight of the ridiculous, sad disaster that her life had become, hanging her head between her knees as she cried.

Turner stopped his truck. "Are you all right, baby?"

And just like that, in her mind she was seventeen. It was that night Turner called to ask her out, that awful night she swore hadn't been real. She felt the sting of her father's hand, but it was nothing compared to the sting of his words. She heard her mother's high-pitched begging. She watched as the red velvet cake dripped down the walls.

Candy quickly sat upright, gasping at the clarity of that memory. She glanced at Turner. He looked worried, doubtful of her sanity, even.

He touched her shoulder. "What is it, Candy?"

She shook her head. Tried to swallow. Felt panic rise in her throat.

"Tell me."

"That night you called . . ." Her voice sounded far away to her own ears, as if it belonged to someone else. Candy stared out the window. "I have to tell you about that night you called and my father answered. I have to explain to you why I forgot. I have to—"

"You don't have to do anything, sweetheart. I'm here and I'm listening if there's something you want me to know, but you don't have to do or say anything."

She looked sideways at Turner. He was so calm. Sensible. He just didn't know. "My parents were having a dinner party for some of Daddy's clients. My mom

asked me to bake a red velvet cake for dessert. I did that
a lot for those parties, you know, and I'd have to sit there
and look nice and not say much. I hated those dinners.
Daddy would be so charming and nice and it would be
like he was showing off his lovely, happy family and his
daughter's cakes so these suckers would feel good buying an insurance policy from him. It was awful."

"Sounds like it."

"You called during dessert."

"Bad timing, I bet."

Candy nodded. She couldn't look at him for the rest
of it. She stared down at her hands, twisting on each
other in her wet lap. "He called me to the phone and
stood over me while I spoke to you. He was wearing a
suit and tie. He smelled like that horrible cologne he
wore mixed with Jack Daniel's and anger. I could feel it
rolling off him in waves."

Turner moved a section of wet hair from her cheek.
It felt reassuring. She continued.

"Daddy pressed up so close to me. I had to get off the
phone. I was shaking all over when I hung up and had to
go back to the table and pretend like nothing was wrong.
The whole time my mother was laughing a little too
much and trying to cover over Daddy's anger. When the
clients finally left . . ."

Candy took a big breath. She had wanted to calm
herself but it sounded like a hysterical gasp for air instead. All she wanted to do was get the whole story out
before she lost it completely.

"He hit me in the face. He called me a white trash
whore. He threw me up against the wall."

"Your father beat you. You never told me."

Candy nodded. "I never told anyone. But it only happened sometimes. That night was the worst ever. And when he was done hitting me, he grabbed the cake stand from the table and threw it against the wall right by my head and there was cake and icing everywhere, all over the carpet and my dress and in my hair . . ."

"Oh, Candy. No. I'm so sorry."

"And he just kept screaming at me saying, 'I'm not sending you to some damn college to whore your way through life! You might as well just stay home and bake cookies! That's what you want anyway, right? A bakery? Hell, you can be some stupid hillbilly girl and bake cakes and slut around Bigler without me wasting my hard-earned money on college! Why don't you just do that?' "

Candy let her head drop into her hands and she began to cry again.

"I threw up all that night and again at school the next day, just sick with fear of my dad and guilt about how I treated you, and . . . I remember praying that you would never, ever talk about what had happened. I wouldn't have been able to deal with it. And you never did . . . Turner, you never brought it up again, and that made it easier for me to forget the whole night . . . forget that it ever happened."

His hand remained on her back. She could feel the heat and strength of his palm through the cold, wet fabric stuck to her skin. She continued to heave and cry like a toddler throwing a temper tantrum in the cereal aisle of the Piggly Wiggly, feeling more ashamed than she had a few minutes ago, with her butt on display for half of Cataloochee County, if that was even possible.

"Oh, Candy. Baby."

She bolted straight up at the sound of Turner's voice. For a moment, she'd almost forgotten he was there. Oh, God, the last thing in the world she wanted was to let him see her like this.

She peered through the windshield and saw her car. She dug her hand into the front pocket of her denim skirt, located her key, and pulled on the door handle.

Turner grabbed her upper arm. "Where are you going?"

She ignored him and turned away.

"Candy, look at me. Seriously. Where the hell are you going? You're wet to the bone. You're traumatized. Please, let me take you—"

"Thank you for everything, Turner." She managed to get the words out in between gasps for air. She didn't dare look at him. "I am sorry if . . . I embarrassed you . . . in front of your coworkers."

"What? I don't give a rat's ass about them. I only—"

"I'll be fine. I'll talk to you tomorrow." She jumped out the door and ran to her car, throwing herself behind the wheel.

With a loud backfire, the car started. She turned on her windshield wipers, swiped at her eyes again, and hit the gas. Right then she made a bargain with herself. *Keep it together until you reach the Tip Top,* she told herself. *Then you can grab your toiletries and a towel, buy yourself a dollar-fifty shower, and spend the entire fifteen minutes of hot water behind the locked shower stall door, alone, where you can totally lose your shit in peace.*

* * *

Turner phoned in his brief report to the dispatcher while he followed Candy—at a respectable distance—out of Cherokee Pines. He had no choice but to follow. For starters, she was hysterical and trying to drive a death trap of a vehicle through mountain roads during a downpour. Also, he just didn't think she should be alone. If ever a woman needed someone to hold her and tell her everything was going to be all right, it was Candy Carmichael, on this particular night. That story she'd just told him left him vibrating with anger and numb with sadness. If he had seen even a hint of what was going on in that house when they were kids, Turner would have killed the man with his bare hands.

Candy had hidden it so well.

And now Turner had the overwhelming urge to bring her home with him and keep her close. Keep her safe. The way he hadn't been able to do when they were kids.

When Turner received that call from Wainright Miller about a break-in at the senior home, his heart had dropped like a rock. His first thought was it had something to do with the Spiveys and that Candy was in danger. He'd contacted O'Connor, who called in other members of the task force already in town. Happily, his hunch turned out to be a little off target.

Once he'd helped Candy out of the window, Miller had given him the details—he'd discovered that Gerrall Spivey was helping Candy stay longer than guests were permitted, working out a deal where Candy baked him a cake for every night he sneaked her inside. At least that explained how her cakes had made their way into the meth lab.

"Shocking," is how Miller described Gerrall's behavior. "I fired him on the spot, needless to say."

Turner couldn't say he was sad to see Gerrall leave the place.

He craned his neck, searching out Candy's car. Where the hell was she headed? He might have been three cars behind, but there was no way in hell he'd lose her—all he had to do was follow the cloud of smoke and the rancid odor, now worse than when he'd written her up for an emissions inspection weeks ago. Turner sighed, thinking that the old Chevy was a lot like Candy's life in general—it needed quality parts and a lot of skilled labor.

"Damn, girl," Turner mumbled to himself, watching her pull into the Tip Top. Why there, of all places? He just prayed Gerrall wasn't there for a drop—that would be a little awkward. Turner parked his SUV on the other side of the diesel pumps and waited to see what she'd do.

After a few minutes, Candy exited the car with a large shoulder bag and headed for the entrance. Turner pulled around until his SUV blocked her way to the building. She looked up and shook her head slowly, then tried to walk around his vehicle. Turner got out.

"Candy, please. Just talk to me for a minute."

"I need to be alone right now, Turner."

"Really?" Turner heard the snarkiness in his own voice but didn't feel like hiding it—especially since he'd had enough standing around in the rain for one night. "Because I'd think by this point you'd be good and sick of being alone, handling everything by yourself." He paused. He ran a hand over his chin as the truth hit him. "I know I am."

Candy stood clutching her bag, shaking her head as her lips trembled.

He decided she had to be the most bullheaded woman he'd ever laid eyes on, and that was saying something considering he had been married to and raised by two of the most stubborn women God ever created. Turner approached her slowly, then wrapped her tight in his arms and kissed her wet hair. "Just get in my damn truck, okay?" When he felt her body relax and her head nod in surrender, he opened the door and got her settled.

A few minutes later they were parked at the edge of the truck stop lot under a huge old pawpaw tree. Candy was sipping hot coffee with her bag of shower supplies at her feet, snuggled under a blanket Turner had fetched from her car. It nearly broke his heart to see that the Chevy was crammed with everything the girl owned.

The way Candy now sat, hunched over and protective of herself, made Turner think of some kind of exotic, graceful bird nursing a broken wing. He knew her bones were intact. It was her spirit he was worried about.

Turner had asked her several times to tell him what was going on, but she'd remained silent. As frustrating as it was, he had nowhere else he had to be. His cell and radio were on, and save for the call to Cherokee Pines, the night had been quiet.

"You know, Candy, I got all the time in the world, but you're going to catch pneumonia if you don't get out of those wet clothes."

Finally, he got a response. She peered over the rim of her paper cup and looked him up and down. "You're as wet as me," she whispered.

"I know. And I'd sure like to get dry. So I'll tell you what. How about we both drive to my house. It's only about five minutes from here and you can get a hot shower that you don't have to share with a gang of female truck drivers, not that I have anything against showering with female truck drivers, per se."

That got a small smile from her.

"This will be a completely legitimate arrangement, Candy. Just come home and get some rest and we'll figure this out together."

She glanced sideways at him, doubt lingering in her eyes. At that instant, with her wet curls plastered to the sides of her face, she looked like she was about seven years old.

"What will people say?"

Turner laughed. "Probably the same shit they said after you kissed me at the counter at Lenny's today."

Candy's eyes went huge. "You heard about that?"

"Of course I did. I hear everything. That was why I was so shocked that I somehow missed the news that you'd left Viv's house over two weeks ago to stay with your mother! It hacked me off something awful."

Candy's brows met in consternation. "Why?"

Turner backtracked, knowing he had to stay cool. He shrugged. "I just wanted to keep an eye on you. Make sure you were all right."

She nodded. "I appreciate that."

"Candy. C'mon now. Let's go home. Enough of this foolishness. We're grown-ups. I care for you. I am not taking you to my house to get you in bed—although I'd be a damn liar if I said the thought had never crossed my mind, because you know it has—but not tonight. Please. Trust me. Come home with me."

Turner watched her stare straight out the windshield, the muscles of her jaw working. He figured it was time to play his best card. "I've got a wall safe at the house," he said.

Her head snapped around and her eyes widened in excitement. "Are you serious?"

"Serious as a heart attack."

But just as quickly as Candy had perked up she scowled again. "Why do you think that would be important to me?"

Turner laughed once more and shook his head. He was still trying to recover from the vision that had greeted him upon arrival at Cherokee Pines earlier that night—Candy's perfect, round, luscious, snow-white ass covered in a tiny pair of pink panties, sticking right in his face, some kind of money belt contraption secured around the juiciest part of her left thigh. Whatever she had in there she wanted to keep close by. Real close by.

"Oh," she said, her voice flat. "I guess you saw it."

"Whatever *it* is, yeah, I saw it, and I figure that any thing that important to you should be in a safe and not tied to your thigh. Although don't get me wrong, I think your thigh would be a fine place to be tied to." Turner cleared his throat, thinking that might not have come out right.

After Candy stared at him for a moment in bewildered silence, he was sure it hadn't.

"But you don't know me," Candy said, her voice barely above a whisper.

"Huh?" Turner reared his head back. "What're you talking about, girl? I've known you since—"

"I'm a failure," she said, cutting him off. "I showed up in Bigler with about sixteen dollars to my name and nowhere to go. I lived in my car for a few days before I agreed to stay with Gladys Harbison, which is how I knew I could buy a hot shower at the Tip Top for a dollar-fifty. *That's* who I am. *That's* who you'd be taking home with you." Candy jutted out her chin in challenge.

"And you immediately set about changing that. Which you've done. That's not failure, Candy."

"I'm greedy and shallow and materialistic." She sniffed. "I brought Cheri down with me because I kept pushing for more and more success and more and more money! It was my fault we lost everything in the real estate crash. I'm one hundred percent to blame!" Candy emitted a sound that was part wail and part hiccup, and Turner decided to retrieve the small package of tissues from the center console of his SUV.

"Here, darlin'," he said. "Have you talked to Cheri about this?"

"Oh, sure," she said with a dismissive wave of her hand. "She told me I'm nuts, that we made decisions on the way up together and we went down together. But that's a bunch of crap." Candy grabbed the pack of tissues and began twisting the plastic in her hands. "I transferred to three colleges down in Florida, did you know that, Turner? I owned six houses while I lived down there. I started a bunch of businesses for the sole purpose of selling them—what does that tell you about me?"

Turner shrugged. "That you're an entrepreneur?"

"Ha!" Candy grabbed a few tissues and blew her nose. "I didn't care about those businesses. They were stupid! They never helped anyone! All I cared about was the money they made! What I'm trying to tell you is that I'm greedy!"

"Okay," Turner said. "But you provided a legitimate product or service someone needed, right? It wasn't like you were out selling drugs or something."

She grimaced. "My most successful business was a dog poop removal service, okay? Rich people paid money so they didn't have to bend over and clean up their own damned backyards!"

"Wow," was all Turner could think to say. "There are companies that do that?"

"And when I sold Doo-Away I had sixteen full-time employees, a fleet of eight cars, and over two hundred and fifty clients so lazy that they'd pay a hundred bucks month to have someone else pick up their dog's crap!"

Turner laughed. "What a great name," he said.

Candy cocked her head to the side and produced a smirk. "What I'm telling you is that my businesses weren't created to save the world. They were created to make me rich. I'm materialistic, like I said."

"Hey, some of my best friends are capitalists."

"And I've dated a whole bunch of men, but no one for very long," she said, obviously too far gone to appreciate his sense of humor. "I got bored with them, Turner, that's what I'm trying to tell you! I've never been big on commitment!"

He nodded. "They weren't right for you, I guess."

"And my family—my God!" Candy waved her hands

around. "You know my mother and I have never been close, and I'm just now understanding what a racist ass- hole my father was. But here's the thing, Turner, here's what you need to know—I was a *coward*! I didn't stick up for you with Daddy! I didn't stand up for what I knew was right! Is that the kind of woman you want staying in your house? Is that the kind of woman you want *kissing* you in public?"

"Candy," he said, reaching out for her hand. "You were a kid. You were scared of your dad. It's over and done with."

"I hurt you," she said, shaking her head, the tears slipping down her cheeks.

"You've already apologized. I accepted your apology. It's done." Turner squeezed her hand until she raised her eyes to him again. "Anything else you want me to know?"

Candy laughed. "Oh, Lord-ee! Seriously? You can take more?"

Turner smiled and plied a fresh tissue from her clutches to dab at her tears. "I'm a pretty strong man. I can take a lot, darlin'."

She rolled her eyes. "Okay, well, I should tell you about the thing on my thigh."

"If you'd like to."

"I've got a bracelet in there."

"Okay."

She laughed again. "A really valuable one—over twenty thousand dollars' worth of pavé diamonds and sapphires in platinum."

If Candy's goal had been to shock him, she'd finally done it. Turner felt his jaw unhinge.

"Yeah. That's what I was trying to tell you—I'm shallow! When Cheri and I were hocking everything to stay alive, I kept it, and I never told her I had it. I just couldn't part with it. To me it symbolizes everything I ever wanted, it symbolizes success. Sophie is my lucky charm. I thought if I kept her, I could keep my dream alive, and someday she'll provide the seed money to make my dreams come true."

"The bracelet has a name?"

"Sophie. I thought it sounded like a nickname for sapphire."

"Ah."

"That's it?" Candy's eyes went huge. She gestured toward him. "That's all you have to say to me?"

"I'll add one thing—thank you. Thank you for telling me all that. You're right—there was a lot I didn't know and I'm sure there's a lot yet to find out." Turner leaned closer to her. "I'm looking forward to the adventure."

Candy pulled her mouth tight. "I do not want to interfere with your life. I will be gone as soon as I find a place."

"If anything, you make my life more interesting. You add spark to it. And I'm in no hurry to kick you out."

It happened slowly, but Candy finally smiled, and once it started it couldn't be stopped. The smile plumped the apple of her cheeks and filled her beautiful eyes with light. "Okay, then," she said. "What are we waiting for?"

She threw off the blanket, placed her coffee in his cup holder, and ran through the rain to her car.

And just like that, Candy Carmichael was coming home with him. Turner's hands gripped the steering wheel as his heart banged around in his chest like a just caught fish in the bottom of a boat.

Chapter 15

The hot water beat against the clenched muscles of her body. Candy leaned her palms against the tile of Turner's shower and let the warmth penetrate her skin and soothe her jangled nerves. If she'd learned anything in the last few weeks, it was that she couldn't predict what the next day might bring, so that's why she'd decided to allow herself a few moments simply to feel where she was in the here and now. Candy savored the heat seeping into her bones. She breathed deeply, aware of the expansion of her lungs. She sensed her legs and feet strong beneath her, reliable and balanced.

Sure, she'd had a wild day, but Candy reminded herself that she still had everything a person needed to get by. She had her friends. She had her dreams—with Sophie tucked away in Turner's safe. She had a job. She had a car. She had cash in her pocket.

Candy had herself.

After she shampooed and conditioned her hair, dried off on a fluffy towel, and rubbed moisturizer all over, she felt almost normal—whatever normal was for her lately. She put on a pair of yoga pants and a hoodie, which she zipped up to her clavicle. It wasn't because she didn't want Turner to want her. She did. She just wasn't sure she was one hundred percent ready for everything that would come *after.* What would they say to each other? Would their friendship ever feel natural again? Would they discover a new natural?

One thing was certain—once they went there, there would be no going back.

She exited Turner's bathroom and immediately headed into the guest room, deciding that she needed a couple of minutes before she faced him. But she rounded the corner and there he was, in a dry and pressed navy blue sheriff's department uniform, bent over the far side of the guest bed, smoothing out a top sheet. He glanced up when she entered the doorway.

Turner was a gentleman, which she'd always loved about him, so he didn't feel compelled to say something about the obvious "man-woman-bed" moment they were having. He simply smiled up at her and assured her he was almost done. Oh, but in that instant his eyes had connected with hers, Turner told Candy all she needed to know.

He wanted her *bad.* And bringing her home with him was a very big deal for him.

"I can finish up," she said.

"Hell, no," he said, chuckling. "You're my guest. My mama would kill me if I let a guest make their own bed."

"Please. Let me do it."

His hands stopped tugging on the sheet and he stood

straight. His eyes and smile were soft. "Sure. I'll be out in the living room if you need me."

It was a small bedroom, so Candy felt Turner's big body brush against hers on his way out. Instinctively, she stretched her fingers out as he walked by and the brief contact sent a shiver through her. Shamelessly, she peered over her shoulder to stare at him as he walked away, only to find he was looking back at her.

They both laughed.

She sat down on the edge of the bed and peeked around. Clearly, Turner must not get a lot of overnight visitors, because before he could even put sheets on the bed he'd had to remove a jumble of CDs, newspapers, and magazines, which were now stacked against the wall under the window. The room held a dresser and mirror, an upholstered chair, and boxes stacked along every bit of open wall space to at least five feet high. Candy had a funny feeling that if she were to look inside those boxes she'd find Junie's belongings. It was going to take a concerted effort for her not to feel like an intruder in another woman's house.

When they'd arrived about a half hour before, Candy noticed immediately that Turner's place felt serene. Peaceful. It was an older log home tucked into the woods about ten minutes from the Bigler town line, surrounded by tall pines and bordered by a creek. They'd had to drive over a small private bridge to reach the lane leading uphill to the house.

The inside was small but didn't feel cramped. It was cozy, with pine walls and floors, a large stone fireplace, and a thoroughly modern kitchen with stainless steel appliances and granite countertops. She asked Turner if he'd recently remodeled and he'd told her yes—it was his and Junie's first project after they got married.

The kitchen wasn't the only indication that a woman had lovingly turned this little house into a home. There were feminine touches everywhere, little details that made it obvious a man hadn't created the space alone. The dark brown leather couch and chair were accented with colorful kilim-patterned toss pillows. The windows were framed in generous swags of sheer ivory fabric held open with scrolled brass tiebacks. The artwork on the walls was muted and perfectly complementary to both the interior and the view Candy imagined would present itself with every sunrise.

"It's really lovely," she'd said.

"It's home," he'd replied. "And it's yours for as long as you need it."

Candy gave a quick check in the dresser mirror before she joined Turner. She had to laugh. She looked like a worn-out chick with wet hair and a few dozen major life issues to sort through, which about covered it. At least it was truth in advertising.

"Hi," she said, walking around the end of the couch where Turner was sprawled under the soft glow of a floor lamp. As she settled down in the chair Turner shot up to a sitting position, startled. Obviously, he'd fallen asleep. "Oh." Candy immediately stood again, already feeling like she was intruding. "You're very tired, so you rest and we'll talk tomorrow, okay?"

Turner's long arm reached out and he gripped her hand in his. "Please don't go. Sit for a minute."

"Are you sure?"

"Very." With his free hand he patted the sofa next to him.

Candy sighed in surrender and let herself be pulled down at his side, immediately tucking her legs under her and turning to face him. Turner did look tired, but there was so much more in his expression than physical exhaustion. He looked content.

"I'm glad you're here, Candy," he said, keeping her hand tucked in his.

"Thank you for this, Turner."

A strange little smile crept onto his face and several moments went by without them feeling the need to speak. It was a rare opportunity for Candy to simply gaze at him, relaxed, in his element, his expression open and calm. She was mesmerized by the color of his skin—like a perfectly toasted marshmallow, like a two-thousand-calorie mocha latte, like the warm brown of an autumn leaf. She'd never known his father—he'd passed away when they were kids—but she wondered if that's where Turner got those extraordinary hazel eyes. And his broad shoulders. And the sensual shape of his mouth.

Without thinking, Candy reached up and brushed her fingertips down the side of his face, and Turner's reaction was equally spontaneous. He closed his eyes and leaned into her touch, the softest moan escaping from his throat.

She snatched her hand away, embarrassed. That was the kind of touch a man receives from the woman he loves, the woman who belongs to him and cherishes him in return. Junie had been that woman to him. Candy looked around the living room apprehensively, almost expecting Junie to pop up from behind the chair and give Candy a piece of her mind.

"So," she said, trying her best to cover up for her awkwardness. "I don't want to get under your feet in the morning. What time do you have to leave for work?"

Turner's eyes opened reluctantly and she watched him struggle to make the transition from the sweetest of touches to the most mundane of small talk.

"Uh," he said, shifting on the couch. "Technically, I'm at work right now since I'm still covering for Pauline. But I'll need to be back in the office about seven."

"Okay. I need to show up at Lenny's at seven-thirty, so that will work out perfect." Candy looked down at her hand in his. "Um, Turner? Is Miller going to press charges against me?"

"Naw. I wouldn't worry about him. He'll cool down in time."

"Really?"

"Sure. I told him it would hardly be worth his trouble since the charges would probably get downgraded to misdemeanor trespassing."

Candy was surprised by that. "With all those people who showed up I thought for sure I was headed to prison. Who were they, anyway? They looked like they belonged on some FBI TV show."

"Right." Turner straightened up a little more and cleared his throat. "They were in the area, you know, working on something else."

"But why would they care about some chick trying to climb in a window at a nursing home?"

Turner shrugged, as though the subject bored him, which made Candy even more curious.

"Okay. So I was right?" Candy asked. "They're FBI people?"

"Hey, would you like a cup of tea or something?" Turner dropped her hand, jumped from the couch, and was in the kitchen before she could answer. "I've got chamomile, mint, green, green decaf . . ."

"Are they from the IRS?" Candy spun around on her knees and rested her arms on the back of the sofa so she could watch his reaction. She was starting to get a little paranoid. "Is this about my bankruptcy or something?"

"What?" Turner looked over his shoulder and laughed. "Of course not, Candy!"

"But you're not telling me something. I can tell. Why did a whole bunch of cops show up at Cherokee Pines?"

Turner twisted around to lean his palms on the countertop. "Darlin', they have nothing to do with you. Seriously."

She frowned.

Turner came back to the living room and lowered his face to her level. He kissed her softly, his lips warm and tender on hers. She would have been happy to have more, but he pulled away. "Listen, there's something we should probably deal with right now so we can get it out of the way, all right?" Candy nodded and watched Turner return to his spot on the couch. "There are a lot of things about my job that I can never share. I don't tell Reggie or J.J. or my mom or anyone. And I can't tell you."

"Oh. No problem." Candy could understand that. "So you can't tell me why the FBI people are in town?"

Turner laughed. "Baby, I can't even tell you that FBI people *are* in town. I can't answer any of your questions, but I can assure you one hundred percent that they're not here about you. You haven't done anything that would interest them."

She sighed deeply and fell back against the couch. "Thank you," she said. "That's all I need to know." As soon as the words came out of her mouth she realized they weren't true. "Except for one more thing—did Gerrall Spivey get in trouble because of me?"

"He was fired."

"*Fired?* Oh, great."

"Does that worry you?"

Candy shrugged, not wanting to dwell on the whole Gerrall drama with Turner. "Of course it does. He lost his job because he did me a favor, which makes it my fault, so yeah, it worries me."

"You don't think he'll do anything crazy, do you?"

Candy glanced at Turner to be sure he was being serious. "You mean like come after me with a meat cleaver or something?" She laughed. "Of course not. He's weird, but he's not a psycho case."

"Always good to hear." With that, Turner pulled Candy closer to him, wrapped both arms around her and kissed the top of her head. "Are you sleepy?" he asked.

Candy smiled. If they hadn't already discussed the fact that they wouldn't be sleeping together tonight, she would have assumed that's what he was asking. "I am, but this is so nice I don't want to move."

"Good, 'cause I don't, either," he whispered.

Candy let her head snuggle back into the sweet spot in the crook of Turner's arm and closed her eyes. And it was all pleasant enough, but something was bugging her. It was Junie again. Candy sighed, and in the stillness of her heart she asked Junie to come closer for a little girl-to-girl chat. She didn't believe in ghosts, but she did believe that some things were more powerful than whatever thin veil divided life and death, and love was one of them.

"I know Turner is a truly special man," she told Junie in silence. "He will always know exactly where I'm coming from and what I'm feeling. I will never intentionally hurt him. And as long as I'm here I will treat this man and this home with respect."

It could have been in her imagination, but Candy swore a sweet fragrance moved through the room. It wasn't disturbing—it was lovely and kind and reassuring.

Turner tightened his arms around her and the solid weight of his body made her feel anchored. Candy felt safe—for the first time in years. And as the rhythm of his breathing gently rocked her, she realized she couldn't remember the last time she'd fallen asleep in a man's arms but knew it hadn't felt this wonderful.

Because nothing ever had.

"He fired your ass?"

Gerrall hung his head. He knew this was going to be a nightmare, but he hadn't really done anything *that* bad. All he'd done was make it easier for Candy to stay a few extra days. It wasn't like he'd stolen money from the Fat Man's stash or gone to the cops about what was really going on out there at that place.

"You fuckin' idiot!" His father paced back and forth along the length of the trailer's living room, a cigarette flopping out between his lips. "Are you kidding me?

That asshole has been holding this whole operation together. You know that, right? He's the middleman. How do you think we got where we are?"

Gerrall shrugged.

His daddy stopped pacing and scowled in his direction. "Please, God, don't tell me this has something to do with that piece of blond pussy you've been jacking off to."

"What?"

"Did you get caught doing her in the supply closet or something?"

"What? *No!*"

"Then what? You worked at that place for a reason, you dick brain. It put you in town every day. It provided a central drop-off and pickup from the Fat Man's orders. You had a really simple job to do—you ran the front desk for that asshole and when your shift was over, you collected the shit and brought it back here. Now tell me—when did that get too hard for you to handle, huh?"

"I'm sorry." Gerrall stuffed his hands in his pants pockets. "Well, I'll talk to you later."

He could hardly believe it, but his daddy just let him walk out of there. Not even a smack on the head or anything. Gerrall wandered out to the barn. Their latest cook was at work and looked up and gave him a sort of friendly nod. The helpers didn't even look up. Dan, the driver, sat in a plastic lawn chair in the corner, reading the latest issue of *Sports Illustrated,* probably waiting for the night's shipment.

"Hey," Gerrall said.

Dan looked up from under his long hair and twitched his lips a little. Then went back to the magazine.

"So, where you from?" Gerrall asked.

Dan shrugged.

"You speak English?"

Dan slapped the magazine closed and glared at Gerrall. *"Poquito."*

"Okay. So, no, right? You don't speak any English?"

Dan looked up to the barn's ceiling then back again. "Yeah, I speak English, ass wipe," he said. "I'm from Brooklyn, okay?"

"Oh. Right." Gerrall wiped his palms on the front of his jeans. Just then, the little girl he'd kicked out of his tree house came wandering in. She tugged on the shirt of one of the dudes on the line, who yelled at her and she walked away, keeping her eyes down. Gerrall kind of felt sorry for her. He didn't know what kind of loser brought his kid to a place like this.

When Gerrall turned around, he saw Dan staring at the kid, but immediately went back to his magazine.

"Hey, have I showed you a picture of my girlfriend?"

Dan nodded. "Yeah."

"When I've got enough money, I'm gonna buy a new car and we're both going to leave this town and never come back."

"That's fuckin' great," Dan said.

One of the helpers called out, "You got some more cake? That shit was good!"

"When you gonna bring her out here so we can get a piece of her?" another one asked.

Gerrall was about to kick that dick's ass when he was knocked to the ground by a blow to the back of his head. When he tried to get up, he felt a boot on his neck.

"Kid didn't do nothing." It was Dan's voice. Gerrall

tried to turn enough to see what was happening but couldn't. His face was being smashed into the disgusting barn floor.

"Stay the fuck out of this."

"Whatever."

Dan got up and left. That's when Gerrall felt his father grab him by the back of his shirt and pull him up.

"You're a worthless piece of shit!" his daddy screamed. "I just found out what you were doing over there, you fuckhead! Are you kidding me? She was giving you a cake every night you let her in the back door? You stupid fuck! Now that asshole says he don't want to do business with us anymore!"

The guys on the line started laughing, and he wasn't even sure how it started, but pretty soon every dude in the barn was hitting and being hit. It went on for at least fifteen minutes, and Dan tried to break it up, but he ended up kicking more ass than everyone else combined.

Gerrall crawled out while everyone was still fighting and someone pulled off a few rounds from a gun. He dug up his cash box and got some clothes and left. He didn't know where he was going or what he was going to do, but he'd had enough of this life. He didn't even care who'd gotten shot that night.

He deserved something better, and so did Candy.

Turner woke up with a start, knowing immediately that he was on his own couch in his own living room but that his whole world had changed. Candy Carmichael was snuggled up in his arms, sound asleep, her freshly washed curls tickling his nose, her ass warm and soft against his left hip, the back of her hand tucked into his open palm. He smiled as the night's events came back to him—rescuing her from the window, hearing her confession in the truck stop parking lot, bringing her back here so she could store her treasure in his wall safe.

Turner chuckled to himself, thinking about the sight of those long legs and that deliciously round booty hanging out of that window. It was Christmas in July. Finally, he was getting exactly what he'd asked Santa for every year of his life between puberty and graduation—and it was already partially unwrapped.

Candy Pants.

Lord, he'd surely done it now. She was in his arms and in his house and he'd be damned if he'd be letting her go anytime soon. J.J.'s advice echoed in his head for the thousandth time: *Make it worth her while to stay.*

The truth was, he had little to entice a woman like Candy, a woman who'd become used to a certain kind of lifestyle. He wasn't rich. He didn't live in an exciting cosmopolitan city full of culture and entertainment. He wasn't a particularly fascinating or charming man. Turner was a cop in the middle of nowhere, battling drunk drivers and meth labs and domestic violence, just trying to find joy in the little things in life—his friends and family, good music, good food, the beauty of the mountains, the comfort and peace of his home.

J.J. was only half right. Turner could make it clear that he wanted Candy, but if she decided to stay in Bigler it would have to be for her own reasons. Candy would have to find something that anchored her here, something important enough for her to want to stay. It might very well be a combination of several things, and if Turner happened to be one of them, great. But he wouldn't put on some kind of front to get the job done. If she decided she wanted to be with him, Turner needed to be certain it was the real him she was interested in.

He placed his lips on Candy's hair and let them linger there a long moment. Obviously, the physical part of this was going to be easy. The attraction they already felt for each other was damn near explosive, and Turner was sure that once she gave him the green light, the sex was going to be off the chain. In fact, simply having her close to him like this had pushed his body to the breaking point. He was hard enough to pound nails and he wanted nothing more than to throw her down and devour her.

Which was why he needed to get her into her own bed and out of his lap.

"Candy," he whispered. "Darlin', wake up."

In response, she turned into his chest and her hand flopped into his lap, her fingers grazing against the straining zipper of his work pants.

"Shee-it," he murmured. "Baby, wake up. You should get in bed."

"Mmm," she moaned.

Turner's eyes began to cross. Maybe he should have left well enough alone. Just then, Candy tilted her head up and her lips grazed the side of his neck.

That was all he could take. In one motion he rose from the couch, turned, and lifted Candy in his arms. He carried her to the guest room and laid her down. It took a minute of tugging, and he might have accidentally brushed his hand against her butt and legs a time or two, but Turner managed to pull the covers down beneath her body so that he could pull them up over her. But before he did so, he paused to gaze at Candy while she slept. She was so long, so lovely, so thoroughly covered in that hoodie and those stretch pants that it made him want to howl in frustration. Her feet were bare, so he admired them for a few seconds, then covered her up.

"Good night, beautiful," he said, as he kissed her cheek.

It was three A.M., too early to go into the office and too late to pretend he'd be getting a decent night's sleep. So Turner lay down in his bed in the dark, fully dressed, and stared into the night. It wasn't long before he felt wave after wave of emotion—loss, grief, desire, loneliness—pummel at his resolve. If he weren't careful, they'd get the best of him. Not tonight, he told himself. Not with Candy in the next room.

Please, not tonight.

He missed Junie with everything in him. He missed the sweetness of her touch and that look she'd give him when he'd said or done something that crossed the line. He missed the way she smelled and the taste of her skin on his tongue. And he'd never forget her. She was a part of him and would stay in his blood until his last breath.

But that didn't mean he didn't have room for another woman in his heart, in his blood, in his being. He knew he did, and the woman he wanted was in the next room. Candy was as different from Junie as two women could be. She was fanciful where Junie was practical. She was disorganized where Junie was precise. She was tall and bodacious and blond where Junie was compact and lithe and brown. Candy was not Junie.

But right there in the darkness, Turner pulled Junie close in his prayers, as he often did, and assured her that he would never attempt to replace her. That would be impossible. But it was time, he told her. He was ready to welcome Candy into his world, not as a substitute for someone else, but for the woman she was.

"I need to live again," he whispered into the night. "And I want Candy." With that, Turner pulled off the gold band he'd worn on his left hand for more than six years, and placed it in the bedside table drawer.

He clasped his hands over his stomach and waited for Junie to release him—or for him to release himself. He had no idea what the process would feel like or how long it would take, so he breathed quietly, pictured that smile Candy had laid on him in the SUV that night, and felt his chest open with light. And slowly, so slowly, that empty place he'd been carrying around for four years began to fill with something unexpected, magnificent. It was *joy*. And Turner found himself grinning even as the tears slipped out of the corners of his eyes.

Chapter 16

The cell phone alarm went off as usual, but Candy opened her eyes and froze. Her arms and legs were stretched out on a soft expanse of comfort, not wedged into the shape of Jacinta's overly stylized sofa. She was in a real bed! In a real bedroom! And the smell of coffee was in the breeze.

She combed her fingers through her hair and staggered out into the hallway, smiling. At some point in the night, Turner had moved her to the bed. He must have carried her, since she had no memory of getting there herself. Something about that made her feel like a princess.

"Turner?" She glanced down the hall to what she figured was his bedroom. The door was open but she saw no movement from within. She went into the kitchen and saw the note immediately. It was propped up against a clean coffee mug, sugar, and cream already poured into a little pitcher.

"Good morning, beautiful," it read. "There's a spare key on the hook near the front door. I hope the coffee is fit for human consumption. Help yourself to anything in the fridge and if all goes to plan I'll see you at lunch." He signed it with a big *T*.

"P.S.," he wrote. "You are lovely when you're asleep."

With a giggle, Candy pocketed the note and poured herself a cup of coffee. She was dressing for work when she thought she heard the front door open.

"Turner?" she called out. There was no response.

For some reason, Candy suddenly felt terrified. It was ridiculous. She was in Turner's house. There was nothing to fear. No one would dare hurt her here, if anyone would want to hurt her at all. She didn't even know where such a ridiculous idea came from.

Candy stepped into hallway and gasped at the large man who loomed over her.

"Excuse me," he said.

It took her a couple seconds to make the connection. "Reggie Halliday?"

"Absolutely. And you're Candy Carmichael."

"I am." Right about then she started to feel really awkward. "Turner's letting me stay in his guest room for a couple days."

"Sure. Of course." Reggie appeared as uncomfortable as Candy felt. She watched as the big man shifted his weight, tried to smile, then walked toward the kitchen. He placed the large Tupperware container he'd been holding down on the countertop, and shoved his hands in the front pockets of his jeans. "Well. It's really nice to see you again. You enjoying your time in Bigler?"

"Oh, absolutely." Candy threw her purse over her shoulder and passed by Reggie on her way to the door, where she remembered to grab a spare key. "It's great to see you, but I'm late for work. Take care!"

Oh, *Lord*! As she ran to her car, Candy went over the situation in her head. Clearly, Turner hadn't told his brother that he had a houseguest, just like he hadn't told his houseguest that his brother was likely to pop in. Candy only hoped she hadn't made a total fool of herself.

Just as she reached Lenny's, her cell phone rang. The first call was from Jacinta. "Are you okay?" she screeched before Candy could even say hello.

"I'm fine. I apologize for what happened last night."

"Well, you certainly know how to make an entrance," she said, not even bothering to hide her giggle. "You got that Spivey boy fired, you know."

"I know," Candy said, cutting the ignition and stepping out of the car. "I feel bad about it."

Jacinta laughed outright. "Well, don't! I heard at breakfast this morning that he's been going around telling everyone you're his girlfriend. He has a picture of you in his cell phone. He claims you make him special cakes because the two of you are in love!"

Candy nearly dropped the phone. "Are you sure you heard right?"

"Oh, good. It isn't true."

Candy's jaw unhinged. "Mother! Of course it's not true! My God!"

"Well, that's what I told people at breakfast but they didn't listen."

"Great. Well, I'm late for work."

"Wait," Jacinta said. "Listen. I want to talk to you

about something. Come out to visit me this week some-
time, would you?"

Candy laughed. "Yeah, sure. I haven't been arrested
enough lately."

"Oh, Miller can stick his bylaws up his big, fat ass,"
she said. "My daughter can come by for a visit if she
wants. I'd like to see him stop you!"

Great, Candy thought. That sounded fun.

She'd just ended the call with Jacinta when Cheri
called.

"Is it true?" she asked, out of breath.

"Uh . . ." Candy was afraid to ask exactly what she
was referring to, though she had a good idea. "You mean
the window thing?"

"Oh, my God! I told J.J. that there had to be a mistake! But he read about it in the overnight police
reports. Are you all right?"

She had been until that second. "Please tell me it's
not going to be in the paper." Candy pulled open the
employee door to find Lenny waiting for her. "Cheri,
I'm going to have to call you back on my break."

"No!" she shouted into the phone. "You can't! What
happened? You've got to tell me."

"Nothing happened," Candy answered Cheri as she
nodded to Lenny. "I got locked out of Jacinta's apartment and tried to get in through the window, but it
turned out to be her neighbor's apartment and the old
buzzard called the police. It was a simple misunder-
standing."

Right then, Lenny started to laugh. The laugh turned
into a howl. The howl turned into a guffaw.

"I gotta go," Candy said. She hung up on Cheri and clocked in. She felt Lenny's hand on her shoulder.

"Can I just say how much I enjoy you working for me?" he asked.

"Sure," Candy said. "Go ahead."

"I already did!" Lenny said, continuing to laugh as he disappeared into the kitchen.

One of the reasons Turner chose to pursue a law enforcement career in his hometown was the pace. Compared to a major city, Bigler was downright boring, which gave Turner the latitude to focus on one thing at a time and really sit down with folks in their time of trouble and try to get them back on their feet. A small-town job gave him room to think.

But on that particular morning, Bigler might as well have been the Big Apple.

J.J. was waiting for Turner in his regular spot, a look on his face that guaranteed a lively encounter. "Morning, Jay," Turner said, jogging up the back steps to the municipal building.

"Sheriff," J.J. said, falling into step with Turner as they made their way through the early-morning hallways. "Sleep well?"

Turner ignored him. He greeted Bitsy, accepted a stack of mail from her hands along with a mug of fresh coffee. "You're my girl, Bits," Turner said to his secretary, smiling. "Close the door behind you," he said to J.J.

"So." J.J. sat in the chair across from Turner's desk. "Seems you had an interesting night."

"Kinda slow, really," Turner answered him, sorting

his mail. "I think a lot of people stayed indoors because of the rain."

"Right, yeah, except for the ones who were kind of half indoors and half outdoors. You know, like hanging out of a window."

Turner didn't look at him. "There was that."

J.J. laughed. "Damn, Halliday! You mind telling me what was going on out at Cherokee Pines last night? I read your report about Candy and then I get a call from Lorraine Estes telling me that the parking lot out there was crawling with federal agents."

Turner shrugged, peering at his stack of mail as if it were the most fascinating thing in the world. "That lady's a couple fries short of a Happy Meal, Jay. So you gonna put the story about Candy in the newspaper?"

J.J. chuckled. "I could. I *should*. The incident is part of the public record. But I spoke to Wainright Miller this morning and he said he's undecided about filing charges, so I'm not sure how much of a story there really is."

Turner tossed the pile of mail to the desk and smiled at J.J. "And what does Cheri say about all this?"

"Oh, nothing much. Just that she'll smother me in my sleep if I run it."

"You da man, Jay!"

When they stopped laughing, J.J. leaned his elbows on his knees and looked up at Turner with a no-nonsense kind of stare. "Is this another drug task force operation? Is it related to the shooting out at the Tip Top? When can we expect a bust?"

Turner frowned at him. "You know I can't say."

J.J. whipped out his notebook. "It's impossible to

hide shit like that around here, especially since there are just two nice bed-and-breakfasts in town and one decent motel, so it ain't hard to figure out where everyone's staying. And anyway, I remember Kelly O'Connor from the Waynesville bust last year—she's kind of hard to forget. I saw her driving around town the other day, and don't tell me she's here for the scenery."

Turner laced his fingers behind his head and leaned back in his chair. "What do you want me to say? I'll tell you the minute we've made a bust and nothing before. That's how it has to be, Jay."

His friend sighed. "How soon?"

"Can't be soon enough if you ask me. I'll rest easier when this thing is shut down."

"Meth?"

Turner shook his head. "You know I can't say anything more. I can't jeopardize this investigation. Please just sit tight and as soon as I got something that can go public you'll be the first to know. Same as always, all right?"

J.J. shoved his notebook in his back pocket, suddenly very quiet. When he looked up at Turner again, he saw grave seriousness in his friend's eyes.

"What?" Turner asked.

"Where's your wedding ring, man?"

Just then, Bitsy knocked on the door. "It's Reggie," she said, barely getting the words out before Turner's brother pushed past her through the office door.

"Jay!"

Turner observed his brother and J.J. greet each other with enthusiasm and nodded to Bitsy that it was okay. He mouthed a "thank you" to his secretary.

"Hey, come on in, Reg. Really." Turner waved his arm around the office. "It's not that I was in here with the door closed engaged in official department business or anything."

Reggie laughed. "Yeah, whatever. Bitsy told me it was just J.J. so I knew damn well I wouldn't be interrupting shit. So . . ." The way Reggie smiled at Turner made him squirm with discomfort. "I ran into someone interesting this morning."

Turner glanced quickly at J.J. before he looked to Reggie again. "That's nice. Can this wait?"

"Oh, *hell*, no!" Without being invited, Reggie pulled up a spare chair and bent himself in half, resting his elbows on his knees. "See, the thing is, I went by your house this morning, T. Mama asked me to drop off some leftover pot roast for you."

Turner shot up out of his chair, knowing all too well where this was headed. "Listen, Reg, I'm going to have to discuss this with you later." He stood over his brother and glared down at him. "You should go."

Reggie only leaned back in the chair, scooted his butt forward, and crossed his legs like he was fixin' to stay put a while. He smiled up at Turner. "Don't worry, little brother. I got a few extra minutes before I gotta be in the showroom. I'm in no rush."

"Yes you are."

"No, not really."

J.J. laughed. "What's all this about?"

"Oh, it seems Turner had a sleepover last night." Reggie delivered that news with a heavy dose of swagger.

"It's not what you think," Turner snapped.

J.J.'s eyes got big, "Say what?"

"Yep." Reggie's grin spread. "The lovely Candace Carmichael was just on her way out when I came in. And listen, I haven't seen that girl in a long, long time, and all I gotta say is, *damn,* she turned out *fine*."

Turner shook his head in disgust and returned to his chair. He knew that no matter how much he tried to explain himself to Reggie he'd only dig the hole deeper. It was a lesson he'd learned a long time ago.

J.J. coughed. Turner looked up at him and nodded his admission.

"Wow," J.J. whispered.

"Don't worry, I won't tell Mama," Reggie said.

Just then, Bitsy tapped on the door and poked her head in. "May I have a word, Sheriff?"

"Absolutely!" Turner was glad for the interruption. "Gentlemen," he said, standing. "So sorry but it's time you—"

"No." Bitsy cut him off. Her eyes were quite big. "It would be best if they stay in there and you come out here."

Turner left Reggie and J.J. behind, knowing the two of them would have a rip-roaring good time in his absence. But he couldn't worry about that now because Bitsy looked dead serious.

"The conference room," she said with a crisp nod. "I'll make sure your visitors are escorted out."

Without delay, Turner opened the conference room door, where he found Kelly O'Connor and undercover agent Dante Cabrera, who had been beaten black and blue.

* * *

Candy knew it was ridiculous to feel this way, but she couldn't help it—she felt a little disappointed. It was after ten o'clock and Turner wasn't home. He hadn't shown up at Lenny's for lunch as he'd promised. He hadn't even called. She'd spent the evening by herself in his house, watching satellite TV, eating a chef's salad she'd brought home from the diner, and scribbling in her notebook.

Of course, he didn't owe her an explanation as to where he was and when he'd be back. She wasn't his wife—hell, she wasn't even his girlfriend. Not really. In fact, the longer she thought about it, the more Candy realized she didn't know what she was to him. What did it mean when a man called you "beautiful" and "baby" and brought you back to his house where he snuggled with you until you fell asleep? What did it mean when a man licked ice cream off your cleavage in a park and told you that you drove him fuckin' crazy? What did it mean when a man made it perfectly clear that when the opportunity presented itself the two of you were going to go ravish each other?

Candy supposed all those things made her Turner Halliday's *potential* girlfriend.

Okay, then. His potential girlfriend missed him, and she was disappointed that he hadn't come home.

Candy wandered through the house, careful not to do anything that might be considered "nosy" while still getting herself acquainted with her surroundings. Turner's bedroom was decorated in typical bachelor style—a brown and blue striped comforter, bare wood floors, very little on the walls. She guessed that he'd changed the look after Junie died, maybe to spare him from memories too painful to deal with every morning when he woke and every night when he tried to fall asleep.

Interestingly enough, there was only one photo of Turner and Junie that Candy had seen in the house. It was on the living room fireplace mantel, and it was a photograph from their wedding reception. The two of them were beaming, breathless, dancing with each other like no one else in the world existed.

Candy picked up the silver-plated frame so she could examine it closer. Junie had certainly been an attractive woman, her dark curls clipped loose at the back of her head, her exquisite white lace wedding dress tight on her slim frame. It struck her how perfectly Junie seemed to fit in Turner's embrace, and how much love was conveyed in the way she looked into her new husband's eyes.

And then there was Turner. She felt the slightest shiver of jealousy at his expression. He appeared transfixed by the woman in his arms. His handsome face was radiant. His smile was dazzling. Every bit of his attention was focused on her, his wife.

With a sigh, Candy placed the frame back where it had been, and in doing so noticed that a thin film of dust had settled on the mantel. She smiled. She could clean! It would pass the time. It would help earn her keep.

An hour and a half later, Turner's house was spotless. She'd vacuumed, dusted, made beds, mopped the kitchen, and scoured both bathrooms, and all the while she'd let her mind swing back and forth between the questions and answers that haunted her.

Could Turner ever love her?

What a ridiculous question—she was leaving in two and a half months and that was that.

How would she compare to Junie? What if she wasn't as sexy as Turner's wife or as funny or as smart?

What a ridiculous question—she was probably leaving in a couple months.

And what if Candy fell hopelessly, madly, passionately in love with Turner Halliday? What would she do? What would happen?

What a ridiculous question. She probably would be leaving at some point.

To celebrate a job well done—and to clear her head—Candy took a long, hot shower. Then she painted her toenails in a dusky pink Lancôme shade she found at the bottom of one of her boxes.

It was twelve-thirty. Still no word from Turner.

Eventually, Candy gave up waiting. She checked to make sure the front door was locked and fell into the guest bed, exhausted, lonely, all her thoughts on Turner.

And she dreamed his arms encircled her, his weight was heavy against her, and the rhythm of his breathing rocked her to sleep.

Turner opened the front door and entered the house as quietly as possible, something he hadn't needed to do for more than four years. He tossed his ball cap on the kitchen counter and took off his work shoes, leaving them on the rug by the front door. As he moved through the living room he stopped, sniffed, and whirled around.

The place was *clean*. Not that he'd ever let it get disgusting, but its current condition went way beyond tidy. It was immaculate.

He sighed. Candy shouldn't have done this. He didn't want her doing anything for him. She was his guest. She was . . .

Turner stopped in the hallway and peeked into the guest room. She'd fallen asleep with the bedside lamp on, a notebook and pen tossed aside, and one of her bare legs stretched out on top of the covers. A lump formed in his throat as he gazed at her. He itched to brush his fingertips down the back of her thigh, knee, calf. He yearned to put his nose in her blond curls and breathe deep. He ached to feel his lips on her soft and warm cheek.

Turner had to smile at how fast and completely he responded to Candy. His body was already humming and buzzing to life, simply being in close proximity to her.

Using all the self-restraint he possessed, Turner stepped into the room and turned off her lamp, then closed the guest room door.

He was so tired his body hurt. The day had been a crazy rush of emergency meetings with the task force and prosecutors, with efforts to obtain search warrants for the Spivey property and an arrest warrant for Gerrall, who had gone missing after the ruckus. With the picture Dante painted for them today, everyone agreed they were going to have to move fast before someone got killed in the chaos out in Preston Valley. Dante insisted it was safe for him to go back in, that no one had any suspicions about his identity, but Kelly fought him hard. Finally, it was agreed that he go to the Western Carolina Medical Center's emergency room under his assumed identity, and go back to work with Spivey once he was patched up.

This entire operation was making Turner increasingly uncomfortable. Gerrall being unaccounted for made him anxious as hell, especially after Dante's description of his erratic behavior the night he got fired. He wanted nothing more than to arrest Bobby Ray and his crew, shut down the meth lab, and get Gerrall behind bars.

Turner stripped out of his uniform and took a quick shower. He set his alarm for six and pulled down the neatly made bedcovers, slipping inside with a groan of relief. The weeks of pulling double shifts were really starting to wear him down. He closed his eyes and waited for sleep to come.

And he waited.

A half hour later, Turner sat up in bed and flipped on the light, knowing there was no way in hell his mind and spirit could rest while his physical form was on alert the way it was. His dick was so hard it was uncomfortable. It was as if his body instinctively sensed Candy's presence through the wall, down the hall, behind the shut door. He was nuts if he thought sleep would find him.

Turner rubbed his hands over his face and sighed with frustration. He looked up in surprise when he thought he heard a soft tapping at his bedroom door. He listened carefully. There it was again.

"Yes?" he asked, his blood pounding in his head.

Candy pushed the door open a crack and peered in, a smile on her sleepy face. "Are you okay?" she asked, blinking into the light.

Turner couldn't speak at first. She stood there in an old T-shirt and a pair of panties—at least he assumed there were panties involved but the shirt came down to the tops of her thighs so he couldn't be sure—and he could see the outline of her breasts. He could see her hard little nipples under the thin cotton fabric. Turner bunched the covers up over his erection, suddenly, painfully aware of his own nakedness.

This felt way too dangerous.

"Fine. Good."

"I was worried about you," she said, yawning, raking her fingers through all that thick hair. Turner noticed that she shifted her weight and stretched out one of those gloriously long legs, letting it poke through the crack in the door. He had to believe she didn't know what she was doing to him. He had to believe that she was half asleep and didn't realize she was driving him insane.

"I'm sorry I didn't call," he said, hearing a scratchy desperation in his own voice. "It was absolutely wild today."

She nodded, then shrugged. "Okay." Candy tilted her head slightly. "Sleep well, Turner. Good night."

And she was gone. The door shut. He heard her footsteps heading down the hallway. He listened for the click as her door closed.

"Oh, fuck," he whispered, rubbing his hands hard over his head. He felt as if he were going to die if he didn't find release for all the pent-up lust inside him—lust for Candy—even if he had to do it himself. How pitiful could a man get?

Turner threw the covers off and staggered into the bathroom. He ran cold water in the sink, splashing it in his face until he'd knocked some sense into himself. He returned to his bedroom, but couldn't put himself back in bed. Instead, he threw on some boxers, went to the door, pressed his ear against it, and listened.

What did he expect to hear? The sound of her breathing? Her voice calling out to him, begging him to come to her? Morse code?

This was ridiculous, he knew. He wanted her. She wanted him. He'd have to go get her.

Turner opened his bedroom door and gasped. Candy stood in the center of the hallway, eyes wide, biting her bottom lip, pulling down on the front hem of her T-shirt to cover her crossed thighs.

"Hi," she squeaked.

"Oh, hell, yes," he said, moving toward her.

Chapter 17

Candy couldn't move and she couldn't breathe. Turner was coming right at her, that slow and sensual walk of his sending electric jolts right into the sweet spot between her legs. He was mesmerizing, his body exquisitely naked from the waist up, his black boxer briefs revealing nearly as much as they hid.

She tried not to whimper, but she failed.

Candy swallowed, her mouth suddenly dry. She stared at him, illuminated by the overhead hall light fixture, unashamed that she was staring, determined not to miss a detail of that gleaming, smooth brown skin, the muscles and tendons rolling beneath the surface, the confidence in how he carried himself. Turner was surely tall and strong and masculine, but he was beautiful at the same time. He'd always been so.

She'd seen Turner in swim trunks a thousand times out at the lake, and it had been impossible not to notice his agility and grace. Whether he was swimming, diving, rowing, running—he'd always seemed to take joy in what his body could do. But those days had been a dozen years and a good twenty-five pounds of muscle ago, and Candy could honestly say that she'd never seen a man as fine as Turner in the flesh. No one in her life had even come close. And though she wasn't a particularly religious woman, she said a prayer right then that she'd have other opportunities to study every facet of him, because right at that moment, she was too nervous to pay close attention. And she was running out of time.

Turner moved closer. His eyelids were heavy. His smile was sly. His hips rolled and the muscles in his torso and thighs rippled. She noticed he didn't have much body hair at all. Oh, God, she planned to lick him *everywhere*.

Only a few seconds remained before he was right in front of her and the choice would be made. They would choose to touch each other. They would kiss and caress and devour each other—this time in private and barely dressed—and everything would change. Her life would change. His life would change.

Oh, God, *it was happening*.

Turner put his hands on her. He gripped her by the upper arms. He slid his grip up to her neck and down again to her wrists, where he clutched her tight. She thought she saw him nod ever so slightly before he lowered his mouth to hers, as if to reassure her that, oh, yes—he was fixin' to have his way with her and there wasn't a damn thing she could do to put a stop to it.

And that was okay with her. Candy didn't want to stop him. She wanted nothing more than to finally, truly, fully feel what it was like to be taken. Somewhere in the back of her brain this moment felt familiar. It felt ancient, like she'd dreamed of it and wanted it for as long as she'd been alive, like she'd always wanted Turner in exactly this way.

His lips landed on hers. The kiss started gently. Candy decided it felt like a kind of introduction, where Turner explained to her how it would be. With only the use of his lips and tongue and teeth and varying pressures and angles, Turner explained to her that she was his, and that he'd be taking her somewhere she'd never been but had always belonged.

He released her wrists. She raised them up, skimming her palms along the smooth front of his body, groaning in appreciation as the kiss intensified and her fingertips encountered firm muscle, tender nipples, a hard clavicle. Eventually she brought her hands up along the ridge of his shoulders, along the sides of his neck, then clasped her hands on either side of his head.

He used his tongue to nudge Candy's mouth open, and she made everything available to him, everything delicate and vulnerable was his. He could have it. And he pushed his tongue into her and she felt it as intensely as if he'd just entered her pussy.

Turner began to walk forward, forcing Candy back. She had no concern about that. She didn't need to know where he was pushing her. Whatever he chose was fine. She continued to edge backward until she felt her heel hit the baseboard. He pushed her until her butt thudded against the log paneling of the wall, then, more gently, the back of her head.

"Feel me," he whispered. "Put your hands on me." And though the instruction wasn't specific, Candy knew exactly what he wanted. Slowly, she trailed her hands back down the front of his body, feeling the places she missed on the way up—his sternum, his ribs, his rigid abs, the protrusion of his hipbones. She slid her fingers down the front of his boxers, and opened her grasp to accommodate his width.

She had to keep opening.

"Oh, my God," Candy whispered, looking down to where her hand linked their bodies.

"Let me get hard in your hand."

Candy glanced up at Turner's face, seeing the pleasure wash over him as he stared at the ceiling. His Adam's apple danced as he concentrated on the gentle movement and squeeze of her hand.

"Um, you mean you aren't hard?"

"No."

Candy let her head fall back against the wall.

"Does that scare you?" Turner looked down at her, nothing but seriousness in his eyes—serious lust.

"Not at all."

"Good," he said, propping his hands on the wall over her head and leaning closer to her. "Because you're going to be spending a lot of time with that big dick and the last thing you need to be is scared of it."

She swallowed and nodded.

"I want you to love it. Crave it. I want you to get to the point where you can't go a day without it."

Candy tilted her head to the side as she cupped his balls in her hand. "A day? How about an hour? How about five minutes?" Then she nipped his bottom lip.

That's when Turner kicked her feet apart, almost causing her to lose her balance. "I need this off of you," he said, using his teeth to pull at the neckline of her T-shirt. As soon as Candy nodded, she felt his hands at the bottom hem. He ripped it over her head and she stood wearing only a pair of white bikini panties, breathing hard, her legs wide apart.

Turner's mouth opened. "Lord have mercy," he said. "You are the most beautiful thing I've ever seen."

"I'm glad you think so."

"Ha!" She watched him rub his hand roughly over his mouth, his chin, cheek.

"Is something the matter?"

"Ah, no." When he rubbed his hand over the top of his head she knew he wasn't telling the truth. She recognized his little dance of anxiety. She'd seen it the night he pulled her over and she kissed him for the very first time. She saw it again when they'd kissed in the parking lot of the municipal building. And now. She knew what it was—he hadn't been with a woman since Junie died and it was a lot to process for him.

Right then she noticed that his hands were shaking. And that he was no longer wearing his wedding band. The realization hit her with a thud. She had no idea when he'd decided to remove the ring or why. All she knew was that it was a very big deal, and it was because of her.

"We can go as slow as you want," Candy whispered, touching him gently along the side of his face, along his chin.

Turner chuckled. He shook his head slowly. "That's not what I'm worried about, darlin'."

"Tell me then," she said. "Your hands are shaking. Your ring is gone."

Candy sucked in air as she felt his fingers trail up the inside of her thigh. He leaned in and hovered over her, his lips grazing hers when he spoke. "Yes, I took off my ring. But my hands are shaking because I'm trying to hold back. I'm afraid I won't be able to stop once I start." His finger skimmed over the damp crotch of her panties and slid down the inside of her other thigh. "I'm afraid I'll go at you so hard and for so long that you'll run away and never come back."

She laughed. "There's only one way to know if you're right."

"Hmph." Turner raised an eyebrow. "You're in for it now, baby."

Turner began kissing down her throat, across her chest, then dragged his lips and tongue to her breasts. Slowly, gently, he kissed and caressed each breast, cupped their weight in his palms, nuzzled his nose into her cleavage. After paying homage to them like that he began to suck on her nipples, first softly, then with more pull, his teeth nipping and tugging at her until she began to cry out.

Just when she didn't think she could take any more, Turner skimmed his tongue down from her sternum to the middle of her belly, then went to his knees in front of her. Candy stroked his head as her breath went shallow. "Oh, God," she said. "Oh, Turner. Oh, your touch feels so good."

He flicked his tongue into her belly button. He ran the tip of his tongue along the elastic band at the top of her panties. When Candy felt his fingers push away the crotch panel, her knees began to give, but Turner slapped his free hand up against the inside of one of her thighs and propped her up. Then his tongue found her wet and swollen outer lips.

"Ohhhhh," Candy moaned. It had been so long since she'd been touched like this that she felt shock waves run through her. Then Turner opened her up with his tongue and began to flick at her swollen clitoris and it really didn't matter how strong he was.

She was going to fall.

"Gotcha."

Turner caught Candy as she began to crumble, picking her up and carrying her in his arms to the guest room. With extreme care he laid her back on the bed, almost every inch of her beautiful body exposed to his view under the bedside lamp.

Candy opened her eyes. She lay there and gazed at him, her big, vulnerable blue eyes fixed on every move he made. There was such hunger in her expression, so much need that he fell to his knees on the bed and picked up where he left off, this time removing the soaking wet, skimpy white panties, dragging them down her silky legs and off the ends of her painted toes.

And she was finally, perfectly bare for him, her breasts heaving in anticipation as he pulled her legs apart and back. He felt like a man dying of thirst as he buried his face between her pale thighs and drank from her.

She was everything he'd ever imagined Candy would be. She was sweet—oh, definitely sweet—but she was salty, too, like the ocean, and slick with arousal and so swollen that she blossomed like a flower in his mouth, her clitoris a little hard bud at her center. The experience was almost too beautiful, too delicious, and he felt his whole being tremble with emotion.

This was Candy. She was giving herself to him. After all this time, all these years, this luscious woman of his fantasies was finally his to lick and kiss and suck and fuck.

God, how I want to fuck her.

And just then, she cried out and came in his mouth. Turner jerked back in surprise as her juices squirted all over his chin.

"Oh! Whaa—"

Candy quickly sat up, a horrified look on her face. "I'm sorry!"

"What?" Turner was still trying to figure out what had just happened, but one thing he was sure of— Candy had nothing to apologize for. He licked his lips.

"I didn't mean to do that . . ." she stammered. "I'm not sure . . . I don't know what that was . . ."

Turner slammed his mouth onto hers to stop her from talking. He kissed her with all the desire and love he felt welling up inside of him. He kissed her until her mouth opened to him, until she enthusiastically shared in the taste of her own juices.

"Baby," he said, catching his breath and holding her face in his hands. "Never, *ever* apologize for coming like that. I've never experienced it—I've heard about it, but never known it firsthand and I gotta tell you—I fuckin' *love* it." He began leaving little kisses all over her face and throat.

"It's never happened to me before," she whispered.

Hearing that made Turner want to pump his fist in victory, and he promised himself right then that his goal would be to make that kind of response commonplace.

"Squirt all over me, baby. I want to drown in Candy juice."

Her laugh might have been shy but her hands were boldly trying to tug off his boxer shorts. He decided to help her, since getting them off was going to be a trick in his present condition.

Turner pushed himself off the edge of the bed and stood, looking down on Candy's ivory-skinned beauty accented with pink, pink everywhere. A pink blush of arousal had spread across her cheeks and chest. She had little pink painted toenails. And she had beautiful, pouty pink lips—two sets. He focused on her face as he pulled down his boxers, and he couldn't help but smile as Candy's eyes flew wide and her mouth formed an O of astonishment. She pushed herself up to a sitting position on the bed, then scooted until her legs hung over the edge.

"C'mere, Halliday," she said, looking up at him with mischievous crystal-blue eyes.

Turner was happy to comply.

The instant Candy's fingers brushed the length of him, Turner heard himself call out in delight. Her caress was achingly good. A shock to his body. It had seemed like a lifetime since he'd felt a woman's loving touch, and he knew it would take intense concentration to keep from exploding in her hand. "Damn, Candy," he moaned.

Her hands roamed all over his belly and hips and grabbed on to his ass, all while she pressed her lips to a variety of places—around his navel, on his quadriceps—she even nipped at the inside of his thigh with her teeth.

But none of those small thrills could prepare him for the bliss he experienced when her hot, wet mouth slid down upon the head of his dick.

She was a natural. She alternately swirled her tongue, gently sucked, and took him deep, all while her silky curls brushed down over his thighs. To better witness this performance, Turner gathered up her hair in one hand and held it back away from her face. She looked up at him, her eyes smiling and her mouth full of his dick.

Too much. Too much.

He had no choice but to press his hands against her shoulders and encourage her to move away. Just like in his dreams, he knew he couldn't last if she continued to do that. The combination of physical sensation and visual delight was overwhelming. And he wanted to be inside her when he came, especially tonight. He wanted their eyes to be locked as their bodies came together for the first time.

Turner bent at the waist and pushed Candy back upon the bed. He propped himself over her, kissing her neck and lips and breasts, enjoying it each time a faint sigh escaped her mouth, loving how she arched her back to give him her nipples, then yielded to his pressure. Candy was a playground of ripe feminine flesh, curves and hollows and velvet planes of softness. His body and mind drove him on with only one objective: devour her, consume her, enter her, meld with her.

Turner was on automatic pilot now. He felt his knees push her legs farther apart and he hovered just above her sweet opening, so swollen and slippery with desire. "Put me in," he said. "Now. Do it."

* * *

Candy slipped her hand around his hardness and pulled him close. She wanted nothing more than to feel him buried inside her, filling her up, making her whole. When she arched her hips to meet him, the very tip of Turner's cock began to nudge into her, but it was a tight fit. He pushed. As her pussy opened for him, they gasped in unison and began to rock together.

"It's so good," Candy breathed, clutching at the back of his neck with her hand and pulling him closer, shock waves of pleasure rushing through her limbs, her belly, her chest, her mind. Turner felt just right on top of her—solid, hard, masculine, but all the while gentle. She gazed up at his intensely beautiful eyes and saw him experience his own rush of bliss as he pressed deeper into her.

"Candy," Turner whispered, his gaze locked with hers. "I've wanted you all my life. Give yourself to me. Don't hold anything back."

She spread her legs wide and threw her thighs around his waist. Candy locked her heels together at the small of his back and felt her body soften and open under him.

"*Yessss . . .* " Turner threw his head back and thrust once more. "Oh, damn, yes."

When he cupped Candy's buttocks in his hands and thrust into her once more, she wailed with pleasure. With each inward push of his cock he made further headway, and soon Candy felt his big testicles tap against her bottom. All she could do was breathe, feel, *be* in the extreme enjoyment of the moment, the abundance of sensation exploding from inside her pussy.

Then Turner kissed her. It was wild and hard and demanding and somewhere in the back of her brain she realized this was how it felt to be taken by a man. Claimed. She'd never felt so ravished in her life, so forced open, so pinned down, so thoroughly fucked.

She hadn't known it would be like this with Turner! She hadn't known it would be like this with *anyone*!

Turner dragged his lips from her mouth down the side of her throat, to her collarbone, the tops of her breasts, her nipples again, all while he moved into her, insistent, demanding.

Candy let her hands roam all over his beautiful body as he moved, feeling the muscles ripple and the bone and sinew work. He was languid. He was sensual and graceful. Turner made love the way he walked, and the thought of that pushed her higher.

"You're so tight. So perfect." As Turner rose above her and thrust into her again, Candy rested her palms on his rock-hard abdomen, slick with sweat. She slid her fingers all over the surface of his skin, fascinated by the ripple of his muscles, the sleek way he was made. And though her eyes had been shut as she concentrated on the feel of him, she decided she had to see. She had to know how he looked in this moment and commit it to memory.

Candy heard herself gasp. In the light of the bedside lamp, Turner's flesh was shining, dark and rich as milk chocolate, hard as polished wood. The sight of her pale hands on his dark flesh sent a flash of lust through her so extreme she felt a small orgasm ripple through her.

"You are the most beautiful man I've ever seen," she heard herself whisper, her voice raspy with emotion. "Turner, you are extraordinary."

He looked down at her then, his eyes hooded, his smile soft, all his concentration on how deep he could get inside her. Suddenly, she felt herself wrapped in his arms, picked up, and flipped over, and the transition was so unexpected that her foot clipped the bedside lamp and sent it crashing to the floor.

"Oh, no!" She began to reach for it.

"Leave it," Turner said, slapping his hands on her ass and pushing her down on his cock. "Ride me, Candy. I want to watch you move on me while I'm all the way up in you, can you do that, baby?"

Of course she could. So she did. And as Candy began to grind down on him, the jolt of lust was so concentrated and intense that it wasn't long before she cried out, half drunk with joy, and began to buck and shiver as she came, wetness exploding all over his abdomen and thighs.

"Fuck, yes!" Turner yelled, holding her down tight as she continued to tremble and jerk, the searing pleasure rolling through her again and again. She gulped down air and collapsed on top of him.

But Turner didn't let her rest. Immediately Candy was grabbed and flipped over on her back, and somewhere in the recesses of her mind she thought she heard another crash. Was that the headboard? Had something fallen off a wall somewhere? Then there was nothing but more pleasure, more Turner, deeper, his mouth on hers, his hands all over her, his cock inside her . . . so good, so good . . . and then she was on her hands and knees . . . and she suddenly felt herself being rhythmically pushed off the edge of the bed. She caught herself, hands outstretched against a stack of boxes, but the boxes started to tumble just as she was pulled back onto the bed.

Candy opened her eyes. Turner's gaze locked with hers. He was completely present, completely focused, and he smiled down on her, chuckling. "You all right, baby?"

Candy nodded. "Please don't stop," she said.

Her body was soft and silky. Her hair smelled like flowers. Her eyes were innocent and sexy. And Turner knew he might as well surrender right then and there because Candy Carmichael was going to own him with that pussy of hers. She was going to break him down into a slobbering fool with that pussy, take him to heaven and back with that pussy.

Oh, how he loved the sensation of being fully buried inside of her, as she lay beneath him now, eyes half open, little mewls of pleasure releasing with each plunge, until she went silent and rigid for what had to be the fifth time since they started making love.

"Do it, Candy," he said. "One more time. This time I'll go with you. Don't keep anything back. I want you so much. I've wanted you for so long—"

Turner felt her grip his cock with one long, hard shudder, followed by a series of rolling, clutching waves, and that's when she let go with a cry that came from deep inside her chest. Once more, she squirted all over his stomach.

He came with her, a roaring, bucking, whole-body spasm of joy that threw him outside of his own physical form for an instant. Where he went, he had no words for. And after, they lay together, belly to belly, kissing softly and letting their hands roam all over each other's bodies, while Turner let the realization settle over him—they had officially started on this journey together. He hoped and prayed there would be all the time in the world to build on this beginning.

After a long while, Turner pulled himself from Candy and rolled to his side. He repositioned them so they lay lengthwise in the bed and placed the covers over them both.

Candy snuggled into his chest. He reached around her back and held her tight, feeling her breath soft against his skin. Everything about her—her scent, the way her body molded to his, the way she tasted—it was all absolute pleasure for him. She was everything he'd longed for, and more.

"Turner?" Her voice was faint and muffled against his chest.

"Yes, darlin'?"

"I didn't run away."

He smiled and kissed the top of her head. "Are you sure about that?"

She nodded. "Yes, but I think you tried to kick me out of bed at one point."

Turner laughed softly. "Uh, no. I just got a little carried away. Sorry about that."

"No apology necessary." He could feel her cheek press against his chest when she smiled. "Turner?"

"Hmm?"

"That was pretty wild. Did something fall off the wall?"

"Uh, yeah. I think. I'll have to check."

"Maybe we should make love in an empty room from now on," Candy said, giggling.

"Yeah. Nothing but a wrestling mat and padded walls." Turner pulled back a bit to look down into her face. He pushed hair away from her eyes. "Was it too crazy for you?"

She smiled up at him. "No. Can I can have some more?"

"Sure, baby," he said, reaching down over the side of the bed to unplug the twisted lamp. "I'll be good to go as soon as I get the feeling back in my hands and feet."

They laughed together, softly at first then loud and rowdy, but their laughter soon faded into sighs, and the last thought Turner had before he fell asleep was that there was no point in lying to himself another minute.

He was going to fall in love with Candy Carmichael—if he hadn't already.

Chapter 18

Apparently, Turner regained the feeling in his limbs about four-thirty that morning, because that's when Candy woke up to find his face between her legs. She returned the favor, learning more about what pleased him, what brought him to the edge, and what would push him over.

They made love in the shower—twice—and Turner made coffee while Candy threw together some scrambled eggs, toast, and grits. They sat at the dining room table and ate as if they were starving, and when it was time for Turner to leave he grabbed her and kissed the hell out of her.

"What's on your agenda today?" he asked.

"Oh, you know, same as every other day—feed the hungry, rescue the oppressed, make a couple chocolate cakes."

Turner chuckled into her hair, and Candy felt the vibration travel all the way down to her toes. It felt so damn good to be in his arms that she wanted to cry.

"You know, you poke fun at your talent, but you

shouldn't," Turner said. "You've got a real gift, Candy Pants."

She pulled away and stared at him. "What did you just call me?" It was fun to watch Turner's eyes widen in alarm.

"Did I just say that aloud?"

Candy blew out air. "Yeah."

"Okay, well, that's what J.J. and I always called you back in the day. Hope you're not offended. It was meant as a compliment. Still is."

Candy tried not to smile but she was wholly unsuccessful. She busted out laughing.

"You knew?" Turner looked shocked.

"Of course I did," she said. "You and J.J. might have thought you were superbad back in seventh grade but I'm here to tell you—you weren't. You were goofy and loud. I've always known that's what you called me."

Turner wrapped his arms around her waist and smiled down at her. "And you still liked me, even after all that?"

Candy chuckled. "Yeah. Go figure."

"Ever had a nickname for me?"

"Not yet." She wiggled her eyebrows. "But it shouldn't be hard to come up with one."

Turner laughed, and when he did his dimples deepened and his eyes sparkled and Candy suddenly felt light-headed and giddy as a girl. His joy was a beautiful thing to see. His happiness was contagious.

If she ever caused him pain she would hate herself.

"I'll see you tonight," he said, kissing her forehead one last time before opening the front door. "I'll try to come in for lunch."

* * *

"Hey!"

Turner slid onto a stool at Lenny's counter and inwardly sighed with relief at the sight of Candy. She was real. He hadn't made her up. And she looked as happy to see him as he was to see her.

"Can you recommend anything particularly tasty today? I'm in the mood for something sweet but savory."

Candy pursed her lips. She leaned her elbows on the counter and whispered to him. "I believe the item you're referring to isn't on the menu here at Lenny's."

"Damn, that's good to hear."

Candy broke out into a wide grin, her blue eyes alive. She looked happy, Turner thought, happier than he'd seen her since she came back to town. He liked to think it was partly because of him.

He had to eat fast, so ordered the soup and sandwich combo. He had a lead about Gerrall being spotted in Winston, a town about five miles away, and he thought he'd drive out to have a look-see. When he got up a few minutes later to pay his check, Turner felt a few sets of unfriendly eyes on him. With a smile, he acknowledged the glares of Ed Hamilton, Haywood Buckston, and Junior Schneider, three good ole boys long retired from the county public works department.

"Gentlemen," he said, nodding in their direction.

Only Junior responded to the greeting. "Sheriff," he said.

With a sigh, Turner decided he should defuse the situation. The diner was plenty crowded and the last thing he wanted to do was appear guilty about his relationship with Candy. He wasn't and never would be.

And besides, everyone in town already knew about them.

Turner strolled over to the booth where the three old men were finishing their lunches, aware that every eye in the place was on him. "How ya'll been?" he asked.

"Good enough," Junior said.

"I heard they're going to have to rip out the Pigeon Creek bridge out past Highway 25. Now, weren't ya'll on the crew that built it back in the sixties?"

"Hell, yes, we were!" Haywood said. "And there ain't a damn thing wrong with it, either. Just a bunch of bureaucratic horse manure if you ask me, saying bridges gotta be replaced every so many years."

"Hmph," Ed said. "The '75 flood banged it up pretty good, though. It had to be shored up. I say it probably needs to be replaced."

"Well, you can't be too safe when it comes to bridges," Turner said.

"Now that's true," Junior agreed.

"Looks like you're getting pretty friendly with Jonesy Carmichael's girl these days."

Turner was grateful for Ed's abrupt redirection of the conversation—he had a limited amount of time built into his day for bullshit. "Candy is a wonderful woman, Ed. We've been friends all our lives, you know, so it was wonderful to reconnect after all these years."

"Hmph," Ed said.

"How long's Junie been gone now?" Haywood asked.

"Four years in May."

"Long time," Junior said. "God rest her soul."

"Thank you, Junior," Turner said.

"Hmph," was Ed's contribution again. "My Rowena's been gone seven years now."

"Well, all I got to say is it's a damn good thing Jonesy ain't around," Junior said, nodding with the gravity of his statement. "He wouldn't be none too happy."

Turner made sure his smile was in place and answered with a friendly lilt in his voice. "Our families and friends are supportive and happy for us, which is a blessing. Now ya'll have a good day. Enjoy this beautiful weather we're having."

"You, too, Sheriff," Ed said.

"Take care now," Junior said.

By the time Turner got to the cash register, whatever tension had been present in the diner had dissipated. He handed Candy his money and winked at her.

"Smooth talker," she whispered.

"You ain't seen nothing yet, baby."

Chapter 19

"You know I don't usually do this," Lenny said as he escorted Cheri back into the prep kitchen. Candy wiped her hands on her apron in surprise as Cheri waved to her. "This here space is sacred," Lenny was telling Cheri. "It's where all the magic happens."

Cheri smiled and nodded. "I know that's true. I've been eating your magic since I was a toddler, remember."

Lenny laughed, shaking his head. "You girls are cruel! You never miss a chance to remind me that I'm old as Methuselah and just about as good-lookin'. Ya'll have a nice visit, now," he said, heading to the back.

Candy leaned her butt against the steel counter. "To what do I owe this honor?"

"Oh, please," Cheri said, hooking her purse strap on a cabinet knob and pulling up an old metal stool. "I came by to tell you we're going to have our engagement party Saturday afternoon and I wanted to make sure you can still do cupcakes."

"Of course!" Candy said that with a smile, but she

was not yet sure she was safe. This could be a trap, since she'd been sure Cheri showed up not to talk about cupcakes but to pump her for details on what was going on with Turner. That was a subject Candy would rather not get into due to the simple fact that there would be no way to discuss it without sounding reckless, wanton, and just plain bad mannered. After all, what kind of woman starts something so beautiful and amazing with a man she intends to leave?

A depraved woman. A woman without a lick of decency. That's who.

"What exactly did you have in mind?" Candy grabbed notebook and pencil from the countertop. "Do you have a color scheme or a decorating theme?"

Cheri chuckled. "Sure. Our colors are lake blue and grass green and our decorating theme is summer at Newberry Lake."

Candy pursed her lips and let the notebook drop against her thigh. "Sounds like you're going all out."

Cheri laughed again. "Oh, you know how J.J. and I feel about all the wedding pomp and circumstance. We're doing it mostly so we can say we had an engagement party, so Viv will stop pestering us."

"Hmm. So what kind of cupcakes did you have in mind and how many should I plan on?"

"I was thinking both chocolate and white, with both kinds of icing, and the confetti kind of sprinkles on top."

"That sounds simple enough."

"About two hundred should do it—in case people want more than one."

Candy immediately began her mental calculations—how much flour, sugar, and butter she would need and how much baking and decorating time she'd have to build into the schedule. "No problem," she said.

Cheri smiled at her. "Hey, did you hear the hot gossip?"

"No." Candy crossed her arms over her chest, wary of where this was going.

Cheri wiggled her eyebrows. "Tater Wayne up and went missing for a couple weeks, and he called Viv to tell her he'd have to get to her chores at some other time—*when he gets back to town!*"

Candy was shocked. Tater was the quintessential Bigler boy, a guy who'd barely graduated from high school, who thought haircuts given by a licensed barber and dental care were for sissies, and who'd been plagued his whole life by an eyeball that wouldn't sit still. He was the nicest guy in the world—he'd give you the shirt off his back if you could stand the smell—but Tater had never been known to travel. Anywhere. Like anywhere outside Cataloochee County.

"Where did he go?" Candy asked.

"That's the thing—nobody knows," Cheri said. "And since his barbecue wagon is key to the engagement party, we had to be sure he'd be back here in time. That's why we just now have a date."

Candy wasn't falling for it. Cheri was being far too chatty this morning. There was something else going on.

"And there's something else," Cheri said.

I knew it! Candy busied herself by checking the cakes in the oven. "Oh, yeah?"

"Yeah. Tanyalee is supposed to be coming home over the weekend."

Candy spun around, stood up straight, and blinked a few times. "Just in time for the engagement party."

Cheri shook her head slowly. "We'll have to see about that. Emily Post doesn't have much to say about situations like this one—'does one invite the groom's nutso ex-wife to the engagement party if she happens to be the bride's sister?' "

Candy scrunched up her mouth and nose. "Sounds a little risky."

"Yeah, but maybe she's . . . you know . . . *recovered*."

"Hey," Candy offered, "stranger things have happened."

"Okay. I guess I should be going." Cheri hopped off the stool, grabbed her purse, and hung the strap on her shoulder. She went over to Candy and gave her a tight hug.

"You doing okay?" she asked, her voice pleasant.

"Oh, sure."

"Good."

Her best friend turned to leave. Candy was about to release the breath she'd been holding for the last several minutes when Cheri whipped around and shouted, "You weren't even going to tell me? What are you—freakin' crazy?"

Candy's mouth fell open.

"You're living with Turner!"

"Shh," Candy said, rushing to Cheri and steadying her by the upper arms. "Keep your voice down, please."

"Why?" Cheri asked. "So Lenny doesn't find out? He already knows! Candy, I got news for you—*everyone knows*!"

"Oh, jeez."

"Uh-huh. I heard it from J.J. first, followed promptly by Gladys, then Viv, and then Granddaddy Garland, who heard it from Turner's *mother*. And then I got a call from Tater Wayne asking if it were true."

"Huh?"

"Yeah. He called long distance. He also asked if your car was running all right."

"Oh, Lord."

"So you weren't going to mention this to me? Really?"

"I swear I was. I just—"

"I'm so mad I could chew up nails and spit out a barbed-wire fence!"

Candy huffed in frustration and backed away from Cheri. "I'm sorry," she said, meaning it. "The truth is, I don't know what the hell I'm doing, Cheri. I plan to leave Bigler. I have nothing holding me here. But at the same time, I'm having all these feelings for Turner. He took off his wedding ring. He makes me . . . I'm thinking maybe . . . he makes me want to—"

"You slept with him."

Candy nodded. "Last night. And this morning. It was like we couldn't wait any longer, like we were both tortured being in the same house and not . . . you know . . ."

"Oh, shee-it," Cheri said, running a hand through her stylish cut and spinning around on her boot heels. "How is Turner doing with all this?"

Candy laughed. "What kind of question is *that*? He's doing *great*. Better than great. He's amazing. He's incredible. He's the most—" Candy stopped herself when it became apparent that wasn't exactly what her friend was asking. "Uh, if you mean doing *emotionally*—how he's doing being with someone for the first time since Junie died—I'd have to say he's doing pretty well."

"Okay." Cheri frowned and fiddled with her purse strap. "It's just that—"

"I know," Candy said, cutting her off. "You don't want to see Turner hurt. Nobody does, especially me. That's why I've been completely up front with him about my plans. He knows I intend to leave town as soon as my time here at Lenny's is done."

Cheri laughed. "You make it sound like a prison sentence. Is Bigler really that bad?"

Candy didn't want to have to go there, but it seemed she had no choice. She sighed. "Yeah, Cheri, it's that bad—for me. Not you. It's perfect for you—you're in love with a wonderful man. You have a home filled with memories and a job that means something and a family that adores you and is proud of you. Bigler is great if you're Cheri Newberry. If you're Candy Carmichael? Not so much."

"Oh, Candy." Cheri took a step closer to her but Candy shook her head.

"I'm going to be okay. Like you said just a few weeks ago, I always land on my feet and I will this time. If it makes you feel any better, I don't plan to stay at Turner's house for long. One more paycheck and I should be able to swing a deposit and first month's rent somewhere."

Cheri let go with a bitter laugh. "That's the stupidest damn thing I've ever heard," she said. "You're going to spend all that money just to live somewhere for a little over a month? And then you're gonna pack up and go?"

"I don't want to mooch off my friends."

Cheri shook her head and gave Candy a shriveling look. "You don't get it, do you, girl? People *love* you, you ninny. J.J. and I have offered for you to stay with us because we love you. Turner offered because he loves you. Viv, too. And even Jacinta. Do you think she would have taken you in over there if she didn't love you?"

Candy shrugged. "I really need to get these cakes out of the oven."

"You know what, Candace Carmichael? You need to open your damn eyes." Cheri put her hands on her hips and glared. "You're supposed to be the queen of seeing possibilities where other people see nothing but problems, right? Well, maybe it's time you used that skill with your own life."

Cheri turned and reached for the door, but she looked over her shoulder while making her dramatic exit. "You know why I get to say that to you?"

Candy huffed in impatience. "Why?"

"Because *I* love you. And you're going to listen because you love me, too."

She slammed the door.

A little while later, while the cakes cooled, Candy went out to the front of the diner to finish her daily cleanup. She was sorting silverware when the bell jangled and the diner door opened.

Gerrall Spivey walked in. He looked like hell.

"Gerrall?" Candy dropped the forks and stared. "Are you okay? Are you hurt?" She asked herself which emotion had the upper hand at that particular moment—the guilt she felt for getting him fired or the anger she felt at how he'd been spreading lies about her. She decided it was a draw.

His face seemed strangely vacant. "Can I get a cup of coffee?"

"Sure. Of course." Candy gestured for him to have a seat and turned her back to him to pour him a cup. "Cream or sugar?"

"You know what I like."

Candy froze. There it was again—that vaguely threatening tone he'd used with her from the very first time they met. It reeked of entitlement, an intimacy that didn't actually exist. Now, suddenly, it made sense to her. After what Jacinta told her about the photo in his phone and the lies he was telling people, she realized that Gerrall lived in some kind of fantasy world. Now was the time to set him straight.

"I would have no way of knowing what you take in your coffee, Gerrall." Candy set his cup and saucer down in front of him along with the sugar and cream. "I'm sorry for what happened at Cherokee Pines."

"Really?" He stared at the spoon as he twirled it around in his hot coffee. He made no move to take a sip.

"Of course," Candy said, going back to sorting silverware. She discreetly checked to make sure she could see Lenny in the kitchen. He was out of the line of sight, which left her feeling a little uncomfortable. "Have you started looking for another job?"

Gerrall produced a nasty laugh and glanced up at her. His pale eyes looked a little wild and his smile was more of a snarl. "You've really disappointed me, Candy. I thought we had an understanding."

A cold shiver went up her spine. What if Gerrall was more than just an eccentric nerd who lived in a fantasy world? What if he was a whack job? Or on drugs? And what did it mean if a whack-job junkie was carrying around your photo and telling people you were his girlfriend?

Not a good thing.

"Gerrall, look, I heard that you've been telling people we're in a relationship. Please stop. And I don't know how you got my picture, but I'd appreciate it if you deleted it from your phone."

This time when he laughed it was laced with an unnerving disgust. He shook his head. "You're with Turner Halliday now? Really, Candy? I thought you had higher standards than that."

"Everything okay out there?" Lenny poked his head out the serving window and Candy spun around to face him, widening her eyes in a plea for help. He got the message and immediately headed her way.

Gerrall stood up. "You were supposed to have my back, but don't worry about it." He leaned on the counter to finish his sentence before Lenny appeared. "You're gonna make it up to me, Candy. I'll be in touch to let you know how."

And with that he headed for the exit.

Candy jumped when Lenny placed his hand on her shoulder. "What was that about?" he asked her.

"Uh, not sure," she said, "but he's really pissed I got him fired."

"Yeah, well, stay away from him. That Spivey kid has never been right in the head."

She shuddered. Well, at least she had confirmation.

"Can't say I blame him, though. With a daddy like his he's lucky he ain't in the state pen for murder."

Candy looked at Lenny like he was joking. "Come on, now."

He held up his hands. "I'm telling you the God's truth, honey. It's a miracle that kid ain't blown his daddy's brains out with a shotgun. Bobby Ray Spivey deserves it—crazy, ignernt bastard that he is, beating on that kid since he was small. All the Spiveys been crazy, far back as I know."

Chapter 20

Candy pulled through the pretentious circular drive of Cherokee Pines and entered the front door like she had every right to be there, because, as Jacinta had assured her again only moments ago on the cell phone, she did.

Miller sat at the reception desk. He looked up with a pleasant expression, but the instant he saw it was Candy, his face fell.

"Hello, Mr. Miller. I'm here to see my mother."

"You've got some nerve, Miss Carmichael." A red splotch of rage popped up on his cheeks.

"Could you let her know I'm here, please?"

He smirked. "Now why in the world would I do you any favors?"

Jacinta rounded the corner and without delay smacked Miller right on his bald spot.

"Ow!" he screamed.

Candy suppressed a snicker. "Hello, Mother. How did you know I was here?"

"Are you kidding?" Jacinta reached for Candy's hand and pulled her down the hall. "I can hear that car coming from miles away." She smiled at Candy. "I'm glad to see you. It's been too normal around here since you moved out."

"Since I was dragged away in a police car, you mean."

Jacinta laughed loudly as she opened the door to her apartment. "You looked like a willing prisoner, if you get my drift."

Candy noticed immediately that the coffee table was covered with what looked like legal documents. "Having me deported?"

"Ha!" Jacinta headed into the kitchen. "Would you like a cup of tea or something?"

"Sure." Candy wondered for a moment if she'd been dropped into some kind of alternate universe. Her mother seemed chummy tonight, truly glad to see her. And watching Jacinta smack Wainright Miller upside the head made the experience that much more surreal— fun, but still surreal.

Her mother toddled in with two mugs of Lipton. "What's new in your world, Candace?"

Candy accepted her tea with a frown. "Somehow, I have a feeling you already know."

As Jacinta settled into the chair, she shook her head and chuckled. "Shoo!" she said, shaking her head some more. "Lordy, Lordy," she added.

"Feel like elaborating?"

Jacinta thought that was the funniest thing she'd ever heard, apparently, because she broke into a series of snorts and chortles punctuated by a few more "Shoos!" and "Lordy, Lordies." When she'd sufficiently calmed herself, she set down her mug and shot Candy a serious look.

"Candace," she said. "Your father was the biggest racist son of a bitch this side of the Mason-Dixon line."

That wasn't the conversation starter Candy had expected. "Oookay."

"And thank God above he's not here to see you shackin' up with our handsome sheriff."

Candy's mouth fell open for an instant, but she pulled herself together quickly. "I am not shacking up, Jacinta. I'm staying with him temporarily, and as soon as—"

She waved her arm around until Candy stopped talking. "Darling girl, do not try to bullshit me. Do you think I'm not sitting here tonight looking at a completely different woman than I saw two nights ago? The lines are gone from your face. Your eyes are sparkling. Frankly, whatever Turner Halliday is doing to you and for you I say, bravo! You look absolutely radiant."

Pod people, Candy thought. Her mother had been taken away by the pod people, and this creature sitting in the chair across from her was an alien substitute, an imposter rockin' one of Jacinta's caftans. Her mother had never mentioned sex or referred to Candy as "darling girl," and she'd certainly never spoken ill of her late husband, at least not to Candy.

"Now, I realize we've never discussed Turner, but this is not exactly unexpected news."

Candy cocked her head to the side. "It isn't?"

Jacinta chuckled to herself. "Oh, my. How do I even begin?"

"Begin what?"

Jacinta took a sip of tea, then rested her palms on her knees. Candy thought the posture made her mother look like a Buddha with a beehive. "Now, you have to understand, Candace. We all saw how Turner looked at you when ya'll were in school. He was one lovesick puppy! And, of course, Rosemary and I discussed it sometimes, and we did what we could to keep a lid on the situation."

Candy's mouth fell open. "You and Turner's mother *discussed* us? You tried to keep us apart? What *situation* are you talking about, exactly?"

"Oh, you make it sound like some kind of evil plot." Jacinta shook her head. "We were just two mamas trying to protect their chicks, is all. Now, I've known Rosemary all my life—as lovely a woman as there is in this county—and she was beside herself with worry for Turner. She didn't want him hurt and, well, she knew your *father.* She knew what a disaster that would have been for Turner."

Candy's lips parted but she was too stunned to speak.

"Frankly, Rosemary and I were relieved when the two of you went your own ways after school. We thought it was for the best."

Sadness and anger welled up in Candy's chest. It wasn't enough that her father had crushed her when she'd been a kid. Now she discovered her mother had manipulated her emotional life, as well. "I don't believe what I'm hearing."

"Candace, that was then, honey. You and Turner are grown-ups now and your father is no longer walking this earth making life miserable for everyone." She sighed deeply. "What I'm telling you is that I'm happy for the two of you. So is Rosemary. We think it's . . .

oh, I don't know what the word is . . . fate, maybe? What I'm saying is that it's nice that the two of you found each other after all this time."

Candy jutted her head forward in disbelief. This was too much to handle all at once, out of nowhere. Candy felt like she'd been hijacked. "Is this why you called me over here? To give me your blessing to do the nasty with Turner?"

"Oh, heavens no." Jacinta reached over and picked up the documents from the coffee table, then thought better of her answer. "Well, on second thought, everything's connected, I suppose, but no. I didn't necessarily call you over here to talk about Turner Halliday. I wanted to show you these."

Jacinta held out the papers and waited until Candy accepted them with a groan. "What's all this?" She scanned the top document and knew immediately that she was looking at a deed. But to what? And why was her name on it? "I don't understand," Candy said, flipping through the pages. She glanced up at Jacinta and frowned.

"Look at the second set of papers."

Candy pulled at the document tucked in a robin's-egg-blue folder. "Daddy's will?" Candy skimmed through it as quickly as she could until she got to a page marked with a sticky yellow arrow, where she saw her name in bold print. It took only seconds to read and then reread the pertinent sentences. With shaking hands, Candy placed both the deed and the will on the coffee table.

"Why didn't you tell me about this when he died?"

Jacinta shrugged. "Why would I have? You read what it says. You inherit that building only if you're a resident of Cataloochee County, and until a few weeks ago, you were a resident of Florida and intended to remain so. And if you didn't return within twenty years of his death, the building would have been given to the city."

"But—" Candy's mind was reeling. It was complete insanity! "I can never sell it? What the hell is that all about? He can't do that! Why would he give me something of value and then tell me what I could and couldn't do with it?"

Jacinta laughed. "You do know what building we're talking about, right?"

"Of course! It's the old dump where the insurance office was. I just walked by it the other day. But I didn't know he actually owned the property."

Jacinta smiled sweetly. "Well, he did."

Candy tossed the papers to the coffee table and shook her head. The place was awful—dark and dingy and cut up into half a dozen small offices, all covered in cheap wood paneling and industrial-brown carpet. She could still smell the stale cigarette smoke and copier toner. "Why in the world would he leave me that building?"

"Don't you see?" Jacinta reached out for her hand. "Your daddy never did anything out of the kindness of his heart. There were always strings attached. Listen, I need to explain something to you, and I'm not telling you this because I expect you to praise me or nominate me for mother of the year or anything . . ." Jacinta stopped. Candy watched her mother fail to fight back tears.

Another first.

"Go on," Candy reassured her, squeezing her hand. "Tell me."

Jacinta jumped up from her chair and walked to her living room window. She was still a tall and elegant woman, Candy saw, still beautiful in a kind of over-the-top way, with her heavily sprayed bouffant and dramatic makeup. She turned around just then, her face looking younger in sadness. "Candace, did you ever wonder why your father was never home?"

She shrugged. "You told me it was because he was busy at work and had all those important civic duties."

"Yes, I did tell you that," Jacinta said, a sad smile touching her lips. "And do you know how it came to be that Jonesy Carmichael was such a busy, important man?"

Candy shook her head, almost afraid of what this new mother of hers was about to tell her.

"Because I made damn sure he was," Jacinta said, the bitterness detectable behind her smile. "I made sure he spent as little time around you as possible. I got him nominated to serve on every board and committee and panel within hundreds of miles. I set up client meetings in the evenings. And do you know why? Because I didn't want him poisoning you, Candace! Do you understand what I'm saying?"

She blinked a few times and nodded, trying her best to follow along.

"You see, I fixed it so that you spent hardly any time with your own father. I was protecting you. And that's why I tried to keep you and Turner apart while your daddy was alive, because he would have killed that boy and locked you up and thrown away the key."

She felt stunned, like someone had slapped her. Suddenly, her mother didn't fit into the tidy description

Candy had always chosen for her—a cool and aloof woman focused on her husband and not her child. Candy felt a trembling begin in her belly, and it moved through her until her chest felt tight and her hands began to shake.

"I'm sorry if this upsets you, but I knew I'd have to explain it should you ever decide to come back to Bigler. And, well, here you are."

She looked up at her mother and nodded faintly. "It's a little overwhelming."

Jacinta offered her a tentative smile. "I suppose it is." She walked over to the couch and sat down next to Candy, taking her hand in hers once more. "So. What are you going to do with the building?"

Candy laughed. "I have no idea, Mother. What the hell would I want with a dingy, vacant, hundred-year-old warehouse in downtown Bigler that I can't even sell?"

Jacinta shook her head. "That's for you to decide."

"But why?" Candy stared at her mother with wide eyes. "Why would he leave this to me? I still don't get it."

Jacinta patted her hand. "I've thought long and hard about this, and I've come to believe that your father left you that ugly thing to get the last laugh."

"Like a sick joke."

"Right. Think about it, Candace. No one can say he didn't provide for his only child, right? But you and I know your inheritance was practically worthless to you."

"What a guy," Candy mumbled.

Jacinta looked down at their joined hands. "I could have done much better for myself, obviously. But I don't regret it, since that marriage brought me you."

Candy let go with a bitter laugh. "Why did you marry someone you knew was such a jerk?"

Jacinta looked away and blinked. "Well, I suppose you have every right to ask that, and the only thing I can say in my defense is I didn't know." She turned her gaze to Candy again. "I knew he was a Bigler good ole boy, of course, but he didn't seem any worse than anyone else around here."

Candy was listening.

"I was young and stupid," she continued. "I didn't ask enough questions before we got married. I didn't pay close enough attention to the men he kept company with and how they saw the world. And then one day, I woke up and realized I'd married a man with a twisted soul, a shriveled-up little heart. And . . ." Jacinta began to cry in earnest now. "I was pregnant with you, Candace. I . . . I tried to make the best of a bad situation, and in the process I lost you. I pushed you away in my effort to keep you safe, and you never found it in your heart to love me. I don't blame you."

Candace felt that tight feeling in her chest begin to dissolve into a hot flood of sadness, and before she knew what was happening, she and Jacinta were hugging. She wasn't sure who initiated it, and she supposed it didn't matter, but they were now sitting on the sofa holding each other as they cried.

"I'm so sorry for everything," Jacinta said into Candy's shoulder.

"It's okay, Mother." Candy hugged her tighter, smiling to herself through her tears, knowing that it really was all right, because now she knew that her mother had done her best. Jacinta did what she thought she had to do to protect Candy and keep Turner off Jonesy's radar screen. It was a damn shame that so many people had been forced to dance around that angry bully of a man, but he was gone now. He no longer factored into their lives.

But Jacinta was still here. Turner was still here. And right at that moment, Candy realized she'd been given another chance with both of them.

She would have so much to share with Turner when she got home.

Candy stayed through the evening. Jacinta called her attorney and set up an appointment for Candy to meet with him about the building. Mother and daughter had dinner in the dining room, and Candy's appearance attracted quite a crowd. The bocce ball crew was thrilled to see her. The bridge club asked if it were true she was staying with the sheriff. Lorraine Estes snubbed her nose at Candy on her way to the salad bar.

Candy hugged and kissed her mother good-bye after dinner, and as she strolled through the lobby toward the exit she smiled in Mr. Miller's direction. Even he couldn't ruin this incredible evening, and the happiness in her heart.

"Good night!" she said cheerfully.

"Hmmph," was his reply.

Chapter 21

Candy drove up the hill to Turner's house in the woods and saw his SUV parked out front. She smiled so big her face hurt. She practically ran up to the front door.

His lips were on her before she had both feet inside.

Turner spun her around in his arms a few times, put her down, then began peeling off her Lenny's T-shirt. Candy tugged up on the shirttail of his sheriff's department uniform.

"Let me get all this shit off first," Turner said, removing the electronic gadgets and weapons that hung from his waist and placing them on the entryway table—gun and holster, radio, cell phone, stun gun, and billy club.

"How do you even walk with all that crap?"

"You get used to it," he said, starting to unbutton the waist of her jeans.

"I love the way you walk, by the way," Candy said, unbuttoning the front of his shirt.

"Really?"

"Hell, yes. It's a swagger. I get wet just watching you walk across a room."

"Good," Turner said, unhooking her bra and licking and sucking on her nipples. "Because you make me hard when I see you walk."

"For real? I never really thought I had much of a walk." Candy pulled the shirt off his shoulders and ripped his undershirt over his head, then licked his pectoral muscles. "I always thought I walk like a hillbilly white girl."

"Oh, you do," Turner said, chuckling as he yanked open the snap of her jeans. "But you've got an ass that could cause a five-car pileup."

She tossed her head back to laugh and Turner attacked her throat with a series of voracious kisses and nibbles and sucks.

"I know I probably smell like carrot cake. Sorry about that," Candy said, tugging on Turner's trousers even though she couldn't lower her head to see what she was doing.

"Fine by me. I love your carrot cake." Turner shoved his hands down the back of her jeans and panties and grabbed at her ass cheeks. "But not as much as I love your pussy." He pushed her jeans and underwear to the floor, and Candy stepped out of them as Turner stepped out of his.

"I've been waiting all damn day for this," Turner said, his mouth once more on her lips, her throat, her breasts. All the while Candy ran her hands over the hard muscles and soft skin of Turner's body—wide, strong shoulders, cut biceps, rippling abs, the firm swells of his back and butt. She felt like a starving woman who could only be satisfied through the sense of touch, and she wanted more, more, more . . .

Candy was lifted. She threw her legs around Turner's hips and felt herself being carried to the back of the leather sofa, where she was lowered. Immediately, she became lost in the vortex of hot and wet kisses, the pressure of his hands on her flesh. It was almost too much joy when he entered her, pushing deep, spreading her open to her very being. She looked up into Turner's face, transformed by pleasure, and she saw everything she had ever desired in a man.

Kindness. Truth. Beauty. Goodness.

His eyes flew open and his hazel gaze locked with hers as he thrust deeper into her, body and soul. She felt his hands locked behind her back. She hung on to his neck. And even as he began to take her harder, with a desperate determination to have all of her, she knew she would not slip through his grasp. He had her. Turner would not let her fall.

Suddenly, she knew with certainty that he would never let her fall. No matter what.

"You are mine, Candy," he whispered. "You've always been mine. Do you understand that?"

"Yes," she said, unable to say more. The physical pleasure was acute and building higher, but all the while she felt emotion rush through her, strong and insistent, and she couldn't ignore it if she wanted to. So she let it flow. The tears welled in her eyes and she knew they were for everything and everyone . . . for her mistakes, for her mother's choices, for her father's malevolence. Candy cried for all the pain Turner had gone through without her being there to help him. She cried for Junie's death.

She didn't understand any of it. None of it was part

of any kind of grand plan that she could accept. God wasn't that cruel. It just . . . *was*.

Candy gasped. Turner was taking her to the edge. She was so close. And right as she felt she was about to reach orgasm, she saw it.

All of it—the pain and the mistakes and the loss—it belonged to the past. It did not belong to this moment, this beautiful, perfect slice of time. In Turner's eyes she was reminded what this moment was all about. It was so simple.

"I think I'm in love with you," she whispered.

Oh, God, she hoped Turner had heard her because she didn't think she could say it again—sharp, deep waves of pleasure had left her breathless. She was coming.

Turner grabbed her by the back of her head and lifted her close to his face. "Candy," he said, his eyes boring into hers. "I don't *think*. I know. I love you, baby. I always have and I always will."

He slammed his mouth on hers and shoved his cock into her and she was gone. It felt as if she'd hit a wall of bliss, a million pieces of her soul flying out through the world and into Turner.

The man who loved her.

Gerrall pulled his girl's picture up on his cell phone for the thousandth time. But now, seeing it filled him with anger. Anger for the way she'd flirted with him every time they were together. Led him on. Made him believe she wanted him the same way he wanted her. Then she'd gone off with Turner Halliday, making a mockery of their relationship and leaving Gerrall feeling empty, alone, and filled with unbearable rage.

Earlier that day, he'd hidden in the trees outside Turner Halliday's house, and he'd seen all he'd needed to. Candy was a whore and a liar. And it was made worse by the fact that Turner Halliday was the one who'd stolen Candy away from him. This wasn't the first time the man has stolen his woman.

First it was Miss Junie Halliday, his favorite teacher. Gerrall knew that he was special to her, too. They'd spent long hours together after school while she helped him with his homework, and she always invited him to her house for dinner. Even back then, Gerrall had hated Turner for being so close to her. Resented the fact that he had to share Miss Junie's attention and affection with that cocky son-of-a-bitch cop, walking around all smug and conceited like he could have any woman he wanted.

The truth was, Turner could never love Miss Junie the way Gerrall did. Just thinking about her filled him with a deep sense of loss that Turner could never understand.

That was another reason Gerrall hated his dad. The night Miss Halliday was killed, Bobby Ray got blind drunk and admitted that he was the one who ran her off the road. He'd meant to send her a message—stay away from my house, my son, and mind your own damn business. But instead of leaving her running scared, he'd left her dead. And Gerrall would never, ever forgive him for it. Even worse was his father's complete lack of remorse as he drunkenly bragged about what he'd done. Laughing and mocking Gerrall the whole time.

Gerrall put the phone away and grabbed the wig from the floor of his dingy rented room. Gerrall had gotten the wig—along with a dress and some makeup—from the second-hand store down the street. It was his disguise for when he needed to go out for food, or just to clear his head.

The gang his father worked with had surely gotten wind of his disappearance, and he knew there must be a lot of people looking for him right now. He hadn't gone far. He was just in the next town over. But they'd never think to look for him in his current disguise, he thought with a grin. And they'd never imagine what he had planned next.

He knew exactly what to do to outsmart everyone who had hurt him. He just needed to wait a little longer. He'd have his opportunity soon enough.

While Candy talked a blue streak, she folded another piece of pancake in half and dipped it into a puddle of syrup on her plate. Turner sipped his coffee, trying not to laugh, but honestly, he'd never seen anyone eat a pancake like that. He supposed it was one of a million little things he would be learning about Candy along the way.

It was six A.M. and he'd not slept much, but Turner was a happy man. His body was humming with the kind of deep satisfaction that comes only with incredible sex and good company, and he'd had a whole lot of both in the last eight hours. Candy was a sensual miracle, a woman open and giving of herself, sweet and light-hearted, a girl who loved to laugh.

But she was also a woman of substance. They'd talked long into the night about their mothers' plot to keep them apart when they'd been young, and when Turner expressed his anger, Candy reminded him that their mothers had acted in the best interest of their children.

"What would you have done if it were your son?" Candy had asked him.

Turner thought about it and said, "I'd have done exactly what my mother did."

He smiled at Candy now as she sat across from him at the table, holding up her little pancake roll, a line of syrup dribbling down her forearm. "So what do you think I should do about the building?"

Instead of answering her, Turner snatched Candy's wrist, licked her from her elbow up, then chomped down on the pancake.

"Hey!" she said, laughing.

Turner swallowed, then grinned. "I think you should take your time making a decision. Look at it. Talk to your mother's attorney. And then just sit on it a while. Something might come to you."

"I'd rather sit on you," she said, arching one of her blond eyebrows.

Before Turner knew it, Candy was in his lap, leaving sweet kisses on his forehead. All he could do was close his eyes and melt from the soft brush of her lips, the firm abundance of her body against his, her scent, her warmth. He would never grow tired of the delight of this woman in his arms. He'd gone too long without this kind of contentment to ever take such a gift for granted.

"I know you have to leave for work soon," Candy whispered in his ear. "I promise I'll be good. I just wanted to hug you one last time."

Turner wrapped his arms around Candy's waist and buried his face in her breasts. He heard himself moan.

He couldn't help it—her words forced him to remember that this woman in his arms still planned to leave.

"You know, I think I've realized something . . ."

"Oh, yeah?" Turner raised his head. This sounded promising.

"Yeah. After my talk with Jacinta I realized that I might have been using material things as a substitute for people. Does that make any sense?"

"Of course it does," Turner said, his heart lightening at the direction the conversation was taking. "Tell me more."

"Well . . ." Candy absently dragged her fingers over his hair. "I think I got my sense of belonging through stuff, you know, like it defined me, like it gave me a place where I fit. Except for Cheri, of course, people had always seemed to be unpredictable—I *expected* them to disappoint me. But stuff was always there. And the more stuff and money I collected around me the safer I felt."

Turner raised one of her hands to his lips and kissed it tenderly. "And then the stuff was gone."

Candy chuckled softly. "Yeah. And what was I left with? Cheri. My mother. My hometown. *You*. It's kind of ironic, isn't it?"

Turner felt his stomach twist in knots. He didn't want to push her. He was afraid to hear how she'd answer his next question, but he had to ask. Turner touched her cheek until she looked down into his face. "Is that a bad thing?"

"No," she said, a tentative smile playing at her lips. "I can't promise you anything, Turner. Please understand that. But I'm . . . I'm starting to see things differently. I am open to . . . possibilities." She cocked her head and let her eyes explore his face. "Please be patient with me. Give me a little time to figure this out."

He nodded, determined that she would not see the fist-pumping celebration going on in his head. "All the time you need, darlin'."

"But Turner, what about your feelings for Junie? Do *you* need more time?"

"No."

Candy blinked at him. "Just like that? You're sure?"

Turner nodded. "I'm absolutely sure."

"How did that happen?"

He fingered one of her blond curls and thought about how he'd answer her. He wanted to tell Candy the truth but didn't want to sound like a nutcase. "I talked to her."

Candy's blue eyes went big. "You did?"

"Yeah. I told Junie I was letting her go and asked her to do the same. And you know what?"

"What?"

"She did. And the next thing I knew, you were waiting for me in the hallway."

Very slowly, a smile spread across Candy's sweet lips. Then she leaned down and touched those lips to his. There was so much tenderness and affection in that kiss that Turner was left wondering how and why he'd gotten so damn lucky—what had he ever done to get another chance at love like this? With a woman as wonderful as Candy?

"There are people who won't like it, you know."

Turner sighed. "Always will be. But it's none of our business what people think of us. Do you know what I'm saying?"

Candy took a big breath. "I think so."

He put his hands on her upper arms and held her tightly. "We have to promise each other right here and now that we won't let them get to us. We can't let them take away any of our happiness. If we do, we let them win."

She nodded. "I promise."

Turner pulled her close to kiss her but Candy resisted. "One more thing," she said. Her eyes clouded. "It's about Junie again."

"Okay," he said.

"Well, Junie and me."

"All right." Turner gave her a smile of encouragement. "Tell me what's on your mind."

"Well, she was so . . . people remember her as a firecracker, you know? She had standing in the community. She was a really good person."

"She was definitely all those things," Turner said, and he realized that he felt peaceful inside as he talked about her. For the first time since her death, Turner felt more peace and acceptance about Junie than grief.

"I'm not her," Candy whispered, biting her bottom lip.

Turner smiled sadly. This had turned out to be one hell of a morning-after talk, and it was because Candy had been game to go there. He loved her for being so open, so willing.

"No, you are not Junie and Junie was not you, but hear me when I tell you this, Candy—you are not a replacement for someone else. I love you for *you*. I want you, Candy Pants Carmichael. I want everything—your zest for life and your courage and your caring spirit. You make me laugh. You make me insane with lust.

You make me happy to be alive. All that is uniquely you. I want *you*."

Candy nodded, her chin trembling as the tears welled in her eyes. She threw herself in his arms and hugged him so tight that she cut off his air supply. He barely heard it when she whispered, "I love you, too."

Once the breakfast rush was over, Candy had the strangest feeling someone was watching her. She tried to shake it off, but it wasn't until she was in the prep kitchen that she could relax. She almost mentioned something to Lenny, but didn't—she'd been a drama queen lately at work. She didn't want to push it.

Turner called about eleven, telling Candy he couldn't make it in for lunch. She was disappointed. "I'll miss you," she told him.

"I'll miss you, too, baby. But I'll see you at home tonight."

The idea of that made Candy so happy that she convinced herself the feeling of being watched was a product of her imagination. It was unnerving, for sure, and it had come back as soon as she'd finished in the prep kitchen and returned to her post behind the counter. But there was no reason for it. She'd gone out into the parking lot and she'd checked the restrooms and even looked under the booths—there was no one lurking in the shadows. She drank a cup of coffee and told herself to snap out of it.

Lunch was crazy. It was probably for the best that Turner couldn't come by—she wouldn't have had time for him. They sold out of every dessert in an hour an a half, and Lenny later told her that his daily receipts had increased twenty-seven percent since Candy started baking. He asked if she'd be willing to work the counter only at breakfast and spend the rest of her day baking. Of course, she accepted.

So at about two o'clock, when Candy found the note propped up near the cash register, she was baffled. How had she not noticed Gerrall in the diner? Was that why she'd been feeling so creeped out? But where had he been? When had he been here?

When she read the letter a second time, she noticed her hands trembled.

My sweet Candy,

I have been watching you. Don't worry if you did not see me because I am in disgize. Some day soon you will see me, tho. We are going to be together.

You are so beautiful that you have to be mine.

Sinsearly,

G. Spivey.

Chapter 22

Turner welcomed the federal agents into his house and told them to make themselves comfortable. He handed the letter over to O'Connor, who immediately slipped it into an evidence envelope. Candy sat on the couch and answered their questions, and Turner could tell she was trying to be calm but was terrified.

Part of Turner was relieved to see she was finally taking this seriously enough to be scared. He couldn't *believe* she didn't tell him that Gerrall had come into the diner the previous week and threatened her. The other part of him wanted desperately to protect her from any fear, any discomfort.

But all that took a backseat to the fact that Gerrall Spivey was fuckin' with her *at all,* and it made him want to smash walls and break heads. Where *was* that little bastard?

"Miss Carmichael, we appreciate you contacting the sheriff right away," O'Connor said.

"And you're sure you didn't see him?" Marshner

asked for probably the fourth time. "You have no idea if he might have been disguised?"

Candy shook her head. "Like I said, I didn't see anybody that stood out in any way. But it was insanely busy today, so I wasn't really paying attention."

O'Connor and Marshner shook Candy's hand and thanked her for her cooperation. Turner showed them to the door.

When he joined Candy on the sofa once again, she looked exhausted. "C'mere," he said, sighing with relief when she fell against him. Turner kissed the top of her head and couldn't help but smile when he caught a whiff of chocolate cake and grilled cheese.

Though Candy snuggled against him for a moment, she was soon restless. She popped up and frowned. "Okay. What's going on? That DEA agent was at Cherokee Pines the night I got stuck in the window. Why?"

Turner nodded, trying to give her a reassuring smile. "First, please understand that I'm putting my ass on the line telling you this, and I'm only doing so because you are in danger. Candy, you cannot share what I am about to tell you with anyone—not even Cheri and J.J. *Especially* not them."

"Why?"

Turner rubbed his chin. "If the newspaper ran a story about this too soon it would jeopardize a large-scale investigation and might even get an undercover agent killed. I hate to put you in a position where you have to keep a secret from your best friend, but it's very important that you give me your word you will not share this information with *anyone*."

Candy pursed her lips. "I understand. You have my word. But what does this have to do with Gerrall Spivey?"

"It's about his daddy, Bobby Ray."

"Oh!" Candy said, perking up. "Lenny told me all about him the other day."

"What?"

"Lenny said Bobby Ray Spivey was crazy and had physically abused Gerrall over the years."

Turner sighed, relieved that was the extent of Lenny's knowledge. "True. Gerrall was one of Junie's students the year she died. She tried to help Gerrall, but Bobby Ray was a real bastard. But nowadays he's manufacturing and distributing methamphetamine. It's a pretty large operation."

"What?" Candy's lips parted with shock.

"Gerrall has been working for him as a kind of errand boy. But the really bad part is they're now mixed up with a couple dangerous international drug cartels. We think the boy who was killed out at the Tip Top got caught between the feuding organizations."

Candy's eyes went huge. "Oh, my God! I thought that kind of stuff only happened in big cities!"

"Maybe fifteen years ago, but not anymore." Turner took her hand. "We are real close to making arrests, and here's how you can help me—are you listening?"

She nodded.

"I do not want you to be alone at any time, except for here in this house, and only for short periods of time. I'll be dropping you off and picking you up from work. This will be just for a few days. Promise me you'll cooperate with me on this, not put up a fuss."

Candy nodded slowly, her eyes not yet back to their normal size.

"I won't let anything happen to you, baby."

"I know you won't."

She opened her arms and was about to hug him when Turner stopped her. "There's something else you need to know." He figured he might as well tell her the whole story. Her own safety depended on Candy knowing what the Spiveys were capable of. And besides, she'd trusted Turner with her ugliest secrets. Now it was his turn.

"The night Junie crashed her car and was killed, she'd just left Bobby Ray's place. Another teacher told me she'd planned to stop by on her way out of town. She didn't tell me because she knew I didn't want her going out there."

"Why didn't she tell you?"

Turner shook his head. He grabbed Candy's hand in his and concentrated on the lovely sight. He needed it to ground him while he got the rest of it out. "I told her never to go out there. Spivey was an ignorant and violent man and a racist on top of it all. But she went anyway."

Candy squeezed his hand. "What are you saying?"

Turner looked up into her intelligent, serious blue eyes. "I have never been able to prove anything, but my gut instinct has always told me that Bobby Ray had something to do with her accident."

"Oh, my God, Turner."

He nodded. "Junie was three months pregnant. I've never told anyone that. Not even my mother and brother know. And I had her autopsy sealed so no one ever would."

There. He'd said it. He waited for the gut-wrenching pain to slam into him, the way it always did. But something different happened this time. He felt Candy's soft lips on his cheek, and she pulled his head down to her breast. She held him there, breathing softly, saying nothing for a very long time. Eventually, she released him and looked deeply into his eyes.

"I am so sorry you suffered like that, Turner. I wish there was something I could do to take the pain away."

He nodded. He even felt himself smile just a little. "You just did," he said. "And the single best thing you can do to help me now is to take these people seriously. Take your own safety seriously until we get them in custody. Will you do that for me?"

"I will."

He kissed her then, and felt her surrender to him in trust and affection. It was an honor to have the love of such a wonderful woman. It was his solemn responsibility to keep her safe.

Never again would he fail to keep his woman safe.

Turner excused himself to make a few calls. The first one was to Reggie.

"What's up, little brother?" Reggie said with a hearty chuckle. "How's the new roommate working out? She paying her rent on time, man?"

"I need your help."

His brother went silent for a moment, clearly catching on that this was no time to joke. "Anything you need. You know that."

"Good. I need you to leave work and come over here.

As soon as you can. Just stay in the house with Candy until I get back. No questions. I need you, man."

"On my way."

The next few days went by without incident. Turner worked late, and since Reggie had apparently been assigned as her after-hours bodyguard, he and Candy got to know each other well. They watched movies, played Uno, and Reggie filled Candy in on what Turner had been through when Junie died. It broke her heart to learn he'd responded to the scene of the accident and was there to see his own wife pronounced dead. But she was grateful that Reggie and Rosemary had been there to see Turner through the worst of it, and she told Reggie so.

"My brother deserves a little happiness in his life," Reggie said, an unspoken question in his eyes.

"I know he does," Candy said.

On Thursday evening, as Reggie sprawled out on the couch watching the news and Candy finished the dinner dishes, she had an epiphany. The very same day Turner lost his wife and unborn child, Candy closed on her first million-dollar real estate deal and marched out with her big wad of cash to buy Sophie, now stashed in Turner's wall safe.

Why hadn't she realized this before? *The same day!* She had to stop what she was doing and take a couple of deep breaths. Right then and there, Candy made a promise to herself: whatever she decided to use Sophie for in the future would be in honor of Junie and the baby, if only in her heart. It would be something good and honorable. Something real. It would be a symbol of something more than vanity or material wealth.

On Friday evening, when Candy had to stay at Lenny's late to finish the engagement party cupcakes, she put Reggie in charge of the sprinkles.

"I've never done this before," he said proudly, distributing the tiny sugar crystals with his giant fingers.

"You'd never know," Candy assured him. "You're a natural."

On Saturday afternoon, Candy and Turner arrived at the lake a good hour before the party was set to start. They pulled the SUV close to the front porch to unload the cupcakes and saw that preparations were almost complete. The band was setting up on the stage. The front lawn was dotted with guest seating, potted plants and flower arrangements, and serving tables. Balloons and streamers were hung on the trees, the porch, and along the dock.

"Need some help with that?"

Together, Candy and Turner looked up to see a man in an eye patch standing near Tater Wayne's infamous hog-shaped portable barbecue. Candy decided he even looked a little like Tater Wayne. He could have been Tater Wayne's well-groomed cousin, if he'd had one of those.

She and Turner reached the same shocked conclusion at exactly the same time. *"Tater Wayne?"* they shouted.

"Haven't seen ya'll in a while. How's it goin'?" Tater removed the tray of cupcakes from Candy's hands and began to carry it into the house.

Turner followed with another tray, wiggling his eyebrows at Candy over his shoulder.

"Oh, my *'effin'* God," Candy said under her breath. Just then Cheri came out the door and headed down the porch steps to lend a hand. Candy stared at her with giant eyes.

"Yeah, I know," she whispered. "Stay cool. I'll tell you what I know a little later, but I don't want Tater to feel self-conscious."

"But—"

"I know. I know. Viv about had a coronary when she saw him, and made such a big deal that he went home real upset. He didn't even finish his usual chores. I don't think he wants the attention."

"But he's so—"

Cheri elbowed her just as Tater and Turner returned for more. Cheri and Candy handed them each a tray.

"The cupcakes look really beautiful," Cheri said to Candy, as they waited for the men to get back inside. The second they were out of earshot, Candy grabbed Cheri's hand.

"His teeth are perfect," she whispered.

"Yeah. A full set of implants. He got them done in Atlanta."

Candy gasped. "But that kind of thing costs a fortune! How the hell did he—" Candy managed to shut her mouth just in time. "Here you go, Tater," she said, handing him the last tray. "That's all of them. Thanks for your help."

"No problem," he said, flashing her a Brad Pittesque grin. That's when Candy noticed a couple other things that were different about her lifelong buddy. He'd had his blond hair cut and styled—professionally— and he was sporting a stylish goatee that set off his new smile. He was wearing a pair of nice jeans, clean sneakers, and a new shirt, with an actual collar. Plus, there was the eye patch.

"I think I'm gonna faint," Candy managed, once Tater was back in the house. "But what's with the pirate patch?"

"He had surgery, apparently. It was just the first round, and Viv says he'll be wearing one until his eye is all the way fixed."

Candy was stunned, but when her friend came back out she gave him a big hug, immediately noting that he was wearing an expensive cologne. The overall effect was mind-boggling. "You look really great, Tater."

"Well, now. Thank you. You do, too." And with that, Tater went back to his hog-shaped barbecue barrel to stoke the coals and check on the marinade.

"Could you lend me a hand in the kitchen?" Cheri put her arm around Candy's waist and directed her up the front steps, giving her a sideways glance.

Candy giggled, noticing the sly smile on Cheri's face. "Well, don't you look cute as a June bug today?" She touched the hem of Cheri's flirty, ivory lace sundress. "Very pretty."

"Thanks," Cheri said, her smile not mellowing. "It's a big day for me, you know."

"It certainly is." Candy slipped her arm around her best friend's shoulders and squeezed. "I couldn't be happier for you and J.J.—well, I can't really say that since I'll be even happier on your actual wedding day, but today is a close second."

"Ha!" Cheri slipped out of Candy's grip and twirled

around in the living room, her arms out at her sides, her frilly dress translucent in the afternoon light. For a moment, Candy had a flashback to when they were little girls, with little-girl dreams.

It seemed some of them were coming true—for both of them.

The two friends laughed and chatted while putting together the plates and napkins, and Candy told Cheri about her father's building on Main Street. After Cheri had regained her ability to speak, she had a thousand questions, most of which Candy had no answer for. When she asked Cheri to go on a walk-through of the building with Jacinta's lawyer on Monday, Cheri enthusiastically agreed.

They were almost done assembling the veggie tray when Cheri suddenly placed her hand over Candy's, which happened to be full of radishes. The little purple balls went rolling all over the wooden kitchen table and onto the floor.

"Is it wonderful?" she asked Candy. "Are you and Turner happy?"

Candy nodded, overcome with a rush of emotions she wasn't sure she could contain. She felt foolish holding back tears like she was, just because her best friend had asked her if she was happy, but the answer wasn't simple. She was happier than she'd ever been in her life. She was deeply in love and loved in return for the first time. And she was scared to death about making the wrong decision about her life.

"Oh, Lord-ee!" Cheri opened her arms and hugged Candy close. "It's going to be okay, girl."

Candy nodded but pushed herself away. "I would just die if I got mascara all over that white dress," she explained.

They laughed, but Cheri patted Candy on the arm. "Nobody is rushing you, you know," she said, gentleness in her voice. "You just do what you think is best for you when you're good and ready to do it. I believe that you'll wake up one day and you'll know what the right thing to do is. Sometimes, it's that simple."

Candy smiled at her friend. "It was that way for you, wasn't it?"

"Oh, yeah."

"How did you know, Cheri?"

Her friend glanced out onto the lawn, where J.J. was chatting it up with Turner and Tater Wayne. "When I looked at that man and realized nothing made any sense in my life without him."

Candy gasped.

Guests began arriving. Everyone was casually dressed and brought a hot dish or drinks. The beer keg was tapped and flowing. The band—featuring one of the *Bugle* reporters on banjo and lead vocals—was playing everything from Merle Haggard to Metallica, and some people were dancing, some were swimming, some were just sittin' and drinkin'.

The guest list was a real cross-section of Bigler society. There was practically everyone from the paper, of course, including Gladys Harbison, who hadn't spoken to Candy since her nighttime getaway.

"Seems you've landed on your feet just fine," Gladys told Candy, eyeing Turner up and down as if he were a Porterhouse steak in the butcher's window.

"I have. Thanks. And again, I appreciate you letting me stay with you for a bit."

Gladys shrugged. "I wish I could say you were the first person to run away from my place in the middle of the night, but you weren't. First woman, though." And with that she wandered off, which allowed Candy to see the strap of one of her bras peeking out from Gladys's shirt.

Turner's mother and brother arrived soon after, and Candy was greeted warmly by Reggie, who gave her a big hug, and introduced her to his eleven-year-old son, Marlon. Rosemary kissed Candy's cheek and told her how good it was to see her and asked if her son was behaving himself.

"Of course he is," Candy said. "He's the sheriff."

That made her laugh.

When Jacinta arrived with Hugo in tow, Candy and Turner were pleased to watch their mothers greet each other warmly and break out into laughter. They had a good idea what was so funny.

When it seemed that just about everyone who was coming was there, Candy blinked in surprise to see the female DEA agent wander onto the lawn. Candy poked Turner in the side and nodded in the woman's direction.

"O'Connor? What the—"

J.J. put his arm around Turner. "Like I said, I knew she was in town so I invited her."

"That's great," Turner said noncommittally. He supposed every party needed a mystery guest.

O'Connor grabbed a beer and strolled over to where J.J., Turner, and Candy stood. They made small talk for a while, Candy admiring O'Connor's idea of "casual" attire—a pair of dress slacks with a sharply pressed seam, a starched cotton blouse, four-inch heels, and full makeup. She looked the part—of an elegant visitor from out of town.

While O'Connor had been chatting, she'd been carefully observing her fellow partygoers. Candy assumed it was part of her training—a hyperawareness of her surroundings. But suddenly she froze. Stood taller. Sniffed the air.

Candy looked down to find that O'Connor's hand had landed on her forearm.

"That man," she said to Candy.

Candy followed to where O'Connor had nodded. "That man? The one by the barbecue?"

O'Connor nodded. "Yes. Him. Do I know him?"

Candy bit her lip, trying not to laugh at the idea that Tater and this hardcore DEA agent might have met socially. "Uh, I doubt it."

"He reminds me of someone." O'Connor started to tug at Candy. "Introduce me. Please. I'd appreciate it."

Candy looked back over her shoulder to Turner, who just shrugged.

Once they reached the stainless steel hog, Candy did her duty. "Kelly O'Connor, this is my lifelong friend T*ayyy*—" She stopped herself. Maybe part of Tater's problem had always been his nickname. The man deserved to be introduced to a beautiful woman by his actual name. "This is Thomas Wayne. Thomas, this is Kelly, a colleague of Turner's."

"Nice to meet you," O'Connor said.

Tater held out a perfectly manicured hand. "The

pleasure is all mine," he said, bringing the agent's fingers to his lips.

Candy wandered away, making sure O'Connor didn't see her shocked expression. She stopped to chat with Cheri's aunt Viv and granddaddy Garland for a moment and then returned to J.J. and Turner, catching the very end of their conversation.

"It's that good?" J.J. asked.

"If it got any better I'd have to hire someone to help me enjoy it," was Turner's answer.

J.J. shook his head. "Damn. You're not going to be obnoxious about this, are you?"

"Hey, you asked."

"I guess I did."

After J.J. went off in search of Cheri, Candy made her presence known by tapping Turner on his back. He spun around and his face immediately filled with delight. Candy felt herself pulled tight and kissed with a sense of purpose.

"What was that all about?" she asked.

"Nothing you don't already know, darlin,' " he said.

The band finished a song and suddenly the air filled with the sound of someone banging on a microphone.

"Is this contraption on?" Garland said, loud enough to send the birds scattering. Everyone laughed. "Oh, well, now, pardon the interruption, folks, but we have a little business we'd like to attend to. On each table ya'll will find some fancy little plastic champagne glasses and a couple bottles of bubbly, so please serve yourself and get situated."

"Tell them where to stand!" Viv screamed from across the yard.

Garland rolled his eyes. "I'm gettin' to it, Vivienne. Anyway, folks, we'd like to ask everyone to gather around the lake edge, if you don't mind. We're gonna do this at the end of the dock."

"I'll get us our drinks," Turner said. "Be right back." When he returned, he had Garland with him.

"Ya'll have special duties today," Garland whispered, a glint in his eye. "You two come with me."

The crowd had started to assemble near the water's edge, and parted when Garland walked toward the dock. "Leave a little opening, if you don't mind," he said to everyone, waving his long arms around. Turner and Candy followed him.

"What's all this?" Turner asked Candy.

And that's when she saw J.J. standing at the end of the dock, now wearing a jacket and a tie, with his hands folded nervously in front of his body.

"Oh, my God," she whispered.

Garland immediately shushed her.

Turner laughed. "Oh, hell. Is this what I think it is?"

"Shh!" Garland said again.

Candy stood where Garland directed her, off to his right, and Turner took his place next to J.J.

"Thank you," was all J.J. had time to say to his best friend.

Garland tapped on the portable microphone. "Friends and family, we are gathered here together for the surprise wedding of Jefferson Jackson Decourcy and Cherise Nancy Newberry!"

About half of the hundred or so guests gathered around began hooting and hollering. The other half were speechless.

"All right. Pull yourselves together. J.J. and Cheri said the most important thing to them was having everyone together and they didn't want much of a fuss made over the wedding details, so here it is, folks—for those of you a little slower than the norm—what I'm telling ya'll is this is not the engagement party. *This is the actual wedding.* And since I've been working as a part-time magistrate since retiring as publisher of the *Bugle,* I am hereby authorized to perform this ceremony." Garland paused and pointed to the band. "Hit it, boys!"

The band immediately began playing the wedding march and Candy saw Cheri begin her walk, first down the front porch steps, then across the lawn, and down the dock. She looked beautiful and happy as she carried the simple bouquet of wildflowers Candy had seen displayed in a pitcher on the kitchen table just moments before. It was all so lovely and simple that Candy started to cry.

It was a short ceremony. J.J. and Cheri exchanged sweet and loving vows and kissed each other with gusto. Then J.J. grabbed the microphone from Garland and thanked everyone for being good sports and asked anyone who felt compelled to give a wedding gift to donate to a charity of their choice.

Then everyone toasted the couple. Cheri and J.J. strolled down the dock as husband and wife, followed by Garland, then Candy and Turner, holding hands at the rear of the procession.

The party continued on as it had begun, even though everyone now thought of it as a wedding reception. O'Connor barely left Tater's side the whole evening, helping him serve up ribs and chicken and dancing with him when the stars came out. The cupcakes were a hit. Cheri and Candy spent a few quiet moments on the porch steps together, laughing and crying.

"I should be mad at you," Candy told her.

"Why?"

"Because—I had, like, two seconds to relish the fact that I'd been asked to be your maid of honor!"

"But you're not mad, right?"

"How could I be?" Candy asked. "It was perfect. It was you and J.J. and it was just as it should have been."

Turner and Candy danced, too, and it felt wonderful to be whirling around the lawn in the middle of dozens of other couples. Just before Turner's family left, Rosemary pulled Turner and Candy aside, embracing them both.

"You make a fine and dignified couple," she told them. "If you choose each other from the heart then that's all that matters. I followed my heart when the whole world told me I was wrong, and I never regretted it for a second."

Candy had barely recovered from that touching encounter with Rosemary, when the crowd became noticeably quieter. It probably didn't help matters that the band was packing up for the night and there was nothing to draw people's attention away from Tanyalee's entrance.

"Oh, shee-it," Turner whispered.

She walked with her head held high, wearing a simple peach-blush summer dress and matching heels, carrying a beautifully wrapped gift. She marched right over to her sister and her former husband, and politely hugged them both.

Anyone who lingered in the front yard got to hear every word that was exchanged.

"Tanyalee!" Cheri said. "When did you get home?"

"This afternoon. I'm staying with Viv until I find a job and a place."

Candy felt for the girl.

"I just wanted to wish you both well," Tanyalee said. There appeared to be no snarkiness whatsoever in her tone of voice. "I am sure you'll have many years of happiness together. Congratulations."

With that, Tanyalee placed her gift on a table and serenely walked back through the yard to Viv's pimp-mobile and drove away.

"I sure hope that package isn't ticking," Turner said.

Candy shook her head slowly. "It's been one hell of a day, hasn't it?"

Turner smiled at her. "The night is young, Candy Pants."

Chapter 23

Today was the big day. Today would be the day that changed the order of everything. Today, Gerrall would finally show the world that he was a man to be respected and admired. And yes, feared.

The first stop was Cherokee Pines and the Fat Man. All it took was a quick phone call and the pig was in the parking lot in ten seconds. It was amazing how fast a big fat slob could move when he thought money was involved.

The hardest part was sticking the needle through all the fat on his ass, then making sure that when he fell he fell onto the backseat, because there was no way he could lift that guy or wrestle him while he was awake.

Gerrall might be a man to be admired, but even he had limits on what he could do.

Next, he'd go pick up Candy. That should be a snap. And then they'd head out to Preston Valley, where he'd take out his daddy and the Fat Man at the same time, get his hands on every dime he could find, and take Candy out of Bigler, forever.

*   *   *

LeRoy Bellfleur, Esquire, stood in front of the Main Street office building and shifted his significant weight impatiently from foot to foot, tapping on his smartphone. He appeared irritated.

"But we're not even late," Candy whispered to Cheri as they approached the front door.

"Lawyers always act like that," Cheri reminded her.

Mr. Bellfleur looked up and smiled. "Ah!" he said, shoving his phone in the front pocket of his suit trousers. "I was just about to call you."

Candy and Cheri shook the attorney's hand and exchanged pleasantries. "Marvelous to see you, ladies. Shall we?" Mr. Bellfleur used two keys to unlock the thick oak door, and pushed it open. "Now, ya'll watch your step. The power's not on, mind you, but there should be plenty of natural light. There's nothing to trip over, since the place has been cleaned to within an inch of its life."

Candy felt her mouth fall open in shock.

"My God," Cheri whispered.

Slowly, Candy stepped inside. She scanned the vast and empty street-level space, trying to sort out what she was seeing. For as long as she'd been alive, this place had been chopped up into a maze of tiny rooms—a small reception area, a half dozen cramped offices, an employee break room, a storage area, and her father's larger suite. The walls had always been covered with that disgusting brown paneling and the floors with that disgusting high-traffic carpeting. But now . . .

"It doesn't even look like the same place," Cheri said.

Candy could only stare in awe. She looked around

again, just to make sure she wasn't seeing things. No. It was real. Obviously, everything had been ripped out. Nothing was left but bare brick walls, newly refinished wood floors, and the huge picture window from which light now poured.

Candy turned her wide-eyed gaze toward Mr. Bellfleur. He chuckled. "Your mama said you'd be surprised."

"What the . . . ?"

"After your daddy died, Jacinta had this place gutted—and I mean *gut*-ted. Took out every sink and commode and every light fixture and doorknob in the place. She worked with an architect from Asheville and had space for a commercial kitchen roughed in in that area back there . . ."—he gestured to his left—"and then she put in new copper plumbing throughout the building, along with new wiring, wireless Internet, cable, heating, and air-conditioning, you name it. She said she didn't want anything left standing but the brick. And then she just left the place like this—empty as a tomb. Said she wanted it to stay like this."

"Whoa," Cheri whispered.

Candy had trouble breathing.

Mr. Bellfleur shrugged. "It's funny what people do when they're deep in the grieving process."

Candy couldn't help it. She snorted with laughter, and then had to attempt to cover it up with a fake sneeze.

"Bless you," the lawyer said.

When Cheri started asking questions, Candy was grateful, since she hadn't managed to regain her ability to speak. "So how soon after her husband died did Jacinta have all this done?" Cheri asked.

"Within a few months."

Cheri gasped. "So this place has been sitting here empty for years? Like *this*?"

"Yes." He directed his answer to Candy. "Your mother never really said, but I assumed she wanted it ready for you, in case you ever came home."

"Ready?" Candy asked. "Ready for what?"

Mr. Bellfleur shrugged. "She never said outright and I was kind of baffled myself. But it didn't take me long to put two and two together once you started working at Lenny's."

Suddenly, it all began to make sense.

"Now, I'd have to say your lemon chiffon cake is my favorite, but I'm also partial to your applesauce cake." A wistful smile appeared on Mr. Bellfleur's wide face. "I haven't tasted a decent applesauce cake since my mother passed, God rest her soul. And mark my words— you're going to make a mint with this place, especially if you attract some of the tourists who wander through on the way to the Smokeys."

"This is your bakery!" Cheri blurted, grabbing onto Candy's forearm. "Oh, my God! This is your *bakery*!"

Candy pulled away and walked into the center of the room. She needed space to think and breathe. She needed a minute to clear her head, to put the pieces together in her mind.

Her father had died and left her an ugly building she wasn't allowed to sell, fine. But then her mother had fixed it up in the hopes that one day Candy would come home to Bigler, claim her inheritance, and open a bakery? What the—

"Shall we take the grand tour?" Mr. Bellfleur gestured

for the women to follow him. Candy wouldn't have been able to move if Cheri hadn't grabbed her wrist and dragged her along. "Two thousand square feet on the main floor, front, rear, and side entrances, as I'm sure you recall, plus the small parking lot in the back." He wiggled an eyebrow. "Jacinta just had it repaved last week!"

"That's fabulous!" Cheri said.

Candy's palms started to sweat. She wasn't going to fall for Jacinta's trap. This wasn't what she'd envisioned for herself. She glanced over her shoulder, out the picture window and to Main Street beyond. Main Street would take her to Highway 25, which would get her to I-40, which would . . .

Her cell phone rang. It was Turner. *Crap!* She was supposed to have called him as soon as she and Cheri met up with the lawyer. Now that the task force was ready to move in at any moment, Turner had become positively paranoid about her safety, as though he were certain Gerrall Spivey would come after her. Candy sighed and answered the phone.

"I'm fine," she said. "Can I call you when I get back to Lenny's?"

Turner didn't reply immediately, and Candy knew he was pissed. "Are you're sure you're fine?" he asked. "Because you don't sound fine."

Candy rolled her eyes, and immediately realized she'd never rolled her eyes at Turner before. Why was she rolling her eyes? He was just worried about her. He had his reasons. She'd promised she'd call and she didn't. But maybe she didn't *want* to be worried about! Maybe she didn't want to be *reporting in* as if she were on probation! Maybe she wasn't ready for all this.

A bakery? A boyfriend? In *Bigler*? What the hell was she doing?

Her eyes darted to the window again.

"I'll call you back," she said, hanging up on Turner and powering off her phone.

"Is everything all right?" Cheri asked, her lips pulled tight.

"Of course," Candy said, then turned her attention to Mr. Bellfleur. "Let's get this over with."

"Well, all right." He looked offended. "As I was saying, the lot has been repaved. Would you like to see it?"

"Not particularly." Candy started to feel a little nauseated. Overheated.

"At any rate, your mother has kept up with the property taxes and all exterior maintenance required by the city's historic district commission," Mr. Bellfleur continued. "Did you have a date when you'd like to take possession?"

Candy froze. Her ears buzzed. She began to feel seriously dizzy.

Turner. What about Turner? What would happen when she left? Oh, God, it would kill him.

She'd made such a horrible mistake.

"Miss Carmichael?" That was Mr. Bellfleur.

"Seriously, are you okay?" That was Cheri.

"Hold up." Candy backed away, her hands held out in front of her. She stopped only when she bumped into the far wall. "Mr. Bellfleur, are you absolutely sure there's no way I can sell this building? Because I most definitely want to sell it. I've researched the comps and I know it's got to be worth over a hundred grand totally restored like this."

The attorney frowned. "I am sorry, Miss Carmichael, but according to the terms of your father's will that will not be an option for you. I thought you understood that."

"But he can't really do that, can he? He can't leave me an asset and then tell me what to do with it, right?" She was pretty sure she had just broken out into a cold sweat.

"Certainly he can," the lawyer said with a shrug. "Your father had a valid will, and those were his wishes. Depending on the whim of the deceased, any number of restrictions can be placed on inherited real property."

"And I couldn't fight it in probate court?"

Mr. Bellfleur smiled at her like she was a slow child.

"Sure you could. It would likely require several years and a boatload of cash to get a judge to tell you the will stands, but that's certainly within your rights."

Cheri chuckled. "Good ole Jonesy wants to run the show even from six feet under, doesn't he?"

Mr. Bellfleur smiled, but said nothing. No need to elaborate, Candy figured, since being her father's lawyer probably wasn't much better than being his daughter.

Suddenly, she saw a flash of red. Red cake. Running down the wall.

"Shall we look at the upper floors?" he asked. "They aren't finished, so don't get your hopes up."

Candy barely paid attention while he gave her the tour. It was just two big empty lofts. So what? She suddenly found it difficult to breathe.

Mercifully, the ordeal was over in about fifteen minutes, and the attorney excused himself to answer a few calls. He told the women he would meet them out front. "No rush. Take your time."

Cheri and Candy waited until they heard him make it down the two flights of steps and open and close the front door. Candy peered out the window to ensure Mr. Bellfleur was truly out on the sidewalk, then turned to face her friend.

"What the hell?" she said, waving her arms around the huge second floor. "I feel like I'm in an episode of *The Twilight Zone!*"

Cheri smiled brightly. "It's pretty amazing, isn't it?"

"Amazing? It's downright *bizarre!* I don't know who to be angrier with—my father or my mother!"

Cheri cocked her head and frowned. "But Jacinta turned lemons into lemonade for you. This place would have been an albatross around your neck, but she transformed it into exactly what you need! She—"

"Who says it's what I need?" Candy felt even dizzier than she had downstairs. "It's not Jacinta's place to tell me what I need!" Her eyes began to sting with tears. "*I* don't even know what I need, Cheri! And now everybody expects me to just start baking cakes and shit and live in Bigler for the rest of my life as Mrs. Halliday? Is that it? Well, I won't do it! I won't let anyone manipulate me!"

Cheri's eyes went big. She took a cautious step toward Candy. "Calm down."

"No! I'm not going to calm down! Oh, my God, this has been such a disaster! I've only been back here a month and I've managed to fuck everything up!" She spun around in a circle and clenched her eyes shut. Her heart was pounding.

"What are you talking about, girl?" Candy felt Cheri's soft touch on her shoulder. "You haven't fucked anything up. You are in love with a wonderful man who loves you back. You have options available to you that you never dreamed were possible. You've rediscovered your talent for baking. You've reconnected with Jacinta. It's a lot to think about, I realize, but—"

"I can't listen to this right now. I'm sorry. I'll be fine, but I just need some space to think this through." Candy gave her best friend a quick hug and tried her best to smile. "Listen, thank you for coming with me. I've got to get back to work."

Candy hustled Cheri downstairs and outside, then told Mr. Bellfleur she'd be in touch. She parted ways with Cheri at Main and Fourth, where Cheri ducked into the *Bugle* building and Candy continued another block to Lenny's.

"Are you sure you're going to be okay?" Cheri hollered down the sidewalk.

"I'm better already!" Candy called back with a wave and a fake smile.

Of course her friend meant well, Candy thought, continuing to walk, but she also had an ulterior motive—she wanted Candy to stay in Bigler. It seemed everyone did. Cheri, Jacinta, Turner . . .

But what did *she* want?

What *did* she want?

What the *hell* did she want?

Rosemary's words hit her hard: *"If you choose from the heart, then that's all that matters."*

Well, that was the problem, obviously. Candy didn't know how a person went about doing that.

"Umph."

A hand had just slapped over her mouth and an arm was squeezing around her waist, and before her brain could begin to process what had just happened, Candy was dragged into the alley behind Lenny's and shoved into the passenger seat of a car she didn't recognize.

She tried to scream. She twisted violently. She tried to free her arm to hit whoever had grabbed her. That's when she stared right into Gerrall Spivey's icy blue eyes and froze. He smiled at her. He released his grip on her waist, but immediately she heard the heavy click of the gun that he pressed into her temple.

Chapter 24

"Drive."

Candy's hands shook so badly she could barely control the wheel. She didn't know what frightened her most—the gun that was now shoved into her side, the psycho glint in Gerrall's eye, or what she'd just seen in the rearview mirror—Wainright Miller hog-tied in the backseat, screaming so violently behind his gag that his face was purple and the tendons in his neck looked like they were about to pop.

Candy was so scared that she didn't even find it particularly interesting that Gerrall was dressed like a girl.

"Don't look at him," Gerrall snapped, nodding his blond wig in Miller's direction. "He's not worth it. He's a piece of shit and I'm going to love seeing him squeal like a pig when I take him out in the field and shoot him."

Miller's muffled screams filled the car. His eyes pleaded for Candy to help him.

Gerrall smiled at her. "You like my disguise? Here we are, just two girls out for a drive. Pure genius, huh?"

Candy blinked rapidly in an attempt to see through her tears. Her mind was checking off escape options so quickly she couldn't keep them straight.

She could try to crash the car and hope Gerrall wouldn't shoot her, but she wasn't wearing a seat belt and neither was Miller. She could try to wrestle the gun from Gerrall and somehow drive at the same time. Or she could try to distract Gerrall and stick her fingers in his eyes. None of these seemed like good bets.

Her cell phone! She could try to speed dial Turner without Gerrall noticing. But the phone was shoved down in her front pocket. And it was turned off.

Oh, God, *why* had she turned off her phone like that? What had she done? Ten minutes ago she had a wonderful man's love, a best friend's support, and her mother's gift from the heart. And how had she responded to all that good fortune? She'd hung up on Turner, got all snarky with Cheri, and panicked at the thought of accepting her mother's help. Ten minutes ago, she wanted to run away from all of it.

She would give anything to have the last ten minutes of her life back.

"If you slow down any more I'll shoot you. Pay attention." Gerrall rammed the gun against her ribs.

"Okay, okay." Candy's chest was so tight with anxiety that she was having trouble getting enough air. "Where are we going?" Maybe if she kept him talking she'd get a little more time to figure something out.

"Preston Valley. No more questions. Just shut up and drive. Where's your cell phone?"

"I don't think I have it with me."

Gerrall laughed and shoved the gun so hard into her

ribs that she gasped. "You are such a lying bitch," he snarled, leaning close enough that the wig tickled the side of her face. "But that's old news, ain't it, Candy Carmichael?"

Gerrall came even closer and sniffed her neck and hair. She thought she might throw up.

"Turn right at the next light," Gerrall snapped, suddenly angry. Candy knew she had to do a better job of hiding her revulsion if she were going to survive. She tried to smile at him.

"It's too late for that shit, Candy. You'll be driving on Preston Road until I tell you to turn, about five miles more. Now, I'm going to find your phone."

Candy stifled a whimper as Gerrall's hands roamed over the front of her T-shirt and down across the zipper of her jeans. It took him about ten seconds to locate the phone and jam his hand down into her pocket. With the gun still poking into her side, he turned the phone on, and laughed.

"Ain't you popular! You have eleven missed calls, all from lover boy Halliday. You think he might be worried about you? Oh, I bet he has no idea how worried he should be, since the cops around here are dumb as goats. Wanna listen to his messages?"

No! Candy's whole body stiffened. It was bad enough that she'd royally screwed up her own life, but if Turner had mentioned the task force in any of those voice mails, Gerrall would warn his father, and the drug dealers would clear out, or worse still, would be lying in wait for the task force. People would be killed. It would all be her fault.

She didn't even pause to think. Simultaneously, Candy slapped her left hand down on the driver's side window button and snatched the phone from Gerrall with her right. She threw it out of the car and grabbed the wheel, bracing herself for the sound of the gun.

Instead she felt a stinging slap to the side of her head, followed by the press of the gun barrel into her temple again.

"Bitch!" Gerrall screamed, jabbing at her head with the gun. "You're going to *make* me shoot you! You *want* to be shot, don't you?"

"Please, no. Don't shoot anyone. Just listen to me." Her thoughts raced. She could die without ever seeing Turner again, or hearing his voice. She might never see Cheri again. Or J.J. Or Jacinta. Or Lenny. Or Hugo. Or Tater Wayne. Or Reggie and Rosemary. Viv. Garland. Tanyalee. Gladys, even.

And she found it fascinating that at this moment, when it could very well be over for her, she didn't care about the five-bedroom stucco with the Gulf of Mexico views or the Infiniti or her bank balance or the Birkin bags and the Louboutin platform pumps and the spa visits.

None of that meant anything. She knew what she wanted now.

What had Cheri said just before her wedding? *"One day you'll wake up and know what to do—it's that simple."*

Well, this must be that day, Candy thought. And *dammit,* she wasn't going to die now, not after she'd just woken up!

"Can we pull over and just talk?" she asked Gerrall. "You don't have to do this. I won't press charges. Just let us go and—"

Gerrall's loud burst of laughter cut her off. "You think I'm just some stupid country boy, don't you? Well, you're wrong about that, Miss Hot Ass. You have no idea who you're dealing with. See, you could have had everything if you'd just given me a chance, but no, you were too good for me. Is that it?"

The gun pressed harder against her head. She saw Miller in the backseat, still purple and sweaty and straining against his gag.

Suddenly she found herself taking a turn a little too fast and hit the brakes. Something was wrong. She heard a metal-on-metal squealing sound and the car wasn't slowing as it should. She didn't know if she could handle the curve at this speed.

Oh, God. She'd tried her best. She really had. But she couldn't keep it together anymore. As she wrestled with the wheel, she began to cry.

"Everything's in place, Sheriff. We're ready to roll. We're waiting for your word."

Turner stared at his phone, anger and fear roiling around in his gut. About twenty minutes earlier, she'd hung up on him. He'd called six times since and she hadn't answered or called back, which meant she'd either turned off her phone or was intentionally making him sweat. None of those things were like her. Candy knew that her safety was everything to him. She'd said she understood. She *promised* him.

O'Connor cleared her throat, which made Turner

glance up from his phone. That's when he noticed that the rest of the task force had exited the conference room. When had that happened?

"Dante's safely out," O'Connor told him, and by the look on her face he imagined it was not the first time she was giving him this bit of news. "He's got the little girl and they're clear. We can move."

Turner blinked at her. "I can't find Candy," was all he could say.

Turner was halfway down the hallway when Bitsy yelled out for him. "Sheriff! You better take this call!"

"I can't," he shouted, pulling his cap down tight and heading for the back door. He'd given the order—the bust was playing out at that very moment. And he was fairly certain that Gerall had Candy. Cheri said they'd parted ways twenty-five minutes earlier and Lenny said she hadn't returned to her shift at the diner but her car was still in the lot. Sure, there was a slight chance Candy might be off by herself sulking, as Cheri suggested, but Turner knew in his bones that it was something far worse than a temper tantrum.

"You have to, Sheriff! Please!"

"Transfer it to my cell, Bitsy."

He was in the SUV when his cell rang.

"Halliday," he said.

"Sheriff, this is Louellen Lukins over at Cherokee Pines, Waintright Miller's secretary. I thought you should know we think something might have happened to Mr. Miller."

Turner flipped on his lights and his siren. He could see the federal agents speeding away just up ahead, traffic moving to the side of the road in their wake. He hit the gas even harder.

The hairs stood up on the back of Turner's neck. "Go on."

"Well, it just don't make sense, is all. Mr. Miller was waiting for the tow truck to come get his car, because the brakes were shot to hell and it wasn't safe to drive. But he got a call a few minutes later, told me he'd be right back, but never did. Then about fifteen minutes later the tow truck driver showed up and was pissed because he couldn't find the car, so's I went with him out back and found Mr. Miller's car gone but his cell phone and wallet tossed on the asphalt, money and credit cards still in there. I called Bitsy right away."

Turner thanked Louellen for her quick thinking and within seconds had an all-points bulletin out for Miller's blue 2009 Buick Lucerne—with shot-to-hell brakes.

"You're trying to kill us!" Gerrall screamed.

"No!" Candy spoke as loud as she could through the panicked sobs. "There's something wrong with the brakes! I swear to God!" Miller's wailing suddenly became louder than ever, and Candy glanced in the rear-view mirror to see him furiously nodding and screeching into his gag. She made eye contact with him for a split second, still fighting to keep control of the car.

"Is there something wrong with the brakes?" she called out.

Miller nodded violently.

"Oh, shee-it," she said.

Gerrall spun around in the seat, the gun still against

Candy's skull. "You fucker!" he screamed at Miller. "I should blow your brains out right now!"

The gun had suddenly become her second most pressing concern. She couldn't find the car's emergency brake, and unfortunately she had been on a steady decline for many long seconds, and the car continued to speed up. She was up to sixty-five miles per hour, a good twenty over the posted speed limit. The only good news was that as she'd groped around she'd located her seat belt, pulled it over her lap, and snapped it. When she spotted the hill up ahead she laughed with joy. It would be her salvation. If she could only make it . . .

"Turn now!" Gerrall screamed.

"What?"

"There! At the flag! Now!" He started waving the gun around and grabbed the steering wheel.

It was a blur. Candy knew she hit something when Gerrall tugged at the steering wheel but hadn't had time to see what it was. The airbag had deployed and the car kept rolling. She couldn't see. She knew Miller had been tossed around in the back. She'd also heard Gerrall scream and slam into the dashboard, but she had no idea how badly either were hurt because she didn't have time to look. The car kept moving downhill. Peering over the airbag, she saw a trailer with men standing around out front. She thought she heard gunshots. Then there was another loud *bang*!

Then, only darkness.

Turner drove, his knuckles white on the wheel, one second following the next, one mile after another, as the bottom fell out of his soul.

He knew this feeling. It was the feeling he promised himself he'd never have again as long as he drew breath. Something horrible had happened to the woman he loved, and he was too late to stop it. Though he was coordinating this response and his radio was crackling with nonstop task force chatter, he felt split in two. One half of him was duty. The other half was Candy. And he knew he had only seconds left before he no longer gave a fuck about duty.

She was still missing. All of his day shift deputies were searching for her, along with everyone at the *Bugle* and half the general population of Bigler. Still nothing. No accident reports. No sightings. With each second that went by, Turner grew more certain that Gerrall had her, and probably Miller, as well. It made perfect sense. Miller had fired him. Candy had turned him down. They had to pay.

Turner radioed the task force one last reminder of how this would play out—half of the team would secure the meth lab while the other half would take the trailer, outbuildings, and property. If Miller's car was spotted on the compound, they were to put Candy's and Miller's safety as priority one. If not, it was standard evidence protection protocol and getting the suspects in custody—alive if at all possible. To help with that, six ambulances were bringing up the rear of the convoy.

Turner slammed his fist on the steering wheel.

How the fuck had he let this happen to her? How could he have failed her so spectacularly?

He would not lose her. He would not lose that sweet laugh, those gentle lips, that velvet skin, that warmth and love and bliss. He would get to her in time. He had no choice. He'd just found her.

Turner's whole body shook with rage and pent-up frustration.

He would not lose her.
He'd just found her.

Candy felt herself coming awake, but had a difficult time getting her eyelids to open. So much noise. Shouting. Such a horrible smell. Oh, and her head throbbed! She hurt from her toes to her hair. She probably was having a nightmare. She was . . .

Her eyes suddenly flew open.

She was tied to a chair and gagged. She was in a room with a half-dozen scuzzy men, one of them Gerrall, no longer dressed as a girl and staggering around smeared with blood and holding his left arm tight to his side like it was broken. He was screaming at someone. It didn't take Candy long to figure out it was the infamous Bobby Ray Spivey.

"You can't do anything right," Bobby Ray hollered. "Why did you bring this stupid bitch here? Huh? And what the *fuck* were you thinking, doing this to the Fat Man? We can't touch him! If we do, we're all dead!"

"Shut up," was Gerrall's comeback.

Candy wasn't following the conversation too well. She felt woozy.

Bobby Ray cracked Gerrall upside his head with a fist. Gerrall crumpled to the floor.

In the middle of all this insanity, Candy sensed she was being stared at. The men not actively beating on each other were sprawled on a collection of filthy chairs and couches, alternating their attention between leering at her and watching the father-son battle of wits.

Oh, God, her head hurt. What had happened? She remembered Gerrall shoving her in some car . . . making her drive . . . then the brakes gave out.

Candy shifted her gaze to her right and jerked in shock. The front end of a car was sticking through the wall of what she now realized was a trailer home. It was the car she'd been driving, and it was twisted and leaking green fluid right onto the dirty carpeting.

And then she checked to her left. It was poor Wainright Miller, in a similar situation, still tied up and gagged. He was breathing, that much she could tell, but unconscious.

Gerrall staggered up from the floor, wincing in pain.

"Well, your little sissy boy is in no shape to take care of that girl so whad'ya say I take a shot at her?" The man who said that was speaking to Bobby Ray but grinning at Candy.

No. As she frantically looked around the trailer, her understanding of the situation became sharper. She was in a load of trouble. First off, she was the only female. There were guns and crumpled beer cans thrown everywhere. Several men were talking shit about how Candy "disrespected" Gerrall and would have to pay. And the leering continued, along with cussing, laughing, and lots of beer.

Her mind began to race. Her body trembled. The perspiration rolled down her face and back. She hadn't survived two kidnappings and a car crash in the last two months to give up now. The question wasn't if she would get out of here alive, but how?

Suddenly, Candy's mind was flooded with memories of Turner—his beautiful face, his intense eyes, his bad-ass walk, the way he smelled out of the shower, his touch, the way he made her feel. She loved him. There was no doubt, not a single shred. And he loved her. It was that simple.

And because of that, she had no choice but to make it out of this hellhole in one piece. Whatever it took.

Candy reared back in the chair as Bobby Ray stepped toward her.

"So you got the hots for Sheriff Halliday, I hear." He bent at the waist and displayed his green teeth to her. Candy could smell several years of cigarette smoke clinging to his hair and clothes. She had to shut her eyes and glance down and away.

"Oh, so I'm not good enough for you? Is that it?" Bobby Ray grabbed her chin and tugged on it but she refused to look at him. That made him laugh something awful. The laugh immediately turned into an awful, hacking cough.

"Let me have a shot at her!" shouted the same man from across the room. Candy figured that must be his standard pickup line.

"I said shut up," Gerrall snapped. "She's my girl-friend!"

Everyone in the room broke up at that.

Bobby Ray didn't pay them any mind. Instead, he studied Candy carefully. "I knowed your daddy pretty good. Me and him was involved in some of the same po-litical groups."

"Is that what y'all called the KKK back then?" one of the men called out, laughing.

Bobby Ray spun around, pulled a gun from his waistband and shot the commentator in the leg. The man wailed in agony and hobbled out of the trailer, dripping blood.

Candy overcame her horror enough to notice a muffled squealing sound coming from her left, and she turned to see that Miller had woken up. He stared at her with huge, questioning eyes—then peed himself.

All right. The situation was going downhill fast. Candy made a quick study of her condition—feet looped around the front legs of the chair and tied tightly to the rear legs. The same rope was crossed many times around her middle and chest and then used to yank her arms tightly and tie them to the back of the chair. Knowing she wouldn't be going anywhere soon, her body sagged in despair.

"You know," Bobby Ray said, returning his attention to Candy. "If Jonesy were alive today, he'd shoot Halliday between the eyes for touching his baby girl." He put a hand on her thigh. "Maybe I ought to be a stand-in for your daddy and protect your honor. Whad'ya think?" His yellow fingers crawled up her leg. "Only maybe I can play with you a little bit beforehand. Huh?"

"Don't touch her!" Gerrall shrieked. "She's mine! Nobody can touch her but me!" He lunged toward his father but Bobby Ray bashed him in the head again.

This was too much. These people were animals. She and Miller were going to die if she didn't figure something out fast.

"I'll do whatever the fuck I want to do. You know damn well that's how it works around here."

Gerrall's face contorted with sadness. "I don't want you killin' her like you did Junie Halliday! She didn't have to die! She didn't do nothing but want to help me! She was the only person who ever wanted to help me! I *hate* you! I *hate* you for running her off the road the way you did!"

Candy hardly had time to react to that terrible revelation. At exactly the same instant, Bobby Ray and Gerrall had pulled out their guns and were locked in a standoff.

They were too late.

That's what Turner thought when they heard the gunshot. But seconds later a man staggered out, obviously hit in the leg, and tumbled down the aluminum front steps of the trailer. An agent plastered up against the outside wall of the trailer shut the door after him, and an emergency medical technician was there to treat the man while Turner interviewed him.

"Is there a woman inside?"

The man's eyes rolled into the back of his head at Turner's question. He howled in agony.

"A woman," Turner repeated, grabbing him by the face. "Is she alive?"

He nodded, wincing in pain. "She's alive," he mumbled. "Help me. Somebody help me."

Turner made one last check. The lab was secure. Seven people were already in custody. Two FBI snipers were on the roof. Four DEA agents were at the back door. Eight were at the front door. And two additional state police snipers had maneuvered into position inside the wrecked car.

He gave the signal, just as two simultaneous gunshots rang out and echoed through the compound.

The trailer door burst open, and Candy raised her eyes from the carnage on the floor to a burst of sunlight, followed by chaos. There was nowhere she could hide. She could only sit and hope she wasn't shot or trampled in the melee. But it unfolded seamlessly, and within seconds, every man who had been lounging in the room was facedown on the floor and handcuffed. She blinked into the bright light, hoping what she was seeing wasn't some kind of apparition brought on by her injuries.

There could be no mistaking that walk. Smooth and determined, it was the walk she loved with all her heart. And suddenly, Turner was there, kneeling at her feet, tenderly unwrapping her gag and cutting her loose as he spoke to her, his voice contained and calm on the surface.

"Did they hurt you? Did they touch you? Did the brakes fail? Where are your injuries?"

Turner began to run his hands all over her body, and she wasn't sure if it was relief or exhaustion or just the need to feel his arms around her, but Candy collapsed against him.

He picked her up and carried her in his arms out the door. She hung on to him, in pain, weak, but the happiest she'd ever been in her life.

"I didn't lose you. I didn't lose you," Turner said over and over, his nose and mouth buried in her hair as he walked.

Candy felt herself lifted into an ambulance, but

Turner shooed the workers out and shut the door. He sat down on the gurney and put Candy back in his lap, so he could hold her closer, tighter.

"I'm okay. I got banged up in the car, but I'm okay," she assured him. "Turner, they didn't hurt me. The Spiveys killed each other. It was awful, Turner. So awful."

He cradled her face in his hands and examined her from her hairline to her chin. It made her smile. "See? I'm all right."

He nodded.

"I have to tell you what they were fighting over."

Turner shook his head. "Later. The details can wait, baby. Let's get you—"

"You were right," she said, stopping his protests. "Turner, Bobby Ray Spivey ran Junie off the road, and Gerrall absolutely hated his father for doing that. Right before his daddy shot him, Gerrall said that Junie was the only person who ever wanted to help him."

Turner's face went hard as stone. Candy couldn't tell if he was even breathing. She worried she was intruding on a private moment. "Maybe you want to be alone for a minute while you sort this out. I can—"

He pulled her down and crushed her mouth with a kiss. Candy felt his love and passion, but also gratitude, amazement, wonder. Turner released her and looked up at her with tears welling in his eyes.

"I've been alone a very long time, Candy. Not any more." He brushed his fingertip down the side of her face. "Please do me the honor of staying by my side while I put away this last piece."

Candy nodded. "Of course."

"Thank you."

"I love you, Turner."

"I love you. And it's changed everything," he said. Then he rested his head against her breast, shaking in silence.

Epilogue

Candy stood on the sidewalk and made one last critical analysis of the curb appeal factor. People would be arriving any minute, and she knew if she wasn't ready now she never would be.

The autumn pansies, mums, and sedums overflowed from the window boxes. Three sets of wrought-iron café tables and matching chairs were arranged in the sunshine. The brightly striped awning hung straight over the window but left plenty of room for the large gilded letters to sparkle in the light: CANDY PANTS BAKERY.

It brought a smile to her face to see the old building's exterior looking so tidy and fresh, the result of a thorough power washing of the brick, tuck-pointing, and a careful scraping and painting of the wood trim. The sidewalk under her feet had been bleached and the heavy oak and leaded glass door refinished. Truly, it was a relief to see that the storefront looked nothing like it had back when Jonesy Carmichael ran his insurance business from inside—which had been the whole point, she supposed. And soon, their lovely second-story loft apartment would be ready to move into while their house received a few upgrades—two more bedrooms, a family room, an attached garage, and a fenced-in yard—things that would allow their new family to make it their own.

Tanyalee opened the door and poked her head out. "I've done everything on the grand opening list. Anything else you need?"

"Nope," Candy said to her only full-time employee. "Just put on your customer service smile and a fresh apron. We're about ready to rock 'n' roll."

"You got it!" Tanyalee grinned pleasantly and disappeared back inside.

A moment later, Candy felt a pair of strong arms encircle her from the back and large hands come to rest directly on top of her expanding belly. With a sigh of contentment, she let her head fall back against Turner's chest, and snuggled her butt against the front of his body.

"So beautiful," he whispered into her ear.

"It really does look great, doesn't it?"

"I'm talking about you, darlin.'" He began to leave a trail of kisses down her cheek, jaw, and neck. She heard herself purr. "You make me absolutely crazy, Candy Carmichael."

She laughed. "Thanks. Let's hope you still feel that way in another couple months, when I'm extremely large and people are callin' me Candy Halliday."

"Always. Forever. Don't you ever doubt that." Turner tightened his grip on her and pulled her closer. "I am so proud of you. Seriously. It's been a thrill to see you make something out of nothing, to bring this dream to life the way you have."

"I had some help, as you might recall."

That was an understatement, of course. Sophie brought just a little over sixteen thousand at auction, which was barely enough to pay for commercial ovens and other kitchen fixtures, so, for the last three months, Candy had relied heavily on the volunteer labor of friends and family working in shifts from dawn to dusk, doing everything from painting and decorating to heavy lifting.

Hugo and the bocce ball crowd from Cherokee Pines came out of retirement to offer their collective expertise in everything from plumbing to drywall and tile work. The ladies of the bridge club set Candy up with window coverings, antique tables and chairs, and regional folk art and decorative touches. Viv and Gladys did what they did best and told everyone they knew in North Carolina about the business. Lenny had a line to gently used restaurant equipment and fixtures, and he helped Hugo with installation. Tater Wayne built the front counter and all the storage shelves, plus the huge chalkboard menu display. Cheri, J.J., Turner, Rosemary, and Reggie worked tirelessly priming, painting, and hanging light fixtures.

And Tanyalee had been invaluable in her suggestions for the design of display cases and the menu, and Cheri and Candy discovered that as long as they made sure J.J. and Tanyalee were rarely in the same place at the same time, her contribution was nearly drama-free. Since she'd needed a job in the worst way, Candy decided to hire her. So far, so good.

Perhaps the biggest shock came the day Jacinta handed Candy a check, saying she wanted to invest in the business. "I have all the faith in the world in you, Candace," her mother had said. "I know you'll turn that place into something beautiful and good for this town."

And in an ironic twist, one of Candy's first commercial contracts came via Wainright Miller, who decided to outsource the senior home's daily desserts to Candy.

During all these weeks of help and support, Candy often found herself more focused on her morning sickness than her own business plan. She sometimes felt guilty for not pulling her own weight, which everyone told her was nonsense.

"Just make Turner work harder," J.J. suggested.

Candy closed her eyes now, enjoying the last quiet moment before the big event. She savored the warm and comforting touch of the finest and bravest man she'd ever known.

"I couldn't have done any of this without you, Sweet T," she told him, turning in his arms so that she could see his face. "I wouldn't have any of this good stuff in my life if it weren't for your love. You know that, right? You are why I'm here. You are everything to me, Turner. You're my anchor."

His mouth hitched up, and he stroked the side of her face. "And soon to be your ball and chain," he said, laughing.

The grand opening was a huge success. They sold out of everything except for the poppy seed muffins, and Candy took thirty-four advance orders for Thanksgiving and Christmas pies, cakes, and pastries. Perhaps the biggest compliment she received that day came from Rosemary, who tasted her apple pie and said, "You're gonna put me out of business," as she gave her a hug and a kiss.

Among the last customers to arrive that day were Kelly O'Connor and Dante Cabrera, who showed up about a half hour before the event was scheduled to end. Both DEA agents were now permanently stationed in a new field office in Asheville, and since Dante was no longer working undercover, he'd starting coming out of the shadows a bit. Turner had described him as a good cop but a New Yorker who didn't trust many people and absolutely hated the South, so it was a shock when they watched him make a beeline directly toward Tanyalee, who was working the register.

"Have they met before?" Candy whispered to Turner, perplexed.

Turner then turned to J.J. "Should we warn him?"

J.J. shook his head. "Looks like we're already too late for that, and besides, warnings don't work with the Newberry women."

Everyone stared as Tanyalee greeted him with a huge smile and fluttering lashes. "What a shame," she told him, in her over-the-top Southern-girl voice. "We're sold out. I don't think there's a single thing I could offer you."

Dante paused for a long moment, in which he let his eyes travel all over her. "I beg to differ," he said.

Turner sighed. "Oh, boy."

Once everyone had gone and Tanyalee had clocked out, Candy and Turner sat at one of the tables, listening to the silence of the old building and the hum of the commercial refrigerator-freezer. She was curled up in his lap and his arms were around her. Turner had his cheek resting on her breast.

"Are you exhausted?" he asked.

"Very."

"But are you happy?" Turner looked up at her, those hazel eyes filled with a question. "Are you happy you're right here, right now, back in your hometown? You don't have any plans to run away on me, do you?"

Candy brought her hands to either side of his face and cradled him like that, feeling the perfect curve of his skull and the warmth of his skin. She saw in his eyes the depth of love he had for her. She leaned down and kissed him tenderly, smiling softly to herself.

It was true that most everyone saw Candy as a resident and business owner in the city of Bigler, North Carolina, the place of her birth. But she knew better. This wasn't the Bigler of her childhood. It wasn't the Bigler of the past. It was a town of present and future only, a place she'd created from scratch, with love and a boatload of help.

"I am happy because I'm with you," Candy whispered to Turner. "Besides, where would I run to? I'm already here."